AF424774

"A heartbreaking, and heartwarming, tale of youth, war, loss and redemption, and the irrefutable value of family."

Eliot Kleinberg, Author - www.ekfla.com

"A love story centered around a pivotal war in American History, and the human stories surrounding these major events. The story is unique."

Leah Orr, Author

WOW!!! It has been quite a while since I enjoyed reading a story as much as I did "Because of Rachel." Alan Grossman's novel is so beautifully written, so heartwarming, and so descriptive. My emotions ran the gamut from surprise to tears, and to laughter. It's definitely a winner!

Erin Proctor

A must read for baby boomers as Alan Grossman will take you on a walk down memory lane! From the time I picked up this book, I could not stop reading. The twists and turns of this love story takes place in the 70's during the Vietnam War will have you on the edge of your seat for the entire book. I learned a lot from the author's incredible knowledge, loved his story telling and really look forward to his next book. Bravo Alan Grossman!!!

Jeffrey S. Richman

Great twists and turns! Quick weekend read that you will enjoy. Wish there was a film made from this!

G. Mitchell

Captivating! This novel is so well written. The depth of character development and how the layers of their lives unfold is compelling and moving. The story will prompt a great deal of self-reflection about life and love.

Shaun Randall

Every bit real and tangible! Wow! This book has instantly become my all time favorite military romance story. The plot was great, it kept me eagerly turning the pages, it was action packed yet the romance never took a back seat, there was a lot of interaction between the lead characters were beyond great, he has become my all time favorite. The reader is taken into a wild, fun ride (at least for me).

Yet for all the things I loved about this book, it was the heroine who made this story so enjoyable for me. *Because of Rachel* by Alan Bryce Grossman is a wonderfully moving tale some are romantic, some are familial, but all are deeply complicated. Dealing with love, Vietnam war, war times emotions this stirring tale is utterly engaging and ultimately hopeful. Because of Rachel will sweep you away with the difficult times, bold flavors, and sweeping views of the region and transport you to a world you won't be in any hurry to leave.

I will reread this book for sure. I have favorites but since I have read this one, I think to myself, this was great, can't wait for the next one to come out. Read this book, I believe you will not be disappointed. A beautiful tale of love, loss, family and the healing power inside each of us.

Because of Rachel by Alan Bryce Grossman is every bit real and tangible. It's a story you can't walk away from, yet you're breaking into pieces the deeper you read. My only objection is that I wanted more. More of interesting characters and their lives intertwined together. It's a slow burn, a sizzle, a spark, a big gush of wind threatening to blow you away.

Rohan

Compelling read!! The author's writing transported me to Chicago and to the jungle of Viet Nam with his vivid descriptions. He has me in that time period with all the protests and conflicts.

I can't wait to read whatever he writes next!

PokerSusie

I loved this book! Because of Rachel is a gripping story that follows Will Stanford through his journey of self-discovery. Will is a complex and compelling character, and I found it easy to connect with him and his struggles. The well-crafted plot moves between the 1960s and Vietnam, and the descriptions of the war-torn jungle were vivid and powerful. I think this book is a must-read for everyone, as it offers an insightful look into the human experience and how sometimes the choices we make shape our lives. Highly recommended! 5 stars!

Adam

Beautiful love story! Really enjoyed this book. Romances that take place over decades are a favourite of mine, and following these characters was a great way to spend a weekend.

JP

Deeply moving story. *Because of Rachel* is a beautifully written and deeply moving story about the uncertainties of life and the journey towards finding oneself. Set in the late 1960s, the book takes the reader on a journey from suburban Chicago to the war-torn jungles of Vietnam and beyond. The main character, Will, is relatable and his struggles with finding direction and purpose in life are both poignant and thought-provoking. The author's writing style is atmospheric and evocative, transporting the reader to the different locations in the story. The themes of love, loss, and self-discovery are expertly woven throughout the book, making it a must-read for anyone who appreciates well-written and emotionally engaging stories. I highly recommend this book to anyone looking for a thought-provoking and deeply moving reading experience.

KH

It's an amazing read full of unexpected twists. The story of Will is sad, heartbreaking, and full of horror and adventure, but also love and hope. It's a strong story about a man that decided to escape from his trouble his way. This book makes you think a lot about the importance of your family in your life. Great book.

Monika

Five Stars! Excellent! I could not put it down! The imagery had me hooked from the beginning. Very fast read and I highly recommend it!
Paula Bergman

Outstanding! This story was so well developed. The characters, both male and female, had real depth that grew with their years and experiences. Those experiences were typical of human nature and yet unique to the extraordinary times. Chicago, music, poetry, journalism, and the Viet Nam war were all included in amazing detail. Honestly, I couldn't put the book down. And now I'm looking forward to this author's future work.
Cyndi

Good Read! This story spans multiple decades. It starts during the Vietnam war and the main character ends up enlisting in the army. He's a new father and also newly married. This life is not working out for him at all. He ends up on the frontlines and meets with tragedy. The US Army declares him missing and he fights for his life in the jungle. Decades later, him and his new lady return to America to take a step into the life he abandoned. Very compelling read.
Danelle Hagan

Good book to get comfortable with a cup of coffee. Captivating, and will take you back in time into a world you never knew.
Kristin O'Connor

This definitely appeals to those who lived in these times. It brings up so many emotions that are familiar.
Katie Henderson

The book highlights the brutal reality of survival while building a sprawling, emotional story. I could relate to the main characters. I could see myself living then. It was a hard life but people react the same to circumstances.
S Kumar Mishra

It is a unique story of the freedom of the late 1960s, offering lively scenes throughout Chicagoland, yet moving onto exotic locales, telling the story of the tribulations that both Will and Glory encounter, yet ultimately finding their way.

Avimanyu Datta

I recently read *Because of Rachel* by Alan Byrce Grossman, it was a thrilling read! The plot of the book is filled with action and romance, and the interactions between the lead characters are captivating. The author has managed to create a deeply moving story that deals with love, loss, family, and the complicated emotions that arise during wartime.

If you're looking for a book that will sweep you away and leave you wanting more, then read *Because of Rachel* by Alan Byrce Grossman. I can't wait for his next novel!

Jill Lefkowitz

A Time Honored Tale of Americana. The book describes the life and choices made by a young man searching for his path in life. Finding the expected road of job, family, church unfulfilling, the hero enlists in the Army and find himself engulfed in the horrors of Vietnam. The book offers vivid images of 1960s middle American and Southeast Asia and has a number of memorable characters.

Kenneth Leo Maher

A story about life's uncertainties. This book tells the story of Will's journey from suburban Chicago, to the war in Vietnam, and finally to the South of France. With a reluctant marriage and a daughter that challenges him, Will must navigate life's uncertainties and make a choice that will change his life forever. I really enjoyed the whole journey.

Sung Sik Yoon

This is a well written and creative tale. I'll be looking for more by this author. Would love to read a space opera or fantasy by him.

John Justice

Emotional. Engaging! This book has a real appeal for me, one of the reasons being the deep development of the characters. Will is a complex and compelling figure, and his struggles to find meaning and direction in life are both poignant and thought-provoking. The story moves effortlessly through different times and places, even taking us to the battlefields of Vietnam.

Grossman's writing style is truly evocative, painting vivid pictures of the story's various settings. Themes of love, loss, and self-discovery are skillfully woven throughout the book, making it essential reading for those who enjoy well-written, emotionally-engaging stories.

Stoic Putto

Alan Grossman bats it out of the park with his first novel. A thoroughly worthwhile read. An engrossing tale using vivid characters and descriptive settings to tell the story of two young lovers and the trials that make up their lives.

Kindle Customer

This is a great book. The characters are so well written that it's easy to feel involved with their story. I'd highly recommend this to anyone who loves a great love story.

David

Because of Rachel was a great read. This story was beautifully written. I couldn't put it down. I loved taken back into the 60s and 70s. Great romance novel with history which I thoroughly enjoyed. Life takes twist and turns, very interesting characters and many different settings to explore.

Biography Lover

Because of Rachel

ALAN BRYCE GROSSMAN

To Debbie, With Love
Without Her, This Would Be Half A Book,
With Her, I Am A Whole Man
We Would Not Want It Any Other Way.

"Qui va à la chasse, perd sa place."[1]

—French proverb

---

[1]   "Move your feet, lose your seat."

PART I:
CHICAGO, ILLINOIS
- SUMMER, 1967

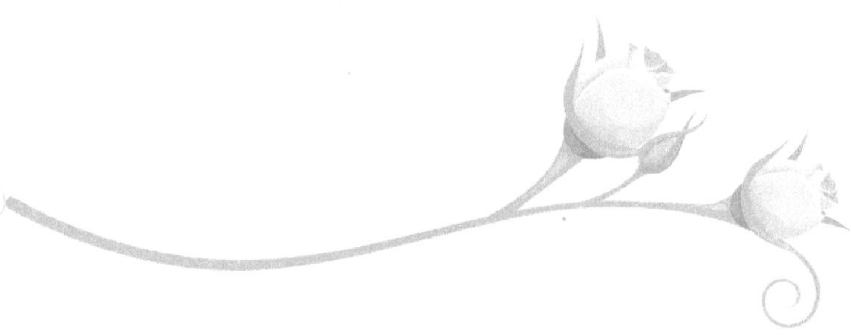

O N E

Glory's destiny could wait no longer. She straightened her hair from the mess created by the outside wind. Then, after arranging her tie-dyed t-shirt and smoothing it down past her waist, she stepped into the fluorescent glare of the sports department, and walked toward the wall of tennis rackets, watching to see if he was nearby.

It was the Summer of Love — a heady time to be twenty and living in Chicago. For Glory Walters, the time was ripe, touching the changes as they greeted her almost daily. She looked back through the glass doors to the parking lot. Her best friend, Teri, was late as usual.

Lodged in front of the wall of tennis rackets, she reached for the pink one, tested it, then another, searching for a feel that she figured she'd know when it happened. Then, out of the corner of her eye, she watched him walk toward her. It was the same walk of confidence Glory noticed the first time his presence grabbed her attention a week ago in that same spot.

He looked more together than when she first saw him a week ago. Now, the pristine white of the corporate-issued dress shirt maintained its place over his trim body. His brown hair had hung in wayward waves that rested on his shoulders, broad in the way that a triangle resting on a point emphasizes the top corners. She stifled a grin recalling the contrasting bulbous look from last time, when his work shift must have been near quitting time, with his tie then askew and his shirt seeking its place elsewhere.

As he approached her, he checked that his solid black tie was in its proper place. She turned around, smiled, and held out the two rackets toward him.

"I can't decide. Which do you think is better for me?" Without thinking, the sales clerk reached for the rackets she held in each hand, took them from her, and looked straight into her eyes, as sparkling green as a dew-nestled Irish lawn. He didn't say anything. He smiled, joined by a pinch at his eyes, the color of robin's eggs, almost periwinkle, tracking his interest in seeing more of her.

"So," she said, "Which one?"

"I'm sorry," he said, focusing on the rackets in his hands. "I think," he continued, "That I'd like to know your name. I'm sorry…What's your name?"

She took the rackets from him. "Glory," she said. "Actually, it's Gloria. Gloria Walters. Glory has more charm to it, don't you agree?"

He smiled, moving his focus back to Glory's eyes. The corners of his eyes added their wrinkled punctuation. "Oh, I think so. Very much."

"Now, William Stanford," Glory said, glancing at the Sears name badge tacked to his shirt pocket. "Is this the right racket?"

"Oh, I think so. Very much."

Across the store, back toward the same door she had entered, Glory heard her name ring out.

"Glory." It was Teri Isaacson, sometimes called Izzy, practically knocking down the door to enter the store. Shouting as she located the tennis section, "I'm so sorry I'm late. The traffic…."

Pivoting toward the door, Glory handed the two rackets back to Will. She rushed toward Teri, hoping to catch Teri's eyes, to shut her up. When that didn't work, Glory sent out a "shhh" that moved faster to Teri than did Glory. As Glory grabbed Teri by her arm, Teri acquiesced to Glory's command.

The two women linked arms and continued in the direction where Will remained, placing the rackets back in place.

Leaning her head closer to Teri, Glory said, "What are you doing? He could have heard you."

"But you told me two o'clock. You know how much I hate being late."

"Shhh."

Nearing Will, who saw them walking toward him, Glory whispered a final instruction to Teri. "That was between us. What if he finds out?"

"What, that you want to buy a tennis racket?"

"I'll have to deal with you later. Just be cool…Hi, Will. This is my friend, Teri."

"So do we need to find her a racket too?" Will asked.

"Uh, no," Teri said.

"Will, Izzy's covered, but I do need one. I can't be seen on campus with my high school racket."

"No doubt," Will said. Then he reached for the rackets he had returned to the wall, while maintaining his focus on Glory and Teri.

Teri stepped closer to Will. "Glory, you didn't tell me how tall he is. He makes me feel like a midget."

Glory grabbed Teri again by her arm and pulled her away from Will. The two women together backed up in the direction of the exit.

Will moved toward them. "These are pretty good rackets," he called out. The girls stopped. And waited.

"Miss…er, Glory…I can help you choose. That is if you want me to."

Glory and Teri stood as if they were frozen to the floor. Then, without warning, Teri took a half-step back behind Glory. She nudged Glory, and whispered into her ear, seeing that the intense gaze had Glory locked onto Will that kept her frozen to her spot.

"Listen, don't blow this," Izzy said into Glory's ear. "From what I can see, he's worth taking the next step."

Glory felt the nudge aimed toward Will. But the next steps conjured an image in her mind that had no business asserting itself. At least not then. She shook her head to clear the memory of her final night with Matt. Her memory was clear of how they had devolved to yelling at each other again. That was then; the end of their rocky year together. This wasn't the time, though, to resume her conversation with herself over the break-up. It's been more than six months. Way past time to move forward.

Teri's right, Glory thought. He is handsome. And strong.

"Do you play? You can show me." Glory asked, accepting Teri's second push that moved her toward Will.

"I have."

"What time are you off today?"

"Why?…Five."

"Groovy. Then you can show me. Seven o'clock. Tonight. Oak Park High School. The tennis courts are in the back. Off Erie Street. You know where it is?"

Will nodded.

Glory smiled at Will, allowing a touch of the smile to connect with her eyes, sending a complete message. She turned around, practically knocking Teri over as she stepped to leave. Looking back, she said, "And don't be late. I need to decide for my tennis class. I'm counting on you."

His smile in response told her everything. It was the same smile she saw last time while spying on Will from the rack of tennis outfits. She watched him help a small boy count his dollars and change to buy a new baseball bat, with the boy's dad hovering overhead. That such a large man shrunk himself down to the boy's size and made him feel special, or so she assumed, smiling as he did it, told her much about this man who, in entering her life, sparked a doused flame.

"Won't be late," he said. "No sweat."

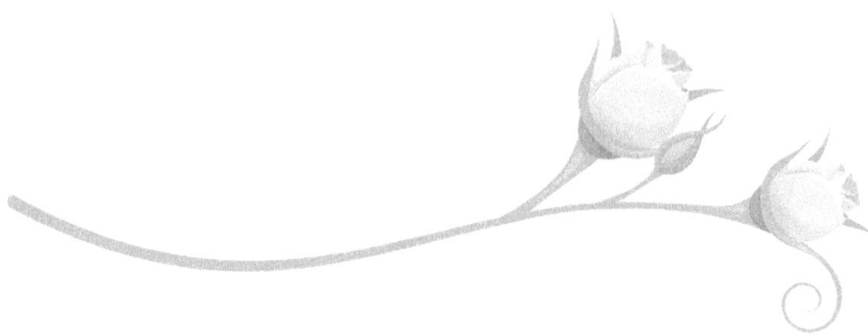

T W O

Will guessed why he told Glory that he was off work at five. While watching Glory and Teri leave the store, he attempted to conjure up all kinds of reasons. When she had asked him to play tennis, Will took a much closer look at Glory. He saw only beauty, both in the way the lights accentuated the gold tones of her hair flowing down over the mounds of her breasts, and in that tilt of her head as she read his name tag. She had focused her sight so tight on him as if the inventory around him instantly disappeared. But it wasn't just her golden hair that shimmered, even in the dismal light. There was more, a current passing between them. He'd make sure the electricity sparked a line between Will and her. She had a way about her that set her apart. He felt it. Maybe it was her ways of persuasion. Whatever it was, it sparked something inside him merely from her gaze boring into him.

Of course, he well knew that he was scheduled to work until closing time. But when she asked, his brain stopped, leaving him with nothing but his heart talking to him. It told him to drop everything; that this chick is extraordinary. He believed that the elusive excuse to lay on his manager, Mr. Harris, would come to him, even as he sauntered back to the register, not sure what's to come next.

It was not an accident that they met today. At least, that was his hope. He had the good fortune to notice Glory a week before. She walked into the store that day, dressed as an ace in tennis whites. Will had watched her promenade through the door and along the aisle that divided the sporting goods department, as did every other guy there. And there she was - a treasure cascading past him, looking as ephemeral as sea spray cresting a wave. Will glanced up to get a better look while he checked out a customer who had handed cash to Will. Glory's entrance grasped Will's concentration, rendering him like a teapot of boiling water, full and ready for something. Handing the cash right back to the customer, the customer looked at Will and asked, "Is your stuff free now? Here's the bread." He handed the money back to Will. "Can we get on with this?" It was only when the customer tapped Will's hand with rolled-up dollar bills that Will refocused. But as he counted out the change, she walked past the counter. The white tennis dress transformed in Will's mind into a glowing white gown to maintain her aura, which held Will's gaze.

Cranking his focus away from her and back to his task, somewhere in there, maybe – he hoped - she looked directly at him for an instant. An instant - how long is an instant? It can't be measured. Like a rock, there's no such thing as half an instant. How each instant is used offers a roadmap through life. Best for humans to take each instant, each moment, and knowing that, with clear intentions to use each moment for good, even if later that good intention turns out to be a mirage, will lead to the next moment. Because if it doesn't, the result can be only that the string of moments that we each experience as life, has ended, with our inevitable demise. We won't know the end when it happens. What we do know is now. And for Will, that instant lingered within him until he saw her again. Her eyes first reflected the store's lights back to Will, penetrating the Irish green deep within Will.

Will had no choice that first day but to turn his attention to a customer at the counter. Finished, he stepped back to the waiting high-top stool, and propped himself on the round, dirt-stained cushion. Will looked out across the store with his hands resting in his lap, his feet resting on the narrow footrest. A shot of the coolness of conditioned air rushed past him. Then he remembered to breathe, took a deep breath, slowed down, and narrowed his vision to keep an eye on the customers.

Then there she was, gliding through the dress aisle. And that's also when Mrs. Guthrie called out from the pools. He had promised her that he'd be right there to help her. Will got off the stool and looked down at his billowed shirttail rising above his belt, portraying a cumulus cloud gathering around his waist. In an effort to tame his shirt, Will contorted his hands to do the best they could to get the white dress shirt in order, but with the primary goal that nobody should be able to see him perform this solo dance. Not a simple task.

The beautiful girl in the tennis outfit was right in front of him, so he had to wait. Then he turned to walk away from her to the pool department, and added spit to his hair to tame it down. That didn't work. At least Mrs. Guthrie didn't care, as she was looking at the pool that Will had put together a few weeks before for the Memorial Day sale. His co-worker, Stan, known as Gimpy, was there to help him. Instead, Gimpy lived up to his name and handed Will a tool, maybe even more than once. Gimpy was a wayward scion who had been banished from his famous family's dry goods empire.

When Will finally stood next to Mrs. Guthrie, she swiped a quick look at Will, then shook her head. Will feigned a slight stumble and snatched a sniff. The Old Spice cologne that he applied in the car on the way to work had long before wore off, leaving little more aroma around Will than the lingering scent of "Old Sears." You stink, was his only thought.

"You said just a minute," Mrs. Guthrie said. "That was a very long minute."

"Was it?"

"What?" she asked in return and turned to look again at Will. The horizontal shake of her head grew large for one last shake. She looked back at the pool and sighed.

"Don't forget I see your Mom once a month. C'mon, son. I need your help. That's why you're here?" Will looked at Mrs. Guthrie, smiled, and reached for the sales tag attached to the pool by a string. "This is Sears' finest above ground pool...."

The moment that she entered Sears, she also entered his life. Neither he nor Glory knew then that a connection had been made in the ether populated by the angels that work for our better selves, anchoring our fates to *terra firma*. What fate awaited them, Will had no clue. If angels were watching down on him, Will hoped they'd hang around for the duration. He knew that they must move on to others, given his history of sliding expectations and his reality that disappoints him.

Back at the register, the dearth of customers allowed Will to sit back and wait. That's when Mr. Harris returned. He caught Will looking again at his watch, apparently waiting for something to do.

"Stanford, what are you doing?"

Will looked up. "Just checking the time, is all."

"I see that. We don't sell time here. We sell sporting goods. I see the new stock isn't on the shelves. Why not?"

"Well, you see, boss...."

"Don't 'boss' me. Stop loafing and get those golf balls where they belong."

Will rose from the stool and started out toward the golf section. Mr. Harris replaced Will on the perch, shook his head, and then looked at his watch.

"Stanford," he called out. "You know you're all I have tonight. Gimpy called in sick and I can't get Marvin on the phone. Got it?"

"Of course, sir. But..."

"No," he interrupted Will. "There is no but. Anyway, get to it."

The clock maintained its ticks toward five o'clock, with the almost-constant turns of his wrist keeping him informed of the passing minutes, Will watched Mr. Harris leave, then moved behind the counter, replacing his manager at the register. When Mr. Harris disappeared outside, Will looked around, pulled out his keys, and locked the register. Will's path then took him through the store, onto the sidewalk along Lawrence Avenue. No sign of Mr. Harris. He started walking the two blocks to his car parked on the street. This will work. But he didn't have much time. Twenty minutes home, then change, make up a story for his Mom, and keep away from Ben and Joey. Then it's forty-five minutes to Oak Park. It then occurred to him that he had never driven to Oak Park. He knew it to be upscale, one of the leafier suburbs rising up west of the city. It's an old neighborhood, so there should be signs showing him the way. Anyway, he'd ask for directions. Who's he kidding. He's never asked. But there are maps somewhere in the car, just in case.

Rushing to his car, he calculated whether he yet had saved enough money to replace the faded paint on the ten-year-old Oldsmobile 88. The original white color of the back fins and the roof of the jalopy was so worn that it showed more of the gray of the metal underneath than the dirty white of the old coat of paint that remained. He repeated to himself the ever-recurring promise to also fix the broken taillight. The dents in the body he could live with, but the crack growing up the center of the windshield he knew would continue to grow until the windshield would one day break into two smaller windshields. But that's not what he wanted to think about. As for the guys, he intended to pass on joining them for the softball game. They'd just have to live with it. Surely there's another first baseman to stand in for him. Hell, Schwartz wanted his spot anyway. This could be Schwartz's big chance in the finest Wally Pippin - Lou Gehrig style.

The driver's side door handle again refused to open, despite Will's repeated tugs of the cold chrome. He struggled with it, all the while thinking about the waste of precious seconds. When his hands found no purchase in cajoling the handle to do its singular job, Will backed up and gave it a swift kick. That knocked it into submission, as his next attempt to open the door resulted in that satisfying click, and the door opened, inviting Will to enter the car's interior.

Will lowered himself into the driver's seat, closed the door, and cranked open the window, which stopped short at the halfway point, as always. Will sighed, but then started the engine, which was the only part of the car he knew would work better than new, thanks to Joey's magic with engines. With the engine started, the radio played, tuned to 790 WLS. The Doors' sultry crooner, Jim Morrison, sang his deep tones of *Light My Fire,* hogging the airwave. He tapped his foot to the music, swaying to the beat. Great song for tennis with Glory - active, sending a strong message. When the chorus rolled around, Will joined in, glancing around to see if anyone would hear him power through. *"Come on baby light my fire. Try to set the night on fi--yure...."* Will held the last note too long and started coughing. He stifled the cough and searched through the overflowing ashtray and found what was left of his joint from the previous night. Just a little, he cautioned. A little is relaxing. But more than that? Well, this was not the time nor the place. He found a cigarette lighter under the clothes on the floor, sat back and looked out to see what was around. The street was quiet. He lit the joint and took his first toke. The scent of marijuana might give him away, but that didn't matter. The moment was right to set him up to be with her. Will put the smoldering joint back into the ashtray, shifted the car into gear and began the six miles north back home, to change, and onto his date; destiny or bust - he'd soon know.

At home, he walked up to the side door. He opened the screen door and stepped into the kitchen, the outer door having been propped open to allow in the fresh summer air. Will stepped toward his mom, Dorothy, known as Dot, washing dishes at the sink. She looked up when she heard the door slam. Dot greeted him as she always did, with a smile, arms out, wet sponge in hand (that isn't always how it was), ready to accept the hug due her from her son. Will bussed a kiss on her cheek, feeling the aromatic grains of her hours-old makeup on his lips. He turned around and stepped back to the stairs, and ran up to his room, looking back as he did. He saw the cookie plate piled high with the results of Dot's recent labors, but the scent that floated with him up to the second floor failed to disclose whether they were chocolate chip or her famous peanut butter cookies.

Will charged through the door in his room, throwing his shirt off his body and onto the floor. He let his trousers drop to the floor, stepped out of them, and grabbed gym shorts and a t-shirt from a dresser drawer. He waded through the laundry on the floor by his nightstand and slid aside the various half-filled glasses and personal detritus to see the alarm clock's hands pointing to 6:05. That's pushing it. He sat on the bed, unrolling the sheet and blanket, flattening them up toward the pillows where they belonged, and put on his socks and white Keds, but now a gray color the same as his Olds, permanently stained from white to gray from overuse. He heard the screen door slam downstairs.

"Hi, Second Mom," Ben Shapiro greeted Dot, entered the kitchen, and walked toward her, eyeing the cookies. "What kind did you make?"

The screen door slammed again and Joey Golden followed Ben's entrance. "Ya slammed the door. Think you're some badass?"

Ben turned around to offer the proper glare to Joey.

"Ben," Dot said, shutting the faucet and reaching for a dishtowel on the counter. "I told you…."

"Yeah, I know. Mom won't like hearing that."

"That's right. I'm a mom. My children…."

"I dig it, Mrs. Stanford."

"That's better. Now, you haven't stopped canoodling with the cookies. Take one. You too, Joey."

They each grabbed one from the plate.

"This is good," Joey mumbled through the crumbles. Ben grunted his agreement.

"Something new, I discovered. Macadamia nuts. Mr. Miller's brother or someone just came back from Hawaii and brought some to the grocery. Good?"

They nodded, the thickness of the cookies still occupying their vocal apparatuses.

"He's upstairs."

The two men turned and started up the stairs when Dot asked a question directed toward Ben.

"Ben, how's your sister? Did she like them? I should go over there and see her."

"Well, she's still recovering. But she's good. Mom's taking good care of her."

Dot placed the towel on the counter, walked to the screen door, and opened it. Ben and Joey stood at the base of the stairs, watching.

"What are you two waiting for? Will's getting ready." They turned and ran up the stairs.

Dot opened the screen door, calling out, "Charlotte, everything okay? Does Samantha want more cookies?"

Dot watched the identical screen door across the passageway open. The subject of Dot's call, Charlotte, walked into her view and opened the screen door. Charlotte's kitchen door was a straight shot across and the same three steps up from the sidewalk.

"Oh, she loved them. But I'll tell you more later," Charlotte returned the call. Something inside caused Charlotte to turn around and respond. Returning to Dot, Charlotte said, "Ben said something about a concert. Do you know anything…?" A second call from inside. Charlotte turned back to Dot. "Never mind. We'll talk later." She backed into the kitchen, turned around, and let the metal-framed screen door slide closed.

Ben and Joey found Will in his room, bent over, leaning inside his closet. Poking through the grand pile that had risen up to meet the shirts and pants hanging from the rod, they heard the thrashing of items thrust asunder.

"Wattya looking for?"

"I know it's here somewhere. My tennis racket."

"Why are you looking for your tennis racket?" Ben asked. "I don't know the last time we played tennis."

Joey piped in. "We're gonna be late. We gotta warm up."

"I'm not going," Will said. He backed out of the right side of the closet, slid the doors over, and resumed his mission on the left side. Still not finding the old racket, the items start flying out from the closet as Will threw dirty remnants of his forgotten wardrobe, landing around the feet of Ben and Joey.

Will emerged from the closet. "You'll be fine without me."

"Where are you going?" Ben asked.

"Oak Park."

"Oak Park? To play tennis? What's gotten into you?"

Instead of responding, Will grabbed his wallet and keys from the desk and turned toward the door. "She did."

"Who?" Ben and Joey asked in unison.

Will headed to the door and shouted back to them. "I don't have time. I gotta go." And the stairs thundered Will's charge down to the kitchen. Ben and Joey stepped to the stairs and watched Will disappear.

"Mom, I'll see you later," he said, standing with his hand ready to open the screen door.

"What about dinner?"

"No time, Ma. But maybe the guys want some." And then he pushed the door open, jumped down to the sidewalk, and galloped to his car, hoping that the damn handle would simply open the door like it's supposed to. That would be a great start.

Ben and Joey came down the stairs and stood at the screen door. The familiar kick of the door handle told them that it was still the same old car and the same old Will. Will jumped into the car and drove away. Ben and Joey returned to Dot in the kitchen.

"So boys," Dot asked. "The stew's about ready. Sit down, and I'll get you some."

"Thanks, Mrs. S," Joey said. "But, we gotta split."

"Ok, do what you want." They walked toward the door, and Dot called to them, grabbing in each hand a paper plate full of warm cookies, covered with silver foil. "Take these," she said, handing each a plate. With their thank-yous, the screen door again opened to lead them to the outdoor world.

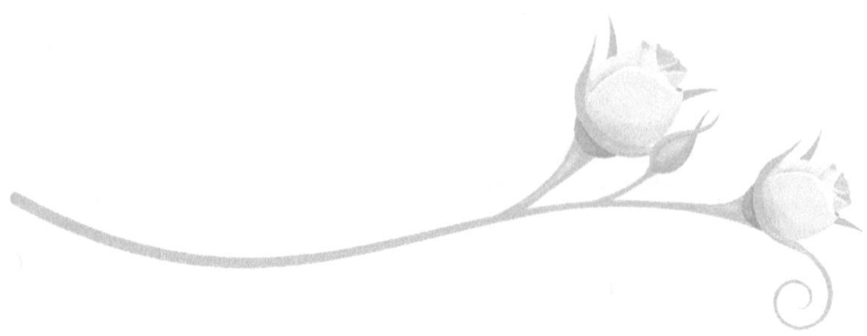

T H R E E

Will turned the Olds east onto Erie Street in Oak Park, slowing down as he did. The high school tennis courts were on his right. Looking for a place to park, he kept driving and made a right turn on Scoville Avenue. Oak Park and River Forest High School stood as an old fortress holding court over the leafy bedroom community. Built with the buff sand color bricks from the dolomite quarries southwest of Chicago, the three-story school took as its footprint the entire block along Scoville. The original century-old building was designed in the Colonial Revival style with Prairie School influences of its most famous neighbor, Frank Lloyd Wright, with the ridge of the center gable pointing skyward. The school interrupted rays from the setting sun, casting its imposing shadow over and across the street onto the oak trees holding a vigil of shade for the two-story homes with the golf-course-green lawns.

Will slowed the Olds 88 in front of the school's main entrance. He looked up at the gable on the roof of the building. Clouds accumulated overhead, showing the darkening grays of heavy rain, for now holding back. Still plenty of light. He remembered that it should stay light until eight or later. Focus, he cautioned himself. The golden-pink sunlight smelled of a promise of grandeur. This is good. Or she won't even show – that she's just playing with him. The thought stopped Will as he completed circling the block, turned back to the far side of Erie Street, and pulled into an open space. Would she show? Should he just go home and join Joey and Ben and take his spot at first base? A motorcycle rushed past him, gunning its engine as Will tasted the metallic power passing by. The sharp report cracked through Will pushing him to take the next step.

Will checked his watch and walked to the tennis courts. He was fifteen minutes early, and nobody else was around. Beyond the far fence of the courts, the Huskies' practice baseball field spread out before him, waiting for him. The welcoming smell of the freshly mowed outfield lawn and the peculiar green glow of the Oregon bluegrass outlining the curve of the infield's blend of sand, silt, and clay invited Will to the inner core of the sport. He walked through a gate, across the tennis courts, through another gate, and stepped onto the field. He stopped for a moment, then walked toward home plate, taking his place in the right-side batter's box. Will spotted a baseball lodged against the base of the backstop. Jogging back to retrieve the ball, Will grabbed it and ran to the pitcher's mound.

When he played ball in high school, Will wanted to pitch more than anything. He could throw a baseball a hundred miles an hour, but when he did, it was just as likely to land on the train tracks that ran just beyond the Niles East High School home field as to dive to the dirt before even reaching home plate. So instead, he found his place at first base, famous for doing whatever it takes to catch the throws from the other infielders, or at least stop errant throws from getting past him.

Will walked up the short mound. He stood atop the mound and toed the rubber, striking the classic pose of a pitcher peering at the catcher's sign. Holding a pretend runner at first base, Will started the abbreviated windup, his hands resting at his waist, holding the baseball with the two-fingered grip of his infamous fastball. Will first stared at the imaginary batter standing at home plate, intent on intimidating the opposition. Will kicked his leg up, strode toward the plate, and let loose the throw, letting out a howl of sharp pain in his elbow he had forgotten existed. The ball reached the backstop, cut short from heading to the street as reported by the resounding chink of the ball hitting the chain link fence halfway up its twenty-foot height, completely missing its target. Typical, he thought. Then another call rang out.

"Stanford. I thought that was you," Glory said, leaning against the side of the open gate of the tennis court. "What are you doing? Living fantasies of spent youth?"

Will looked over at Glory and ran to retrieve the baseball. He grabbed it and then jogged back to the gate and Glory. Slowing his pace, Will meditated on the soiled ball. Without saying anything, he handed her the baseball and grinned.

"What's this?" she asked.

"It's a base...."

"Of course, it's a baseball. I've seen many. With three older brothers, I know how to be a boy, when I want to."

"You have brothers?"

"Three, Jerry, Abe, and Georgie, but don't call him Georgie to his face. Only I can. He's the oldest. He protects me."

"They're not here, are they?" Will looked past Glory to check on the arrival of her cavalry.

"No, but if they were, they'd still be gasping for air from laughing." She reached for the tennis bag at her feet.

"Get with it, Stanford," she said with a chuckle, turning around to head back to the tennis court. "Where are they?" she asked.

"Where are who?" Will responded, following Glory onto the tennis court, again surveying beyond the fence for any hint of intruders.

"Not who. What. Actually two whats," Glory answered.

Will closed his eyes in frustration. He really wanted to impress Glory. But with all the commotion at the store and then at home, with the guys not understanding the import of this new direction for Will, he entirely neglected the central purpose of this meeting, from Glory's view, and forgot to bring the tennis rackets. But anyway, is that really what she wants? To pick a new tennis racket? Maybe it was to pick him? But now...."

"It's cool, Stanford," Glory said, interrupting Will's internal focus. "There's another one in my car. I'll get it, and then you can tell me all about the *ins and outs* of your newest racket."

"I'm hip to that. I'll walk with you."

Their plan was met with objection as then announced by vibrations first felt, then heard, as two enormous rain clouds butted heads close enough to touch. The wind gusted in its invited dance with the thunder. Across the street, the branches of the tall oaks performed their subservient dance to the wind's command. Like the blast of a jet breaking the sound barrier, the first raindrops bombed them, leaving dollar-pancake-size watery lily pads sowed over the entire tennis court and into the distance. The wind picked up its pace, blowing the rain sideways and down.

"Can you run?" Glory asked.

Will tapped Glory on her arm and slid the tennis bag from her shoulder. "Faster than you," he said. "Which way?"

Glory took off to the far gate, with Will following, pushing past curtains of water. In the seconds it took to run to Glory's car, the rain drenched them as if they had jumped into a lake fully clothed.

She unlocked the door and sat on the driver's seat. Will then handed the bag to her, turned, and headed back to his car. Glory threw the sports bag onto the back seat, got out, and stood next to the vehicle in the watery tempest. Glory called for Will to hear her through the storm. "Where are you going?"

Will slowed his pace and turned to see Glory standing at her car, her golden hair dripping onto her clothes.

"Will, come back. Get in."

He stopped to consider her offer. She's inviting me in. He started forward, then stopped again. He wanted this, that much he knew. Then as she called out his name again. He knew that in that call lay his future, whatever it was.

"Stanford, it's wet and I'm cold. Get in the car already." She turned and retreated inside, closed the door, and then leaned to the passenger door to unlock it.

Will ran to the car, and with his watery cloak, jumped inside and slammed the door.

Glory and Will watched nature's chorus play on the windshield as they wiped water from their face and hands. The windows fogged around them. Glory started the engine, and turned to Will. "Take it off," she said. He turned and asked with his eyes what she meant.

"Your shirt. Might as well take it off. There are some napkins in the glove compartment. Hand me some, and you can use some for yourself.

Will obliged, grabbing the napkins.

Glory worked to avoid staring at the water glistening on Will's chest. Broad, as she expected, with a center tuft of hair. That his muscles were so prominent did not surprise her. The unsurprising rise in her temperature, whether physical or not, settled in Glory. Izzie was so right about him, she thought. We know what's on the outside. Glory felt a surprising lightness from the view, shook the dreamscape from her mind and focused on the physical presence that the two of them conjured in that small space, protected from the storm.

Instead of taking the napkins offered by Will, Glory pulled her shirt over her head, then past her arms, and shook the water from her hair. Her breasts followed her lead. She tossed the soaked shirt behind her. Will tried not to stare, with some success.

With no bra, her nipples posted their reaction to the chilled air. Glory brushed water off her arms and chest.

"What're you doing?" Will said, ping-ponging his view from the full roundness and pink crowns of her boobs to the rain slashing the windshield.

"Turning on the heat," Glory answered, reaching to the control. "Don't want to catch a cold."

"That's not what I meant."

"I know. Caught you off guard?"

He nodded, unsure where this was going. The rise that he felt informed Will of one distinct possibility. But…this was neither the time nor place. He had no shred of doubt that this girl was hip. That her approach to life was like nothing he had ever experienced. No girl gave him as much to feel, even if no physical touch had yet connected them. If she wasn't a highly sexual woman, she'd certainly have to modify her actions to show him otherwise.

He turned toward the back and rummaged through her stuff, looking for something to cover her with. "You must have something."

"In the bag," she said, while reaching behind her to attempt to find it without looking.

Glory did not anticipate what happened. She's been known on rare occasion to stroll about braless. It gave her a taste of freedom. Friends of hers were even bolder, shedding their tops at any opportunity, supporting equal rights for women. If men can go topless, why not women? Both have breasts, including nipples, just of different sizes. Teri had cajoled Glory many times to lay on the lawn with her, absent her shirt or bikini top. So far, Glory had maintained her reticence, but each time leaning closer to shucking the modesty and the prurient nature of suburban society.

In this case, it was as much the circumstance as anything. She was cold and soaked and the shirt had to come off. That Will sat next to her with his shirt removed gave her no concern. In fact, it made it easier. His response was the opposite of the first time she was alone with Matt. They were both then seniors in high school. But that was long ago. Still, the memory of that moment when Matt showed the darkness he carried with him keeps her on her guard. She had then been caught entirely unprepared but maintained sufficient strength to fend him off. She learned after that to anticipate – always – the hormonal drive of men, when it takes over both of their little heads. Here caution came with her. Even if her boldness vetoed the small voice standing on her right shoulder, the voice on her left shoulder flattened the otherwise shrill pleas for restraint. Typically, she heard the moment-by-moment evaluation of character when she was with someone in an intimate way. This time her inner voice kept shut. Her impetuousness grabbed Glory and thrust her into a dimension of herself that she had forgotten existed. She wanted, this thing they shared, if only visually, to know that she could trust him. In her experience, the bigger the man, the rougher were his ideas regarding intimacy. However, she saw in Will a philosophy that contradicts that notion. Will is a large man, in tight control of his body, with grace, as she had witnessed firsthand from him. Now she saw an inner side that she suspected to be charming, empathetic, perhaps even gentle. But it remained a question to her. His actions and reticence indicate an underside to Will of honor and restraint. So far, at least.

Glory accepted the small towel from Will and began to dry herself.

"Now what?" Will asked.

"My house."

"Like this?"

"Sure. Nobody's home. My folks left for an art reception."

"Your brothers…?"

"Don't worry."

"Why not?"

"Like I said, nobody's there."

Glory rested the towel over her chest to cover the objects of Will's current desire. She put the car in gear and eased away from the curb onto Erie Street.

"This is nice," Will said, rubbing his hands along the edge of the leather seat. Glory double-checked the towel, shifting it back in position. "I meant the car."

"It was my dad's car. '65 Mercury Comet," Glory said.

"I know."

"You like this model?"

"It's far out. Cool red."

"Yeah. But my dad hates it. It's called carnival red. After a while, he had enough with a red car. And besides, with me living off-campus this year, he thought I'd need a car. He got himself a Lincoln. I think the Continental. A boat of a car."

Will laughed. "I never want that much domestication in my life. Nothing but sports cars for me."

Glory glanced at Will, and shrugged her shoulders. She turned onto Oak Park Avenue. The rain turned to drizzle. Glory lowered her window to let the petrichor scent of the ionized air infiltrate around them.

Will looked outside the driver's side window. "These houses are huge," he said. Glory nodded and a smile curved on her lips. She turned left onto Iowa Street, then a quick right onto Kenilworth Avenue, and pulled over and parked the car at the left side curb in front of 600 Kenilworth, a three-story stucco Prairie School style home that sat behind an ample lawn. Five bedroom windows were set in gables arrayed around the third-story roof. The wide front porch beckoned visitors to come in.

Will rolled down his window and studied Glory and the house behind her. She is a curious woman, he thought. What does she have in mind now?

"See that house there?" Glory asked, looking past Will.

"Sure."

"Ever heard of Ernest Hemingway?"

"Who hasn't?" Will answered. "I had to read a couple of his novels in high school. Something in his writing spoke to me."

"Me too," Glory said, turning to look at Will. "My favorite is *For Whom the Bell Tolls*. I just love the way that he puts the soil, the earth, as part of the love story of Jordan and Maria."

"I am partial to *A Farewell to Arms*. So vivid. The war scenes. I haven't read *For Whom the Bell Tolls*."

"Trust me, you should."

Will resumed studying the entire scene. Trust, she asks for. Will can trust. So why not? But did Will offer trust to Glory? She'll let him know.

"Of course, I trust you," Will said. "I'll get to the bookstore on your word."

The only response came from the breeze flowing through the car's open windows.

"Ok," Will started, "now that the book reviews are done, why are we here? Is this your house? What does this have to do with Ernest Hemingway?"

"Nothing. Anymore."

Then the buzz of the street lamp set high above them on the road verge came to life. The shade surrounding them continued its slow descent to night blue. The perfume of Angels Trumpet blossoms wafted in and out of the car. The aroma presented visions of - well, angels – that the sweet scent battled against the plant's liquid poison was not lost on Glory. Signs she can see, sometimes for good, sometimes for not. Was this such a dichotomous sign?

"Glory," Will said, touching her arm and looking right into her eyes. "What are we doing?"

"I thought you'd like to see this. This is where he lived growing up. His family, as I was told, moved from his birthplace around the corner to this house when Ernie was only seven."

"That's so outta sight." A pause. "Ernie?"

"It gets better. His family lived here all through Ernie's teen years. Then he went to fight in Europe. He came back for a time to convalesce from his war wounds."

"You know a lot about Mr. Hemingway."

"I should," Glory said. "My grandfather was his best friend in high school. They were even on the newspaper staff together. As I am told by family lore, he had a thing for my great-aunt, Florence. But Grandpa Frank would have none of that. Who knows what might have been? I could be a Hemingway right now. Anyway, it's getting dark. We're just around the corner, so onward." And with that, she drove the Mercury around the corner.

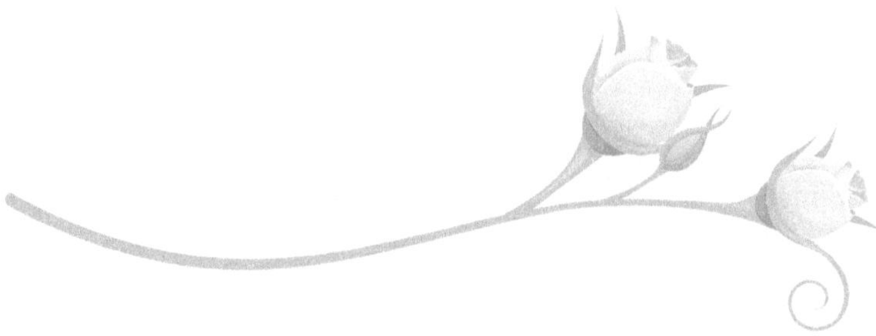

F O U R

Glory pulled into the driveway and stopped the engine. Will got out and strolled to the front sidewalk taking in the rise of the three-story home. The front porch light merged with the overhead street lights painting a golden aura onto the black onset of a starry night. Glory joined Will, holding the towel in front of her, with her tennis bag hanging over her shoulder. They centered themselves on the front walk to better see the symmetry of the two corner towers making up the front wings of the Victorian home.

"Kinda looks like Ernie's home," Will said.

"No reason it shouldn't. The same hands made it. Well, sort of."

"I don't understand."

"Let's go inside, and I'll tell you the story."

Inside the front door, Glory stopped Will and took his shirt from him. "If your shorts are wet, you can go in that bathroom, and I'll get you a robe. But wait here so I can get you a towel."

Will watched her glide over the wood floor and disappear to the back of the house, turning on lights as she went. The chandelier over Will cast its diamond facets of light on and all around Will. Glory called back, "You should take off your shoes. I'll dry your socks with the other clothes."

She returned with a bath towel and a robe, took the socks from Will, and returned to the back. Will made his way to the guest bathroom off the living room.

Will's second impression of her home from inside the bathroom surprised him. It wasn't the marble floor or the high shine chrome of the faucets, but the fact that there seemed to be nothing out of place. A bathroom should be used, and there must be some lingering signs of use – perhaps a towel not folded just so, or a spot of crusted toothpaste on the sink. The contrast to Will's notion of a well-used home started with a scent that he could only guess at the flowers that made it. The knock on the door revived Will from his contemplation of the room.

"You okay in there? Open the door, hand me your shorts and I'll hand you my dad's robe."

Will obliged. With the door opened, Glory asked, "How does tea sound?"

"Sounds like a blast."

"Meet you in the living room."

Will took his seat on the upholstered couch, bookended by two armchairs, centered by a coffee table, with a bouquet of flowers, a bulky glass ashtray, and a large ceramic bowl that looked hand-made, glossed to a dark blue sheen. He didn't know the table's wood, but the glow from the overhead lights revealed a crisp coffee color, with the flowing grains highlighting brown insets. A large Persian woven rug anchored the setting, set across from the dark fireplace. Above the fireplace in a golden frame of ornate swirls and leaves, hung an oil painting of a man with flowing white hair, looking like a stunt double for George Washington, watching Will's every move. Turning his view along the walls of the room and into the adjoining dining room, his view averted into the backyard to the pool, with trees rising beyond, all lit by lighting clearly intended to adorn the exterior for entertaining.

He was satisfied to sit, hoping to avoid a tour of her parents' home. Along the wall leading away from the fireplace, photographs and paintings hung on the walls of different styles and sizes. Faces of people of varying ages and eras all smiled at Will. That their frozen sentiments may be false as directed toward him was not lost on Will. In a small frame, a black and white picture showed a toddler wearing a flowery dress matching the one that Will recalled seeing in a biography he read of Ernie, as Glory called him. His memory prompted the thought of Ernie's misfortune of being born a boy. His mother, Grace, wanting twins, decided that her older daughter, Marcelline, and Ernie were close enough in age at seventeen months apart to serve as twins. To complete the effect, she dressed them alike in dresses. And even as Ernie started grade school, Grace maintained the charade until abuse at school ultimately convinced her that Ernie was, in fact, a boy and should appear as one.

Studying the portraits one at a time around the walls convinced Will that this family's legacy dancing around him would hold his own family in lower regard. No pictures were hanging from the walls from Dot's decoration of their home. The few photo albums tucked away on a shelf in a closet went back only to his grandparents, of which Will recalled conversations with only one, his grandfather, Bertram Stanford. Grandpa B stopped by, often with the sole idea of taking a walk with Will and his brother, Lou, older than Will by a couple of years. Lou followed in his mother's mold, a small man. Will took after his father, both athletic throughout their life.

Reclining back on the couch, Will wondered if the model from which Glory took traits from her family allowed room for his kind. So far, it seems so, he hoped. Just then, the room filled with sounds of scratches from an oft-played record album. The heavy beat of a drum solo emanated from a location that Will could not identify, and bounced around the room. The solo strumming of chords from an electric guitar joined the percussion, introducing the tune. Glory then emerged from the back of the house, carrying a full tray. A robe flowing with large white flowers on a silky orange background covered her from her shoulders to her blue furry slippers.

The song continued. A small chorus of voices sang out the lyrics, which Will did not actually hear from watching Glory walk toward him and put the tray on the coffee table, moving aside the decorative bowl. The melodic sounds continued, offering a sultry comment overseeing their liaison. The chorus of not more than three or four voices sang out,

"It's all for now
The way we are

Will, too, wondered what she wanted him to do. Nothing like the present to find out.

Glory sat next to Will, arranging her robe around her. She reached for the teapot, filled one of the porcelain cups, and handed it to Will. The tea's aroma flowed to Will in advance of the cup, adequately warning him to take caution with the hot cup. Will took Glory's offering, allowing the steam to rise over his face. Glory poured herself a cup and then took a small piece of paper that she had lodged on the plate with the assorted cookies she added to the tray.

"This is called Gyokuro tea. It's like a very rare tea. My folks brought it back from their tour of the Orient last month. It says here that Gyokuro's full flavor, starting with the first notes of slight grassy flavor, a body of umami sweetness, with a long ending."

Will held the cup closer to his nose and sniffed the aroma. It was unlike any tea he ever had. It did not conjure up grass or whatever that other thing was. The warmth felt good, but he worried of spilling the drink. He risked her seeing his hand shake. Besides, it's such a rare drink and one that smells different. This entire scene is different. A cold brew would settle him.

Then the last guitar licks from the song playing around them announced its end, followed by the resumption of the quiet crackles of the record.

"Did you like this one?"

"Pretty good," Will said.

The sounds of a female voice then sang out,

"This is a good song," Will said.

"You like *Image Child*?"

"You bet. Great band. I heard this on the radio."

Glory took a sip of her tea. "What did you think of the first song? I think it's called *"Now and Again*."

"I can dig it," Will said. They both sat back against the couch without a prompt, listening to the music.

Glory turned to angle herself toward Will. What must he be thinking? Is he listening to the words, or just the music, or is his mind somewhere else? She likes him, and he is easy on the eyes. But she wants to learn more about what's inside Will. She tried to create a comfortable place for Will, given the strange circumstances that she created that put them together, sipping tea wearing nothing but bathrobes. Maybe it is too much, she worried. Teri tells her that she is too controlling. That men don't like it and want to be in control. Still, here we are, and he seems comfortable. Yet…

"Will," she said, "You're not drinking your tea."

Will looked at Glory, then at the cup. Her eyes followed his moves. Will put the cup to his lips and tried the strange brew. He turned to Glory and smiled. Then glanced at the plate loaded with cookies.

Glory laughed and reached for the plate. "Don't worry, these aren't rare, nor expensive. Take one. They're just cookies." Will took one.

His silence felt to Glory like it took on a presence joining her in the armchair. She had to do something.

"So, Will. Who are you?"

"Just Will," he said.

"Will. William. Stanford. You have a middle name, I suppose, right?"

"Blythe."

"That's beautiful. Are you named for someone?

"Yes."

Glory looked closer at Will's face, wondering where she'd locate the switch to turn on to get him to talk. The tea wasn't working. Wrong move; a clear setback. The cookie probably helped. But he still was elsewhere. His reaction to her was unusual. Most guys would be all over her by now. After all, he's already seen her breasts. He's probably just shy. But being more forthright with herself, she conceded that he may feel intimidated by his surroundings.

Will then shifted in his seat, and as Glory watched this movement, Will's physicality rendered itself again to Glory. The rock song that had been playing ended again with a silent pause. The music then played a blue-purple guitar riff, accompanied by the angelic notes of the lead guitar, accompanied by the ethereal beat offered by a tambourine.

"What is this?" Will asked. "It's so unusual."

He likes this, Glory considered. "It's beautiful," she said. Then the lyrics rang out in a ballad with the trippy tempo matching the beating of a heart.

This day
Exists for you
Unlike yesterdays
And those to come
It's a wonder that time exists at all…

"It's called *This Day*," Glory said. "This album has so many gems."

"I've never heard anything like this."

Will swayed to the music and closed his eyes, breathing deeply, taking in the aroma of the tea.

Glory had a thought. "Dance with me," she said.

Will opened his eyes. "I don't dance."

"Of course you do. Everyone dances. I just saw you dancing, at least a little. Anyway, there's nobody here but you and me, and I promise I won't watch."

The sultry music continued through them. Will leaned forward to put the teacup down but then stopped.

Glory sensed that the moment was ripe for a deeper connection. She reached to Will and placed her hand on his shoulder. Will responded by returning the cup to the tray. Then without saying anything, she caressed his arm and felt the goosebumps rise up in reaction to her touch. She pondered where else Will experienced a rise. The thought tingled inside her, the wetness arranging its debut between her legs. Then her fingers coiled themselves around his fingers. Glory sensed the slightest return squeeze from Will's fingers to hers.

Will had never felt so much in one moment as was then happening to him. The second she put her hand on his arm, the couch disappeared, the table and flowers and bowl and tray were gone, and the photos and paintings slid to the ether. Even old George's understudy, waiting in his

34

crinkled painted venue, slipped into the distance, the penetrating dark eyes of Glory's long gone relative too far away to see them. It was just her. When he later tried to recreate this moment from his memory, the thing that stood out for him was her touch, the energy passing back and forth. Their fingers plugged into each other, creating the current of electricity that even Will, Mr. Stoic as he's been called, could not deny.

Glory stood up from the couch, keeping hold of Will's hand.

"William Blythe Stanford. Will you please get up and dance with me? Before the song ends."

With a smile, Will stood, assisted by Glory's pull of his hand. They moved into the center of the room, joined by the crooning of how *This Day* would be different, Will agreed, now with his heart aflame.

The couple stood with their hands locked together, face to face. Will moved with an instinctive skill that he had locked back in his mind. His right hand resting on her hip, he raised his left hand, holding hers in the classic waltz position. Their moves blended, and when she looked up at him, his whole body felt like it was lifting off the floor. They swayed as the music carried them to a place of pure emotion. The song slowed and ended. Instead of stepping back in anticipation of an ending, Glory leaned into Will. His robe parted at his chest where she had rested the side of her face. His black hair gave her a tickle before yielding to her. She wrapped her arms around his waist, clasping her forearms behind him. Will, too pulled her closer, his arms crossing hers in an embrace.

The next song started up, another ballad with a light plucking that emphasized the deep tones from guitar strings five and six. They resumed their movements to and fro; small, as imperceptible to anyone but them. Glory and Will remained centered in their space, allowing the music to move with them, through them. A man's voice sang in measured cadence,

> *"I know you*
> *You're the one for me*
> *You've said that it is so*
> *Now it's there to see."*

The voice faded to silence. A flute sent out its singular notes, one tone after another. Will thought that the tones were made just for them.

Closing his eyes and feeling Glory lean in even closer, he worried that his growing erection would send her the wrong message. This was a moment that had never been a vision in his mind. What is next? Glory then pulled her head back and looked up at Will.

What Glory knew then was the magic that accompanied Will to that spot. Or maybe it was something their electricity created that would not exist from them alone. They added more sway to better match the tempo. Then Glory stepped back, released her hands, and placed them on his shoulders.

"You can dance," she said.

"Seventh-grade cotillion is all. Thought I'd forgotten it."

"You didn't forget."

"And that's not all I can do," Will said.

Glory reached her hand to caress Will's cheek. "There's more? Can you show me?"

When the next song started, they pulled back into their hug, swaying in dissonance with the feisty tempo of the rock music.

Glory stopped the motion. "This music isn't working. Do you want to see something?"

"See what?" Will wondered what she had next for him. When he thought that he understood her, she made another left turn. But each turn put him in a place that, while entirely unexpected, showed him a part of her world. He was in.

"Sure."

Glory led Will toward the dining room and then turned into a hallway. They stopped in front of a door, and Glory slid the door open. She stepped through and flipped a switch that turned on an overhead light. Still holding Glory's hand, Will followed. They stood side by side, facing the door. The room was the size of a closet, with the walls and ceiling covered in brown paneling. Glory pushed a button on the wall by the door and closed it. The song of a metal apparatus then flared up. The bottom of the room pushed them upward.

Will laughed. "You have an elevator? That's crazy."

"Yeah, I know, but my folks got it for grandma."

"Is she here?"

"No, her apartment is in the carriage house. But I don't want to talk about her."

"Nope."

Will pulled Glory closer to him, released her hand, and reached around to pull her in by her waist. Glory helped by leaning into him. When the elevator stopped, she opened the door and exited with him into a small hallway. Together they walked to one of the doors, and Glory opened it and stepped into a bedroom. Inside the room, she turned around and looked at Will.

"This is my room."

They remained where they were and surveyed the room. This is Glory's inner sanctum. And she wants me here. What else does she want? The lightness of her perfume floated to Will; lavender, as he felt it, like the colors of her Laura Ashley bedspread of lavender and seafoam green flowers, coordinated with the curtains covering the windows. Surprisingly, Will did not feel like dashing out the door. The depth of his breaths, though, matched the moment.

Glory walked over to the stereo and selected a record to play. "Now, Will," she said. "I think your clothes are dry. Just wait here, and I'll get them. Let me clear the chair, and you can sit while I run downstairs."

"Don't."

"Why not?" Will turned to Glory, cradled her cheeks, leaned in, and kissed her. Glory accepted his kiss, parting her lips to allow in his lips and tongue. The scent of warm cookies combined with his uniqueness as she tasted her first introduction to Will's sex. His hands caressed her back through the silk robe. Their kiss grew its intensity, as they shuffled as one toward the bed. Glory pulled back, untied the knot of Will's robe, and ran her hand down his chest, lower and lower, stopping to sparkle his pubic hairs. Will let out a slight moan when Glory completed her manual search, pulling his throbbing penis out from the robe and sliding it into her cuffed hand.

Together they lowered themselves to Glory's bed. Will submitted to her nudges that he lay back. She let go and slid her robe to the floor. Then she crawled to Will, and he leaned up and watched the fullness of her breasts lead the way. Glory climbed onto the bed, separating her knees to lie outside Will's thighs, his erection ready at attention.

"Don't we need…."

"Shhh," Glory replied. "I'm on the pill."

He started to ask her a question but stopped when she raised herself over Will, her vagina wet and open for him. Instead, he lay back as she lowered herself and slid him inside her. Rocking with him in tempo to match the music that she barely heard, she savored his tight fit that, as she moved, filled her. Will rocked his hips up, offering himself to her even more. Their motion rocked through them as if they were one person. Will leaned up and pulled Glory to him. Kissing her, mouth open and ready, she pulled him closer still. Together they rolled on the bed, with Glory now beneath him. Will pushed, rocking further inside her. Glory moaned with each thrust. Then she let out a small and powerful cry. The pressure in him reached the point of no return, with Will's cries joining the burst from within followed by another, his orgasm shooting through him.

His panting matched Glory's. He lowered himself onto her chest, laying his head to her side, the stillness of the bed then incomprehensible to the energy in Will. That energy flowed into Glory, emptying Will, leaving him spent. He raised himself and rolled to lay next to her.

"Wow." Will worked to control his beating heart. He turned and watched Glory. "That was amazing. You are so beautiful."

Glory reached her hand to wipe strands of his hair, away from Will's forehead. His gulping breaths reminded her of the pounding of waves at the seashore. Her smile sent Will the only message that mattered. Together they lay still, and Glory maintained her focus on Will. He closed his eyes, adding a smile to his face. His breathing returned to normal.

"Say something," he said to Glory.

She kissed his hand. "I'm happy. Not just happy – ecstatic. That was amazing. Seeing you smile like that…oooh, I just want to keep you."

"Did you…?

"I'm happy; that's what I did. Pure joy. What else matters?"

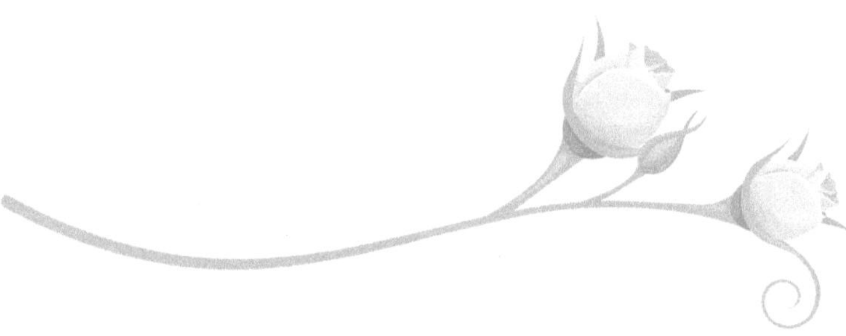

FIVE

The same matching seafoam green and lavender pillows had been pushed off the bed during their lovemaking. Glory leaned over the bedside, looking for the bed throw. The air chilled her. She knew that Will would be getting cold. At this very moment, she knew, the key required that he be made warm. She grabbed the blanket from the pile, and swung it up until it landed on them.

"Perfect," he said, accepting her toss and arranging it over both of them. Underneath, they wriggled themselves to touch their arms, hips, and legs. Their hands found each other lying between them.

Glory shifted her foot to brush her toes over his lower leg, hunting for his foot. She thought she heard him chuckle when his toes found hers. The match solidified, and their feet completed their physical tie.

The music stopped, replaced by a calm coated with the slight ringing in their ears, fading to silence. The only sounds were their rhythmic breathing, the rises and falling of their chests marking time. The quiet, the cool air, and the found warmth surrounding their connecting bodies gave Glory a feeling of serenity. Seeking a closeness prevented by the fact that they lived in separate bodies, Glory turned to her side and reached her arm over Will. Will turned, accepting the offering of her spirit, the place in them where the connection began.

They held each other; their eyes remained closed. The last thing Glory remembered was reaching up to brush her hand against Will's bushy sideburn stroking it with the care that told him far more than words could.

Glory sparked to sitting. Her heart pounded, her breathing deep and labored, yet she knew she was in her bedroom. But the watery landscape from her dream and children running in all directions replayed itself in her mind. A crack she heard must have been the reason for the children's haste to leave, but she wasn't sure if it was in her dream. She slowed down her breath. Will slept on his side, turned away from her. A wisp of air escaped his lips on each exhale. The throw covered Will from the waist up, exposing his butt and legs.

She rolled off the bed, grabbed her robe, and sat at her desk. On a sheet of stationery embossed with Victorian lettering, "GGW," for Glory Ginevra Walters, she wrote a few lines in robin's egg blue. She put the pen down and folded the paper, not one or two times but four, for effect.

Then she realized, with a flash of anguish, that she had no idea what time it was. How long was she asleep? Through the quiet, she listened for outside noise. Were her parents already home? What a disaster if her mother saw their clothes sitting in the dryer. It was then that she heard them come home; that very instant. Then she heard the shimmy of the walls from the garage door closing, and jumped off the chair.

"Will, get up. You gotta go."

No sound came from Will, so she made her way to his side of the bed and rocked him by his arm. His eyes opened, and from the pillow, Will looked at Glory.

"What's going on?" Will sat up, rubbing his eyes.

"They're home. My parents. They won't come up here. But you gotta leave. You can't be here."

Will looked at the blue fleece robe crumpled over the foot of the bed.

"I'll get your clothes," she said, taking off her robe and pulling clothes from her dresser drawers. "Just wait here. And don't make any noise." She opened the door and stepped out.

"What the fuck…?" Will called out, as Glory slid the door shut.

Will knew that he didn't belong there. Glory was fantastic, but this place, these things, were too far out for him. It looked like the matching bedding cost more than his entire bedroom furniture set. And now she wanted him to leave like he's a scraggly dog she let in for a charity meal. He's no charity, Will concluded.

She's not really like this. He knows it, feels it. What they shared over the last hours replayed for him as he lay back and stared at the ceiling. Hands clasped behind his head, the smile that returned again to his face arrived before the thought that prompted it. She had something – a vivaciousness, spunk, even freedom to do what she wanted. Her sensuality attracted him as much as the beauty she carried with her. That she gave herself to him turned the corner on whatever made him then shout out. Then he became nervous that his blast cut through the quiet. He conjectured that it must have stopped in this room, letting his thoughts slide back to the downpour at the tennis courts, the view in her car, a cookie, and a single song that will forever take him back to this chamber.

"They're in their room," Glory said as she entered the room, closing the door. She hid the note in the pocket of his shorts and handed Will his clothes. Then she remembered his shoes. Where did he leave them? Oh crap, what if her parents saw them? They'd hold that nugget of information close to their chests to throw at her at a most inopportune moment. She settled down, remembering that his shoes were hidden by furniture in the living room.

"Too late to meet them?" Will asked.

Glory's laugh landed in him much apart from her usual playful chuckles and laughter. There was more underneath that expression.

"You gotta be quiet," she said. "You can't use the elevator. They'll hear it, and I never use it, so they'll probably come out thinking Grandma wants to see them."

"So you want me to leave? Hide me from them?"

"Well…."

"Whatever," Will said, getting up from the bed and putting on his clothes. When he finished, she handed his socks to him. "So now what?" Will asked.

"I'll take you to the stairs and go down with you, get your shoes, and you can leave by the back door. Simple. But don't say a thing. My mom, she hears. She hears everything, even things I don't say."

"You sure?"

"That's it. Then I'll check in with my folks and tell them that I need to stop by Teri's house. They'll believe me if I tell them that she's having another one of her tizzies, which is why I call her Izzy. Cute. Right? She loves it 'cause it's just for us."

Glory brought Will his shoes in the laundry room with the back door waiting. Keeping her voice low that it wouldn't go beyond the room, she told Will to walk to the street and that she'd pick him up at the corner to take him back to his car.

"Never mind," Will said, keeping his voice at a whisper. "I feel like walking."

"Ok. I can walk with you."

"No. Sometimes I like the street to myself. I love the night air, the anonymity of the darkness. It's only a couple of blocks."

"Will, please don't be upset. You don't know them. For them to meet you this way, trust me, you don't want them to. They are very old-fashioned, even if mom makes her living as a poet. They're actually romantics. But more like the courts in 1800 England than in 1960s America. I suppose it's a Catholic thing."

"As you say," Will said, moving toward her. He pulled her close, and they built the silence around them as a coat bundling them as one. Then Glory leaned up and kissed Will, first on his lips, then his cheek, his cleft chin, the other cheek, and back to his mouth. His day-old beard scratched her face in a series of tingles that splayed through her. Will let out a single moan.

"William Stanford, keep these kisses with you. And don't worry. I know what I'm doing."

One last kiss and the opening door beckoned Will outside. Glory closed the door. Will heard a man's voice from a distance calling out from behind her, "Firefly, where are you going?"

"Thought I heard something, Dad," she called back. "I'm okay."

Will bound to the street, avoiding the lights in front of the house. The half-moon provided enough light without man-made moonlight. The wind gusted and every so often blew Will to the side. It didn't make him cold, except that his hands tingled from the rush of chilled air. He shoved his hands in his pockets, and felt something resting at the bottom, under his keys. He pulled out the folded paper, rubbing the richly formed parchment as he unfolded it. He moved into a pool of light, and read Glory's looping cursive handwriting, "Will, I want to see you again. You – we – were amazing This Day. Call me. OA2-2002. Glory." The note finished with a peace sign under her name.

Will arrived home but had no memory of his return trip, traveling on automatic pilot, allowing his heart to bounce in his chest. He held her note closer and closer, breathing the other-worldly scent of Glory infused in the paper.

Glory heard her father call her again by her nickname. "Firefly," Fred Walters said, "Is everything all right out there?"

"It's more than all right, Dad. It's super groovy." Then Glory rushed inside up the stairs, two at a time, and into her parent's room. She pushed open the door and sat on a nearby chair. Fred and Beth were in bed, sitting up, with each holding a book and the twin lamps on the night tables providing the only light.

"What's so super, princess?" Fred asked.

"It's super groovy like I said. It's a beautiful night, and I feel so fine."

Beth looked up from her book, her reading glasses perched on her nose. "Groovy? What is that? Why can't you use real words?"

"Aw, Mom. That's how we talk. It's the sixties, and life is far out. You know, outside."

"Ok," Beth said. "I suppose so, but you made so much noise. I know we taught you better. But anyway, tomorrow's a new day, and it's late, and I need my sleep."

"Sure, Mom." Glory got up from the chair and walked to Beth's side of the bed. She leaned to kiss her mom and then hugged her, both arms wrapped around Beth in a big squeeze. Beth coughed, then nudged Glory to move her back.

"What's gotten into you, Gloria?"

"Ah, the question. It's life."

Fred placed his bookmark in his book, closed it, laid it on the night table, and reached to turn off the lamp. "Are you high on something? There's so much of that marijuana and who knows what around."

"Of course not, Dad," Glory said, leaving Beth's side for a hug with her father. A hug, a kiss, and Glory made haste up to her room.

Back inside her room, with the fallen pillows and blanket reminding her, a warm wave rose up, recalling their moments together when she felt like she was outside of herself. The tide receded. Glory sat at her desk and opened her diary, and started writing. That's when the bells of her white and gold princess telephone rang. It could only be Izzie unless Will couldn't wait even for the sunrise. When she picked up the phone, Teri had already started before her second syllable of "hello" found its electronic destination.

"You gotta hear this," Teri said.

"My God, Teri, how about at least a hello, a hi, maybe a simple yeah."

"Right. Hi. Yeah. You gotta hear this."

"Not now," Glory said. She remembered who was on the other end of the line, and settled in her chair, laying her pen down. "Okay," she said, "but can we do this quick. I've got something to tell you."

"Sure. They want you back."

"Who?" Glory asked.

"Sy and Arista, they want you to write again. They loved the piece you gave them on your meeting Dr. King."

"Glad for that, but that was a fluke. You know I was too late for his talk. I couldn't even get in. So when I waited by the side door, all of a sudden, there he was."

"I was there, remember. But you managed to get him to talk with only you. Longer than even you could've imagined. It still amazes me. Must be your natural charm. But your article. There's still a buzz. Every time his name comes up, they mention you."

"Great, but can we talk about this later. I gotta tell you what happened to me today." Glory recounted her day with Will, smoothing over the intimate details. And Teri understood. She always understood Glory.

A loud, sustained ringing. Glory pushed her head out from the comforter and reached for the phone."

"Hello." Will.

"Hello," she answered, laying back on her pillow. Her bedroom was immersed in early morning darkness colored by a faint stream of sunlight peeking from behind the curtains.

"It's me. Will."

"Hi-iiy." Glory sang the single dipthong as if opening a line from a movie melody. "What time is it?"

When Will responded, the clarity of his voice gave Glory pause to ponder if he was nearby.

"I don't know. Early. Everybody's still asleep."

"Where are you?"

"Home. I wanted to hear your voice," Will said.

Glory rolled to her side to watch the sun rays build up the light around her room. With her smile reacting to the night's end and the enveloping serenity, she heard a long *cheeka* call followed by the shorter *cheeka cheeka* from the oriole nesting in the branches of the elm tree only a couple of arms lengths from her window. She listened to the tones, and recalled describing her happiness to Will. They had been separated for hours but remained connected, by spirit, by shrunken time, and by technology, considering the phone resting on the side of her head. Was it a new day, like her mom predicted? Or was there more here than a new day, maybe a new way, poetic in its hold on Glory?

"You still there?" Will's voice, spiced by the crackle from the electric phone lines.

"Yeah. I'm glad you called."

"Me too. I wanted to get you before you left for work or whatever. I can make this quick."

"No work. Just stuff to do. You know."

"Sure. Anyway, just one question. Do you like pizza?

"Now. Pizza for breakfast. Cute. Like you."

Glory heard Will smile over the line.

"Dinner. I thought we could go for pizza. Like a real date. Tonight?"

"Deep dish. It can only be deep dish."

"Thought as much. You are a Chicago girl, right? Through and through. Anyway, the best is Gino Mantia's, but only the original in Rogers Park. So I thought we'd tackle their best -- sausage with extra cheese. You okay with Rogers Park?"

"That's near the lake, right? I heard of Gino – whatever it is. I've never been there. Are you sure it's the best? Can I trust you on that?"

"It's the best. You can trust me."

"Then I do."

"Great. We're set. Seven. I'll pick you up."

"Can I go back to sleep now?" Glory asked.

"Can I join you?"

Glory smiled at the thought. "If we both go back to sleep, does that mean we have to tell people that we're sleeping together?"

Glory heard that chuckle from Will that she is quickly learning lands in her the same as his smile.

"I suppose. But who do we tell? We can tell each other, right?"

"Yeah, and I'll listen to us."

"Me too."

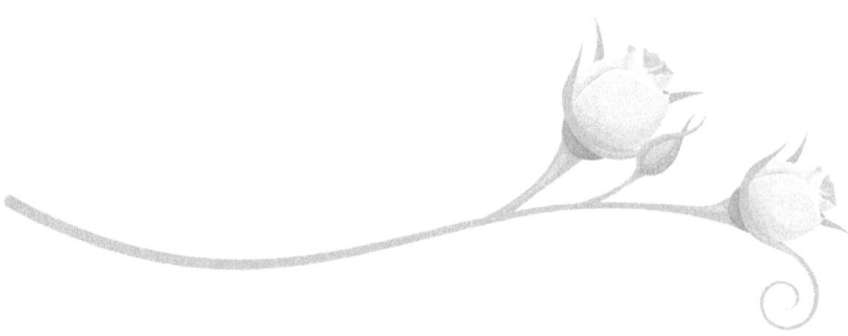

S I X

When Gino Mantia opened his pizza restaurant on Clark Street in the northern neighborhood of Rogers Park, he carried with him the tradition of the deep dish pizza pioneered by his father, Angelo, from an old recipe brought over from Naples. The calendar turned the page on the old century when Angelo first sold pizza on Maxwell Street to the peddlers selling their wares from pushcarts. To generate interest, he gave away slices. Soon he opened his full-service restaurant in the garment district. The family business thrived, taking over the entire lower floor of a nearby office building. When Angelo died, he left the restaurant to his two sons, Ambrogino and Lorenzo. Lorenzo didn't share Gino's dream of expanding the business throughout Chicagoland. This disagreement grew into a dispute. Their sister convinced Renz to buy out Gino's interest to mediate the problem, with both men sharing the secret recipes that provided so much following from their customers. Renz agreed, but only if Gino promised not to open a restaurant near the original Angelo's. With his keen business mind, Gino agreed. Thus, Gino Mantia's was born in Rogers Park.

The summer sky showed indigo blue with the fading sunlight. Will and Glory were in Will's father's car, cleaned and polished by Will for the occasion in exchange for his father agreeing to let Will borrow the Impala. Will had no interest in treating Glory to the charm of his crapped-out excuse for a car. Will pulled in front of her house. Ready, and watching through the large plate glass window, Glory didn't wait for the old-fashioned walk up to the door, the ringing of the bell, and the formality of a greeting. Instead, before the car fully stopped, Glory left her house, jumped down the steps, and ran to the car. Will scrambled to turn off the car, run out and rush around to her door. Maybe he was left out of that formal greeting at the door, but he knew how to be a gentleman. Glory let Will open the door for her. She stopped and reached up and hugged Will, then got into the car.

When Will pulled the car in front of the restaurant, his luck started as a parking space opened. Will parked mere steps from the entrance. Inside, the dark wood-paneled walls dimmed the restaurant clatter. For a Tuesday night, the place had a good crowd. They sat at a gingham-covered table for two along the wall. Above them, hanging on the wall, was a large, framed, black and white photo of a kneeling baseball player, leaning on a bat, with the silhouette of a bear cub lodged within a large "C" adorning the front of the uniform.

Will turned down the hostess's offer of help with his chair but instead stood for a moment to gaze at the large photo.

"Do you know who that is?" Glory asked.

Will took his seat, alternating his glance from the photo to Glory.

"Not sure."

Glory leaned closer to the framed print, spotting the soot-colored placard attached to the bottom of the wooden frame. "Says here, 'Gabby Hartnett - 1922-1940.'"

"I shoulda known. Probably the best catcher ever, at least for the Cubs. But I don't think I ever saw what he looked like. Strapping young man, right?"

"I see two strapping men."

Will leaned toward Glory and reached for her hands. He took her hands, one in each of his. That's when the waiter arrived; ignored by the engrossed couple.

"I take it then that you are a fan."

"You take that right."

"So you play?"

"No more," Will answered. "My playing days ended. Now it's just softball with the guys."

Will explained to Glory his limitations as a player, adding that he never could throw with any accuracy as she saw, and that challenged to a race with his mom, it would be a close call. He lumbered, rather than ran, so they gave him first base, limiting the territory he had to cover to his small corner of the diamond.

"So no college ball for you? I can see you in the purple and white of Northwestern. Say, I never asked; where do you go?"

"Go? You mean college? Nah, that's not for me. Got through high school okay, but now that I'm done with that, I'm done with homework."

"Oh," Glory said. "I thought…Actually, I don't know what I thought."

The waiter's return to take their order gave Glory a moment to think about this tidbit of information about Will. Before she gathered her thoughts to cohesion, Will leaned forward and started.

"Tell me about yourself. I know what I saw. Your home is amazing. How can your parents afford that?"

Glory told Will the short version of her family history, about her great-grandfather's invention of indelible ink used for magazines that doesn't smudge on your fingers. The winds of fortune blew on her great-grandfather, Grady Laughlin, far beyond that of a mere chemist with the meteoric rise of the printing of magazines and pamphlets. In the right place at the right time, Grady developed Witco Chemicals as the primary ink seller throughout the center of the domestic publication industry that helped build downtown Chicago. When Grady expanded to rubber products and more, the money wouldn't stop. Now, her father ran the business as chairman, which still remains a close family business. She told about her uncles taking posts in New York, St. Louis, Los Angeles, and, more recently, France.

"Whew. No wonder. Why isn't your house bigger?" Will asked.

"I guess so he has enough cash to afford his daughter's lifestyle. He wouldn't want to deprive me." She smiled at Will and then watched as their pizza and beer were served.

"You are not deprived."

"Well…He wouldn't buy me a new car. I'm stuck with his old thing."

Will thought she was serious until he looked at her as he cut himself a bite of the thick crust pizza. Her smile and something he saw in her face, not exactly a physical response but a holistic view that talked through him, told him that the entire money thing meant little to her. Will knew that it was too late to pretend that he came from money himself, not that he would do that because he wouldn't even think of it. And that they met at work at Sears displayed his reality.

"You have a great car. I'd take it in a heartbeat." Will took a long drink of his beer. Then he added, "you don't want to see my car. It's better suited for the junkyard."

"Whose car is that?"

Instead of answering, Will looked at her through the golden liquid of the beer in the clear mug.

"You can't hide from me, Will Stanford," she said as she reached to lower the mug away from Will's face. "I saw you. Remember? All of you. Plus, I know your middle name. Now that's something to hide."

"Now I know you're joking. Blythe is a good name; from my grandfather. I never knew him - my mom's dad. Mom talks about him a lot, though. He died in the war. One day I want to visit his grave somewhere in France."

"Have you been?"

Will shook his head.

"Well, maybe one day," Glory said. "France is beautiful, particularly in the south. The southern air, the colors, and the light. If you go, go in the spring. You'll understand why so many artists made their homes there. You may not want to leave. Who's your favorite?"

"Artist?"

Glory nodded.

"Can't say. What are my choices?"

Glory laughed, prompting Will's smile.

"Love this," Glory said through the pizza she was chewing. "Amazing buttery flavor. It melts in my mouth."

Finished with their meal, Glory and Will walked outside and strolled along Clark Street, slowing to look in the shop windows. The air was still, warming to invite the expected heatwave.

"It'll be hot tomorrow," Will said.

"Seems like it."

"There's probably a breeze by the lake. It's just a couple of blocks down the street. Can I take you there?"

Will drove the Impala to Lake Michigan, heading east on Morse Avenue. The street dead-ended at the beach. The last vestiges of sundown had disappeared. Will helped Glory out of the car, and together they started along the sidewalk. Where the sidewalk and sand met, Glory sat on a bench and beckoned Will to join her. They sat in the blended light from the half-moon playing out over the grays of the sand and the overhead street light. Seeing Glory unraveling the leather straps wrapped around her calves and ankles to take off her sandals, Will sat next to her and untied his shoes, pulling off his black socks and rolling up his slacks.

Will and Glory remained on the bench, holding their shoes in their laps. The unseen waves in the distance, beyond the vast stretch of sand spread out before them, sent to the couple echoes of the waves ceaselessly unrolling along the wet sand. The lingering scent of the sea rested among them and was soon ignored. A man and woman passed by with their shaggy golden retriever leading the way. Syllables only, not fully formed as words to Glory's ears, floated away from the strolling threesome.

"Looks pretty safe here," Glory said.

"Yeah. We'll probably see the fuzz drive by to take a look. They keep a pretty good eye on things."

Glory jumped up with no verbal warning and was already three steps toward the beach when she spun around, her skirt swirled along with its dance, and walking backward, Glory waved to Will to join her.

"C'mon, Will. Let's see this beach of yours. You brought me here, so it's gotta be good."

Will rushed next to Glory. She turned in the direction of the waves, and together, shoes in hand, they stepped through the pliable sand.

"You're not afraid, are you," Glory asked.

"Of what?"

"Well, I don't know. Of a stranger rushing out and grabbing my…" and Glory realized all she had was her sandals, the brown leather straps dangling down to brush against the sand, "…shoes."

"I will protect your shoes, my fair maiden," Will said, reaching for the sandals, taking them from her, and turning around in a full circle.

"Will, bring them back." He back-pedaled, holding the sandals by their long straps. She chased after him.

"I will do no such thing. My dear lady has charged me to protect this precious cargo at all costs. And you cannot convince me that they are free from danger. Look around you. See over there?"

Will pointed, and Glory turned to look. A maple tree, loaded with leaves, each fighting to stay awake in the stillness of the night, cast its complete, round shadow over the sand.

"There is darkness there, m'lady. But worry not, these…," and as Will searched for his adjective to describe the sandals, the straps twisted around his arm. One of the sandals slipped past his hand, and Will jerked the strap up to keep the shoe from hitting the sand.

"That's good, sir knight. If protecting them means ripping them to shreds, I'll take care of it."

Glory walked toward Will, who was wrapping the straps around each shoe, which he then handed to Glory. "You, good sir, are relieved of your cobbleristic duty," Glory said.

"Foiled, again," he said. And they started back toward the shoreline.

"So you are not afraid?" Glory repeated the question.

"Of the tree?"

The tandem of their laugh sounded as two-part harmony.

"Of anything?"

"Well, not of the tree. Let's see. There's these three guys, whose names I don't remember."

"Jerry, Abe…."

"And Georgie," Will said. "I remember: stick to George."

They stepped into the last gasp of a wave melting into the sand. Their feet sank lower in the sand. The next wave rolled over their feet and ankles, splashing on the bottom of Glory's skirt and on Will's pants.

"Let me tell you about the men in my life. They love me. They'll protect me. But they know that I can beat the crap out of them."

"Seriously?"

"That's no jive. Well, maybe they let me think that. Anyway, we have a solid relationship. When you meet them, you'll see that they're only to be respected, not feared. And that's even more true about my Dad. He wouldn't hurt anyone, unless pushed."

"No pushing from me. That's a fact."

"So shadows don't scare you, and my big bad brothers aren't even here. What about the war?"

"What about it?"

"You're not afraid of the war? You're old enough to get drafted, and there you'd be, sent to die."

"Yeah, that's why we gotta get rid of Johnson. All he wants to do is send us all to die in Vietnam."

"So you hate the war too?"

"You could say that. But afraid? I don't think I'm afraid. I don't want to get drafted about as much as I want to stay away from a classroom. Both could be bad trips."

A large wave crested on the shore, spraying Will and Glory as they bounced backward, lightly rinsed.

With their dance of evasion complete, Glory leaned into Will and put her arm around his waist. Will complied, pulling her closer to him and reaching his arm around her shoulders.

"Will," Glory asked, turning up to see his face. "Are you going to Canada?"

Instead of answering her question, he leaned down and kissed her lips. Their second kiss opened each to the other, connecting their softness in sensual exploration. Will bent his knees to lower himself with the idea of making their bed on the wet sand, and as he did, he urged her to join him with his full hug.

Glory resisted. She straightened her knees to counter Will's insistence.

"Will, let's not. We don't have a blanket."

She remained in Will's embrace. Then reached up and kissed Will's neck, lingering there, the salty taste of his skin adding the perfect flavor to the moment.

"This was beautiful," Glory said. "But I'm getting cold. Can we go back?"

"Of course," Will answered. The couple turned back toward the street. Will pulled her in even closer while rubbing her back, hoping that the warmth he could offer would flow through them. He, too, felt a chill but was unable to detect if the water and wind chilled him or was it something even closer? Was that a rejection? He felt the beating of her heart while they were kissing. But was she scared of something? She kept asking him if he was afraid. He thought she was asking about him. About what he was feeling. Maybe what she was doing was leaking her own fear through her words, her questions.

"Glory, are you okay?"

The car was a few steps away. They crossed those few yards surrounded by a *weltschmerz* of world weariness that settled over their spirits. When Will later remembered that moment, he felt the warning signs of a train about to cross; the guard gates, the flashing lights, the distant rumble of the approaching train, saying to Will, "stop," "danger," "don't cross." Maybe he should have listened more carefully.

They walked to Glory's side of the car. Glory remained attached to Will as Will put his shoes on the car's roof to take out his keys. He unlocked the door, and felt a squeeze of Glory's arm reaching around him. Together they backed up as the door swung open.

"What happened out there?" Will slid his free hand to reach Glory's hand.

Glory shivered under Will's touch and got in the car. She looked up at Will as he leaned on the open car door window.

"Will, I'm cold. Can we go? Please."

Will nodded and started to smile, but the look on Glory's face stopped the smile in mid-formation. He closed the door and got in on the driver's side.

He turned on the engine and started the heater.

"This'll only take a minute, and you should feel better," Will said to Glory. She wiped saltwater off her face and arms, then reached both arms around in a self-hug.

Will put the car in reverse and swiveled toward Glory to look through the rear windshield. Instead, Glory placed her hand over Will's hand on the steering wheel.

"Can we wait a minute?" Glory asked.

He checked Glory to see what she meant. Her eyes and nose were lost to the shadow created by the overhead visor. He could see only her mouth, so to get any sense of what Glory was thinking became a far more significant challenge, being little more than her words.

"Okay. Why?" Will asked.

"I need to know something."

"What do you need to know? I know stuff."

"This you might know. But maybe not."

"Well then, let me have it, and you'll be tied for the first to know."

"What do you want, Will?"

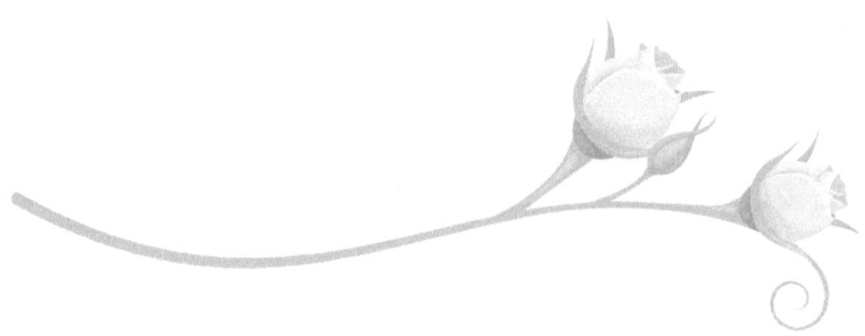

SEVEN

There are few questions posed to one that are more difficult to answer. There are the all-time number one standards, "Why are we here?" and "What's the meaning of life?" To be asked what one wants comes in at a close second. To hear other questions is to consider an internal autobiography, replete with faces and place and paths, all of which swirl around in concentric circles to the point that is the now, so an answer can be formed. Will sat still in his car, the dashboard light casting a glow that Will saw as a shade lighter than dungeon walls, its gray light oozing through the heat bumping up against the chilled air, leaving Will cold.

Will's steady breathing joined with Glory's breaths, and the windshield fog began to bloom. So the question started with "what" does he want. Is it a thing? On considering things to fit the bill as to what he wants other than a towel, perhaps, there is nothing that comes to mind. Of course, she doesn't mean they should drive to Clark Street and hope that Grossman Variety is still open and that he can buy a towel. Here, the "what" is not a thing that can be touched. So what is this "what"? The big things – peace on earth, clean air and water, an end to the war – he wants those. The impersonality of that short list is even further away from Glory's meaning. She asks him to look inside, to find an answer, here, now, sitting on a lamp-lit street, with only half the moon reflecting sparks off the outgoing tide.

Then there's the notion of Will "wanting" something. The car – she's not asking about his car. She's never even seen it. And she already heard his view of that rolling pile of cast-offs. And let's say there's some non-thing, say something far-out – a better memory, more athletic grace – Glory wouldn't ask about these things yet. There will be ample time for those all-night, "I won't hang up first" phone calls. Or is she trying to tell Will that such anticipation may not be realized?

"What do you want, Will?" she asked him. Simple. Few words. But the pile of thoughts followed by words – and, yes, feelings – propped that inquiry up to get in his face. It's no coincidence that the asker intends that the receiver "face" what is put in his face.

And Will did that to himself more than once. But as graduation approached in his last high school semester, that was the only question. Until college admission deadlines came and went, and other than writing his name at the top of one application, NIU, as he recalls, all the other pages with their blank spaces remained just that. He walked away from the whole thing. So, the question repeated in his head, over and over. Scooping up ground balls, there it was. Lapping up a sundae, the question was there, mocking him. In the middle of a test, it would shout out in his head to answer the fucking question. But he brought his fight to this nag, and in time, the echo diminished to the sound of snow landing on ice. And he forgot that such question was still there, waiting, until now.

And then there's the idea that he "wants" something. *"What do you want, Will?"* There is wanting – he wanted Glory. Like in the movies, when the spotlight shines on the star and the rest of the scene fades away, the moment he saw her, Sears faded away, leaving Glory walking not through sporting goods but in a space made only for her, inviting him in. So he stepped into her, and the gods were kind enough to grant him that oneness with her, time and space giving way to ecstasy.

Glory did not ask what Will needs or where his future lie. What he wants is inches away from him, but is she moving another inch farther and then another? But he can't "want" her in the traditional sense. He can't own her. Glory won't be owned; he already knows that about her. She's an unusual woman. Without trying, she can surprise, in ways that make everyone smile at her cleverness; at the way that her next move surpassed the one before. So that's what he wants – her, where immersion in Glory's life would doubtlessly spice his world, if he can keep up.

"I can answer that," Will said, ending the heavy silence.

Glory turned toward Will, her face blank. Glory's scent of French perfume mixed with sea salt escaped to Will as she turned. The sweet-salty smell gave Will a slight boost, with the two opposing scents mingling together in a yin-yang way. It's a sign that there can be a way for them.

"What I want..." Will searched for the thought. "This is what I want. This, right here, you and me."

"Look at me, Will," Glory said. "Do I look to you like this is the best moment? How can this be what you want? We just had a nighttime beach moment, classic, like we should be on a greeting card. But then...."

Will understood the romantic side Glory described and the question hanging above them. The time on the beach was beautiful; a time to remember – that's why Polaroid exists. But this is now more. This is real.

"Don't you see, Glory? Here we are. In this car, together, talking. You're sharing how you feel."

"I don't really know you, seems," Glory said.

"Oh, but you do. I am not complicated."

"Guess not. But what do you see for your life? You don't want to go to college – I don't get that. Where's your future? What about your education?"

"Glory...my future? When Dad convinced me to get a job or I'd have to move out, I actually followed his suggestion. Knowing my sports craze, I thought I'd like to work in sporting goods."

"Do you?"

Will paused for a moment. "Not really. But I can sell. People like me. You don't know how many ask for me. For that, I don't need college."

Glory cranked down the window for a breath of the night air.

"You're a salesman, then?" Glory posed the question to Will. Then she answered it. "I can see that. Well, I actually did. See that, I mean. You sold me, but forgot about the rackets."

"Yeah, I suppose so."

"Do you intend a career in sales?"

"No." Will rolled down his window, leaned his head out, and took in a deep breath. "People see me," he said. "And what do they see? Always a big jock. I don't mind. They often have low expectations. It makes my life easier. I know that I don't have much to prove with this idea that people generally have about me. Actually, what I really want to do is buy for Sears. My dad is a manager at Polk Brothers...."

"I know that store. On Skokie Boulevard, right. Near Gross Point."

"Yeah, that's the place."

"My parents bought our TV there, I think. They seemed to like it."

"Right. So anyway, my Dad's been selling the stuff for my whole life. One of his best friends is Saul. He's a buyer. TVs. He tells stories of all the places he's been, some very far away that I never even heard of. It's, like, a cool gig - traveling, spending other people's money. I don't see the point of going to college."

"You'd be gone a lot."

"That's part of the fun of buying."

"So you want to do that?"

"Well...I think so."

"If you go to college, you won't get drafted."

"I know. I'll take my chances. Maybe we'll end the war first."

And they talked into the night, still sitting in the parked car at the beach, with the sky's darkness hinting at the oncoming dawn. The morning calls of the seagulls chirped Will awake. They both had nodded off, still sitting in their seats. While they were sleeping, Will shut off the engine. Instinctively, overnight they snuggled closer to each other on the bench seat of the Impala, sharing their body heat, their heads resting on each other. When Will opened his eyes, the gold of Glory's hair draped in front of him like a pair of golden sunglasses. He reached for her hair so as not to wake her.

Glory stirred underneath Will's arm. She sat up, yawned, and rubbed her eyes.

"We slept?" Glory asked.

"Yeah. Good morning."

Glory reached for Will, hugging him with a kiss and holding him tight.

"I'm glad we talked, Will."

"Me too."

"What time is it?"

"Does it matter?"

"Depends on what day it is. It's Thursday now, right."

"Yep."

"So, does it matter?

Glory looked at Will, rushing her hands along her hair to set it right. "Probably not."

"So then…breakfast?"

Glory watched a flock of seagulls circling over the beach not far from them.

"Will, I need to stretch. And I want to change."

"So do I."

Will backed out of their embrace and stepped out of the car. He circled around to open Glory's door. Then they walked back to sit on the same bench from which they had begun their beach excursion the night before.

"Today is Thursday, you say?" Will asked.

"As best as I can recall."

"Well, then we can go together."

"Where? What are you thinking, Mr. Stanford."

"Ladies' Day."

Glory's look questioning Will did not require words.

"The Cubs. At Wrigley Field. On Thursday, it's Ladies' Day. Ladies get in free."

Will stood up and turned to reach for Glory. She took his hands and stood. The couple remained in place, watching the sun peeking over the horizon somewhere over Michigan.

"The Giants, right?" Glory asked Will. "I'd hate to be the Giants today; how the Cubs lost to the Braves? The ump was wrong. The catcher blocked the plate. It was clear obstruction. But still, I'd love to see Willie Mays and McCovey. It's too bad they aren't Cubs."

"You're a fan?"

"Three generations a fan. The story is Grandpa Dave once tried out for the Cubs. Apparently, he didn't make the cut. But he always loved the game. Dad, too."

"Who's your favorite?"

"It's between Ernie and Billy Williams. And I have no interest in choosing, so don't ask."

"I wouldn't think of putting you in that position."

"Take me home, Will. Then pick me up. In your car."

"Uh…I can keep the Impala. My dad has the jalopy."

"Then switch back. I want to see the real William Blythe Stanford in all his glory. Get it, in all his…."

Will laughed. "You are clever. Let's get you home. The arena awaits, m'lady."

"Where were you last night?" Teri asked Glory through the princess phone, back in Glory's room.

"We had a date."

"All night? Who is this guy? Must be pretty special for you to be out all night."

Glory sat up in her bed, pulling a pillow over her lap. After Will dropped her off, she skipped past breakfast and went right up and slept. The late morning sun woke her. When Teri called, Glory was already working out what she would wear. Thursday afternoon, the day was partly cloudy, with a slight chance of rain. At Wrigley, it's not the rain but the wind to prepare for. When the wind blows off Lake Michigan, the chill can arrive without any warning. Or the wind may be still. Only the grand dame of the largest fresh body of water on earth knows, and she'll tell you when she wants to.

"He's Will. And, yes, we spent time together. But last night, we fell asleep in his car at Morse Beach."

"Okay. I'll hear more from you later. Don't forget, we start at eleven."

"Right. Totally forgot. What are we doing, again?"

"It's for the protest this weekend. You promised to help make the posters. Everybody will be here."

"I'll see you in twenty minutes. Is there any of your Mom's banana cake left? I'm starving."

"You know there is. She saved a piece for you."

"I can't stay the whole time, Izzie. I'm going to the game. Will's taking me. But I'll have him pick me up at your house so you can meet him."

"I don't think she liked me," Will said. Will followed Glory down the front steps leading from the front door of Teri's home. Glory knew why Will would think that, as she used to feel the same way. Teri often makes people believe that she doesn't like them. Glory knows Teri to be a serious woman. Rarely does she smile or crack a joke. She'll laugh, but only when something is genuinely witty. To her, trying to be funny is a quick path to her dark side. But she would do anything for Glory. Following Teri's lead in the fall of their sophomore year Glory allied herself with Yuna, and abandoned her prior station as a cheerleader.

When they started high school at Oak Park, Teri had recently moved from the city. Glory joined in with her friends in harassing Teri. Day after day, they made fun of her looks – her pear-shaped body supporting the dark curls commanding a mop of hair that Teri was forever pushing away from her eyes. And there was the nose, prominent and dominating her comely face. Glory never gave much thought to her feelings about Jews. But she hated things she heard from some of the other girls, and almost all of her cheerleading teammates - hateful words, ignorant of their impact of the hurt they could inflict. Glory lowered her head thinking about how she and her "friends" treated Teri. But then Teri showed that there is more to a person than how they look or how they call themselves. Or even their religion. Her dad taught Glory about the worth of all people and that she was taught that everyone has merit. Then what happened to Yuna Sunshin changed everything. Glory knew nothing of Yuna when she started at Oak Park in tenth grade other than her Oriental appearance, her accented English, and that she was brilliant. She didn't even think to inquire further. But what happened to Yuna prompted Glory to learn the story of her family escaping from Korea, deathly afraid. Yuna later explained the abuse they suffered in Korea and the fear of much more significant harm from the simple fact that her father worked as a translator for the Americans stationed at Osan Air Force Base near her home in Songtan.

When it happened, it was Teri who stepped up. For Glory, on the other hand, living in her Oak Park bubble, when she saw Yuna and Teri walking into school together was the first time she saw firsthand how people can suffer. Sure she read the newspaper and kept an eye on the TV news. The tragedies that occurred all over the globe bothered her but stayed in her distant view. Until they didn't.

Because one day, Yuna wasn't in class. Teri later told Glory what had happened. In their speech and debate class, Yuna was Teri's partner and was worried that she hadn't heard anything from Yuna. Nobody who Teri asked knew anything. Teri checked on her when the third day came and she had no partner to practice with. She called and was relieved to find out that Yuna was home. Teri went to see her. She walked into Yuna's home. The shock of seeing Yuna almost brought Teri to her knees. There she was, in the living room, with gray light seeping through the shaded windows. The sight of Yuna sitting in the armchair, with her face wrapped in bandages, her arm in a sling, shocked Teri. Looking back, only then did Teri notice that her mom's eyes were red, accompanied by a slight sniffle. Teri rushed to sit on the couch next to the armchair.

"Yuna. My god. What happened? Are you okay?"

Yuna dabbed her free eye with a tissue, and explained through tears about the attack in the city. Her family was driving through downtown and got lost looking for a gas station. When they stopped to ask for directions, instead of helping, the gang hanging out on the street pushed her father. Yuna's brother got out to help, and he was attacked. She and her mother were forced out of the car and roughed up. In the melee, Yuna's face was sliced from the flying glass of a shattered window, and she suffered a broken arm. Someone had gouged her father, and he was in the hospital. He may lose his eye, Yuna explained. Fortunately, her mom was not hurt, except for the scar of reliving the attack. In her tragedy, Teri saw Yuna as a girl in pain, regardless of where she came from or how she looked.

"Yuna, I am so sorry this happened to you," Teri said.

Yuna looked back at Teri. Teri saw the single tear dropping from Yuna's free eye.

The day Yuna returned to school, Teri walked with her through the staring crowd of teenagers. Shed of the face bandages, the scars running down her face were in the darkest stages of healing, rendering a fierceness to one side of her face. Glory couldn't believe what she saw. Two obvious misfits, yet they walked through the crowd like they were on their way to a coronation. Teri explained afterward that the two girls made a pact, even practicing their walk and their stoic facial expressions, knowing that everyone would watch them.

The sight shook up Glory, watching from a distance, trying to comprehend what happened to Yuna. And the way they walked as if they owned the school struck Glory as acts of strength that Glory doubted she would match in similar circumstances. For the rest of that day, whenever she saw Yuna, Teri was close by. Teri and Yuna sat together during lunch. Glory's cheerleader captain, Amanda, got up from the cheerleader table, followed, of course, by Holly – captain and her first mate – and made their way to Yuna and Teri, who were gathering their lunch trays to return to the kitchen. Glory rose with the rest of the cheerleaders as they followed their leaders, but slowly separated herself as she sauntered toward the table, hoping that her break from the gang would not be noticed.

"What happened to you? You are even more freaky now." That was Amanda.

Holly, ever the loyal lieutenant, added her own vitriol. "How do you say Frankenstein in Chinese?"

The two girls leaned into each other, cackling, and walked back to their waiting minions. As they did, Glory edged backward, away from the cafeteria doors, and watched the prima donnas of Oak Park High School exit, all proud of their latest triumph. Glory slowly turned as if to join them. She made it only as far as the hallway, found the restroom door, and snuck inside. In a stall, she locked the door, cried, and wondered what was next for her. But as part of the clique, Glory felt twisted inside. This couldn't be real. Who was she? How could people treat each other like that? They are her friends, so what does that say about her?

Later that night, after dinner, she told her parents what had happened. Unsurprisingly, her father agreed that the other girls' actions were uncalled for. Her mother dismissed the incident as kids being kids; that people learn from what they do.

"Mother, we're not kids. I'm almost seventeen and practically an adult."

"That's how you think now," Beth said. "When you're older, you'll understand."

"Dad…" Glory answered both of them.

"Glory, your mother is right, too. You can't truly understand why people act the way they do, even your friends. Sometimes especially your friends."

Was she like her friends? She didn't feel that way watching the leaders confront Yuna. And anyway, what did she have in common with them, other than the absurdity of cheerleading. Plus, she didn't even like the Beatles all that much. Come to think of it, she didn't care much for cheerleading either, jumping around and screaming at a game that she didn't really understand nor care about. Most of the football players acted like jerks much of the time, too.

With nighttime descending over the household, Glory stayed up in the den, sitting in the recliner, then moving on to the couch to better view the books lined up on the bookcase nearby. She took to studying the titles and the authors' names. The books spoke to Glory, inviting her to open the pages and enter the worlds created by the authors' solo efforts. The titles from their collection of Hemingway's novels sang out to her. She knew his story, coming from Oak Park as he did, always remembering the crazy mother who wanted Ernie to be a twin with her daughter. Glory understood that Ernie overcompensated for the rest of his life for those years of confusion, constantly working hard to show the world that he was a man. She found the tragedy of his recent suicide at age sixty-one to be only sad; that the man never became a whole person. When he could no longer write nor play the role to the world of the drinking, hunting *übermensch* who no longer existed in Ernie, he had no reason to exist either.

By dawn, after sleeping a couple of hours, Glory woke up with not only a plan but as an entirely different person. This was a new day, a day to start becoming real, not the Barbie doll for the entertainment of the high school crowd. Despite the lack of sleep, Glory felt fresh, encouraged with her new idea by the blast of autumn air, spiced with the scent of falling leaves, blowing through her window.

She arrived at school early and waited against a tree in front of the entrance. It was impossible to miss the show of the cheerleaders walking by in complete navy blue and white uniforms with the "OP" emblazoned on the front. They looked like clowns ready to perform in the circus instead of a pep rally. When Amanda summoned Holly to find out why Glory wasn't with them and why she wasn't wearing her uniform, Glory told Holly to let her boss know that she wasn't participating. Glory handed a paper bag to Holly. She opened it and saw inside Glory's uniform crumpled at the bottom. When pressed for more information from Holly, Glory dismissed her with a wave of her hand. Holly walked back to the waiting girls, who looked at Glory. Together they turned away to head into school. That was fine by Glory. Then saw Teri and Yuna get out of a car nearby. She didn't wait for an invitation.

Glory left her base of the tree trunk and walked toward the two girls. Teri and Yuna stopped in their path, but didn't say anything, instead watching Glory come in closer.

"Hi," Glory said.

In unison, Teri and Yuna returned the greeting.

Then silence. Standing no more than three feet apart, with the brick facade of the school rising above them, the quiet continued. It was Teri who broke the short trance.

"Can we help you?" she asked. "Your friends are inside. You should be with them."

"No I shouldn't," Glory said. "I should be here. I am sorry for how they acted yesterday."

"Really," said Yuna. "You were part of it. You're in that group."

"I was. I turned in my uniform."

"Why?"

Glory didn't answer directly. She walked to close the gap, dropped her books, and reached to Yuna, arms open. Yuna backed away. Teri stood where she was, watching.

"I need a hug," Glory said. Yuna stopped and let Glory reach her arms around her. Then Glory backed away.

"Can I walk with you?" Glory asked.

Yuna and Teri looked at each other. Then Teri answered Glory.

"We don't understand. Yesterday you were a cheerleader with them. Now you're not."

"No. I'm not."

"Then let's walk to school." And they did. The twitter of voices shadowed them the rest of that day.

Teri and Yuna aced their speech class. Teri coached Yuna to erase her accent, and Yuna taught Teri and Glory how to speak certain choice phrases in Korean. They were all selected for the yearbook staff in their junior year. Yuna borrowed her dad's Tachihara field camera, already demonstrating artistry as a photographer. By their senior year, they were in charge of the yearbook, with Teri, of course, being the editor in chief and Glory her assistant editor. Over those years, they shed the conservative attire leftover from the Fifties, adopting a modern look as the Sixties evolved in opposition to the war and police brutality and in support of civil rights. Their paths diverged as their graduation approached, and Yuna announced her acceptance to Cal Berkeley. By the summer's end, with the onset of their college careers, the girls gathered at Yuna's home and said goodbye to her in a group hug that none wanted to end. But as the friends they were, Glory and Teri felt proud through their tears as they watched Yuna leave in her parent's car, that their friend was moving up, and promised to visit her in California.

Teri and Glory roomed together in the woman's dorm on the Northwestern campus, entering as freshmen in the fall term of 1966. Focusing on their schoolwork, they committed to helping each other, and by the end of their first year, their grades showed that their devotion paid off. They supported President Johnson's signing of the civil rights act, participating in campus rallies. When Students for a Democratic Society organized on campus, they both joined, determined that the new law was only the beginning of the changes they had in mind, not only for their school but well beyond.

Glory, Teri, and Yuna all returned home over the summer. Not long after, they read the news of the West Side Riots in Lawndale. Together they joined the march in Marquette Park on the South Side organized by Martin Luther King, Jr. Yuna captured an image of Dr. King speaking face to face with Chief of Police Wilson that the Tribune accepted and published on its front page. Glory kept a notebook with her and took notes of the various events over the summer, intent on submitting a piece to *The Daily Northwestern,* which both Glory and Teri vowed to join as staff reporters once the school year began.

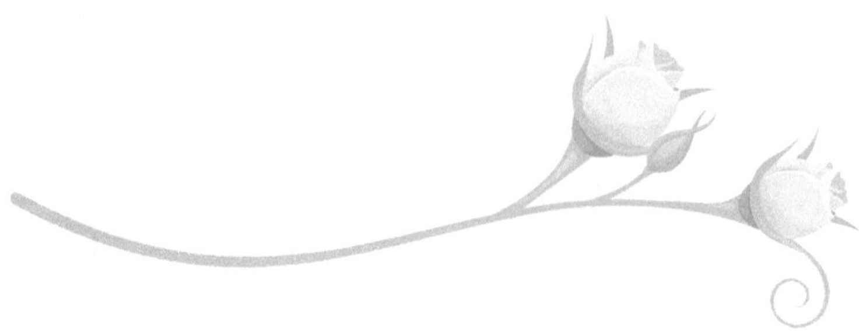

E I G H T

By the time Will followed Glory's directions to Teri's house to pick her up for the game, Teri's leadership in the local SDS chapter was in full swing. As Teri opened the door, the smell of marijuana drifted to Will, in harmony with the music of The Doors playing on the stereo.

"Hi, again, Will," Teri said as she stepped back from the open door. Teri was wearing a full-length tie-dyed dress, her hair crowned with a single row of braided pink and yellow peonies.

Will reached out his hand in a formal greeting. Teri ignored the gesture, reached her arms around Will's neck, and pulled him into a hug. Separating, she called out to the room full of people, "Hey everybody. This is Will. He's come to help. Will this is everybody." Teri looked at Will and winked at him. The announcement was met with a chorus of "thank you"s, with a smattering of "groovy" and "far out."

Glory emerged from the side of the room, wearing jeans and a t-shirt with the Cubs' logo. She added her own voice. "He's here for me," she declared, to oohs and aahs from the group which Glory could not decide if the sentiments were attempts at sarcasm or acknowledgment of the physical presence that always accompanied Will.

Will whispered to Glory, following a quick hug, "We don't have much time. Why did you tell her that I am here to help?"

They held hands, and Glory responded to Will. "I don't ever know what she'll say. Let's show her and make a poster. Something positive."

Glory led him to a spot on the floor. She grabbed a poster board and some markers and handed one to Will as she urged him to sit with her.

"What are we gonna write?" Will asked.

"I don't know…maybe you can come up with something." Glory was handed a joint, took a hit, and passed it to Will, who did the same. They sat together discussing the message they wanted to write. The music stopped, and off to the side of the room, a man with straight hair hanging past his shoulder blades, wearing a leather vest with fringes hanging down and no shirt, started playing a guitar and singing. Glory took another hit. Will declined.

"I know this song," Will said. "Give me a minute."

"You like Bob Dylan?" Glory asked, leaning over the poster board and drawing letters in purple ink.

"This is not Dylan. Phil Ochs. I picked up his album. Great songs. That guy singing, do you know him? He's pretty good."

"That's Garfield. A music major, as you might guess. But unfortunately, he's heading back to Indiana soon, so you'll have to soak in his music now before he leaves."

"Hey, Glory. Don't Teri's parents mind what's going on here?"

"No. They're very cool. That's why we can do this here. Not many of the over thirty crowd support what we're doing, even if they agree with our position."

Will rolled the marker in his hands while Glory finished her work on the poster. Will stood and followed. "That's it, guys," Glory said. "We gotta go. Can someone tell Teri we left, and I'll call her tonight?"

Yuna stood up and walked over to Glory and Will. "Hi, Will. I'm Yuna." She shook Will's hand.

"Hello," Will replied.

Yuna said, "I think she's outside with Oran, working on the arrangements for Saturday. Will, are you coming with us? We don't have enough cars? Can you can be a driver? You have a car, right?"

Will looked at Yuna, who barely came up to Will's chin, giving Will a better view of the shine of Yuna's black hair. "I guess," Will answered. "What are we doing?"

"I'll fill him in," Glory interjected. She turned past them and took a blue Cubs baseball cap with the red "C" and a worn baseball glove from a table near the front door. Will joined her and reached for the glove. "Mine's in the car. I never would've thought that you'd bring one too. Far out. Is it yours?"

"Like I told you, I have three brothers. What do you think?"

"Between the two of us, we have to catch at least one foul ball," Will said, handing the glove back to Glory. "I've tried, but I only got close once in all the games I've been to."

"It's my karma, I think," Glory said. "I have a few, but the very first one I caught I gave to my cousin. He was seven, and I was already a teen, but that's what you do, right? Let's get going. The lot at the Ridgeland station could be crowded already."

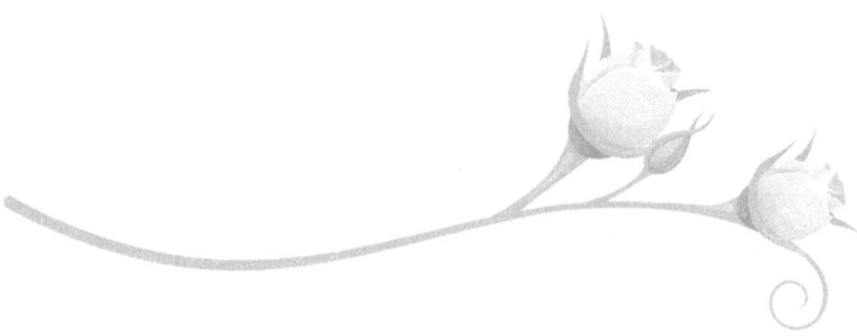

N I N E

Together they walked to Will's car. "This is great," Glory said.
"What's great?"
"Your car."
"You're kidding."
"No, I mean it. I love these older cars. And like you said, if the engine is smooth, there's nothing that a good paint job and a better seamstress couldn't fix."

Will opened her door. "You're serious," Will said.

"Serious as my mother. Oh, but you haven't met her yet."

Glory lowered herself into the seat, and Will shrugged and eased the door closed. In typical fashion, his door required the heavy prompting of Will's foot. Getting in the car, Will noticed that Glory did not laugh but merely watched. Then she said, "well, maybe a mechanical fix or two."

On the ride to the subway station, Will looked over at Glory with her hat perched on her head. He alternated between his views of the road and that of her hat. He had to take a closer look. "Is that a real hat?"

"Of course, it's a hat. It's on my head, isn't it?"
"That's not what I…You're sassin' me?"
"I know. It's fun, huh?"
"Well…Anyway, let me see it."

She handed the cap to him. An inscription was written on the inside of the visor: "To Glory, keep the magic. Ron Santo."

"You know Santo?"

"My dad does. In the off-season he sells insurance. Dad's been his client for a couple of years. Groovy guy."

"And fun to watch," Will said. "They all are. What a team, right? This is going to be good. Plus, we can watch the Willies at work too."

"I've discussed this with my dad, you know. He says Willie Mays is the greatest player ever. I don't know why he says that. Look at Ty Cobb, Lou Gehrig, and Babe Ruth. Now there's something special about him. There was, I mean. A top pitcher and then the greatest home run hitter this game will ever know. Plus, how can he ignore Ernie Banks. I mean, c'mon. It's Ernie."

"Yeah, and sweet swingin' Billy Williams. I copied my swing after him. Smooth and always in control."

"So we will probably never agree," Glory said. Will glanced over at her. "I don't mean you and me," she continued. "Pop is enamored of Willie. Plus, he's still upset that the Giants left for the left coast. He loved the competition. The Giants don't come to Wrigley as often."

"You know today's starters, then?"

"And do you?" she asked.

"Nope. Thought I'd let you tell me, how you read the newspaper and all."

"You don't?"

Will kept his focus on the road, his stoicism answering her question.

"I do know," Glory said. "You probably never heard of him. Bill Stoneman. He's actually a local kid from Oak Park, but he grew up in L.A., I think. Durocher gave him his first appearance against the Giants last week in San Francisco, and he did pretty good. So now he gets the start. We'll see. But up against those guys for his sophomore outing…I don't know."

"You know a lot about the game, I see. Very impressive."

"Thanks, Will. What's not to love about the Cubbies."

The Ridgeland station was crowded as Glory predicted. The plethora of Cubs shirts and hats and pennants rendered the subway car as a rolling advertisement for the Cubs. After transferring to the Red Line, they exited at Addison Street at the southeast corner nearest Wrigley Field, closest to the right-field corner. Glory and Will joined the teeming crowd down the stairs from the elevated platform and walked along Addison. With Wrigley Field on their right, they aimed for the main entrance. Closing toward the main gate, Will pulled Glory away from the stadium.

"What's up, Will?" Glory asked.

"Let's step back and take a look. I'll explain in a minute."

They walked toward the center in line with the main entrance and crossed the street. On the sidewalk, the entire facade of the stadium stood before them, ranging to the left and to the right, the light sand color of the cement walls offering a bland presence. The only color came from the red of the old sign, welcoming them to *"Wrigley Field Home of the Chicago Cubs"* in curved lettering as a reminder of the early days of Chicago Cubs baseball.

"What Santo wrote on your hat gave me an idea," Will said. "The magic of this place."

"I get it."

"Probably you do. See how gray it all looks. Not just the stadium walls, but the street, the buildings."

"Sure. But there's color. Look at all the Cubs blue walking by."

"Right. But when we walk in, let's remember the grayness outside."

"As you say, boss."

They bought Will's ticket and entered through the turnstile. Inside, the lower level was jammed with people going in two directions. The smells mixed together – popcorn, hot dogs smothered Chicago style with grilled onions and sauerkraut, spilt beer, and the aroma emanating from the mass of humans gathering together. They felt the buzz in the air that joins the fans in celebrating their team and the excitement of being at the ballpark. They passed a small, hand-made wooden counter painted in blue, with a line of people, mostly kids, stretching through the crowd. Behind the small counter were three players in full uniform greeting the fans and signing autographs.

"I love that they do that," Will said. "It's too late today, but when Mom used to bring me, we'd get here early, and I'd get to meet the players."

"Yeah," Glory said. "That's Culp. Yesterday's starter against the Braves. And Don Kessinger. What a great shortstop."

"I met him. Super cool. And if Hundley's not behind the plate…"

"…I'd rather not watch," Glory finished for him. "Not exactly correct, but I feel the same."

When they found the ramp leading up to their section, Will again pulled Glory away from the ramp to lean against the far wall. "So here's what I was saying," Will said. "This is the super cool part, given how dark it is under here. When we get up the ramp, into the sunlight, don't rush."

"Oh, I know what you're saying. Let's do this."

Glory pulled Will by the hand, and they worked their way through the crowd and up the ramp. At the top, they stopped and showed the usher their tickets. The organist playing the Beatles' *All You Need Is Love* filled the charged atmosphere. They then took two more steps and stopped again. There, the sparkle of the Kelly green of the Wrigley Field diamond and outfield turf spread out before them, an image of what the Emerald City of Oz would be if it were horizontal. The pitcher's mound sat nestled in the center of the infield grass. The brown dirt of the infield contrasted with the brightness of the green lawn surrounding it. Past the outfield, rising up along the wall curving at the edge of the outfield grass, the green leaves of the thick ivy hid the red brick of the outfield walls, with the cut-outs expertly highlighting the white block numbers showing the distance in feet from home plate to the wall. The manual scoreboard, the crown of the stadium, stood perched atop the center field bleachers, green with the white and yellow lettering and numbers, displaying the game status and the scores of all the games that day. The centerfield flag was blowing in, predicting a pitcher's duel. Halfway down the flagpole, as on a sailboat mast, the scorekeeper hung the blue "L" flag from yesterday's loss to Atlanta. Around the stadium, the seats were filling for a sold-out Ladies' Day crowd.

"This is a wonder," Glory said.

Will let out a low whistle in agreement. "I love this place. I've felt only magic every time I come here."

They climbed up to their seats as the grounds crew completed hosing down the infield dirt and inserted the reflective white bases in their spots. They settled into their seats as the public address announcer announced the starting lineups. Will opened his scorecard and, with the short pencil that came with it, followed along and wrote in the lineups.

"You keep score?" Glory asked.

"Every game. I've got a whole stack of these at home."

"Well, you got me there. I've seen dad keep score now and again, but I prefer to watch and root for the home team." A boy about nine years old sat next to Will, and next to him was a woman who was obviously the boy's mother. They wore the standard blue Cubs hat with the red emblem. The boy had a mitt in his right hand and peered at the field, pounding the glove with his left hand. The crowd roared and stood as one as the Cubs ran onto the field.

"*...And the home – of the – brave*" sang out through the fans. With the last note, they resumed their seats. When the warmups ended, the home plate umpire's instruction to *"play ball"* bellowed through the stadium.

Will looked at the boy and noticed that his mitt was the same brand as Will's. He leaned toward the boy. "Ever catch one?" he asked. The boy looked at Will and shook his head. "Well, maybe today's your day."

"Yeah," the boy answered. "Santo and Banks can hit it here."

"And we get the bonus of Mays too."

The boy smiled and turned his view back to the field.

"What's your name?" Will asked. Then leaning further, he asked the mom, "It's okay, ma'am, if I talk with your son?"

The mom gave Will a once over and saw Glory leaning toward them.

"It's okay. It's up to him. He doesn't like to miss anything so he can keep score."

The crowd roared as the first pitch from Stoneman was fouled off by Jesus Alou to start the game with strike one. The boy forgot about Will, but Will saw a small smile leap onto the boy's face. The first two innings went by quickly. In the bottom of the third, Santo singled back up the middle, scoring Popovich from second base. The fans rose as one at the excitement of the Cubs' first run. The Giants tied the game in the fifth inning. In the sixth, Santo popped one foul ball after another, one falling only a few rows from Will, with fans scrambling to get it as it bounced high above the seats. Then Santo managed to straighten one out that landed in the back rows of the left-field bleachers for a solo home run.

After Santo circled the bases, the crowd settled back into their seats, but the twittering continued. Will leaned to Glory. "That's your guy." Glory smiled and patted Will on his arm, turning her attention to Ernie Banks taking his turn at bat. During play, Will noticed that the boy next to him never varied from his gaze toward the field, taking in every pitch and writing down each batter's results. Will admired the kid's focus, as Will had missed a few batters, talking with Glory and leaving for hot dogs and drinks. The kid denied his offer of a hot dog, but mom accepted, offering Will cash, which he refused.

It was the bottom of the sixth, with Ernie Banks batting, when Will turned his attention to the boy next to him. "Hey, kid," Will said. "What's your name? You're pretty good at keeping score."

Ernie took the first pitch, easy to pass on as it bounced off the dirt to the catcher.

"Thanks," the boy answered. "Alan."

"Far out," Will said. Then he leaned closer and asked the boy, "Who's your favorite."

"Don't got one." Down below, Ernie took a huge cut at an outside fastball. Will and Alan watched the ball arc up toward them. Looking to Will as the kind of lazy fly ball he knew too well, he joined the small crowd around them rising to their feet as the ball reached the top of its parabola and began its descent. Will reached up with his glove hand and snagged the fly ball. Alan stood and reached up with his mitt under Will's considerable shadow.

They all sat back in their green-painted seats. Will looked at the ball and showed it to Glory. "You got one," Glory said, taking the ball from him and twirling it in her hand. "You must be excited. I can see that."

Will nodded and retrieved the ball from her. He rubbed his finger along the raised red stitching of the ball, noticing the small bruise on the otherwise white ball where Ernie's bat knocked it into the stands. Will's heart remained pounding from the dual thrills of Santo's home run and catching the foul ball. Looking again at the ball, the feeling he expected evaded him. Maybe ten years ago, he'd still be jumping up and down from catching the ball. Then Alan leaned to grab his scorecard from the ground and bumped his arm. The boy would probably have had his first foul ball if Will wasn't there. He's a kid, Will considered. Then with a sudden move, Will reached the ball toward Alan. Alan looked up at him, smiled, and opened his glove toward Will. Will dropped the ball into the glove. Alan took the ball, and repeatedly tossed it into his glove. His mom watched the interaction. "What do you say, Alan?"

"Thank you, sir," Alan complied with his mom's urging.

"Glad to do it, young man," Will said as they joined the crowd standing as Banks hit a deep fly ball to the right-field corner, not far from them. It could've been a second homer in a row but fell short of the bleachers, caught by the right fielder.

Inning fell by after inning, and more runs scored with small ball forced by the strengthening wind, with the game tied 4-4 after seven. Neither team could push home the winning run, taking the game into extra innings. The late afternoon shadows reached across the entire infield and much of the outfield, cooling the air to a stark chill and darkening the scene. Alan and his mom left after the eleventh inning. They stood and gathered, as the mom told Will that she wanted to get home before it got dark. Alan then added, "Thanks, mister," showing Will the baseball lodged in his mitt.

The game finally ended in the bottom of the twelfth when McCovey scooped up a ground ball and, instead of taking the sure out by stepping on first base, tried for the double play with a throw to second base. With one out and men on first and second, had it worked, the inning would have been over, and extra innings would have continued. To the Cubs' good fortune, McCovey's throw hit Adolfo Phillips' hand as he raised his arms to protect himself from the throw, diverting the ball into the outfield. By the time the Giants' second baseman tracked down the ball, the throw home was late, and the Cubs backup catcher scored the winning run from second base.

The buzz of the late-inning victory died down, leaving the spent fans to their solitary pursuits, some reliving the error by McCovey and seeing Spangler round third to beat the throw home. The "L" train lurched from one station to the next. When two seats opened, they were already one stop away from the transfer station to the Green line – destination: Oak Park. Glory and Will fell back in their seats, holding hands, with the tracks drumming their lengths passing under the rail car. Will copied

Glory and closed his eyes against the whiteness of the overhead lights. The sweet bark-like scent of marijuana floated past them. At Ridgeland, they roused themselves off the depths of the curve of their plastic seats, exited the train, and walked to Will's car.

Will repeated the pattern from before, including kicking the door handle. This time Glory kept her thoughts to herself. On the way back to Glory's house, Will watched as Glory rose in her seat, turned around, and reached behind Will. When she straightened back up, she was holding a baseball. "Whatcha doin' with that?"

"Is this a game ball?" she asked.

"Yes. I mean no."

"You must be tired."

"Probably. What I mean is we sell the official game balls at Sears. So it's an official game ball. I got a bunch of them. How did you know it was even back there? It's so dark."

"Don't know. I guess the street light and the ball must have been perfectly aligned. The shine's still on it."

They rode together in silence. Will leaned to the radio, turning up the sound on Tim Hardin singing *If I Were A Carpenter*. Glory added her own voice. Not to be left out, Will, too, sang out as he drove along.

The rolling patter of the overhead street lights drew its meandering shapes on the car's dashboard decorating their short ride back to Glory's house. Will pulled the car into the driveway, turned off the engine, and rolled down the window. The dark of the car's interior enhanced the sense of separation, in contrast to the white of the nighttime lights ringing around the vehicle. Yellow light spilled from the house's front windows, adding to the dichotomy of man-made lighting competing with nature's moonless sleep. Only the vibrato of the crickets played as music against the stillness of the night.

On cue as if directed by an orchestra conductor, Glory and Will spoke simultaneously. "I'm not up to coming…" from Will crashed with Glory asking if he "wanted to come inside."

"Maybe another day," Glory concluded the duet.

"I suppose."

Will then realized that Glory held his baseball for the entire ride back to her house. She still tossed the ball from one hand to the other.

Will watched her game of catch. Without warning, she tossed it toward him. Instinctively, he caught it with a swinging motion of his arm.

"Can you sign it?" she asked.

"What?"

"Yeah. You must have a pen in here somewhere."

When Will didn't respond, Glory rummaged through the glove compartment and pulled out a pen. "Try this," she said, handing the pen to him.

"Why? You misunderstand. I'm not anybody. It'll ruin the ball."

"Hardly. That's more than appropriate for my souvenir of our first game together. I'd like it. You can put your mark if that's better."

Will took the pen and brushed his initials on the ball. "Here. Happy now?"

She took the ball back from Will. "That's two from you, Will. What should I do with them?"

Will shrugged.

"Anyway, I thought it was sweet of you to give the ball to that boy."

"That's what's done," Will said.

"But never for you."

"True enough. I've waited all of my twenty years. When I caught that ball and then looked over at Alan, as always pounding his mitt, I couldn't help but wonder how he'd feel with the ball. He could've caught it, you know."

"But you did. Your first ever."

"His smile erased half of my twenty years for a minute."

Glory reached for Will, and he obliged, leaning toward her. Their deep kiss lasted, arms reaching for each other. Glory kept the ball in her hand, rolling it over Will's back. He let out a slight moan, leaning back from Glory.

"That feels great," Will said. His voice revealed the release of tension from the ball's rolling against his back.

"If you want to come up, I can give you a massage after we put together something to eat."

Will thought about it until a breeze came through the window, carrying his hours-old scent to his nose. "Maybe I should go home. It's late. Plus, I need a shower." Will opened his door and walked around the car to open Glory's door.

"You didn't tell me about the protest," Will said.

"What protest?" Glory asked as she got out of the car. "Oh, Teri and Yuna and the SDS gang. There's a war protest on Saturday downtown."

"Sounds great."

Ready to unlock the front door as they stood together on the porch, Glory put her arms around Will. "I had a great time today. When you caught that ball, were you protecting me?"

Will laughed and pulled Glory closer. "I don't remember. And like you like to remind me, with three brothers, I doubt it's you who needs protecting."

"I can see your point. But maybe, one day…." Glory leaned up for one more kiss, then broke away and scampered inside. "Goodnight, William," she said as she leaned against the door jamb with the door swinging to close. Will spun toward the steps and jigged his way back to his car.

T E N

Before she even made it through the front door, Glory smelled the steaks that her father had put on the grill. She found her mother in the kitchen preparing for dinner.

"We didn't know if you would be here. You should take this and add it to the grill. Your father just went out there, so it's fine."

Glory took the plate with the lone steak on it and walked outside onto the patio.

"There you are, Firefly. How was the game?

"We won in twelve. I'm glad McCovey's not a Cub."

"What do you mean? You told me yesterday that you wished he was a Cub. What changed your mind?"

"Only that he didn't take the easy out and instead threw his attempt at a double play right into the runner. He won the game for us."

Fred smiled and stabbed the steak with the grilling fork and laid it on the hot barbecue.

"Who did you go with?" Fred asked, keeping his focus on the steaks.

"Will."

"Who's Will? I haven't heard about that one."

"He's cool, dad. Anyway, I gotta wash up." Glory scampered back inside.

Under the night lights of the patio, Glory sat with Fred and Beth, enjoying their steaks and grilled vegetables.

"Glory tells me she has a new boyfriend," Fred said.

"I didn't say that."

"You told me that this boy took you to the game. If so, that's not the first time you were together. I'm right about that, no?"

Glory laughed. "You always know. It's like you can see inside me. Read my mind. Yeah, since you said so, I guess he is my boyfriend."

"What's his name?" Beth asked.

"Will."

"That's not a name. It's what we wrote for you, so that, one day, all of this will be yours…and your brothers."

"Mom. Why?" Glory shook her head and placed her fork on the plate. "It's his name. Well, part of it."

"There's more?"

"Of course. William Blythe Stanford."

Beth didn't respond. Fred and Glory waited for her to continue.

"So he's from the Cincinnati Stanfords?" Beth asked. "How did you meet him?"

Glory looked at Fred and shook her head. "Mom, no. I don't even know the Cincinnati Stanfords. Is that some kind of baseball team?"

Beth turned to Fred. "Honey, she's your daughter. What is she talking about?"

"Tell us about Will," Fred said. "What's he studying?"

"See, I knew you'd find a guy at Northwestern," Beth added.

"Ugh," Glory uttered. "He's a kind, gentle, thoughtful man."

"Great," Beth said. "What's his major? I bet he's pre-med, with a name like that."

"You should have invited him in for dinner." Fred leaned toward Glory. "I guess you're over Matthew."

"Did you have to bring him up?"

"I liked him. He's on track for a great future. I don't know why it didn't work out between you two."

"Dad, it just didn't. Alright?" Glory thrust her chair back, the legs screeching their complaint of the sudden movement. She got up and took the dirty dinner plates from the table. "I'll get dessert."

When she was gone, Beth spoke with Fred. "Do you know anything about this? I know she talks with you more than me."

"First I heard of this Will. William."

"How long has this been going on?"

"No idea."

Glory returned with the plate of cookies, still warm. She recapped the basics of meeting Will, getting caught in the rain, the two baseballs, and the game. She left out the more intimate details.

"So it's been a couple of weeks," Fred said. "Why keep him a secret?"

"It's not a secret. But it happened fast, and you're always so busy."

"I'm not," Beth said. "You can tell me, you know."

"I know, Mom," Glory said and smiled at her mother.

"So, where did you meet this William?"

"It's Will. At the tennis rackets."

"Well, tennis is an honorable sport. He must be good, then," Beth finished.

Fred's interest rose. "Does he prefer grass or clay? Maybe we can work in a match over at the club."

"Maybe. I guess."

"Well…I don't understand," Beth said.

"Tell us how you met," Fred urged.

Glory looked out toward the rising half-moon. The clouds black, from the dark of night, drifted past to block the little light offered by the glow of the semi-circle.

"He works at Sears," stumbling over her answer to Beth. "He sells tennis rackets and lots of other stuff. Well, Sears does anyway."

"So, where's he from? Not Cincinnati, that's for sure," Beth responded.

"Skokie."

"That's fine. Close enough to Evanston. I guess his commute for class is not bad from there. Just up the road," Fred said, offering his conclusion.

"Is he…" Beth started to ask.

"Mom, leave it. I like him. And he's good at what he does. He's working on a career there."

"A career. At Sears? You didn't meet at school?"

"He's never seen Northwestern."

"So where then?" Beth asked, peering at Glory.

Glory shook her head.

Beth leaned in, glanced at Fred, and continued. "You can't continue with him. This is not the future we planned out for you."

"Oh, stop it, Mother. It's my future. You can't plan my future. Christ almighty. Dad, say something."

Fred shook his head, waiting for his cue from Beth.

"Well, I don't want to meet this Will."

"Then you don't have to. I'm fine with that."

"And you can't see him again." Beth laid down her ruling.

Rising from her seat, Glory placed both hands on the table. "You cannot tell me who, or what, I will be seeing. I can do what I want. Fuu…argh."

She slammed the chair against the table. "I gotta go." Looking at Fred, she said, "Great steak, Dad. As always."

And with that, she was gone.

Fred took a sip of his drink. Beth watched the slammed door vibrate.

"I blame you for this. For her," Beth said.

"Me?"

"You. With your 'everybody is important,' and 'we're all equal.' Blah, blah, blah. You better get her back down to earth. She has no idea what she's doing."

Dot stood on the darkened sidewalk as Will pulled his car into the driveway. It was odd for his mother to greet him on the street, particularly at night. Something must be up, but he hoped it was nothing terrible. Had she heard from Lou? Maybe they finally got a letter from overseas.

She took a few steps toward the car, then waited for Will to emerge, and called out, "Where've you been?"

"Wrigley. The Cubs took the first one from the Giants. Twelve innings."

"I heard. Oscar's been trying to find you."

"Who?" Will asked, not hearing her clearly.

"Your boss. You were supposed to be at work." She paused to find a light to check her watch. "It's after seven, and Mr. Harris said…."

Will didn't wait to hear his manager's plan. Instead, he yelled "Shit" and ran into the house and up the stairs. Dot entered behind him and called up toward Will's room, "Do you want me to call him for you?"

"Yes, mother," came Will's muffled voice from the bathroom as he washed with soapy water. "Fifteen minutes, tell him. I'll be there."

It took Will twice as long as predicted to drive to Sears, clock in, and rush to the floor. Gimpy corralled him by the shoe racks and limped with him to the register.

"Thanks for covering for me," Will said.

"And why not. That's what friends are for. But Harris – he's flipping out after that stunt you pulled on him the other night."

"You know about that?"

"Who do you think closed after you bugged out."

Mr. Harris stormed toward the two men. He let Gimpy go and explained to Will that if it wasn't for his friendship with Dot from their days at E.J. Korvette's he wouldn't have a job. "No more chances, Willy-boy," Mr. Harris said. Will winced at the pejorative that he so hated. "I'm going to be nice here, only because of your mom," Mr. Harris continued. Then, he bulled his way to within inches of Will's face, "And don't fuck up again, mister. Mother or not, you're done." Mr. Harris leaned away from Will, placed his hand on Will's shoulder, and asked, "You understand me, right?" Will nodded, and Mr. Harris backed away from Will and then turned and left the store.

Will flinched when Mr. Harris yelled at him. That's what happens in the real world. But when he's with Glory, the natural world fades away. While they were at the game, he never once thought about Sears. Will had to admit that the same thing happens when he's with the guys, playing softball, or engaging in just about any activity. But he needs this job, and the pay's enough to cover his social life and spend some on the car. So in balance, Harris is right to act the way he did. He won't be late again.

To be sure for the next time, Will checked the schedule, and as he suspected, he was scheduled to open the department on Saturday. Maybe he could switch with Gimpy. Will had promised Glory and Teri that he'd add his car for the protest. If he had to miss it, what would Glory think?

But then, it's not like he volunteered for the job. Best he recalled, he got volunteered. Nothing against protesting the war, as he's certainly not for war, and if Glory is active in demonstrating against it with the SDS crowd, that's something he can support. Since he became eligible for the draft, he's kept an eye on Johnson's call to add more troops into Vietnam. Fortunately for him they're still drafting kids older than Will. But now that he's twenty, the blade that is the draft is soon to come slicing through his life, separating the calm of domestic life with the angst and outright danger of the war overseas.

Will called Gimpy the next day and told Will he had plans for Saturday, Will had no choice but to tell Glory. "There's nothing I can do about it," he said to her the following day on the phone.

"If you have to work, you do," Glory said.

He sighed into the phone. "Thanks, Glory. I thought it'd be a problem. What about Teri and Yuna and the rest? Maybe they want to borrow my car."

Glory stifled a laugh. "We'll figure it out."

Will's first thought as he woke on Friday morning was his desire to see Glory. On the phone, Glory explained that she was going with her parents and Teri to Evanston. Their apartment was ready, so they wanted to get the keys and start cleaning and moving their stuff in. They only had a few days to settle in before classes started. And in there, she had homework to do that had waited for her all summer, and still, the assignments sat on her desk, giving her the daily stink eye, knowing that she continued to ignore them.

On Saturday, Will clocked in at work on time. After work, he called Glory at home on her private line, but it only rang. That gave him a chance to catch up with Ben and Joey. Ben told him about a girl he met while cruising on Rush Street. Jessie, Josie, something that Will couldn't hear well but enough to know that Ben had little time for Will. Joey was already out, and his dad didn't know when he'd be back. So Will stayed in that night, hoping that Glory'd call and tell him how the protest went and whether anyone commented on their poster that Glory thought was far out - *Baseballs and Bats, not Rifles and Bombs.* Yuna told him it was appropriate for a summer rally.

Still, they found time for each other. Will helped Glory move her things into the apartment and set it up. One day that week, they shopped together for her food. By the time they finished in the store the drizzle that colored the morning had given way to a solid rain. They rushed the groceries into her car and climbed into the front seat, dripping wet. "Something about us and rain," Glory said. "Wonder if that means something."

"It means we should have raincoats," Will answered, fighting through the heavy drops back at her apartment, and hauling the food up one flight. The rain stopped by the time they were done. When the wind blew in a touch of coolness, Glory suggested they take a break from the work so she could show Will the campus. She excused herself and left for her bedroom. Will waited for Glory to change and scanned her school books piled on the dining room table. He picked up a paperback book, *Poems and Poets of the English Renaissance.* Will flipped through the first pages, but when he heard Glory come back, he dropped the text on the table and spun around to watch Glory walk into the room.

"What was that?" she asked.

"Nothing."

She curved herself around Will, spotted the book lying upside down, and asked, "Do you like poetry?"

"I guess."

"If you want, we can read together. I like to sit by the lake and do my reading there. It's quite peaceful. But first, let's get you out of that wet shirt and dry you off.

Will pulled the t-shirt over his head. Glory dried his back with a towel she brought with her. But when Glory let the towel fall to the floor and reached around to rub Will's chest, the attraction of the two lovers pulled them into her room, on the new Laura Ashley sheets smoothed over the bed. They fell together, and the mattress crashed against the headboard, still waiting to be attached. Clothes mixed with pillows and with blankets and sheets fell to the floor. The drumbeat of the bed rocking against the headboard was no match for the pounding of Will's heart.

Will's tour of Northwestern University was postponed.

With the calendar turning toward the start of classes, Glory spent little time with Will but called him when she could. Will kept busy with work and tried to catch up with Ben and Joey. But they, too, were less available to put together their lives as college called to them. Otherwise, he caught up on his sleep, ignoring his dad's repeated calls to help around the house. He did get the lawn mowed. But his room, even Lou's half, resisted Will's minimal efforts to clean up, the clothes laying about, preferring to stay right where they were. Lou's absence gave Will that much more room to cover until that time when the beds and floor entirely disappeared. Only then would he shovel the mess into a pile and haul it to the basement to clean the laundry and trash the garbage, hoping he'd recognize the difference in the process.

One late afternoon the three men managed to be free at the same time and met at Cock Robin, on Skokie Boulevard, near Oakton Street. They took their burgers and fries and dessert outside to the covered picnic tables. They talked about their majors, Will's friends poking Will still to find out his plan, other than to be with Glory. Will hated talking about it with them. Being a retail buyer, the only thing he could think of that seemed at least not boring or worse, couldn't match the promise that the future held for his friends. Will had no problem sharing his life with them since before the time they made their secret club back in the fifth grade. But this now felt to Will something that went beyond the image he wanted to portray to his friends. Let them think his life selling sporting goods was about as noble a cause as he could conjure up.

Joey, particularly, kept pushing Will to pursue a career in athletics as a coach. Will reminded him that unless he also taught, there was no money there without Will first moving into the ranks of college athletics. But he was not a teacher. And he reminded his short-viewed friends that his baseball career ended when the ligaments in his throwing elbow blew out. And being able to run only as fast as a beanstalk kept him from consideration by any college football program. Nope, he again concluded, there was no college for him. "All I know is I'm not going," Will said, scooping out a spoonful of what started out as Cock Robin's signature square scoop of ice cream that melted into a more standard rounded scoop mixed with soda water, chocolate syrup, and whipped cream.

The sounds of tires screeching nearby shattered their ruminations of Will's future. The Impala rolled to a quick stop at the curb nearest their table. With his elbow angling through the open window, Will's father, Douglas, leaned toward them and called out, "William, what do you think you're doing?"

Will turned his view back to the Blizzard, focusing on his next scoop. Joey and Ben leaned back in a symbolic attempt to give Will his space to figure out what was next for him.

When Will ignored him, Douglas retreated back into the car and, with tires squealing, pulled around to the parking lot, angling into a space.

"He looks serious this time," Ben said.

"Better you than me," Joey added.

"Always." Will turned his attention back to the Blizzard.

Douglas rushed from the car, leaving the door open, and charged toward Will, stopping in front of him. Instead of responding, Will pulled another scoop from the glass.

Douglas grabbed Will's arm away from his mouth and dumped the loaded spoon back into the glass. "Just leave the ice cream," he commanded. Douglas stood tall next to Will, his fists against his hips. "Let's go. Now." He turned back toward the car.

Will slid the glass to Joey, who eagerly took the spoon for himself. Will made his way through the picnic tables, turning to wave at his friends.

Douglas turned on the ignition, and as Will got in next to him, he turned to look into Will. "When are you going to grow up?

"I was eating with my friends. What's the problem?"

"The problem? The problem?" Douglas added a snicker, then pointed to the clock on the dashboard. "You see the time?" he asked.

"Sure."

"So?"

"What?

"Oh, Will. You don't get it. You're supposed to be…" He shook his head. Douglas shifted to reverse, backing the car out, and drove off. Ben and Joey were already gone.

"You're a better person than this. We raised you right. But now that you're in charge of you…I just don't know. It's almost five-thirty, right?"

"Yes…." Then Will looked again and, recognizing the problem, rubbed his hand down along his face as if to hide.

"That's right," Douglas said.

"Did he fire me?"

"Let's put it this way Will, if you need new sneakers, now you'll pay full price"

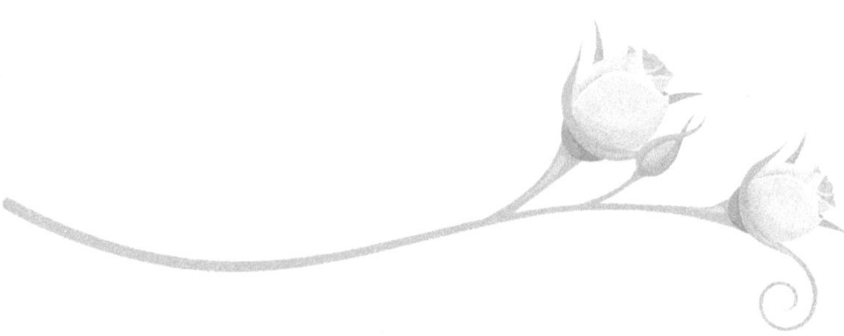

E L E V E N

"Will, it's for you." Dot rested the telephone receiver over the top of its base, hanging on the wall. "She has a nice voice. Who is she?"

He gathered himself off the couch, knocking some of the gathering collection of dirty plates and crumpled wrappers from the coffee table, stopping a half-filled glass from tumbling its contents onto the carpet.

Dot walked in from the kitchen. "You should clean up this mess. I am not your slave, you know."

"Sure, Mom." He started to gather the stuff, then knocked the table, tipping over the glass. He gave up the chore for later and walked to the picture window overlooking the view of the street. Outside, the fall leaves were blowing from the wind. He hoped it would rain soon. The approaching storm promised a deluge but so far held back. He was tired of waiting, preferring the feeling of the darkness, the show of thunder and lightning, and the downpour that would better match his mood.

"Will," Dot said, walking closer, intent on cleaning the mess. "Your lady friend."

"Right," he answered, walked into the kitchen, took the handset, and sat at the table.

"Hello." Will leaned on the table, resting his head in his hand.

"What was all that racket?"

"It's nothing. Just knocked the table."

"You okay?"

"Sure." The slight buzz of the connection grew louder over the pause.

"That's all you have to say?"

"Oh. Yeah. Hi. How are you?"

"C'mon, Will. Are you sure you're okay? You sound different."

"I'm tired."

"I hope so. Anyway, me and Teri and a bunch of us are heading up to Lake Geneva on Sunday. We're staying overnight. I was hoping you'd clear your schedule and come with us."

"Lake Geneva? Wisconsin? Why? What's there?"

"There's a music festival at Majestic Hills. You heard of it?"

"Maybe. It's pretty far, though."

"Not really. A couple of hours. We'll take my car. I'm sure yours would appreciate a little vacation. So, can you go with us? Can you check?"

"I don't know. Give me a minute." Will put the phone down, stood, and pushed the chair around with extra noise that Glory would hear. He pounded his steps through the kitchen and up the stairs. Then at the top, he stood holding the railing, counted to ten, reversed his path, and returned to his seat at the table. "I think so. It shouldn't be a problem."

"Great. I heard The Who will be there. You like them?"

"Of course."

"And the Buckinghams. There'll be lots more. I'll pick you up Sunday morning. We should probably be back on Labor Day before dinner."

"That's good. I'll let my mother know."

"Yeah, do that. She sounded sweet. Did you tell her about me?"

That Will paused to answer, prompted Glory to respond to her own question. "Well, you should. Anyway, I'd like to meet her. I've got stuff to do now, but be ready by ten on Sunday."

Inside her parents' garage, Glory searched through the wooden shelving units that her brothers built when Georgie was in high school. They achieved modest success in creating a properly aligned storage unit.

The familiar scent of old motor oil and well-used sporting equipment welcomed her to rummage through their contents. Then the overhead motor whirred into action as the stark crunch of the door segments lifting the garage door announced the promise of someone's entry.

Beth pulled her car in while Glory backed toward the door leading inside and waited.

"What are you doing here?" Beth asked before she fully emerged from the car.

"I'm looking for Georgie's sleeping bag?"

"Why?"

"'Cause if you remember, mine didn't make it back from Yellowstone once that grizzly finished using it as a napkin."

Beth took her tennis bag from the back seat and walked toward Glory and the door, then stopped.

"Why, pray tell child, do you want to find his sleeping bag?"

"I was going to tell you. Me and Teri and some of our friends are going to Lake Geneva this weekend."

"Okay."

"I'll be back Monday. If you want, I can have dinner with you guys."

"Well. Fine."

Beth stepped toward the wall to push the switch to close the garage door and opened the door to go inside. She asked Glory if she was coming in or staying there as she walked inside. Glory answered by following behind her mother.

"Don't you want to know why I'm going to Wisconsin?" She sat at the kitchen table while Beth grabbed a drink.

"If you want me to know, you'll tell me."

"So there's this music festival Sunday and Monday."

"Wonderful. Who did you say you're going with? And where are you going to stay? I still don't know why you need a sleeping bag. You could stay in a hotel."

"Then I'd miss out," Glory said.

"You mentioned Teri. Do I know the other kids?" Beth joined Glory at the table.

"I don't think so. But there's Luther, Simone, Will, and I think Betsy, but she wasn't sure."

"Don't know them." Then her brow furrowed while she took a sip from her drink. "Is that the same Will guy? He's going with you? You probably paid for his ticket, right?"

Glory leaned on her elbows on the table and looked straight at Beth. "Why are you like this? He doesn't live in the streets. He has a good home."

"So you've been there?"

"Well, no. But he's told me about it. And his parents."

"Glory, I'm sure they are lovely people. But – no."

"No? No to Will?"

"Exactly. He's not like us. You are from some of the finest families in Oak Park. The Walters and the Healeys have been the backbone of this community for generations. And do you want to know why?"

"Ok. I'll bite. Why?"

"Because we know who we are, where we've come from, and where we're going. When you have been part of our class, you know to stay with your own kind."

Glory sat back in her chair and folded her arms over her chest. She'd heard this before, like the time that Abe invited his teammate from the basketball team over for dinner. The team's center, J.K., a tall and very thin black man, had a perpetual wide smile. That night, the only saving grace was that the conversation waited until after he left. And while Fred made it clear that the issue related to J.K.'s class standing and not the color of his skin, Beth was not quite as forthcoming. When Glory heard her mother talking about Abe's poor decision-making in inviting J.K., Glory couldn't take it and rushed out of the room. She was only nine then. It was the first time that Glory became cognizant of her parents' views that showed a disconnect from the things she learned in school, where she had black and Jewish friends and thought nothing of it. And still, she didn't fully understand the notion of class and what money had to do with anything.

But hearing this from Beth now did not surprise Glory. She could have avoided the topic by simply not telling her that Will would be part of the trip. But doing so would be a lie, and for all of her two decades, the one thing that Fred and Beth taught them consistently was to speak the truth. Even the notion of "white lies" was unacceptable, at least within the family. Being so conditioned, when asked the straightforward question about Will, Glory had no capacity to answer other than with the truth.

Then Beth continued telling Glory her truth as the family matriarch. "Girls from families of class don't go out with poor boys. You do understand that?"

"No. I don't. I still don't. But it's not like we're going to get married or anything. We are dating and having fun. I have school. He has work. I don't see the problem."

"Well, I think your father would. And so would your brothers. What do you think they would do if they saw you with this boy?"

This was not the first time that the question of how they would see Will crossed Glory's mind. But each time, she gave it little concern, primarily because she had little idea what they would think. The differences in their ages made Glory's life as their little sister fun when she was growing up, topping a strong sense of security, knowing that they'd do anything for her. The closest in age, Jerry, six years older than her, managed over the years to avoid spending too much time with her and visibly resented those times that Jerry was compelled by parental fiat to take care of Glory. Abe was simply in his own world and floated in and out of Glory's life, applying the same apathy he gave to everything. Then there is Georgie, to whom she feels the closest, with her care often left to him, the age difference of eleven years making him feel to Glory like a junior parent. Their closeness that Glory believed as a child and even into her teens never materialized on a more visceral basis. He was her brother and a friend, but she knows now that she doesn't really know much about his life or what he thinks.

In many ways, as the far younger sibling and only girl, Glory was an only child with two older parents and a widening generation gap. The time they lived in evolved into an unrecognizable epoch for Beth and Fred, tending to leave behind her parents' generation to create a world of inclusion and diversity, matching the ideals of peace and harmony and music.

Glory also knew that this wasn't the time for the more significant debate. There may never be such a time.

"Mom, I gotta go while it's still early."

"So you at least got your schoolwork done. Do you start class on Tuesday? Are you prepared?"

"I am. I have to finish some reading. I'll get it done."

Glory got up from the table and walked around to give Beth a quick hug.

"Where are you staying? In case I need to reach you?"

"Under the stars."

"Do the stars have a phone number?"

"No," Glory answered. "But Luther's aunt lives nearby, and we may end up there, so I can call you." Glory walked toward the front door. Then remembering the sleeping bag, she turned about and headed for the garage. "You sure you don't know where the sleeping bag is?"

Beth shook her head as Glory left for the garage.

Majestic Hills was built to welcome skiers with winter snow to its several ski slopes overlooking Lake Geneva. The grounds turn into a festival site for the summer months. By the time Glory pulled her car into the parking lot, the music echoed over the undulating vista. Joining the many other stragglers, they had no trouble claiming a large enough space for their group.

That night was clear, and the Wisconsin air enveloped them in a brisk chill. Will and Glory zipped their sleeping bags together to share their warmth. Glory had in mind that they could enjoy each other in passion when the only sounds they would hear outside of themselves would be distant snoring.

The brightness of the morning sun woke her. She reached next to her for Will but found only space. Will sat nearby, sipping coffee and eating a muffin.

"I didn't want to wake you. You are even more beautiful sleeping in the light of dawn."

She lay on her side, hugging her pillow. "How long have you been awake?"

"A while. There're some folks selling food and coffee for breakfast. I'll get you some if you want."

"Sure. Is that a muffin?"

"I think it's bulgar wheat with bananas and nuts. It's good. But different. You want one? Coffee?"

Glory nodded. Then she reached both her arms toward Will. Will crouched down on his knees and entered her hug.

The concert resumed much as it left off the night before. By the time Glory and Will walked to the vendors to track down lunch, the clouds gathered overhead, and grew thicker as the afternoon waned. Soon the rain began. At first, it was refreshing, not more than a drizzle. When Glory had located the sleeping bags in her garage, she had also spotted rain ponchos and brought all she found just in case. Even the ponchos failed to keep them dry enough to remain at the concert.

They had burgers with Luther's aunt, uncle, and cousins and then camped out in the living room. Overnight the rain stopped. Hoping that they could still catch The Who, they went back to Majestic Hills. Stopping at the entry gate with their tickets, they were informed that the band would be playing later that day, scheduled to start around 4:00, depending on the other bands.

"I'd hate to miss seeing them," Glory told her friends.

"We can stay," Teri said.

"I know we can, but I told my Mom I'd be home in time for dinner."

"So it will be a late dinner."

"Will," Glory asked, "Do you want to stay? You should be okay. You should have no problem getting to work on Tuesday, right?"

Will nodded.

They decided to stay. Glory went with Will to find a pay phone so she could call home and tell them she would be very late coming home on Monday.

The Who closed the festival as darkness dimmed the afternoon light of the festival grounds. Afterward, Will offered to drive to get the musky crew back to the suburbs, which offer Glory declined, choosing to drive her own car. When she pulled up in front of Will's house, she saw Dot standing on the front stoop under the single porch light. Will pulled his stuff from the trunk and walked with Glory to the front door.

"Hi, Mrs. Stanford," Glory said. "I'm Gloria." She offered her hand, which Dot accepted.

"Why have you been hiding her, Will?" Dot asked, also accepting Will's kiss on her cheek. "She's too pretty not to bring around. Let's go inside."

"I'd very much like that," Glory said. "But I have a car full of exhausted kids who want nothing more than to go home." She turned to Will, pulled him into a full embrace, and then walked toward the car. "What time do you work tomorrow?" she asked.

"Uh," Will stopped. "In the afternoon."

"Well, good. So you can sleep in. We all need it. Good night, Mrs. Stanford."

Will dropped his gear inside the front door. "Are you hungry?" Dot asked. "I can heat up some meatloaf. I think there's some leftover soup."

"No thanks, Ma. I'm gonna shower and crash," Will said and headed toward the stairs.

"Oh, Will," Dot said, "I didn't know you got your job back. When did that happen?"

He moved up only one step, then stopped. He closed his eyes, and trudged up the next step, then the next, hoping that his Mom would leave him alone.

"I know you, son. You didn't get your job back. I'm right, right? Oscar would have told me."

He looked back at Dot, who waited at the base of the stairs.

"Why didn't you tell her?"

"I don't know. Maybe you can tell me."

"You have to let her know. If you can't be truthful with her, what kind of relationship do you think you have? Do you even want one with her?"

"Mom, I don't know what I want. But with a hot shower, maybe I'll figure it out."

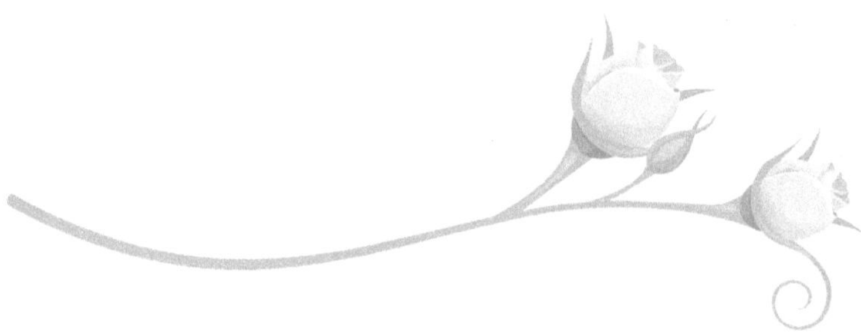

T W E L V E

The hot shower eased Will to sleep before he gained insight into finding a path that made any sense to him. By the time he roused himself from his slumber late the next day, he felt more tired than before he fell asleep. He stayed in bed, staring at the ceiling. He knew his mom was right, but that didn't make things any easier for him. He checked the clock to confirm that what he smelled from downstairs was his dinner. His hunger woke him, but he had no interest in having dinner with Dot and Douglas. Will knew that his father would have choice words for him, his way of offering the course correction that Douglas's historical failures in running his own businesses offered as the constant theme of his attempts at fatherly advice, or worse.

Maybe he'd sneak out the back. But then there's the chance that he'd run into Ben or Joey. How could he be friends with those guys for so long and not rub off some of their character on him? What was wrong with him? He knew he tried. He worked hard, helped people, smiled, and said polite things. So what did they have that he didn't? He'd never ask. Their constant banter as guys being guys prevented any deeper conversations.

Then he heard noise from downstairs that didn't fall into the normal dinner prep sounds. Voices below rose up the stairs, muffled and mixed. The familiar clogging of his father climbing the stairs prompted Will to check to see if he was dressed. He answered, "Come in," to the expected knock on his door.

"Will," Douglas said, entering his room. "There's someone here for you."

Will threw off the covers and slid his feet to the floor.

"You might want to put on something nice. And brush your hair." Douglas turned and left, leaving the door open.

Did her brothers gather to invoke their protective doctrine for their sister? Will dressed in slacks and a short-sleeved dress shirt and put on his penny loafers. Halfway to the stairs, he noticed that he had forgotten to put on his socks in the tumult. That that's just as well, giving his appearance an unconventional punctuation to the standard dress code.

In the kitchen, Dot waited for him. On the table was a terra cotta pot hosting a spider cactus plant with pink flowers. "She brought this for me. Isn't that nice?"

"She's here? Glory."

"Talking with Dad. In the living room. I like her name. I like her. Well done, son. I invited her to stay for dinner. She told that me that chicken-a-la-king is one of her favorite meals. I hope she likes my recipe."

Glory and Douglas sat together in the living room talking about the Cubs, lamenting that they fell ten games behind the league-leading Cardinals. When Will entered the room, Glory stood and walked to Will, giving him a small hug and a peck on his cheek. Her touch was rougher than he had experienced before. Once he saw that squint of her eyes, a new look for her, he couldn't un-see it. But she carried her role of the dutiful new girlfriend to the audience of one, striving to keep Douglas from gaining insight into any tension between Glory and Will. Her performance expertly hid the true nature of her visit.

They all sat together over Dot's dinner. "Mrs. Stanford, this is delicious," Glory said. "This may be the best chicken-a-la-king I have ever tasted. What's the secret."

"Well, if I told you, then it wouldn't be a secret, would it?" Dot answered. "It's an old family recipe. Stick around, and I'll teach you one day."

"I just might do that. If only for this dish," Glory added. "How can Will stay so fit with meals like this?" She looked at Will, who added his up and down nod to affirm that her question was valid.

"So, Will," Douglas said. "How do you stay so fit?"

Will chose to avoid eye contact with everyone except his fork. "Don't know. Good genes, I guess."

"Speak up, son," Douglas commanded.

"Doug, leave the boy alone. He's tired."

The conversation over dinner continued in much the same vein. Banter and playful comments flowed between Glory, Douglas, and Dot, with Will adding little more than grunts and sighs. By the time it ended, an outside observer would have thought that Will was the guest.

When the dishes were cleared and dessert offered, Glory spoke for her and Will and declined. "Neither one of us needs the extra calories. Keeping fit is a full-time job. It'll be extra time on the tennis court for me to work off this amazing dinner."

"Sounds about right," Dot said. "You two run along. Do you have plans for the evening?"

"I have class early tomorrow. So not really. Maybe a walk, Will?" The squint of her eyes gave Will no choice but to nod his agreement.

The evening sky displayed the lingering remnants of the setting sun as pink clouds off to the west colored their view. They walked along Lee Street to the linear park lining the west edge of the North Shore Channel and turned to the south, following the path. Neither said anything. A few minutes later, they reached the Main Street intersection. It was Will who broke the silence. "You want to head back?"

Glory surveyed the street and the park to their left. Saying nothing, she walked to a bench in the narrow park and sat facing the canal. Not sure of his next step, Will waited for some sign of what he was supposed to do.

"Will, are you coming?"

He joined her on the bench, his knee on the bench taking up the space between Will and Glory.

"You lied to me," Glory said, turning to better see him. The calm of her voice unnerved Will. He understood that his lack of social grace at dinner sent Glory a message. He felt uncomfortable around her, which accounted for the spinning he felt inside. How was he to respond to her accusation? When did he lie?

"You told me you were working today. You don't remember that?"

"I was tired," he uttered.

"You embarrassed me."

"How? What do you mean?"

Before continuing, Glory tapped Will's knee to prompt him to lower his knee. He did, and she switched her position, with her knee resting on the bench, as she turned toward Will.

"You also lied by not telling me you were fired. How do you think I know that?"

"My Dad?"

Glory tilted her head back, letting out a blast of air.

"I don't think he even knows. No, Will. I was there at the store. I still need a new tennis racket and decided to surprise you. That's one of the reasons I asked you about your work schedule. I walked in, and you weren't there. I went to the counter and spoke with a friend of yours. Stan."

"Gimpy."

"What?"

"We call him Gimpy."

"Really? Not a very nice name."

"He's okay with it. He likes it 'cause it's unique. He was born with one leg shorter than the other. He knows what he is."

"Do you, Will?"

He did not know how to answer that. Somehow Glory knew what he was thinking.

"Don't answer that. But tell me this, did you have any intention of telling me you were fired?"

"I don't know."

"So as long as I didn't find out, you would've been living a lie, at least with me. Do your friends know?"

"Doubt it."

"I want to know something. This is important. Why couldn't you just tell me? I thought we had something special. We talked. We laughed. We had great sex."

Will looked up at her with that last comment and couldn't help but smile.

"Well, we did," Glory said. "For two people who were getting to know each other, our bodies knew more than we did." He nodded.

"Anyway, that's not the issue now. The issue here, Will, is trust. You didn't trust me. Without trust, what we had was playtime. There could've been more."

"Could have?" Will felt his heart increase its pace inside him. His breathing failed to hide the angst that flared within. He heard Glory's repeated use of the past tense, putting their relationship behind them. The words don't lie, he knew. He understood that she was incapable of telling anything but the truth. Plus, there is nothing like the present to discuss the past. Even if the past doesn't know it already happened and can't be changed.

"I am sorry, Will, but I cannot be with someone who doesn't trust me. Who would hide the truth from me? You don't think I would have understood? When did I ever give you a hard time about anything?"

When Glory stopped, the quiet of the night gave him a chance to think. A few moments passed with the sounds of the distant traffic providing its atonal background.

"It's so embarrassing," Will said. "You are so together. So perfect. From the first second I watched you walk into Sears, I saw that."

"Will, I'm not perfect, I can assure you. Just talk to my brothers. They can inventory all of my many flaws. You put me on a pedestal. I know that. It's been happening to me all my life, and I stopped caring. But I never lied to you."

"I suppose. But your family. Your parents. I was afraid of what they'd think as well."

Glory sat up straight and reached her hand toward Will. He looked at it without response. When she wiggled her fingers, he obliged and held her hand.

"So here's a truth, Will. I won't lie to you." Will closed his eyes and lowered his head.

"Look at me, Will." And he did.

"My family is from old money. My mother's family is the Healeys. You may have heard of them."

"No."

"Rails. Trains. Do you want to hear this?"

"I do."

"When my great-grandparents had only girls, they decided to cash out, to keep their daughters, including my grandmother, away from the bad elements that came with the railroad business. So life was good, as I have heard from the stories. But still, Mom never stops talking about her days wanting to be a flapper."

"Flapper?"

"You know. The Roaring Twenties. Mom was only a teenager then, and it was the style. It must've been exciting, but because she was too young to be part of it, she would pretend, waiting for the day when she could bust out of her cage and join the good life. Then everything came crashing down."

"The Depression."

"Exactly. Black Tuesday. October 29th. Which also happens to be my grandmother's birthday. Mom never fails to tell me that she believes, to this day, that her mother had something to do with it, just to spite her."

"Wow."

"Yeah, wow. It's twisted. But for Mom, it's as real as this bench."

"So your Mom's family lost everything?"

"No. Not everything, but they took a major hit. My dad's family weathered the storm of the Depression much better than some. The ink and chemicals they produced apparently were immune to the financial problems wrecking so many businesses."

"Then there was no problem?"

"I guess. The thing is, Will, Mom never left the twenties. She may look like a mature, sophisticated woman of the sixties, but I can tell you that she wishes that she could've lived the life of the Jazz Age."

"I get it. But what does all this have to do with us?"

"Let me spell it out for you."

"Please…"

"You do not come from the right class."

"What does that mean?"

"That means that society women marry only within society. It was unheard of in mom's day, for wealthy single women to even look at boys from the other parts of town."

"What parts would those be."

"Pretty much everywhere that's not Oak Park or River Forest."

"That's right next to Oak Park."

"Correct. And that's the direction that Mom aimed for when she met my father. She would never even look in the direction of Skokie."

"But it's a nice town."

"Sure, for the common folk. But, that's not me, not how I feel, Will. You know that to be true."

Will nodded his agreement.

"They don't want me to see you," Glory said.

"Who's they?"

"My parents."

"But they don't even know me. I haven't met them…"

Will leaned back on the bench and slid down, resting his head on the back of the bench, looking up at the sky and the stars. "Then you're breaking up with me for your mother? Your parents? I bet even your brothers, too."

"Not them. They'd be cool with you, so long as you treat me right."

"But I do treat you right, right?"

"You did. But you also lied. You don't know how much that matters to me. Until today, my parents' feelings about you – not you really you, but anyone who's not in their same class – well, I would do what I want, even with you. They don't control me. But it's way more complicated than that."

"How so?"

"Consider that we are still young. I have a lot to do. You don't seem to have anything to do. How is that going to work out?"

Will returned to sitting upright, and pulled his jacket closer around him. The chill that settled over them since they sat on the bench washed through him.

"I'm cold," Will said.

"Will, I know one day you'll figure things out. Maybe you'll learn in time to trust. But I can't wait, not knowing if or when I can trust you. I'm sorry."

Glory rose and turned toward the canal, watching the street lights from across the canal glimmer off the slow-flowing channel. Then Will joined her, and they walked back toward Will's house. The longest walk that Will could ever remember was not only him with Glory, but included, as if it were a living being, the presence of silence and coldness. This was a different Glory than he had experienced to that point. When they got back to his house, they stood by Glory's car parked on the street. Instinctively they both kept their hands in their coat pockets. "Goodbye, Will," she said and took her keys from her purse.

"Glory," was all Will said, turning and shuffling to the back door and climbing the three steps as Glory started the car and pulled away. Will heard the engine. He didn't watch the car drive away.

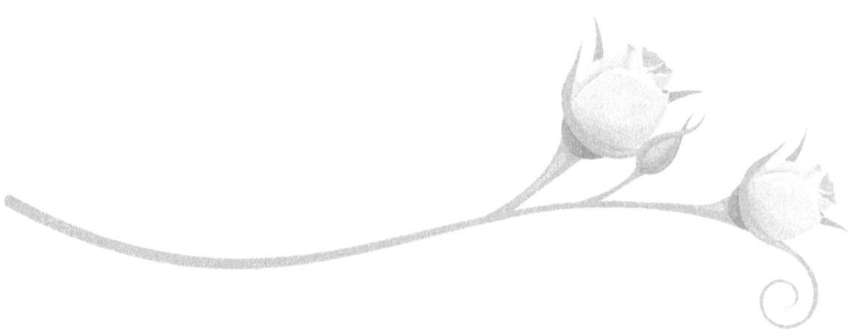

THIRTEEN

Over several days, Ben attempted to check on Will. The answer from Dot was always that Will was sleeping. Finally, he gave up and, with Joey, pulled Will from his bed, made him put on clothes, and, as they had many times before, landed at Ben's house to watch Bulls basketball. Will succumbed to his friends' prodding.

They gathered under the white fluorescent lights of Ben's basement, with the slick dark brown paneling reflecting the white lights in the windowless room. The shag carpet soaked up the remaining light, with patchouli incense coiling up from the end table.

In front of the small TV, Ben once again gave it a kick, hoping this time they'd see the lay-up that kept the Bulls from being destroyed by the Lakers.

"Ben, ole boy," said Joey, "Nice kick there. You're getting pretty good at keeping that TV in line."

Ben grinned and took a swig of his beer. Since Will joined them to watch the basketball game, he said nothing, focusing his gaze more on the scuffed basketball in his hands than the game. Every once in a while he tossed the basketball to himself.

The game ended with the Bulls snatching defeat from the jaws of humiliation once again. Ben shut off the TV. Only the scratches of Will catching his own tosses of the basketball broke the prevailing silence.

Joey tried to cheer up his friend. "Will, try her again. I doubt she's avoiding you. She's swamped. Classes. Studying." Will looked at Joey, then studied the basketball, spinning in his hands.

"Yeah," said Ben. "She'll be happy you found a good job. A real job this time. It's not about sports, but you'll work hard and get paid well. I told you that the factory would suit you."

Will rose and took his jacket off the peg hanging by the stairs. Then he asked his friends to join him outside while enough light remained for a walk. They made their way out, into the soft glow of the late afternoon sun, with heavy clouds rolling across the horizon. The touch of a breeze brushed the bare branches of the trees lining the suburban streets.

Will's brooding flowed into Ben and Joey like an electrical current. Their good nature suffered as Will suffered. The three friends strolled toward the shops on Dempster Street in silence. The autumn air rolled over Will, washing out much of his anguish as his thoughts bounced around in his head. Surely Glory could share in the happiness of his new job. After a solid two weeks, working in the factory put him solidly in the huddle of the camaraderie of the men around him.

Glory was right when she broke up with him that he wasn't doing anything. But now he was. There was hope that she'd take him back. After all, if the job works out, he could move up in the company. Maybe become a manager, and then who knows how far he'd go. This was good, hard work. For Will, the labor forging construction nails suited him. But it's too new to honestly know whether he has a future there. With the job market as weak as it was, Will had little confidence that he'd even find a job. Hopefully, he'll be able to keep this one.

Then he thought of the world in which Glory lived and where she was raised. He'd always be the odd man out. Maybe one of her brothers will be on his side, if there are sides. Why would there even be sides? This isn't war.

Will wondered if he would ever again know the silky feel of Glory's skin, or the warmth of her lips on his, unfolding to the passion of their kisses. He suspected that renewing Glory's former attempts to include Will in her world would fail. Still, he had to try and find out, if she'd let him. Then there is the overhanging dagger of the parents. Could Glory go against her parents' direct wishes to marry some country club jerk?

How can she ignore her heart? Or maybe there is no room in her heart for him. He would sure like to find out.

With Ben and Joey busy with school, and Glory remaining only in his mind, Will felt so alone with himself like a polar bear who falls asleep on an ice floe, only to wake surrounded by nothing but the icy waters of the deep blue. Then one day, on his way home from work, Will heard the clang of the railroad bells while the gates lowered to the street. Their flashing lights forced Will to stop to wait for the Skokie Swift on its run to the Howard Street Station in the northern neighborhood of Rogers Park, to connect with the sprawling Chicago Transit Authority "L" trains. While waiting, many of the memories of riding that rail car flashed in his head at the same speed, conjuring up snapshots of his memories of downtown Chicago. That moment started Will on his solo excursions into the city. A tourist in his hometown, Will aimed for the many locations in Chicago as recommended by the guidebook he had bought at the bookstore one day on his way to the train.

The train marked tracks southbound. It never ceased to amaze Will how close the old brick apartment buildings were to the fleeting rail car. It was as if he could reach out and touch the walls and reach inside the windows as he watched various scenes of apartment living flash by, the windows open, the residents long before learning to ignore the trains rushing by two and three to the hour.

One such excursion started with Will exiting the Red Line at the Jackson Street Station downtown - destination: Grant Park and the Buckingham Fountain.

Buckingham Fountain had crowned the Chicago lakefront for forty years. It was always a favorite destination of his parents for a fun evening out with Will and Lou before they hit their teen years. They loved the moon glow lights of the rococo fountain and the choreography of the sprays arching high overhead, competing with the watery center spire blowing yards up straight to the moon. Those were magical times, fueling his imagination of kings and queens and knights on horseback, swords flashing. Lou told him that was why the police patrolled on horses, for the tourists. Will had believed him. Hoping their treats of popcorn and the music from an accordion player playing patiently for his meal money were everlasting, they had always hated to leave.

That autumn evening, as he walked the promenade along Michigan Avenue, toward the Art Institute, Will vowed, as he passed the imposing Gothic building, that he'd soon plan a day for his immersion in the world of fine art. Then, after walking to the lake, he found a seat on a bench directly in front of the fountain. The bench had been placed at an angle to give equal views of the fountain and Lake Michigan. The glow of the lights enhanced the mastery of the seahorses and the three cascading layers of flowing water, reminiscent of a wedding cake. Around him were parents with their children, the same as always, but for the 60s style colorful clothing and hair longer than allowed when he was six. When he watched a group of girls roller skate by, he made a mental note to bring his skates next time and not forget the skate key so he could make sure the tabs to secure the stainless steel toe grips held his shoes tight.

The night was still and perfect, his shirtsleeves more than enough cover as the warmth of summer refused to fade away gracefully as challenged by the October night.

A woman came by carrying a box held by straps over her shoulders filled with snacks. He picked the caramel popcorn and a pop - root beer. He unrolled the top of the paper cone filled with popcorn, and heard the unmistakable sound of metal wheels rolling over the concrete walkway, increasing in volume. Then coming into his vision near his shoes, a sneaker and its attached skate rolled to a stop mere inches from him.

He looked up. And the magic became real.

"It is you," Glory said. "I told Teri that I thought that was you on the bench."

"I have 20-20 vision," Teri said as she rolled to a stop next to Glory.

Will tried to get up from the bench. Before he managed to corral the open popcorn from spilling, Glory rested her hand on his shoulder and swiveled to sit next to him.

"I'm gonna get myself something to drink," Teri said, backing away in the direction of the fountain. "You want anything?"

"Sure. Can you find me some water?" Teri nodded and turned around, skating at an energetic pace away from them.

He tilted the open popcorn toward Glory, who accepted the offering and pulled out a handful. Will copied the motion. They sat with their popcorn, watching the show from the fountain.

Will popped open the root beer and took a quick drink.

"This is a surprise," Will said.

"Yep, for me too."

"I thought you didn't want to see me anymore."

She laughed and stifled it with more popcorn.

"Sorry. I didn't really laugh. Not at you."

"Of course."

"But it's not literal. Not seeing you again, that is. I couldn't ignore that somehow we were both here on this beautiful evening."

"I guess we both read the weather reports."

She turned to Will and smiled.

"Still, here we are."

"Yes. We are."

Will offered the last of the popcorn to Glory. Then he crumpled the paper cone and threw it toward the garbage can in his best pitching motion. It missed. He picked up the pop for one last drink.

"You're not going to leave it there, are you?" Glory asked, watching him.

He emptied the can, then got up, retrieved the rolled paper, and dropped them both into the garbage.

"Better?" he asked, sitting back next to her.

She nodded.

Then they both said as one, "So what's new?"

A full stop. Then Will jumped in. "I found a job. It's a good one, I think."

"Where?"

"Skokie. They make construction nails and other stuff. They are teaching me the machines. Pretty groovy."

They watched Teri roll toward them gingerly, carrying cups of water. Will and Glory both stood, with Will offering his hand to assist Glory's efforts to stand on her skates.

"I'm happy for you, Will," Glory said. "Why don't you come by, and we can share a drink together."

"And we'll talk," Will said. "The truth. About us."

"Exactly. I will always tell you the truth. Tomorrow night. Are you free?"

"I'll be there. What time?"

"Come after dinner. That will give me enough time to get my work done."

"You guys won't have to worry about me," Teri said. "I'll make myself scarce."

That Saturday morning broke as the sun started its daily trek above the plumb-line straightness of the far eastern horizon. This daily treat was the bonus of the apartment that Beth and Fred helped Glory pick out. The saving grace was the efficient window blinds that blocked the morning sun's burst of light when the early morning of the night before remained a warm presence to the passed-out roommates. Too tired from her busy day, Glory made it a quick evening the night before at a fraternity party that Teri talked her into going. It wasn't long before Glory told Teri that she needed to head back to get sleep so she could tackle her work fresh in the morning. In moments, once Glory rested her head on her pillow, sleep overtook her. The next sound Glory heard was the blasts of her alarm clock, with the night resisting its stage presence to the morning's influence.

Glory put up coffee in the kitchen under the energetic glare of the ceiling lights battling her eyelids, when the phone rang. She knew it was Will. Her calculated delay in answering the call intended to send him a gentle message that she has a life that doesn't involve waiting by the phone for his call.

But then, her enthusiastic greeting belied her plan. "Hello, Will. I'm so thrilled that you called," she said in a far less calculated tone than planned. The energy employed to express those few words surprised Glory. Usually, when she was up before the sun, she slow-walked her conversations, the few that there were, more in line with the quiet of dawn. After the cheery greeting, she explained to Will that her classwork had already taken center stage and had to be done that day. She also had to cover a story for the *Daily Northwestern*. Omitted from her verbal itinerary to Will was the doctor's appointment that Glory managed to plug into her schedule for later that morning. By the time Will stopped by that night, she'd know the real truth that she promised Will. Regardless of the results, the news would then be a fact to dictate her reality…and Will's.

By the time Glory packed up her things to head to the library, her to-do list had expanded. She walked to the library to clear her head, ignoring one of her less honored rules for herself by buying a Coke on the way to give her something to keep her moving to help her brain stay on topic.

By the time she finished her work and was free for the day, as she packed up in the library, Glory counted fourteen pages of random doodles. She was not ordinarily much of a doodler. But given her endless jitters that day, with her pen filling so many pages, she decided to save the collection in her Literary Theory course notebook – drawings of stars and boxes and curlicues and some scribbles that defy description. She thought that the images could later be analyzed in case, somewhere along the way, her mental state was questioned, the same as she had been questioning herself as the day unfolded.

Glory walked back to the apartment across campus. Along the way, she smiled at the activity around her. Games of catch, students in varying numbers lying among blankets and resting their heads on their books, all arising from the universal appreciation of the ending days of summer, allowing one last blast of fun on the lawn. Her energy level surprised her. She ran up the stairs two at a time to the landing of their apartment.

Saturday night turned dark by the time Will arrived in Evanston. Will entered Glory's apartment, dark except for a variety of candles on the coffee table, scents of jasmine wafting about, with Frankie Valli's *Can't Take My Eyes Off You* playing on the record player enhancing the romantic ambiance. Glory led Will to the couch, then retreated to the small kitchen. She returned with a beer for Will and a cup of Ceylon tea for herself and sat next to Will.

"You don't like beer? Since when?" Will asked.

"I like beer just fine. It's only temporary. Tea is healthy anyway."

Will fought off sleep, given the dream-like qualities of the room. The heavy light from the candles gave Will the impression of something ominous that the feel-good sound of the music and the passion of Frankie Valli's vocals masked something darker, the way a bandage covers a bloody wound.

Glory divided her gaze between Will and the candles. As the song ended, the silence gave Glory the moment she needed.

"Will, I don't want you to think of me as rude. I didn't know what to say to you. So, I told Teri to tell you I stepped out when you called."

"Did you? Step out, I mean?"

"Well. Yes, I did. Technically. I told Teri that whenever the phone rang to give me a sec to run into the hall. That way, she was telling the truth."

"I see."

"But it wasn't the real truth. I'm sorry. It wasn't right that I didn't take your calls. You're too nice for me to treat you that way."

Glory looked at Will, who returned her look. Glory felt herself blush and closed her eyes.

"Apology accepted," Will said. "But now you've got me confused. You played with the truth after you broke up with me. And I thought it was because I lost my job."

"It was that…"

"But not all of that, right? "

"I told you then that there was the matter of trust. We can live with hardships, but only if we talk to each other. You didn't do that. How was that supposed to work?"

"I guess it's a problem.

"Is it, Will? How hard is it to tell me things? To talk to me? If I can bare my breasts to you when I hardly knew you, doesn't that tell you something?"

"Oh, it did all right. So when you said that you made Teri wait to answer the phone, you manufactured a story. That's no different, is it?"

"Maybe not. It's a matter of scale. But your point is well taken."

"We can give it another start, bare breasts and all," Will said.

"That's why I wanted to see you. I don't believe in accidents, and running into you by the lake happened for a reason. I didn't know the reason at the time, but it is quite apparent now. But this is hard for me."

"What? Did something happen?"

"You could say that. You have no idea what it's been like for me these past weeks. I didn't plan for what happened, and I know you didn't either, but it's a fact, and we have to live with it."

"Glory, I'm doing better now. I have a good job. At least it seems good. Anyway...."

She interrupted Will. "It's not about your job. Although I am happy that you're happy."

"What then?"

Will turned away from the strange stare pursuing him from Glory's gaze, cutting right through Will.

"You're not sick, are you?"

"Not really. No. I'm just the opposite. I thought maybe you'd be able to tell by now. I'm pregnant." Glory let the news hang there in the darkened atmosphere.

Will tried to sip his drink, but his shaking hand prevented his usual stoic movement.

She rested her hand on Will's leg and continued, "Will, it's true. It's our baby. It came as a shock to me too."

"I can't believe it," Will whispered. "I have some money. You can have it for the doctor. I don't want you to have any trouble."

"It's far from trouble. And no, I don't need money for a doctor. The insurance will cover the pregnancy and delivery. It's after that, though, that we need to plan for medical care, not only for the baby but for ourselves. She'll need both of us."

"Both of us?"

Will sat back on the couch, his chest rising and falling. Closing his eyes, Will spoke. "You're keeping this baby? But we broke up. You insisted." Unsure what to say next, he hoped that Glory would do something to help him. She watched him stumble through his thoughts. Given no help to clear his mind, Will considered what Glory had told him. "You didn't want to be with me. I wasn't good enough for you. Now you changed your mind because of the baby?"

"Will, I have no choice but to have my baby. Ours. We made her. Try to remember that moment."

"I think of it almost every day."

"So then we share something that's been hiding inside of us. We do care about each other. Maybe I was impulsive with you."

"And maybe I need to learn to open up to you."

"See, we share our caring – love – let's call it what it is?"

"Love, yes. I love you and will do whatever it takes to stay together. For you."

"And for her," Glory said, patting her belly. "And – I think that we should be married to give our child a proper home."

"See, there you got me. I don't know, Glory. And that's the truth," Will said more to his beer than to her. "I don't know. What we have is special, no doubt. But there's so much outside of us that tells me that this can't work. In many ways, we are very different. Plus, I'm not really the father type, you know?"

"Will, that's your reaction talking. You're probably still in shock."

"We used protection," Will sighed. "This was not supposed to happen."

"But it did. And now we have to be there for the baby and for each other. We do have something, and we can make a life together. Plus, she really will need us. Think about that. This is a gift of life. This is what God wanted for us. Don't you see, it's not just about you anymore. It's not even about me or us. It's about this life that's growing inside me. A life that we created and are now responsible for. The only way that I can live with myself, and the only way to raise this child, is for us to be married."

Will put his bottle down, stood up, and walked toward the window across the room. Looking at the traffic below, Will said, "How can I when I still don't know where my life is going?"

"I guess we'll have to figure that out. You and I may not be perfect for each other, Will, but what's inside me trumps all that. I know we'll do the right thing."

"The right thing," Will repeated. Being a father was not a concept that Will had spent much time thinking about to that point in his life. And now that it was his new reality, he had very little understanding of what to do. Glory was so strong, so sure of herself in everything she did, that she knew that their fates were now forever connected. He did enjoy being with her; that was no doubt. And he thinks about her all the time. Are his feelings and their good times enough? How is he to know what to do around her parents? He hadn't met them yet, and until that moment, it wasn't even an option they talked about.

"Now that you know I can tell my parents. And then you can meet them, maybe dinner at the house."

"Of course. But did they invite me?"

"Does it really matter? They think of themselves as so aristocratic. It's been hard for me at times. But they are my parents, and I really want them to like you. So you'll come to dinner, yes?"

Will nodded and took a large drink of his beer. "Whatever you think is best. What do I do now?"

"You stay with me," Glory said. "Come back here. Sit with me." He did.

She leaned to Will, removed the beer from his hand, and with the force of passion, pushed him back to the armrest and lay on top of him, her kiss deep and full.

FOURTEEN

Monday at lunchtime, Glory entered the two-bedroom student apartment and called out for Teri, but saw no sign that she was home. A rumble in her belly grabbed her attention. She tossed her school bag to the dining room table, which missed and crashed to the floor with a thud. Glory didn't hear it, not for the pounding in her that demanded immediate release, and she complied, crashing through the bathroom door to bow over the toilet, vomiting into the waiting bowl.

Finished, she sat on the tub's edge, wiping her face with a towel while rebuilding her strength. She thought she heard Teri calling her from her bedroom. With care to steady herself, Glory poured herself a cup of water from the sink and again heard Teri.

"Is that you?" Glory heard the question through Teri's closed door.

Glory composed herself and then went into Teri's room. Teri lay on the made-up bed, covered with a knitted Afghan blanket, crouched into her pillow.

"Teri, what's going on? What happened?"

Streaks of tears washed over Teri's face. Her hair, wet from the tears, washed around her face, shading the creeping redness of her eyes. When Teri tried to speak, her sobs overwhelmed her, and she turned her face back into the damp pillow. Glory crawled onto the bed and lay next to her best friend.

"Teri? Why are you crying? What's going on?"

Teri responded with sobs and attempts to breathe. Glory leaned in closer and held Teri. She shifted herself, pulled Teri into the cradle of her lap, hugged her, and swayed as if in a rocking chair.

They stayed that way until Glory's caresses and calm words helped Teri stifle her tears. Then in her voice intended to soothe Teri even further, Glory asked Teri to talk to her. That all finally worked. Teri sat up higher under Glory's protective arm.

"Tell me, please, Teri. You're my best friend. This is killing me to see you like this. What happened?"

Teri leaned to the night table for a tissue. Then settling back into Glory's embrace, she found her voice.

"Bumba's dead."

Glory stopped breathing. Then she remembered to catch her breath. "Your brother? What? What are you talking about?"

"I just got off the phone with Mom. They came to the door this morning and told her."

"Who did?" Glory pulled Teri into a closer hug. "My God, what happened?"

"I don't know," Teri said through her sniffles. "Something about a major battle. He was killed."

"Hold on. The last I heard, Bumba was still in the States. He shipped out?"

"I guess."

"When?"

"Don't know," Teri answered. "He wasn't supposed to join. What an idiot."

When the tears started again, Glory handed Teri a tissue and leaned closer.

"I tried to change his mind," Teri continued through the tears and sniffles. "I told him not to. Begged him. But he wouldn't listen. Said he had to fight the Commies. That he couldn't stand going to class and pretending that there wasn't a war."

Teri's cries turned on again, powering through her.

"What was he thinking?" Glory asked, but she didn't think Teri heard her.

When Teri again found her voice, she told Glory what she heard from her mother, which wasn't much. She couldn't remember the name of the place, other than it was somewhere in Vietnam. "He was such a good kid. Why did he have to do that? What was wrong with him?"

Of course, Glory had no answer other than to rock on the bed with Teri. Glory teared up too. "I am so sorry," she said through sniffles. But they were only words.

When their tears ceased, they climbed off the bed and went into the kitchen to make sandwiches, which they took to the living room. It was a clear day. The warmth of sunshine at first felt unwelcome, but then as the sun's light floated through the window and warmed them, their moods shifted in the direction of the sun's life-giving light.

"I still don't understand, Izzie," Glory said. "When did he decide this? He couldn't have been there very long."

"He wasn't. But it seems that war doesn't know from time, now does it?"

"Probably not. I hope I never have to find out. So what are you going to do?"

"What do you mean? What can I do?"

"Your folks. They'll need you now. And what does Marsha think?"

"She won't come to the phone. Mom says she can't get her out of her room. She's so young to lose her brother like that."

"No kidding. So are you, my friend." Glory offered her hand to Teri, who accepted, bringing both clasped hands to her cheek.

"How's your mom? Is she okay?"

"So far, I guess. But she didn't want to stay on the phone with me."

"When you want, we'll go there. I don't care if I miss class."

"I can't believe it."

"Me neither. And I thought I had problems."

"You? Problems? Why as long as I know you I thought you didn't know the word."

Glory first suppressed a laugh but then let it out, looking straight into Teri's eyes. That clashing joviality found a place in Teri, and she added her own giggle. For reasons that neither girl understood, they found themselves in a fit of laughter. They ended up falling to the floor, spent of all their energy.

Later that day, they drove in Glory's car back to Oak Park. "I'll put the top down," Glory suggested as they got in the car. "I think the wind will do us both good."

"Sure."

"See," Glory said, putting the car in gear and working it into traffic. "You already sound better. It's a horrible loss, of course."

"He was my only brother. I can't believe he's gone. Maybe they got it wrong. Maybe it was somebody else with his name."

"Bryant Isaacson? Well…maybe."

Teri let out a large sigh, shook her head, and leaned her head against the door, wiping her eyes with the back of her hand. Stopped at a traffic light, Glory reached over to Teri and pulled her back toward her. "Izzie, it's tough, but stay with me." She returned to upright and smiled at Glory. "Besides, I forgot to tell you my news. It's a bit different," Glory said.

"You're pregnant."

Glory's jaw lowered. When the light turned green, she hesitated to push on the accelerator, only acquiescing in response to the honking car behind her.

"What the…." She continued along McCormick Boulevard until she found a side street, drove into the neighborhood, and pulled over. "Nobody knows. How do you know?"

"I see it."

"But I'm not showing. At least, I don't think I am. My clothes still fit. Sorta'."

"It's not physical. Remember when my cousin had her baby? Don't you remember that I told you she was pregnant?" Glory nodded. "And the next day, Mom called to tell me the good news right after she got off the phone with Aunt Suzy."

"Sure, but I thought that was some kind of fluke or something. But how?"

"I don't know, sister, I just know."

It didn't surprise Glory that Teri picked up on her condition. There was always something different about her - clairvoyance - that showed up at critical moments. Even Bumba's death was not entirely a new topic. When Teri told her several times that something was up with her brother, Glory didn't pry for more. When Teri wanted her to know more, she'd tell her. Over the years, Glory learned to trust Teri's instincts, more often than not a harbinger of the vicissitudes of life, offering a chance to make a course correction before the worst of the storm would throw one irredeemably off course. Maybe, soon, Teri'd give her a hint of what was in store for her and Will.

"What did Cinderella say?" Teri asked. Cinderella was their secret name for Beth. Teri came up with it once she got to know Glory's parents, thinking that they treated Glory like she was the step-daughter and Beth was the wicked step-mom, except Teri couldn't remember the name of the step-mother, so they went with what was easy.

"You didn't tell her, did you? What are you waiting for?" Teri asked. "You are getting back together with Will."

"That's right. You're right, of course."

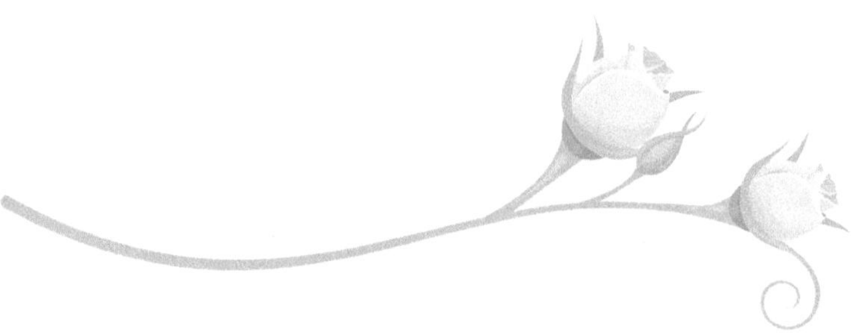

FIFTEEN

As they continued through the suburbs toward Teri's home, their speed picked up, as did the sound of the wind around them. This worked out for the two girls to give them a chance to catch up with their thoughts. Still, Glory kept a view out of her peripheral vision if something about Teri needed her attention.

Then something shifted inside Teri that became visible to Glory as they passed through Irving Park. Glory saw Teri sit up with no warning, correcting her posture from mourning to what looked like aggression. Concerned about what she observed, Glory attempted a close look while she was driving, noticing that Teri was saying something that she couldn't hear. She had a firm grip on the door armrest.

Glory tried to ask her what was happening, but the wind cut her voice into shatters. This continued until they slowed as the car ahead waited to turn.

"What are you doing?" Glory asked, turning toward Teri.

"I'm pissed."

"Huh?"

"Johnson. He killed Bumba."

"You really believe that?" Glory answered. "Let's talk about this later."

Teri nodded.

The street around Teri's house was packed with cars, taking every available parking space and making some new ones. Around them, the autumn leaves paced with them like ushers greeting worshipers. The bending of the air played a somber tune to accompany their broken gait to the house and into the front door.

Inside, the room spoke feelings of empathy, with whispers and furrowed brows combating the incongruent baked warmth emanating from the kitchen that begged for respect. Teri walked to her parents sitting on the couch, surrounded by family and friends. Waving to them to stay seated, she slid in between and invoked a three-way hug. Glory followed and leaned to join in, then backed away to give them room.

Teri soon rose and headed to Glory. "They think I can get to Marsha. I'll be back." Glory took that time to speak with Teri's parents, but few words were spoken, for how does one say anything that can genuinely help in such a time? Glory sat, holding hands with Teri's Mom.

When Teri returned, Glory retreated and leaned against a wall giving up her coveted spot to other well-wishers. Teri handed her Mom a paper, then waved to Glory to join her.

Glory heard Teri tell her Mom that Marsha wanted to see her cousin, that she did manage to write the note. The smile from Teri's Mom competed with the afternoon sun to light up her face. That moment of love faded just as fast, though. Teri followed with another hug, at the same time urging Glory to hug her too. Teri's father walked up to them and suggested that they could bring their cousin over and probably head back to school before it got too late. Teri concluded the thought. "Life does go on," she said, with a tear gaining strength and sliding along her cheek.

They had rounded up Teri's cousin. Then the balm of familial sympathy soothed Marsha into emerging arm in arm with her cousin. The scene at Teri's house settled into a softness that cut the edges off the angled gate of mourning that slammed into them by the Army's uniformed appearance earlier that day.

Walking back to the car, Glory asked Teri if she wanted to go straight back to their apartment or was there somewhere else. The surprising response gave Glory pause, wondering where Teri found such strength. "Let's take a visit to Cinderella," Teri said.

"Are you sure? Now?"

"Yes. I'm sure. We can complete the cycle of life in one day, giving her the headlines. And for this, we cannot avoid a double-banner headline for today's news."

"Oh, Teri…Izzie…."

"Cinderella will see both of today's headlines as equal until you tell her the second part of the baby story."

"Which part is that?"

"The one you haven't told me yet."

"But you know everything."

"Really. And Will? Won't the sub-headline read 'Walters to wed Skokie native'?"

"There is that. But how do you know that, too?"

"You're Catholic, right?" Glory nodded. "So there will be this little person in about nine months. It's Will's little person, too." Glory could only watch the turning of Teri's mind convert into direct statements and indisputable truths.

"You don't know any single moms," Teri said. "You've never even met one, is my guess. So the only vision you have is you and Will as parents for little Will."

"Willa." They both laughed.

"Do you love him?" Teri asked. They had made it only as far as the car and were leaning against the fender, neither taking the initiative to open the doors. Glory knew that question would make its appearance sooner or later. Is there love in here somewhere? Love? Yeah, there's something electrical that they share when they are together. Unless the lust and sexuality masquerade as love, then she fails to fully understand.

"It's something," Glory said. "Maybe love. Maybe that's just a label, and what Will means to me, and now her, defies labeling. You can understand that. I know so."

"Sure. There's life, love, all that. My only other question is who will be quicker to the bank to close your trust fund, Mom or Dad?"

"I told you how many times it's a rumor."

"Yeah," Teri said with a grin. "Prove it."

"How do you prove a rumor?"

The night descended as the girls arrived at the Walters' home. Glory and Teri stopped at the entrance to the dining room, where they shared greetings that bounced off the ceiling. Inside, Beth and Fred were finishing their dinner.

"What are you two doing here?" Fred asked, wiping his face with his cotton napkin. They sat at each end of the table, and both were able to easily see the girls posing at the entrance. "Is everything okay?" The statuesque views of the faces of all four of them gave nothing away.

"Something's wrong," Beth said, taking a sip of wine. "Please, girls, sit. There's still some dinner left for you."

"We're not hungry," Glory answered, moving toward a chair and indicating to Teri that she should sit as well.

"Maybe you're thirsty. Let me get you wine glasses."

"No, Dad," Glory said. "We don't want wine. We're fine."

"So, you aren't hungry, not thirsty, and look like someone stole your best shoes," Beth said. "This doesn't feel like a social call. What do you think, Fred?"

The only answer came from the ticking of the grandfather clock. Glory played with the fringes of the striped tablecloth. "Where do we start?" she asked and then looked over at Teri.

"Well," Teri started. "We have some news."

Beth toyed with her fork. The scratches against the plate cut through the layer of uncertainty that had fallen over the foursome.

"We?" Beth finally asked.

"First me," Teri said. Glory saw a steeliness in Teri's eyes that had moved in, replacing the fog that had dropped in on the news of Bryant's death. Teri's signature look to Glory was always a signal that Glory picked up when what was next to come from Teri would be firm, having no ability to slide into doubt.

"Today, they told my parents that Bumba was killed in Vietnam." Teri neither smiled nor frowned, but hung onto the steel that propped her up, straight and cold.

Fred then turned off the silence. "That is horrible news. What happened? Beth," he turned to his wife, "can you believe it?"

"We didn't know he was in Vietnam," Beth said. "I am so sorry to hear this. He was a nice boy."

"But you," Fred continued. "Look at you. Are you okay? I mean, wow. To lose your brother. You guys were close, right?"

"Dad," Glory said, "It's devastating, but Teri's strong. Too strong, I think."

"Mr. Walters, Mrs. Walters, I hate what happened." Teri leaned forward, taking control of her voice. "I cried. We all did. And no doubt I'll have more tears. But I prefer to think of my brother in his goodness, his love for me, our family, life. Even now, I can hear his laugh. The tricks he used to play on me. I cherish all of that. I'm not going to let this country ruin what I have of Bryant. No way. Not now. Not ever."

When she finished, Teri looked at Glory and, with her eyes, smiled at her. Glory saw her parents catch the look, and they, too, allowed a smile to reach out from the angst that only is known from death.

Teri continued. "And your daughter here never left me. Without her – and you should be so proud – the person you see now would not exist without the true friendship that we have...."

"And love. Don't forget," Glory finished Teri's thought.

"Yes. There is love."

"And as the sisters we are, we have always been there for each other; that's the 'we.'"

"Absolutely," Fred said and then closed his eyes and prayed. "Let's thank God for that, and for his love and protection over us and his comfort knowing that his open arms welcomed Bryant home."

"Amen," Beth added.

"So then, you're both okay," Fred said, getting up from his chair to clear the table. "How about a drink or something. We can celebrate Bryant's life starting now. How does that sound?"

"Celebrate...yes. We'll celebrate," Teri said.

Glory stood and said, "Maybe coffee."

"And dessert, too," Teri said, and then she looked at Glory and added, "And there is more, much better news."

"I prefer good news," Beth said.

"Let's wait for Dad," Glory welcomed the extra ticks of the clock to delay the inevitable tempest that she knew would soon foul the scene.

Glory cleared the table, giving her a chance to arrange her thoughts. She found half of an apple pie to heat up in the kitchen and put on coffee. Not only would this give her even more time to get this right, but it would help give the mood the helium to lift them up in comparison to those imaginary black balloons leaking darkness that landed all around them as bouts of anguish.

Soon they moved into the family room on Glory's suggestion. She added the sounds of Herb Alpert's trumpeted energetic ode to *A Taste of Honey*. Between the jauntiness of the pop melody, the silky taste of the cream and sugar in their coffee, combined with the melted apples bedded in a flaky crust, Glory was fully armed to carry them over the bridge that would be Beth's vitriol once woken.

When she saw that they all were comfortable in the very domestic scene, Glory started. "This is very good news," she said.

"We know," Beth responded. "What we don't know is the news."

"It's good."

"Gloria, please. Say it."

"You're going to be grandparents."

"We are?" Fred asked. "Again? You heard something from George?"

Beth responded to her husband, "It must be Abe. George would have told us himself."

"It's me," Glory declared.

What Glory heard at that moment she could later describe as the opening of cracks revealing a deep crevasse. The fissures began at the narrowing of Beth's eyes. Then the blasts of oxygen that blew out from Beth grew so loud that, to Glory, a train had magically appeared in place of the couch. She felt a slow rumble of power charging toward her, like the front cowcatcher of a train engine moving up and down like a steel jaw searching for more fuel to keep the locomotive moving.

At that moment, Glory understood that Teri being with her at that time was no accident. Bumba's death, or at least the news finally reaching them, came at this very time for a reason. Then, warmth pulsed in Glory, rippling outward. It was all she could do to not rush over and smother Teri with hugs upon hearing her next words that burst the nightmarish vision as a floating balloon vaporized into thin air.

"What a miracle!" Teri declared. Those words of spirit burst from Teri, added by the opening of her palms as they slightly parted, leaving the permanent impression of an angel settling over them.

"God is here with us," Fred said, holding Beth's hand; his head nodding in further agreement.

Beth yanked away Fred's touch. "Frederick, how is the child's careless life a miracle?"

"Beth, dear, you know that God leaves nothing to chance. Whatever made this happen was his design. If he intended for Glory to be a mom, and bring her child from God to us, then we accept God's blessings. When he joins us, we'll welcome him as a beautiful gift from God."

What Glory heard next confirmed the mysticism that then overtook the room. It began with silence, and Glory realized that all four of them were breathing in tandem. Then as if God decided that he wanted to be part of the group, the boom-boom-boom of a bass drumbeat as written by Mr. Alpert, matched the timing of her heartbeat. The prelude completed, with the quiet enhancing the volume from the stereo even though nobody turned it up, the lifted notes of *Rise* from Herb Alpert's solo trumpet washed through them. The lights flickered brighter.

Glory watched her mother, her stare aimed off to the distance. But then she saw it, like a front-line soldier crawling into enemy territory — the tapping of Beth's index finger in rhythm with the music. The beat matched the taps of Glory's foot. When Glory smiled, Beth saw this and asked, "What?"

"Feel how the sound lifts up. That's a sign, Mom. The sign that Dad is absolutely right. Feel the blasts at Jericho. Hear the tambourine that we can still hear from Miriam at the Red Sea many millennia ago."

"The long blast of the shofar on Rosh Hashanah," Teri interjected.

Glory continued without pause. "That God is with us, and as with most of life, what we are now, this moment with my baby, is truly not an accident."

"Amen," Teri and Fred said together.

Beth looked at Fred. "Fred, you're smiling too? Okay, it's three on one. I get it."

"Four," Teri corrected, raising her index finger to point toward God's chamber. "Soon to be five."

That prompted Beth to divert her glare to Teri, initiating a test of inner power. Beth blinked.

Beth settled back on the couch, closer to Fred. "There is a father, right? I mean, we are not now renaming you Mary or anything?" Beth said, dripping the irreverent meme over to Fred as if tossing a basketball for him to take the shot.

It begins now. Seeing no point in dragging this out further, Glory leaned toward her parents.

"It's…"

Before the next sound came out, Beth blurted, "You've got to be kidding. That boy? Bill?"

"Will."

"I don't care. Fred, you're the man, the father, do something. We can't have this." She leaned forward, looking back and forth between Glory and Teri. "Never in all my years have I heard of such a thing. My family – your family, your heritage – requires restraint, proper upbringing."

"Beth," Fred said, which she ignored.

"Our women have always dedicated their lives to their families and brought honor with their actions. How can you dishonor me so much?"

"This is not about you, Mom. Dad, you agree with me that I have my own life? How can you turn it around and make it about you, Mother? My world does not revolve around Elizabeth Walters. Dad? That's right?"

Fred didn't respond. However, Beth leaned her elbow on her knee, pointing at Glory with her other hand. "I am your mother. You're my daughter. Now you will be the mother. You'll see. You'll see, child - and it better be soon - that a baby needs a mother and a father. Bill, Will, whatever, cannot be the one."

"Oh, but he is. And in a short time, we will be one, as husband and wife."

"We'll have a great party," Teri said.

Fred rubbed his hands back and forth on the tops of his pants leg, and looked at Beth, then at Glory. He cleared his throat. "I have to talk with your mother." To Glory, hundreds of ticks of the clock she imagined were, in reality, not more than three or four, with the four adults momentarily frozen as they sat around the coffee table. Not planned words, but the coldness of Fred's comment sunk right through Glory. Typically, her dad was fun-loving, always with a quip or lighthearted observations of human follies, finding the many ironies that life presents. But the darkness of his voice and the stern words caused Glory to shiver, the chill spiking up her spine, sparked by thoughts of how her mother influenced Fred. In Glory's world, Fred was always the last leg, the bottom line, the "buck stops here" dad, always the hopeful veto to her mother's more draconian family legislation. She never hoped more than she did at that moment that such a notion was true. She knew that they'd talk alone, and then let her know their verdict on what the next step in Glory's life would be. This form of edict traditionally came down as if in stone. Case closed. For now, she'd have to wait and hope they'd get it, get what this gift from the divine actually means for her. And for Will.

"We'll meet him," Fred said, getting up to mark the end of the discussion. "Invite him over."

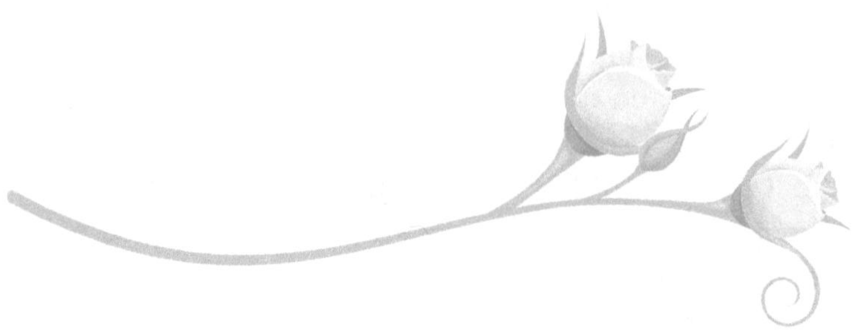

SIXTEEN

The next few days until dinner at the Walters' house felt to Will like the entirety of his childhood zooming underneath his feet as if he could only stand and watch. He prepared to approach the growing abyss by the afternoon, starting with meeting the parents. The way behind him was blocked. No exit sign manifested. There was no rope to swing him over the fissure opening in his life. His search through his personal toolbox of mental props on which he relied failed to help him. What felt more like the day of a convict's sentencing, as the clock ticked, passing one second after another, each second seemed longer than the one before. Yet, he had no choice, no other options, but to walk up and meet this challenge. Somehow.

Drops of water still lingered on his hair. Will walked from the bathroom to the bedroom with a towel wrapped around his waist. He heard Joey mooch another cookie off Dot and then climb the stairs. Will sat on his bed and grabbed a smaller towel from a pile of clothes on the floor. He was drying his hair when Joey entered the room. Joey pulled the chair from the desk, swept the clothes off the seat, turned the seat back toward Will, then sat, leaning his crossed arms on the upright.

"So, what's the big event?" Joey asked.

"I told you," Will answered, laying the towel over his head. "She wants me to meet her parents. And her brothers, too. I think the younger, and the older one, Georgie."

"That'll be a trip."

"Exactly. And I have no idea what to wear."

"So, I'm here as your fashion designer?"

"Go for it."

And between the two of them, they managed to cull through the random selection of garments that primarily served as a science experiment asking how many articles of clothing need to congeal to learn how to walk themselves to the washing machine.

"Remember, you have to be yourself," Joey said, handing Will a shirt with the sheen of a blue and yellow paisley design.

"I don't think that's the right message," Will said. "But I do want color. Something with a dimmer switch, perhaps."

They settled on a long-sleeve shirt in a solid dark blue.

On the ride to Oak Park, Joey's hand-drawn map on the seat next to him, Will passed along Oak Park Avenue, remembering Glory's suggestion that he bring something. Of course, he would, he told her. He is not entirely without social graces.

He picked a fall bouquet with bursts of orange Gerber daisies surrounded by yellow chrysanthemums.

At the Walters' home, Glory answered the door, reached up to hug Will, and accepted the flowers.

She stepped back. "You look very nice, Will."

"Thank you."

She pulled Will by his hand, and walked with him past the living room. The room looked exactly as it was when he left it that one and only time he was there – the couch with the table and the things she had so carefully pushed to one side. There was the corner by the chair where his shoes hid. Will recalled how scared Glory looked when they were in her room, and she realized that her parents might have seen his shoes The stronger memories carried him two flights up. *You have to leave,* she had told him in her bedroom. He could still feel her when Glory had said that, remembering what it was like to be inside her. Then she tossed those four words at him. But now he's back. His leaving was only temporary. She wanted him back, and there he was, to now be thrown into the pit, waiting his turn on the coliseum floor, lions at the ready. He could not tell if he was adequately armed or blissfully unarmed entering the fray.

She had promised him that it would all be okay. He had charmed her, she reminded him. No reason he can't do the same for her family.

"Even your mother?" Will asked.

"Yes, even her." Glory had told him. "You're a charmer. Know it."

He kept that thought right in front, where he could keep an eye on it. This charmer that he is supposed to be, is it real? Or is he acting a part? This felt more like a test than a social dinner. It's a test. He'll pass.

They walked into the family room. Seated on the sofa were Fred and two of Glory's brothers. Beth sat in an upholstered chair, facing the entrance. On the TV a football game kept the men engrossed. Glory walked with Will to the TV and pushed the off button.

Glory straightened herself to square up toward her family. Will followed her lead. "Mom, Dad, guys, this is William Stanford. Will, that's my Mom and Dad, and that's George and Jerry." Each responded with a wave or head nod.

Glory broke away from Will and walked toward Beth. "Mom, Will brought these. Aren't they beautiful?"

Beth took the basket from Glory. "Thank you, Mr. Stanford." Beth then handed the basket back to Glory. "Put them on the table."

She walked back to Will and led him to sit in the love seat across from Beth. They sat together. Glory made sure to edge toward the armrest so that there was a gap between her and Will.

Jerry got up from the couch. He was a man of average height, and kept his hair straight, parted in the middle, cut to the tops of his shoulders. He walked to the TV to turn it on.

"Turn the sound down," Fred instructed. Then he turned toward Glory and Will.

"Where are you from, Mr. Stanford?" Fred asked.

"Fred, we already know that," Beth said before Will answered. "More importantly, what does your father do?"

"Mom." Glory rushed her disapproval.

Everybody waited for Will to say something. "He sells appliances. Well, TVs mostly."

"He owns retail stores. Which ones?"

"No, ma'am. He did own one once, but that didn't work out. He works at Polk Brothers."

"You like that store, Mom. We got our TV there, remember?"

"Oh."

Off in the distance, the doorbell rang. From the minute the food arrived from Beth's favorite Italian caterer, the scent of baked garlic and oregano warmed by the tomato sauce and pasta prompted them to shift to a more relaxed environment. The talk stayed in safe neighborhoods – football, the weather, and what it must be like in Vietnam. That last topic came from Jerry, who was on his way back from a protest march in St. Louis, to Philadelphia and his job teaching American history. He shared stories of the protest and many people taking to the streets. Then he segued to death from the war and how it affects everyone. "I heard about Bumba," Jerry said. "Such a tragedy. How is Teri taking it? She must have a lot to say about the war."

"She does," Glory said. "I've never seen her so mad for so long. Right, Will?"

"I think so."

Jerry and George took their desserts to the family room, leaving Glory and Will to their parents.

Fred sat back in his chair and spoke to Will. "So, what are your plans?"

Will reached for his coffee cup sitting on the saucer, the white curl of steam fading skyward. Having trouble seeing the cup well, Will changed his mind and placed his hands on the white and blue table cloth.

"I…I'm not sure what you mean." He stopped, trying to understand if he was really looking for an answer or if it was merely the beginning of a more general conversation. The silence that waited gave him no information.

"I have a job. I'm learning how to make construction products."

"A worthy endeavor," Beth said, in a whisper, that Will heard, deflating from the moment it was released.

"I think so. Seems steady."

"I hope you're steady," Beth said. "We heard about Sears. Don't bother explaining. It doesn't matter."

"Mom, Dad, Will has ideas. He wants to be in business. Maybe own his own one day."

"Well, that's good. What kind of business?"

Before Will could answer, Beth cleared her throat. "Never in our business," Beth said. "You are not one of us, Mr. Stanford. Our daughter. Your future wife…" Beth coughed, then took a sip of water. "Our daughter has a very high lifestyle. I don't see how you are going to make her happy."

Then Fred cut in. "So long as you are taking care of Glory and your child, keeping your job, not getting in trouble, that's what I want."

"But if you don't…" Beth said. Her eyes narrowed, aimed at both Will and Glory. Will looked down, wiping his hair away from his eyes. What could he say to that? It's his biggest fear. When he thinks about having to take care of Glory and a baby, the inside of his stomach turns in knots, spiraling inside him. This was a massive one, mid-wifed by Beth's vote of no confidence. He hoped nobody could see how he was feeling.

Then the sentence for his crime of forcing Glory to have a baby was passed down from Beth. "Mr. Stanford," she said, "I cannot agree to this."

"Mom…."

Beth ignored Glory's cry. "If this happens, if you too are foolish enough to attempt this folly, well, we can't be part of it. Mr. Stanford, I don't know you. But I see you in front of me, attempting to insert yourself in our lives. No." And Beth stopped there, shaking her head. "If Glory intends on marrying you, we have little say in the matter. But you will be her husband. Only." Then she stopped and sat back, folding her hands in her lap.

"Mom. Please. Stop. Dad, is she speaking for both of you?" Fred didn't say anything. But Glory noticed the tiniest of movement from Fred, perceptible only through a sixth sense. As Fred's only daughter, Glory had long been aware that there was a line between them, telegraph or radio, something flowing through the air. He would be there, Glory concluded. He can't say it, but she knows Fred is with her.

"Dad, how's November fifth?" Glory asked. "It's a Sunday, of course. I already cleared it with Father Cavendish. He can be here in the afternoon, and then we can serve a nice dinner."

"We'll do this," Fred said. "You give us little choice."

"And Mom," Glory asked, looking at Beth. "Is she part of 'we'?"

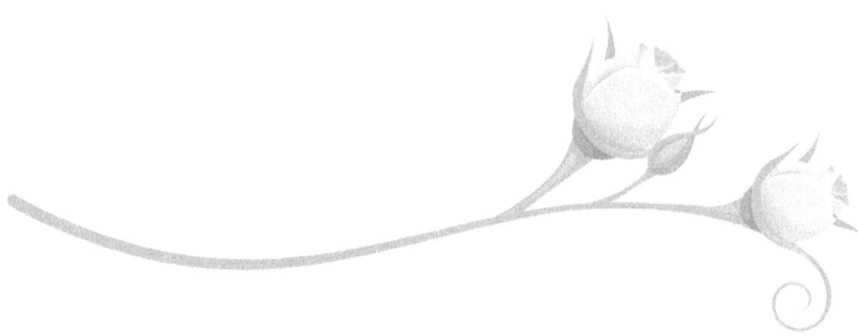

S E V E N T E E N

What served as politeness in the Walters home followed outside with Glory as she walked Will to his car after the evening ended inside.

"That went pretty well, I think," Glory said.

"If you think so."

"Believe me, it could have been much worse."

"Yeah, but she hates me. You know she does."

"Will, she hates everyone that wasn't born on a silver spoon, or whatever that phrase is. Seriously, you did great. I know she's tough. She taught me everything I know. If you can be with me, you'll have no trouble with Beth or Fred."

"That's comforting. I think. You're not so tough."

"Yeah," she laughed. "That's what I want you to think."

"I know. So we agree. If there is anything we ever need to discuss, all I need to know is that you are right. Right?"

"Probably will make things easier."

"There is no doubt."

"But what about your Mom?" Will asked. "We could get married at the courthouse. You, me, and we can ask Teri, Ben, and Joey to join us. Maybe Yuna can be here too."

"No courthouse. She's been my mother for more than two decades. I know what to do with her."

"I sure hope so."

A few days later, back home in his room, Will wrote down November fifth on an index card and taped it to the wall by his desk. He sat to finally write the letter he'd wanted for days to put on paper.

Dear Lou, We haven't heard from you in a long time. I hope you get this letter. The air force should know where you are, even though we don't. Maybe you are writing to me at the very same time that I am sitting at my desk writing to you. I would like to think that anyway. But you probably can't and certainly not sitting at a desk.

Mom and Dad are good. They wish that they would hear something from you. But tell me all the time how proud they are of you. All I know is that you are probably in charge of your outfit by now, maybe even promoted to some officer position. I know that you have that in you, even if maybe you don't see it yourself. We all see it.

Enough about you, big brother. I met a girl, Gloria, but everyone calls her Glory. You would like her. It's a good thing I met her while you were away. You'd fall for her too and then we'd fight over her, like we used to. Remember Melissa? Never mind, that's old news.

But here's new news. Me and Glory are getting married. That's right - the big M. But worry not, she's beautiful. Long blond hair, but not bimbo blond. She has a smile that maybe you could see where you are. And smart. Way smarter than me. Probably you too. Definitly - how do you spell that? Doesn't matter.

It was like Audrey Hepurn and that other guy, you remember that movie? Me and Glory saw each other and that was that. The next thing you know we're planning our wedding. And she's a Cubs fan too. You guys can compete on your Cubs knowledge. She'd give you a good run for your money.

Her parents - maybe I shouldn't put this in writing. Her dad seems ok. Mom, I'll tell you about her. It's easy. She hates me. Were not Oak Park. Glory keeps telling me not to worry about it. But boy. Looks like one day I'll be king of the mother-in-law stories. Enough about her.

But there's this. Soon you will be Uncle Lou!! Do you like the way that sounds? That's right, a baby. We're making a baby. Well, she's doing most of the work now. So how do I do my part? I have no idea. All I know from babies is they start out so small. Tiny even. But moms know what to do. Mom will tell you. She did pretty good with us right?

Can you take a break and be here for the wedding? November 5th. At her house in Oak Park. Not a big thing, but it should be nice. You should see her house. Rich - like ten of our houses. Bet you think I didn't have it in me to marry as far up as I am. I'm not such a little brother anymore, but still and always your brother.

Mom and Dad will understand if they don't let you come home. Me too. But keep an eye on that date. Any chance the war will end before that? You would know better than me.

I hope you're not killing too many people.

When you write back, I'll send you some pictures. But don't get to attached to her when you see her. She's taken.

Write.

Oh Ben and Joey say Hi. (They didn't actually, but I'll make them. They did ask about you.)

Your (little) brother, Will

At the same time that Will wrote to Lou, Glory and Teri bustled about in their apartment, cleaning up from dinner, washing dishes, and getting dressed, with only Glory applying makeup. Instead, Teri tied a leather cord around her hair over her forehead. It was time for them to leave when the phone rang.

"Sure, we have a minute, but then we're heading out," Teri said into the receiver, leaning against the wall that divided the kitchen from the front hallway. She waved to Glory and mouthed that it was Yuna on the phone. Glory slid a chair from the table and sat to wait.

"You'll get her to sign it, right?" Yuna asked.

"I have it right here," Teri said, turning the palm of her free hand up and smiling at Glory at the invisible and unfunny joke on Yuna.

"You guys must be thrilled to meet her."

"We are. But you probably meet writers all the time. You've been to *City Lights*, right? The poets, readings. But you never told me how the coffee is there. Did you meet him?"

"Who?"

"Ferlinghetti. It's his book store, you know. Without him, would we even know Ginsberg, Kerouac, Burroughs?"

"Old news. Anyway, you know how much I love her poems. Can you read me one? Something short before you guys leave?"

Teri covered the mouthpiece with her hand and told Glory, "She wants me to read to her. What a nut." Glory waved her approval and leaned forward to hand Teri one of the books stacked on the table.

"Ok," Teri said into the phone, "but it'll be short. Don't wanna be late."

"Ready."

"A View Through Flow," Teri read, "by Irene Rebhorn."

"I think I know this one."

"Looking at the rainbow's edge," Teri read into the phone.
"Striking in its abundant diversity
Every color represented
Where no color stands alone
The infertile ether plowed for promise
A drop of light, like a firefly's glow
Awaits its mate – hue's its name

So, to see the yellow of the sun
The green of meadow waving in joy
Cheeks of pink spiced by exertion
Its God within seeded in pigment
Painted cell by cell a kernel of energy."
Glory stopped, then added her ending. "That's it."

"Amazing. I could never write like that. But I love the sound of it."

"Me too. But Yuna, you know we love you, but if we don't leave now, we'll be late."

Glory got up from the chair and headed to the door. Teri slammed the book shut, to be heard by Yuna. "Gotta go, Yuna. I'll give you the update later. Bye."

"Where are we going, again?" Glory asked Teri as she drove away from their apartment.

"You have the address, right?"

Glory nodded.

"Anyway, it's called *The Lonely Bean.*"

"I got directions to Hyde Park," Glory said, focused on the nighttime streets. "So we're fine. It was nice of Sy to invite us. To even tell us about it."

"Yeah. You're his star. He's happy it's you taking on the great Irene. But are you sure you want me to write this with you? You've been doing so great with your articles. Wordlings Press is much the better for it."

"I guess," Glory conceded. Then she turned a moment toward Teri. "Izzie, what about Arista's piece last week? Incredible."

"Such insight. We can't win the war and don't want to lose it. So they die for nothing. Or for something that we don't see."

"I know. It kills me." Glory looked over and saw the steel in Teri tighten up again. "Sorry, sweetie. I know. Anyway, let's focus on tonight."

"Just do your magic," Teri said, following her deep exhale. "Do the interview as you always do. The article will write itself. Plus, Sy told me that she's come back home, focusing her work on the problems here. I can't wait to hear her."

When they stepped inside *The Lonely Bean,* they entered a world of constantly changing aesthetics. That night offered the readings by Irene

Rebhorn, about to be appointed as Illinois's poet laureate in place of the laureate, Carl Sandburg, following his death that summer. After Irene's reading, singer-songwriters will take the stage, doing their best to emulate the leads of Dylan and Baez in the hopes that the music mogul that they know is waiting to discover them is among the appreciative audience.

The naked brick walls attested to the age of the building and the rawness of the art within. Single light bulbs hung from the ceiling and cast a golden glow on the scene. The songs, the rhymes, and the prose are given perpetual energy by the ever-brewing pots of coffee. On the street, as they walked to the venue, Teri pulled out a joint and, with Glory, started their evening with the cannabis that gave them a varying awareness of their environment.

The night went as expected. A couple of college student poets braved the expectant crowd who were there to hear from the rare air of a Pulitzer Prize winner. When they had their turns, the apprentices of rhyme and meter kept the audience's attention, who approved the effort with polite applause. But then it was her time.

The house lights were lowered, and the stage lights increased. Gabe, the owner of *The Lonely Bean*, introduced Ms. Rebhorn, laying out the highlights of her years of success. Then she hopped onto the low stage and settled onto the stool behind the microphone.

"My name is Irene Rebhorn," she said. "It's a thrill for me to be here. Thanks, Gabe, for the fine introduction. What I was hoping to do tonight was to give you a preview of my new book. It should be out next month. So here we go."

She lowered glasses from the top of her head and held the papers in her lap to read. "The book is called *Ins and Outs*. This first piece is called *Conflict Set Still*. I wrote it for my friend and beautiful artist, Jillian Parks. Jill recently returned from Africa, I believe Senegal. She took the opportunity to teach the children and paint their portraits. In my admiration for her, I penned this."

She started, "Roaming along

A place I don't know

Arise all you shards

Rough knots of desire

Forge a point

A need in search
Of a bed of seed
Throwing troops to sway
To push away
Infuse, infuse
Through all, is in."

Glory leaned over to Teri while Irene was reading. "Isn't that Sy and Arista over there?" she said, pointing to the side of the small stage.

"Yep. Makes it easy to find them."

When the reading ended, Sy stepped forward from the shadows with Arista to Irene, and moving the mic on its stand, he thanked her. He read from a new poem he was working on to a smattering of approval and then turned the stage back to Gabe for the musical portion of the evening.

Teri watched the change from writing to music, tapped on Glory's arm, and got up from her seat. Glory followed her to the back of the room and made their way to the side door where Sy, Arista, and Irene were talking with several other people. Sy waved them to come over, and then introduced the girls to Irene.

"This is her, then?" Irene asked.

"That's her. She's excellent. Maybe too good for our little newsletter. That right, Teri?"

Both girls smiled.

The interview went as expected, Irene and Glory finding a space of relative quiet. She gave Glory plenty of time, answering her questions, sharing her thoughts of the changes occurring in the South Side, the hopes of everyone that Mayor Daley was speaking not mere words but truths that they'd make him live up to. She hoped. When they finished, Teri remembered to ask her to sign the copies of her Pulitzer Prize winning book. She gave Yuna's book to Glory, knowing that she would be sending it with the invitation to the wedding, such as it was.

EIGHTEEN

When Glory's last class of the day was canceled, she thought it would give her an excellent chance to spend some time with her parents. She figured that Beth would be home, and they'd have some mother-daughter time. Fred would make it in time for dinner.

Inside their home, Glory found Beth sitting at the dining room table. Full-color photos and brochures of flowers and bouquets were displayed on the table in front of Beth. Included in the mix were samples of colors for tablecloths and chair covers.

"What's all this?" Glory asked as she walked into the room. Glory stood behind Beth sitting in the chair, and placed her hands on her mother's shoulders.

"I'm working on the colors for the party. I don't know who has an outdoor wedding in November, but who am I to say?"

"Mom, you can say. Say what you want. I'm sure it's important."

"Well, the problem is the fall colors. They clash with the house and your hot pink theme."

"What hot pink theme? What are you talking about?" Glory sat at the side of the table, careful to not disturb Beth's layout.

"What do you mean? You said you wanted tie-dye, and your favorite shirt has the hot pinks, so I put two and two together."

"Tie-dye is so cool, but hot pink is a choice. It's probably not for everyone."

"I would think not."

"But I don't really care about pink or really the colors at all. Plus, I know that you'll do what you want, right?"

"I already told you. The only way I will be part of this is to make this party, in my home, one of class and style. Your notions of style, frankly, are scary. I know what to do."

"That's what I was afraid of."

"So you might be afraid of the invitation I picked."

"I don't believe it," Glory said, slumping in her chair. "You didn't ask me?"

"No time. You know you didn't exactly form a planning committee or anything. I had no choice."

"Then let me see them." Glory had already considered the problem of the short calendar. The good news about that is that of the close family and friends to be invited, only a handful lived outside Chicago. If Beth was that interested, let her pick. It's the trade-off that Glory made, and a minor one at that, given that Beth promised to stifle her thoughts about Will and his family.

Beth dislodged an envelope from the pile and handed it to Glory. Glory pulled out a baby pink colored card sample and matching envelope. "It's silk paper with an embossed border." Beth said. "How can you not like this? It's classic."

"It's okay, Mom."

"Just okay?"

"Yes. Okay. In fact, it's all okay. It doesn't really matter. Have your party, if that'll make you happy. But give him a chance; he's not a bad person."

"We'll see about that, now, won't we?"

When the rains drowned out Halloween around Chicago, it promised Glory that the weather on the day she cared about most would be clear and dry, only five days hence. Beth directed the deliveries, from the canopy and dance floor, to tables and chairs, and the food, all arriving with near military precision. The setup on the back lawn allowed plenty of room for the fifty guests - another compromise, down from Beth's first guest list of over one hundred people. On seeing the guest list, Glory had asserted her feelings that a small wedding would mean more. "This is not the social occasion of the year," she reminded Beth. Glory truly wished she could find a way to turn Beth's frown upside down when Beth conceded. After that, given free reign over the festivities, Beth reserved her frown to the mention of Will. It had happened so frequently during those last days that Glory worried that the frown would become permanent.

The morning opened clear and calm, as Glory predicted. Beth put George in charge of monitoring the deliveries. Upstairs, fresh from her shower, Beth sat at the dressing table in her drawing-room. Glory pulled up the extra chair.

"You sure that his parents know what to wear?" Beth asked.

"Now, Mom, that's not nice."

"I'm just checking."

"It's childish, and I would think beneath you. But then, again, I am often wrong about you."

Beth turned away from the mirror. "Oh, I think I heard Jerry come back."

"Why didn't you tell me. Is Yuna here?"

"I think upstairs. Probably napping."

"It's the only flight she could get. I'm sure it wasn't easy taking the red-eye. But she'll be fine."

Glory checked the guest room on the third floor and found Yuna asleep on the bed. Glory left Yuna to rest and slipped back into her room. Her dress waited for her on the bed, the white lace smoothed to avoid creases. Her bridal headpiece waited on the hat rack by the door. Glory picked up the wedding dress and held it to her face. The memory of her grandmother flashed in her head, prompted by the perfume that clung to the dress.

Through the many years that she heard shouting devolve into a frosty silence between Grandmum Anabel and Grandpop Dennis, she had wondered if their decision to marry was indeed their own. But because of Anabel's stroke a few years ago, she never had the chance to ask her. Did Grandmum Anabel get cold feet when it was her turn? Would Glory's granddaughter ask the same question about her? Would she tell her daughter the whole story and then one day her granddaughter, or would she gloss over the bad parts, and turn their courtship and wedding into a storybook, complete with full-color photos.

She knew that truth is empowering. But she also understood that leaving all truth unfiltered could cause its own problems. There is the truth. And then there are those little white lies intended to protect feelings. The hard truths, though, matter. Her reaction to Will again rose in her memory. Her infuriated reaction was genuine in her. She needed honesty, as taught to her for so long by Beth and Fred. Can she see it, however, from Will's perspective? Maybe he was simply waiting, hoping that he'd quickly find the next job, and only then tell her his tale of losing and finding employment. He'd make it comedic to then soften the blow of the fact of getting fired. She also was very aware of Will's lack of drive, or ambition, or whatever it is, that she saw clearly as if looking through a magnifying glass. There's that, which contrasts with the good she sees in Will. And the passion they share. Glory again made the same conclusion. "I'll keep him," she said to the dress. "As they say, 'in sickness, and in health'…."

The knock on the door didn't wait for her to finish the saying. Teri pushed her way into the bedroom, her bride's maid dress resting over her shoulder on a hangar. "Are you doing the wedding by yourself?" Teri asked. "I think it's 'till death do us part.' You gonna skip that part?"

"Aw, Teri. You're here. I'll ignore that for now."

Teri laid the dress next to Glory's. "Where is she?"

"Next door. You better go get…."

Teri rushed from the room and ran into the guest room, jumping on Yuna in a massive hug, bouncing the two of them in joy. Glory watched by the door and then joined in when the bouncing stopped.

Together they lounged in the guest room, catching up on their school, travel, and the wedding. "Did she promise to behave?" Yuna asked Glory.

"Sort of. We made a deal. So if you like the party, particularly the colors, you'll know why."

"I hope she's good for it," Teri said.

"She should be. She's transactional. Plus, I think she designed the party to impress the Wrights. Catherine and the children will be here.

Mother told me they were thrilled and even happy they could walk over in this beautiful weather."

"Is she still alive?" Teri asked.

"Frank Lloyd's wife? Yes. She's still in Wisconsin. I meant Catherine, the younger. She'll be here."

"What does Will make of all this?"

"Will?"

"Remember him? He's coming too, right?"

"He'd better."

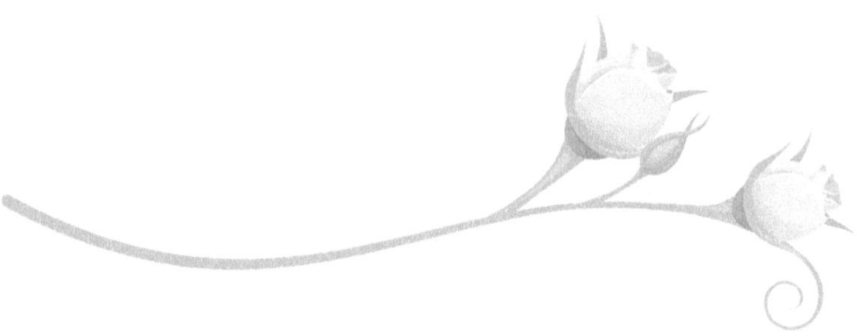

NINETEEN

That Friday morning started the same for Will as every other morning; he was asleep until he woke up. After that, there was nothing the same as any other day he had ever experienced. The first thing he noticed was what he didn't notice. There were no smells of breakfast downstairs. An eerie quiet set over Will. He got out of bed and walked to his parent's room. The door was open and the bed made, but there was no sign of Dot and Douglas.

Will went downstairs and poured himself a bowl of cereal. He heard their car park on the street and the doors closed. A moment later, they walked into the kitchen, engaged in conversation.

"Just tell me the truth, Douglas. Do you like it?"

"Dot, I've told you. Your hair looks great. Why do you have to keep asking me?"

"Oh, there's Will," Dot said, laying her purse on the counter. "Will, do you like my hair?" She turned around. Dot's hair retained a trace of the formerly pronounced dark copper color but had turned primarily white. "Florence was out sick, so they put me with Hazel. I've told Marge many times that I like her and Florence. Of course, today, I had no choice."

"It's nice, Ma," Will said.

"It's an updo."

"I know what an updo is."

"But she did it special. Don't you see it?"

"Dad, is this necessary? I'm trying to eat breakfast."

Douglas smiled at Will. "Is it your mother asking, Will?" Will nodded. "Then it's necessary."

"Got it. Mom, it's perfect. I like the curls on top. Makes you look like Barbra Streisand. Well, maybe her mother. I hear she's pretty good looking too."

"Enough of that, Will," Dot said, sending a friendly slap across Will's shoulders. "I still don't know why we couldn't meet her parents before today. Seems awkward to first meet our new in-laws at the wedding."

"Did they say anything about us?" Douglas asked. "Are you sure you gave them the money?"

"Of course. I told you they refused to accept it, but told me to thank you for it."

"Right, I guess I forgot. But still, I almost feel like they don't want to meet us. What do you think, Dot?"

"All I know is my son is getting married today. And I have a lot to do." And she answered her own cue by walking up the stairs.

Douglas walked toward the table and picked up a section of the newspaper. The only sounds were Will eating his cereal and Douglas arranging the folded newspaper.

"Dad...."

"Will...."

Douglas pulled a chair away from the table and sat, laying down the paper. "Son, do you know what you're doing?"

"I've been meaning to ask you the same question."

"I had no doubt about your mother if that's what you're getting at."

"How'd you know that?"

"From my experience, son, if I was a gambler, I'd wager that it's the only thing in your head. I'm right, no? For about, oh, a month now."

"And you didn't?"

"Of course I did. But it was different. Since sitting across the aisle from her in 12th-grade geography...I know you know this story. We waited almost two years. Not two months."

"I know," Will said. He finished the last of the cereal, placing the spoon in the bowl with a bounced clang. "I hope you're not going to give me the 'you made your bed, you sleep in it' speech. I already heard that from Joey."

"Well, Joey's a smart kid. What else did he say?"

"Really. You're giving me second-hand advice from one of my best friends."

"Maybe."

"As I remember, Dad, all he said was, 'is there anyone out there better than Glory?'"

"And…?"

"I don't know."

"It is getting cold in here."

A little later Joey walked up to the kitchen door and let himself in. "Will," he called. "I hope you're ready." Joey took his time walking up the stairs.

"I thought you were going with Ben," Will said as he emerged from his room, holding one tie in each hand.

"They're not ready yet, so I thought I'd check on you. So far, you seem on track. What am I missing here?"

"What do you think? Solid red tie, or more conservative with the blue and gold stripes?"

"Let me see your suit." Will showed Joey a blue shimmering suit coat hanging on the hook behind the door.

"Blue and gold. It's power. Red is Christmas."

Will smiled and put the tie over the jacket.

"What are you doing?" Joey asked.

"Nothing." Will stood in the center of the room. He looked away from the tie and jacket to his bare feet.

"Socks," Joey said.

"Maybe not," Will said as he sat on the edge of the bed.

"Of course. You have to wear socks."

"I don't. If I'm not going anywhere."

"Okay," Joey stumbled over the syllables, found the desk chair, and then sat down.

"Today is November fifth, right?" Will didn't respond. "Look, you wrote the date on the card and taped it…" Joey stopped when he leaned toward the wall above the desk. The space that held the card showed nothing but a square of wall. "What happened to it?"

"I took it down."

"When? Why would you do that? This is your day. Your time. C'mon Will. We don't get to plan our lives. I already told you that."

"But we do. We make plans, and then they happen."

"You got only the first part right. Even when you don't make plans, they still happen, designed or not."

"Well…not. I think."

"And I'll double you. Not, not. Enough of this big guy," Joey said as he stood. "Get your socks on, put on your tie, and tie your shoes. You have a wedding to go to. You're the star."

"Got it."

Joey headed toward the door. "And don't be late. Me and Ben and his folks, we don't like getting stood up." Then Joey left. Will stayed on the bed, eyeing the tie and jacket. When he heard the screen door slam, the familiar sound soothed Will. Then he heard his parents leaving their room.

"Ready, Will?" Dot called. "We're on time if you are."

Slowly, Will pushed himself off the bed. Picking a pair of socks from the open drawer, he stopped and waited. What Will waited for evaded him. He heard both a call to him and a shout at him in that quiet moment. A few minutes later, the tie squarely knotted, his shoes tied, with socks, Will took the jacket off the hook, put it on, and stepped in front of the mirror. It's time. But is it his time?

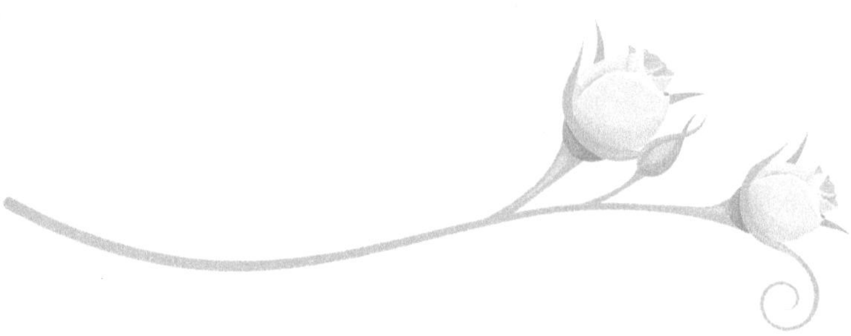

T W E N T Y

When their cars pulled up to the house in Oak Park, a large truck with *'Naomi's Exquisite Caterers'* painted on its side over a depiction of a lush table of gourmet food, pulled out of the driveway. The two families parked and walked up the driveway, to the backyard converted into an outdoor banquet hall.

"This is some place," Douglas said. Will walked behind, with Ben and Joey. Douglas called him to walk with them.

"You've seen this place, Will?" Douglas asked. "It's huge. Have you been inside?"

"Dad, it's just as imposing inside. But don't worry. You know Glory. I'm sure that she's got this figured out."

"So," Dot said. "Can we now finally meet them?"

"Let me check. Let's walk closer, I'm sure we'll see them."

They walked through the round tables arranged on the lawn, covered in pink tablecloths, decked out in flowery china, silver, and crystal. They walked past the tables, following Will toward the pool and the open patio doors. Will saw Fred waiting inside and called to him. Fred turned their way and waved, making his way to them.

"I am so happy to finally meet you," he said. He reached to shake hands with Douglas. It was at that moment that the band struck up their pre-event playlist. "Let's go inside. We can sit for a minute and get to know each other." Will was holding something against his chest.

"What's that?" Fred asked. Will handed Fred a framed picture of Lou and Will standing together in a scene from several summers ago, both men holding fishing poles in front of a lake surrounded by nothing but trees.

"Your brother?"

Will nodded. Inside, they gathered in the family room. Beth didn't make her appearance then. "Something about the wine," Fred explained.

"I'm sure," said Dot. "These events must be hard to get just right."

After a minute or so, silence fell over them. Outside, the guests were arriving. "I guess we can talk more later," Fred offered. "We'll have plenty of time to get to know each other."

The group headed outside. From inside the house, Beth called, "Fred, we have guests arriving. What are you doing?"

They stopped. "Beth," Fred retorted, "You haven't met the Stanfords." She continued toward them, then stopped a few feet away. Beth creeping forward reminded Will of a stalking lion. When Beth paused, it was all Will could do to hold his tongue. What manner of person sees her future in laws more as prey then relations? And as Beth resumed her pace, Will felt the warmth of his father's breath flow across his neck.

Beth walked to Fred, took hold of his arm, then greeted Dot and Douglas. "It's a pleasure," Beth said, but keeping still. The awkward moment lingered in space with Dot and Douglas looking at each other, then back to Beth and Fred.

"She's on edge," Fred said. "But she did a great job putting this together."

"Mrs. Walters," Will answered, "It's amazing, what you've done…."

Beth suddenly broke away from Fred. "Catherine, you look fabulous," Beth called while she walked toward a small group who entering through the front gate.

"That's Catherine," Fred explained. "She's the famous architect's daughter." The Stanfords nodded at the spectacle unveiling itself before them. "And that's her daughter with her. I can't believe she'd come all this way."

"Who? Why?" Will asked.

The answers arrived clear through the early afternoon air. "You didn't tell me Ann would be with you," Beth said to Catherine, the pronouncement ringing across the venue. "Ann, darling, I am so happy you are here. Glory will be thrilled that you managed to escape Hollywood's clutches."

"Of course," Ann answered. "Where is she?

"She's upstairs."

"I have no doubt that she'll be stunning walking up the aisle." Will recognized the new arrival. "Dad, that's Ann Baxter."

"Oh, my God," he said. "You're right. It's Nefertiti. What's she doing here? Dot, look at her, even more perfect…. Sorry dear."

"Don't be," Dot said. "Look at her dress. Stunning."

"Who's Nefertiti?" Will asked. "Oh, wait. You're right. That's Pharaoh's wife. Did she bring Yul Brenner with her?"

"Naw," Fred answered. "I heard they can't stand each other. Walk with me," Fred offered. "She's Catherine's daughter. We've watched her career closely. After *The Ten Commandments*… on fire, says it best. I think that's her husband, but I can't remember his name."

"We can wait," Douglas said, stopping. "If it's all the same to you, Fred, we can meet her later. It's not the time."

"As you wish. Anyway, I think we're starting soon, and I have a few things to take care of." Fred walked away, leaving the Stanfords with their front row seats of the spectacle, and stopping near Beth and Ann Baxter. "We watched you last night, and now you're here. Must have been a super quick flight."

"Actually, Fred, I've been here all week," Ann said. "How are you? Y'all are looking good." She leaned to him with a kiss on his cheek. "I filmed my scenes a few weeks ago. I don't think you've met my husband. Fred and Beth, this is Randolph." They shook hands.

"It's a pleasure to meet you," Fred said. Then instinctively the adults gathered together to pose for the photographer, after which Fred and Beth both excused themselves.

Father Cavendish cleared his throat into the microphone set in front of him at the altar of the outdoor chapel. Lou's photo occupied a seat near the priest.

Will had done little since they walked back to the yard except to look back at the house, particularly the upstairs windows, hoping to see a glimpse of Glory. Teri with Ben and Yuna with Joey, preceded Glory's arrival up the aisle, joining Will and separating on both sides of the priest.

It must have been a solid tradition to keep the bride away from the groom because he didn't see Glory until the band rendered the wedding song. But then there she was, standing with Fred. The veil covered her face. The snug fit of her dress did not disappoint Will, serving instead to remind him of one of the main reasons the event was happening at all. Her train flowed behind her as Glory and Fred paced forward. When they got to where Will stood in front of the priest, Fred lifted the veil, kissed his daughter, and handed her off to Will.

Her hand felt warm in his. Wearing high heels, she was close to his height, balancing the overall look of the wedding party. They stepped to Father Cavendish, who began the ceremony. At that moment, Will overheard Joey whisper to Ben. He asked if he knew whether Beth would want to object to their union. Did Glory work this out in advance? Will didn't hear Ben's answer, but he hoped it was the right one.

Then it happened. Father Cavendish concluded his opening remarks, and then posed the familiar question, asking if there is "anyone present who knows of any reason that this couple should not be joined in holy matrimony." Before he finished, all eyes turned to Beth as she gave out a loud "ohhh." Fred reached to comfort his wife. The crowd murmured its curiosity. Glory leaned to Will and whispered, "I figured that would happen. It's okay; I planned for this." Then Father Cavendish said, "We'll continue." He led the liturgy and the prayers of the Eucharist.

The priest went on. "Will and Glory, have you both…" Glory released Will's hand and stepped closer to Father Cavendish.

"Father, we'd like to change things here. If that's okay with you?"

"Well, I don't know. It's not what we usually do."

"That's right, Father. If you don't mind." Glory turned around to address the audience.

She looked out at the guests. "You all look so good." The gathered group responded to her with a twitter. "Will and I decided to do something different. We privately promised each other those vows that normally are said before you today. We now have something to add." She reached inside the top of her dress and pulled out a folded paper.

"William Blythe Stanford," she said and turned to face Will. "We stand before God and family and friends, and, as you all are witnesses, I pledge myself to you, to our life together as husband and wife, and to our children who one day we will be blessed to have. I ask of God that he protect us, that he grace us with his favor, and that he allow us to make a home filled with love, with peace, and with happiness." She then returned the paper.

"Glory Ginevra Walters," Will said, retrieving his page from his pocket. "Before everyone, I pledge to be your husband, for good and bad, in happiness and in anger, if we must, but short-lived, I hope. We come together here and now, as this major step we are taking means that now our steps match, our paths merge, and together we will make a life and a home full of life and love and peace."

When he finished, Glory stepped closer. "That was beautiful."

More prayers, wine, and the marriage kiss, closed the ceremony. Then the band opened the reception with a ballad. The chairs were cleared off the dance floor. A DJ took the microphone and asked everyone to welcome Mr. and Mrs. William Stanford to the tune of the Bee Gees' hit *To Love Somebody*.

On the dance floor, centered before their family and friends, Will asked, "Are you going to talk to her? I can't be part of that."

"I understand, Will. Forget about it. It's between me and her. A mother-daughter thing. You can't understand."

"So, what do I do?"

"You keep dancing with me," she answered and slowed their motion for their first romantic kiss as husband and wife to the approving chimes of silver on crystal.

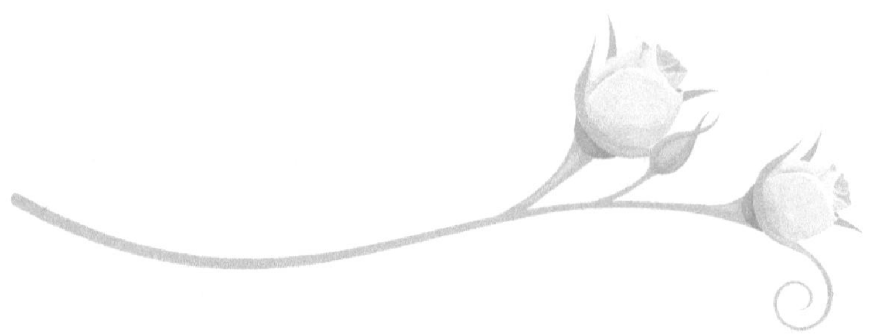

TWENTY-ONE

After the wedding, Will and Glory left that evening for their honeymoon of a few days at the Grand Hotel on Mackinac Island, Michigan. The drive took them into the late night by the time they checked in. For the following three days, when the glow of candles or filtered sunlight fell across the natural silk of Glory's breasts, Will lost himself to Glory's magic.

Otherwise, the days were filled with strolling the carless downtown, walking in and out of shops, and hopping on buggy rides. By the second afternoon, clouds turned to a snow shower, which contrasted with their view from the warmth of a restaurant with the fire lending its flames from the fireplace. Outside, falling snow painted the street scene in tones of whites, lavenders, and pinks.

By the time the third day ended and they packed to leave, the rest and snow and warmth and wine and pasta and cakes and hot chocolate placed them somewhere in a land visited by angels.

Back at Glory's apartment, a bouquet of white and red roses waited for them on the dining room table. The card said it was from Teri and her parents. A blurred photo of two gold rings on a white satin heart pillow was on the cover. Teri had added her own poem inside the cover.

The door to Teri's room opened. She came out, rushed to Glory, and hugged her, almost knocking them to the floor.

"You're back."

"We are. Thanks for the card and the flowers."

"Yeah, thanks," Will said.

"I want you to know, Will," Teri said, breaking away from Glory and walking to Will and hugging him. "This is your home now. You and Glory."

"You're not mad that you have to move?" Glory asked. "You keep telling me that you're not."

"Glory, this is the best thing. I love you, you know that. But this is your place. You and Will now. Besides, your Dad's the best in helping me find my new apartment. The move will be easy."

"I hope so. I care about you."

"I know," Teri said. "Nothing's changed. You're always my best friend."

Glory smiled and said, "All ways. Yes, I remember."

The girls hugged. Then Teri took a jacket from the wall. "You guys settle in. I'm gonna grab a couple of things at the store. Want anything?"

"We're fine. Have fun."

Teri grabbed her purse and left.

"She'll be fine," Will said, still watching the door close.

"I know. We made sure. She's the best."

After 1968 rang in, the spring semester began. Glory returned to school. Will's job held.

With Northwestern on the quarter system, the timing for Glory worked out well. She had discussed with Will that she would take off after the quarter ended at the end of March and then return to school for the fall quarter. That would give her plenty of time to rest, have the baby, and stay home for a while.

It was a late morning in May when Glory reached Will at the factory to rush home that her contractions started and were getting closer together.

Will, Teri, and Fred paced the halls in the maternity ward.

"Where's Beth?" Will asked.

"She said something about finding a phone," Fred answered. "I don't know what's up with her."

Then Dot and Douglas rushed in to join them. The doctor walked to them. "She's fine, and the baby's fine," he said over the surgical mask lowered to his chin. They rushed into the room and watched as the nurse wrapped the baby and handed it to Glory. Will walked to them and then leaned in to encircle them into his embrace.

It was a girl. Maybe now his life mattered because of Rachel.

Rachel arrived home with them smaller than they believed was possible since neither Will nor Glory spent much time around infants. "What do we do with her?" Will asked Glory. Glory didn't provide an answer. Instead, she focused her attention on the infant. After his short fatherhood vacation ended, Will returned to work, instantly worried whether his measly job would be enough to be on their own. But it seemed to be working, despite Will's doubts.

Daily, the range of emotions churned within Will, with the ups and downs of a new baby, the uncertainties of his job, and his new role as father, husband, and son-in-law. Then one day, a new, darker emotion arrived without introduction. It started with the phone ringing. It was the middle of the winter, and Will had just returned from work. Rachel was napping, and Glory was resting with a book.

Will picked up the phone. "Will, can you please come here?" Dot skipped past the customary greetings when she heard Will's voice on the line.

"Mom, I just got home. It's dark, and I think it's snowing."

"Will, please. It's important. We're scared." Her voice cracked as she finished talking.

"Mom. What...? I'm on my way."

Will walked to the couch and sat on the far end, lifting Glory's feet to rest in his lap. She looked up from her book. "What's going on?"

"I don't know. Something. I'm gonna head over there. I don't know how long I'll be, but I'll call you." He got up, went over to kiss her, and then made his way outside to his car.

The car sat under the new layer of snow. What Will thought were mere flurries surprised him with their increased intensity. He drove the white-out streets back to Skokie. At his parents' house, he let himself in. It was dark downstairs, with the only light coming from the night light in the kitchen. He hustled upstairs into his parents' bedroom.

When Dot saw him, she said, "You're here." She started to cry. Will walked to her side of the bed to lean down and hold her. Then leaning back, he asked her what had happened. She took a single piece of paper from the middle of the bed and handed it to Will. Douglas cleared his throat as if to get ready to say something. Will looked at him, but Douglas pointed to the letter, rubbing his eyes.

DEPARTMENT OF THE AIR FORCE
HEADQUARTERS 639th AIR DIVISION

Dear Mr. and Mrs. Stanford:

I am sorry to inform you that search and rescue efforts to locate your son, Staff Sergeant Louis M. Stanford, and his fellow crew members have been suspended.

The C-130 aircraft on which he was a crew member departed DaNang AB, Republic of Vietnam, at 1:10 a.m., DaNang time, November eighth, 1968, on a mission into North Vietnam with landing scheduled at DaNang upon completion of the mission. Operational necessity required a minimum of radio communication.

After a reasonable period following the scheduled landing time had elapsed, it became evident that the aircraft was missing. The aircraft and crew were officially declared missing in action at 5:00 a.m. on November eighth, 1966. An intensive search, involving more than 26 aircraft and ships of the Air Force and Navy, was conducted. We regret that the search was unsuccessful, and that the specific location is not known.

If any other information becomes available to us, I will let you know immediately. If I, or my staff, can be of assistance to you in this time of anxiety, please let me know.

Sincerely,
Signed
W. N. Morris, Brig Gen, USAF
Commander

He stood frozen to the floor, still looking at the black letters typed onto the paper, feeling their impressions on the backside of the page. Will's heart beat a storm inside, forcing him to deepen his breathing. This was when he wished he had superpowers like the heroes from his childhood comics. Lou would appreciate the notion that a superpower would save the day. They had many talks and arguments as kids, as Will recalled, over who's superpower was better. Different powers were intended for different situations. Will wondered what force evaded Lou that now he can't be found.

Will knew why Lou went there in the first place. His fascination with fighter planes showed easily in their room with the completed models hogging the shelf space over their dresser. But Lou never considered that he would disappear. None of them did. And he is probably dead, crashed in some rice paddy or jungle prison. They stopped looking for him. They are not supposed to leave anyone behind, is the idea, at least that's what he's heard. Will's pulse rose with the thought that Lou has now been forgotten by the Air Force. They just don't care. Soldiers, airmen, they die. But not Lou. Not to this family.

He let out a roar of anger, crumpling up the letter and throwing it across the room. He fell into a nearby chair, his chest rising and falling as he rested his face in his hands.

"What do we do?" Will asked, speaking through his fingers.

"We don't know," Douglas said. "I'm gonna call tomorrow."

"They can't stop. He's a good boy," Dot said.

Will sat up. "He's tough and a survivor." He wiped his eyes with the back of his hand. "One day soon, he'll surprise them and walk back into camp, ready for his next mission."

"That is our hope, too," Dot said.

Will called Glory and explained things to her. "How are they taking it?" she asked.

"For now, they seem okay. But I'm gonna stay here tonight. I hope you're okay with the baby and all."

"Of course, Will. Maybe tomorrow I can come there with Rachel. Seeing her will make them feel a little better."

"Sure. They'd like that."

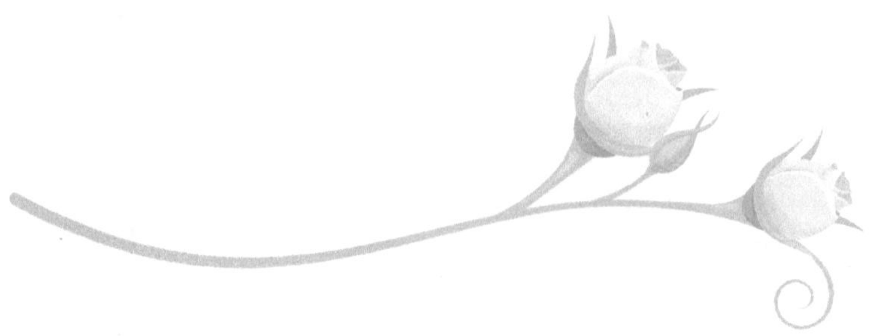

TWENTY-TWO

Glory didn't make it to Skokie the next day. The foot of snow overnight made the brightness outside a museum displaying the art of the earth and of dreams. Will had no choice but to stay with his parents until the snowplow made it past their street. The ride back to the apartment felt upside-down to Will, with the day clear and sunny, the storm having moved eastward to wreak havoc elsewhere. The photo-ready moment outside scrolled past him on his drive through the residential streets, and all Will could see was flames rising up from the underlying darkness of the lower worlds.

Will and his parents had cried over Lou. They talked scenarios trying to guess what happened and where he was. The letter had closed the door on any more information, but together they mused of doing more to look for Lou. But, all told, there was nothing they came up with that made any sense. "If he's out there, he'll come back," Douglas concluded, walking back to sit with Dot.

Afterward, back at his building, Will walked through the drifting snow to make it inside. He kept returning to the idea of doing something. But there is nothing to do, nothing that the Air Force didn't already do.

He could hear Rachel crying from inside the hall as he unlocked the door. He walked past their bedroom and saw Glory with Rachel on the changing table. The goodness imparted from Glory to Rachel contrasted with Will's greater frustration multiplying inside him. Frustration over

Lou that there's nothing he can do to help him. Glory takes care of Rachel. What about Will? What is his part? It's not even the money, really, even though so far it's okay. If he did falter, Fred would come through. So who really needs Will Stanford?

The question turned out to be less rhetorical than Will imagined when it popped into his head, when Will's penchant for difficulty reared itself once again. When trouble arrived this time, it wasn't his fault and came as unexpected as does the sound of a police cruiser's siren when flashing lights fill the rearview mirror.

Will's life was again forced to the curb. The plant at which he found a job had struggled for years. The thirty-year business couldn't keep up with the foreign competition. Despite management taking many austerity steps to keep the business open, Jackson and Sons Metal Works couldn't make it. Then, one morning, Will showed up at work to find workers milling around outside. The doors were locked tight, a paper taped to the door. Dawn broke, near the time of the spring equinox, when the light of day and darkness of night shared the skies equally. The scent in the air of creamy honey and almond from the bloom of the first snowdrop flower of the spring hinted at the nascent thaw from winter's grip, contrasting frosted blackness layered on the tarred remnants of snowfalls past.

Losing his job wasn't what Will imagined for himself, to the extent that he had conjured up any images of his life as an adult. He drove back to Evanston. Back at the apartment, instead of going upstairs, Will took his severance check to the bank and cashed it. Still not wanting to face Glory, he left the bank and headed away from the apartment, walking along Church Street through the small downtown. It was still late morning, with little chance of finding a proper watering hole. So he trudged onward, remembering that there would be no bar in dry Evanston, setting his sights on Skokie.

Then he remembered that an Irish pub had opened on Dempster Street, replacing the old donut shop that had in days past taken from him much of his allowance money in exchange for their overlarge and colorful donuts, often still warm. With his taste changed to crave more of an adult beverage, he also had a much larger allowance for *Kehoe's Irish Pub*.

Inside, the intended darkness, to better hide the time of day and whether or not it was still daytime, gave Will a sense that he had entered a new, timeless world. A two-beer lunch of a burger and fries was followed by rounds of darts. Will did his best to match up with a few of the regulars. At first he held his own, even winning a few matches and chugging the prize beers that followed. Soon though, the darts evaded the bullseye. When he lost a game by not even finding the target, he called it quits and meandered back to the bar. A plate of fish and chips found its way in front of Will. He asked for a green beer for fun, figuring that St. Patrick's Day wasn't that long ago. He could still enjoy the faux Irish tinge to his inebriation. Gil, behind the bar, accepted the twenty that Will slid across to satisfy his whim.

"Will, you can't sleep here." That was Gil, the bartender, slapping the tab in front of him and reaching over to rock Will awake, having fallen asleep on his arms crossed on the bar.

"Uh," Will tried to speak. He sat up, rubbing his eyes.

"It's pretty late. Are you okay, or do you need a ride?"

Will looked around at the few patrons left. "What time is it?" he asked, yawning.

"Late. You should go home. You can't camp out here."

Will paid the tab, then got up from the stool, grabbed a handful of peanuts from a bowl on the bar, and turned to leave. Catching himself from falling, he flipped a short wave of his hand to Gil.

"Good night, Will," Gil said. "You'll find something. But go home and talk to your wife. She's the mother of your daughter. Means something, I think."

Will nodded and pushed the door open to reveal the dark night outside. His walk was anything but straight. But then, a few minutes later, a feeling of comfort and familiarity came over Will as he looked up at the street sign marking the corner of Dempster and Christiana streets. Minutes later he stumbled up to his parent's front door and tried the doorknob. It was locked, so he knocked on the door, slid to the stoop, and sat against it. When Dot opened it, Will fell onto the entrance.

"Oh, Will," Dot said. She called into the house, "Douglas, it's your son. I think he needs some help."

Douglas came out from the family room. "What is this? Will, are you okay?"

Will opened his eyes and looked up from the floor. His parents hovered overhead. "I'm groovy," he said, smiled, then turned and slipped into slumber.

Together, Dot and Douglas dragged Will to the couch, covering him with a blanket, a soft snore confirming that he was out, for the night.

"Yeah, he's here," Dot said into the phone. She was sitting at the kitchen table. It was the following day. Will was still sleeping on the couch when the phone rang. As she expected, it was Glory.

"What's he doing there?"

"I don't know, sweetheart. He came by late last night, drunk. He's still on the couch, fast asleep."

"I'm on my way." Click. Then the ring tone.

After breakfast of toast and a couple of eggs, Will drove Glory home, dropping her off in front of their apartment building, leaving Will to troll the streets for the open space that someone else had dug out from under the snow.

He straggled into the apartment. Glory was busy taking care of Rachel in the kitchen. Will took advantage and fell into bed, and slept. He slept for two days until Glory pulled him out of bed and poured a glass of water on his head. Spurting water, he shouted, "What the hell are you doing?"

She handed him a towel. "First, you don't even tell me you lost your job."

"I didn't lose it," he said, drying himself. "It lost itself. I don't know why."

"And you also don't know what to do." Glory swayed Rachel to nap in her arms. "Why didn't you tell me? What are you going to do?" Will struggled to lift himself off the floor, accidentally pushing Glory in the process.

The unexpected move rankled Glory. "Don't you push me like that. I'm not one of your friends that you can push around. I'm your wife. I have a right to know what you're doing."

When Rachel started crying, Glory hugged her closer and headed toward the door. "Just forget it," Glory said and left the room and closed the door, cutting off the only light to reach into the room. Will could only stare at the closed door from his drip-dry seat on the floor, occupying a momentary body of stone that matched the solidity of his thoughts.

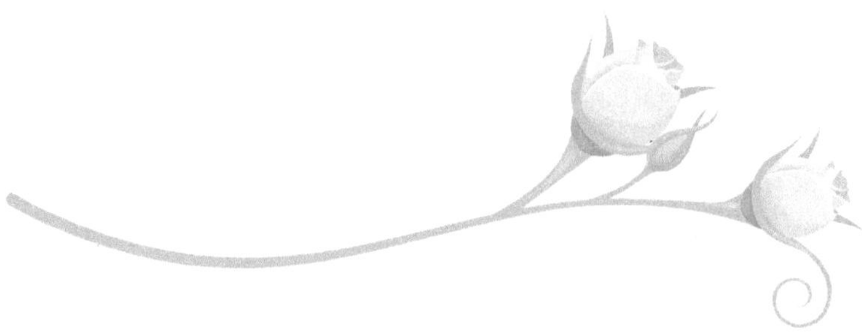

TWENTY-THREE

As week after week passed, they dipped deeper into their savings. The local job market shut its doors to Will. After a couple of quick rejections, he made it only as far as the front door of some of the other factories but never walked inside.

Ben caught up with Will one afternoon several weeks after the plant closed. Glory took Rachel to see her parents, and Will decided to check on Dot and Douglas. When he saw Will's car parked in the driveway, Ben stopped in. After commiserating with them, Will and Ben headed outside to the small backyard. Will sat on the hanging swing of his rusting swing set. Ben sat at the table. "You didn't tell them about your job search," Ben said.

"There's nothing to tell. Nothing."

"If there's nothing around here, maybe you can commute to something," Ben said.

"With my car? Not a chance."

They thought for a moment. Then Ben stood up. "This is stupid. We're going to find something for you. At the library." Ben got up as Will flew off the swing, crashing into his surprised friend. They rolled to a stop, lying flat back on the dry grass.

"Did you say the library?" Will asked.

"That's the place." Ben sat up, then stood and reached down to help Will up. Grunting for added effect, Will pulled himself up. Ben started to leave. "There's lots of information…" He looked around and saw Will not moving.

Ben rushed back to Will and pushed him from behind, erasing Will's inertia, aiming for the gate and the street beyond.

Skokie's library is a central focus of the downtown, central to the many residents living in the apartments and homes near the shops and restaurants that line the streets, protected by the imposing structures of several churches. At the village green in front of the public library, Ben and Will stopped before going inside and sat together on a bench. A bronze statue depicting five victims of the Holocaust, including a kneeling child holding an infant, captured in their stillness, staring at them from across the lawn.

"You really think I'll find something in there?" Will asked.

"Could be."

Will looked at his friend. "Let's not rush."

Will stared at the bronze cast of the victims studying his moves in frozen silence, feeling the presence of their lingering questions of life's miseries.

Ben grabbed Will's forearm, breaking through Will's stupor. Ben said, "Will, look, you got to do something. I mean, we can't just sit here. I'm worried about you. Are you and Glory alright? You can talk to me."

"I don't know. There's, like, no money. We've been eating a whole bunch of macaroni and cheese and pizza. And her parents. You don't want to know. Aw, hell. What did I do to myself?" Will got up and started walking. After a few steps, he turned toward Ben standing in front of the bench. "We gotta figure this out."

"Where're you going?" Ben asked. "The library's that…."

"Screw the library. I need to walk."

So the two friends walked together. They talked through Will's situation. They threw out various ideas for Will. It seemed that nothing they discussed was suitable for Will. Will mentioned to Ben that his life was as viable as a train with no tracks. He wasn't ready for his new role as husband and father, especially with no real career. He reflected that he was barely out of high school, trying to figure things out.

They walked along Oakton Street, talking the whole time. Holding court for the two of them, they ignored the shops as they passed the business fronts that lined the streets. The scene was reminiscent of the imagery of Norman Rockwell's *Carefree Days Ahead* painting, even if Will felt quite the opposite. Shoppers passed Will and Ben as shopkeepers and vendors walked around the pedestrians.

Will looked along the street for a diner or restaurant where they could rest their feet. Down the block, Will watched two men in starched dark blue uniforms leave the storefront no more than forty feet from where Will and Ben were standing. The two men appeared almost identical, with short haircuts, straight creases, and sharply shined shoes. As the two soldiers walked away, Will pointed them out to Ben. They looked back at the storefront and saw that they exited from a recruiting office for the United States Army.

Ben grabbed Will's arm and looked at Will. Will looked back at Ben, and they both walked closer to the office, leaning against the glass front window, and looked inside. The turn of Will's head caught Ben's attention. Will nodded.

"You're not seriously thinking of walking in there, are you?" asked Ben.

Will studied the posters taped to the inside of the store windows. "It all makes sense, Ben," said Will.

"You want to join the Army? They'll send you to Vietnam, and you'll come home in a bag."

"I guess. But with everything we've said, this is something that I know I can do. It fits me. It's good pay. Great benefits. Plus, now I know what to do about Lou."

"You are now certifiable. And crazy."

"Nope. Getting smart is what it is. They'll pay me to get there. Once there, I'll look for him. I'm not giving up as easily as the Air Force did. He's there somewhere."

"But what about Glory? And Rachel? You have a beautiful daughter. What if you don't come back? Don't you want to see your daughter grow up?"

Will began to answer, then stopped. "It's okay. I have a feeling that this is what I'm supposed to do. I'll be right back. Wait here." He turned and pushed the door open, and charged inside the office.

Ben waited for Will on a bench.

After Will signed the papers, he left the office, and they had lunch nearby. Then Will remembered that earlier that morning, Glory had told Will of her plan to buy a puppy for Rachel, giving Will directions to meet her that afternoon at the pet store near Oakton. Will couldn't have thought of a worse idea: bringing home another mouth to feed. Even the challenge of finding the place, hidden down a side street, landed in Will as an omen of worse to come. He had forgotten entirely about the puppy plan when he decided to step into the Army office and sign the papers. The yin of a new puppy joining their family combated within Will the yang of his decision to enlist and march off to war.

Finished with their meal, they left the diner and walked along the streets, approaching the location of the pet store, and Will sent Ben off. What Will really wanted was to run to the nearest flowing body of water and drown out the extremes that his life seemed to be building around him. Returning to reality instead, the looming pet store and Glory's desire for a puppy gave Will no choice. He opened the door and stepped into the world of small living animals.

Will watched Glory with Rachel in her stroller in front of the rows of cages full of puppies before they knew he was there. Glory had kneeled down to Rachel in her stroller, sharing the orange fur ball of a Welsh Corgi puppy.

"I had trouble finding the place," Will said, walking toward them. "Is that the puppy we're getting?"

More interested in Will's job prospects and knowing that she had the puppy situation in hand, Glory asked, "So you found a job?"

"Sorta."

"Will, it's either you did or you didn't."

Will sought for some way to delay the inevitable. He kneeled down and leaned toward Rachel. The glossy blue folder with his enlistment papers fell to the floor. The front of the blue folder displayed the American eagle and "United States Army" emblem like a miniature billboard painted on the floor. Glory handed the puppy to Will, picked up the folder, opened it, and flipped through the papers.

"I see your name is written there, with today's date. The Army? You joined the Army?"

"Shh…"

"Are you crazy?"

Puppies started barking, Rachel cried, and the clerk worked her way up the aisle from the back.

"Cancel it," Glory ordered.

"I can't." The clerk approached, but Will stood and waved her away, as much with the calm of his voice as with his hand.

"It's done."

Glory calmed Rachel and said to Will, "So you're in the army. That's great. What are we gonna do?"

She turned to Will, "Better yet, what am I going to do? I'll just go it alone." Glory kicked off the stroller's brakes, turned it, and strutted toward the door. Will managed a step to follow Glory before the door clanged shut. "What about the puppy?"

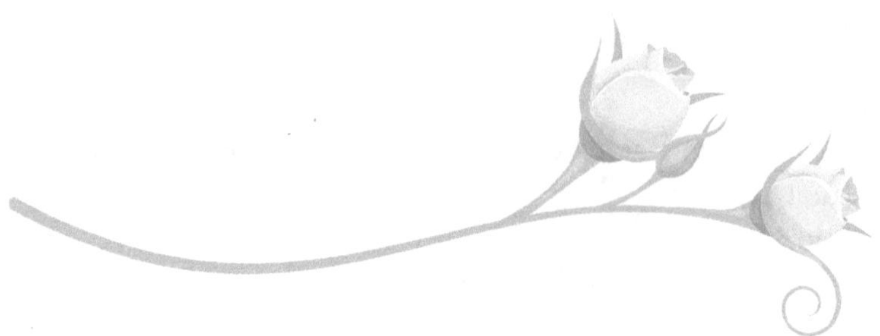

TWENTY-FOUR

Glory wondered if she would see any change in Will from the six months that the Army held onto Will to turn him into a soldier. She waited at the arrival gate to meet him at his flight, as his month of leave brought Will home. She watched the travelers pace down the ramp. It was too late in the evening to bring Rachel, so she left her with Beth. Will's last letter gave her his travel information from Fort Polk in Louisiana through Atlanta to Midway Airport. The departing passengers looked like it was the end of their very long day.

From the few letters she received from Will during basic training followed by advanced training, she learned of the intense environment in which Will was immersed. The end of a day of training pushing the trainees beyond their limits left them tired beyond words. Glory could only try to imagine what the advanced training was like at Tigerland at Fort Polk, somewhere in the northern hinterlands of Louisiana. What level of exhaustion Will must be feeling. Just the moniker bestowed on the camp, *Tigerland,* intended to turn the basic grunts into experts at everything battle-related, gave her pause at how well Will would have handled it. What she knew of Will from their many months together before he left did not give Glory any illusions of Will's fortitude to withstand such grueling conditions.

Through the flowing crowd, she spotted Will, a head taller than everyone else. In his formal dark blue Army uniform, cap placed just so on his head, Will walked in step with a similarly decked soldier, engrossed in conversation. Glory ambled toward the two men.

She overheard Will. "So, yeah, we got plenty of time. If you can come by, I'll grab enough guys for a quick game."

The other soldier replied, "You got it, man. A few beers and shagging some of your towering fly balls should be just the trick to forget drill sergeants, marches, all the crap."

"First, I need to sleep, for a long time."

The two men passed by Glory. She watched them so focused on their conversation. She grabbed Will's arm as he walked right by her, turning him like a beginning ballet student who stumbles through a broken pirouette.

"Will," Glory called as if he was on the other side of the room.

"What the hell are you yelling about?"

"You. You didn't even look at me. Here I am. For you. Who's your friend?"

"I didn't see you."

He leaned down to her, dropped his bag, and reached his arms around her for a hug. She waited, then gave him a hug right back. He landed a kiss on her cheek. Remembering that his friend was waiting, he said, "Glory, this is Tony. We were in basic together at Fort Wood and bunked together for advanced training."

"Will," Tony jumped in, "Everyone bunks together at Tigerland."

"Don't I know it too well. Tony, this is my wife, Gloria, but she prefers it if you call her Glory."

He reached out his hand for Glory. Glory accepted it. "Tony Abruzzi. Pleasure to meet you, Glory. But please, I keep telling Will to call me Two. It's odd, I know, but that's what everybody calls me."

Glory smiled in response.

"Let's get out of here," Will said. "Did you drive here?"

They stepped toward the exit. Glory leaned toward Will and whispered, "You haven't asked about Rachel."

"Where is she?"

"Home with Mom, hopefully asleep."

"Yeah, let's hope so."

Day after day passed, and as advertised, much of his free time found Will fast asleep either in their bed or on the couch, often with the TV blaring. Glory still had to cover her classes, study, and take care of Rachel.

For those weeks, though, most days Will found time with Glory when she returned late in the afternoon, followed by Beth bringing Rachel back to them. Beth had said little to Will, hastily making her exit, leaving the family of three alone in the apartment. Of course, Rachel kept them busy until nighttime. After Rachel went to sleep, the ambiance of the moment lay before them.

Lying in bed in their dark bedroom, Will heard Glory nursing Rachel. Finished, Glory lay her down in the crib across the room, hoping that she was down for the night.

Will asked, "Is she asleep?" Glory's soft shush sought to quiet Will. Glory pushed back the covers and slid next to Will. "I think so. But she still has her cold, so we'll see."

"Yeah, I guess we will." Will turned his naked body toward Glory and reached for her. Glory slid further into the bed and rolled toward Will's embrace. In the dark, she touched Will's lips. He kissed the tips of her fingers, and slid his hand down her nightgown, cascading it up to free Glory from its shroud. Glory responded, caressing Will as he rolled on top of Glory. He began with small grunts. Glory grasped Will's shoulders, digging her nails into his back. Finding the deepest part of Glory, Will's thrusts met Glory's panting, ending in a crescendo of sound and motion. Spent and laying side by side, they turned their glance to the crib, watching Rachel.

The daylight on his last day home broke through the slight parting of the curtains across the room. Will rolled over, and watched as Glory nursed Rachel in the armchair next to their bed. Fighting off sleep, he gave in, closed his eyes, and dozed back off to the hums of Glory's song to Rachel.

The next thing he knew was the sound of Glory's voice. "Shh, Rachel. Daddy's sleeping." Will heard this, opening his eyes as Glory climbed back into bed, holding Rachel in her lap, propped up on her pillow. Will raised his head, hoping for a better view of Glory, her purple nightgown being his favorite, strikingly so when the sunlight behind it displayed the silhouette of Glory's hips. As she turned, he saw the fullness of her breasts. What he saw then, though, was Rachel's hand, reaching for him, taking up his entire view, rendering her hand as large as the room itself.

"Wake up, Daddy," Glory said.

"What time is it?" Will twisted himself in the opposite direction, searching for his watch.

"It's almost dinner time. That was some nap. If you want dinner, maybe we can order pizza."

"Thanks, but I'll be fine. I have to get packed. I don't have much time."

"You have time for this." Glory slid Rachel to Will, who sat up to take her. Instead of holding her, Will placed Rachel on the bed between them. Glory reached to the night table and handed Will a small gift-wrapped box.

"We made something for you."

"We?"

"Yeah. Us girls. Something to remember us by."

Will took the box and tore open the wrapping. Opening the lid, he pulled out a string of wooden beads of light and dark browns. Hanging at the center of the beads was a carved wooden peace sign, about the size of a silver dollar.

Will took the gift from Glory. "It's nice."

"Here," Glory took it from him, "Let me put it on you."

She hung the beaded necklace over Will's neck, and the wooden peace sign swung in the center of Will's chest. Glory laid her head on Will's neck, kissing his face. Their lips met, with both of them keeping their hands on Rachel to hold her steady while she drifted off to sleep. They deepened their kisses, building their sexual energy. Glory slid lower onto the bed as Will followed her lead. Careful to avoid crashing into Rachel, Will climbed over and lowered himself between Glory's open legs, the steel of his desire pulled by Glory's magnetic forces.

Glory stopped moving, checked on Rachel, and motioned to Will to look. As he did, she unraveled herself from beneath him, got up and, being careful not to disturb Rachel, picked her up from the bed and put her in the crib. Rachel didn't move, remaining asleep, apparently content with the world as she knew it.

Glory returned to bed and accepted Will's advances once again. She looked up at Will above her. The peace sign swing against his chest.

"Can I take this off?" Will asked.

"Just for now."

She pulled it over Will's head and dropped it onto the bed. Their lovemaking resumed. Will returned her forward rhythm, joined by their deep breathing. He cried out, blasting the audio climax across the room. On the receiving end, Rachel cried herself awake.

"Shit!" Will let out, confusing his emotional affect. "This won't work," he said. Glory stopped and pushed Will to roll him off her onto the bed. "I'm done," Will added for punctuation. Glory stepped to the floor and to Rachel's crib.

"Will this take long?" Will asked, watching Glory take Rachel from the crib and sit in the armchair as she lowered her nightgown to expose her breast to Rachel.

"I don't know. I think we woke her."

"She's all yours."

Will laid back with his pillow propped behind his head, watching Glory mothering Rachel. Will drifted to sleep, dreaming of images of island beaches underneath swaying palm trees. Rachel's intermittent crying cut into the scenes playing in Will's head as palm trees morphed into street lights, casting a glow over a rainy front entrance to a small home he didn't recognize. His dream of an unknown life continued as the imaginary home opened inside the door to the sights and sounds of children throwing things, running, and shouting. A version of Glory walked into the scene, heavyset, in an apron, wiping her hands on a dishtowel, her face red from her matronly exertions.

Will woke and opened his eyes. He shook his head more violently than he intended. Resigned to the fate that awaited him back at Tigerland, a couple of flights toward tomorrow, Will lay back and waited, doing what he could to shut off the images flowing past his mind's eye, Will focused on counting his breaths while Glory stayed with Rachel.

Outside, the evening light dimmed to the blackness of night, with the ceiling light fighting back with its incandescent glow. Holding Rachel, Glory came back to bed. Will turned to Glory as sleep receded,

"I have to get to the airport." He pushed himself up from the bed and, with the girls watching, dressed in his ironed uniform.

He buttoned his shirt, tied his tie, zipped his duffel bag, and grabbed his cap from the dresser. Glory stood up with Rachel, took the cap from Will, placed it on his head, and asked, "You have time for a photo, still, right?"

Will adjusted the cap more to his liking. "Sure, but then I gotta go." Outside they could hear a car honking. "That must be my taxi."

"Sit. Quickly." Glory took the polaroid camera from the dresser and placed Rachel on Will's lap. Glory joined them and the polaroid camera snapped a picture of the three of them sitting on the bed. The taxi honked again. Will started from the bed and jostled Rachel to crying.

At the door, Will stopped and turned to Glory. "You're getting the money, right?" Glory nodded. Not knowing the best way to fully capture this last moment for how long, Glory walked to Will, Rachel in her arms, and wrapped her arms around them. She handed Will the polaroid photo. "You do look the part," she said. "Take this. We'll be with you wherever you go."

Will took the photo and kissed the girls. He opened the door in unison with the last honk of the taxi.

"Be safe," Glory called.

"I will," Will responded as the door closed.

Glory turned to walk to the window to see the last of Will as he headed to points halfway around the world, the final destination of which she could only guess. She put Rachel in her crib to free herself. She spotted Will's peace necklace lying on the bed. Will left it behind in all the commotion to get him to the airport. Glory picked it up and found it a home in her purse. At the window, she waved her last goodbye to Will.

PART II:
SAIGON, VIETNAM –
APRIL 1970.

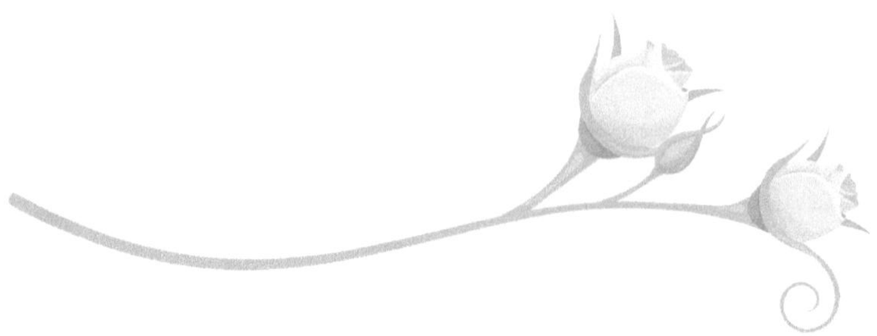

TWENTY-FIVE

Throughout the involvement of the United States in Vietnam in the 1960s, Cambodia remained officially neutral. The Americans at first questioned this neutrality, but the world accepted Cambodia's official state policy, for which the American policymakers were required to acquiesce. This prevented open warfare by the American troops in Cambodia.

However, it was common knowledge among the ground troops that the North Vietnamese Army (NVA) developed sanctuaries inside Cambodia, near its eastern border with Vietnam. To the President, the policymakers in Washington knew that Prince Nordoon Sihanouk's Cambodian government was playing footsies with the NVA and the Viet Cong. It was widely suspected that the new port city of Sihanoukville, on the southern coast of Cambodia, was a central depot for munitions and supplies for the NVA and the Viet Cong. With no proof of any particular acts of war, President Nixon, like President Johnson before him, had no choice – given the court of public opinion worldwide – but to respect Cambodia's stated neutrality.

This official policy was a significant source of frustration for the American troops on the ground and their commanding officers. Their ability to engage the enemy in battle, with any hopes of winning the war, was greatly hampered by the NVA's typical retreat across the Cambodian border to their sanctuaries, knowing that the Americans were forced –

by politics – to stop at the imaginary line that divided Vietnam from Cambodia.

Cambodia's official policy changed because of Prince Sihanouk's legendary – and vivacious – appetite. Though the Prince's policies became the official state position as to the war in Vietnam, he had nonetheless permitted the North Vietnamese access to his country. The emergence of the NVA and the Viet Cong into Cambodia escalated the fear of the ethnic Vietnamese people. By the Spring of 1970, the pressure in Cambodia was building to the breaking point.

Sihanouk's annual spa treatment to France, his annual failing attempt to keep his weight in check, forever changed his life and the lives of millions of Cambodians. With the Prince absent, his prime minister, Lon Nol, deposed him. On March 18, 1970, Lon Nol had the Cambodian parliament officially install his new government.

Lon Nol was an open supporter of America's involvement in Indochina. Given the rapid increase in North Vietnamese involvement in Cambodia, he called on the Americans to protect Cambodia and its people. President Nixon was warm to the idea. It would have been a public relations disaster – not to mention the overall defeat in Vietnam – if the NVA were to capture Phnom Penh, Cambodia's ancient capital.

President Nixon received confirmation of the NVA taking refuge in Cambodia, and authorized the incursion across the border to locate and destroy the sanctuaries of the NVA. The treasure of America's entry across Vietnam's western border was the headquarters of the Central Office of South Vietnam (COSVN), the command and control center of the NVA, which was reported to be somewhere in the Fishhook region of Cambodia. To appease world opinion, Nixon limited the activity in Cambodia to thirty kilometers inside the border. Called operation Rockcrusher, the plan was to carry out a joint operation with the Americans and the South Vietnamese Army (ARVN), involving thousands of troops.

Private William Blythe Stanford didn't hear President Nixon's address to the nation on April 30th when the president declared that the combined American and South Vietnamese forces would "clear out major enemy sanctuaries on the Cambodian-Vietnam border." Will had little knowledge of where Cambodia was, having been in Vietnam for only a few weeks. Saigon's new sights, sounds, and smells enthralled him.

Immediately whisked to a nearby ammunition depot not far from the city, introduced Will to the flatness of the rice paddies and the hills set back to frame the scene that seemed saturated in every known shade of green. Of course, he was at the whim of his superior officer, marching as ordered.

"Private Stanford," his CO called out weeks later. "Pack your gear, you and Abruzzi are heading out." Then in a flash, Will found himself transported by helicopter to join up with Alpha Company in the central plains.

The very night that Will joined Alpha Company, as ordered, he settled into the foxhole in the eastern perimeter of Fire Station Base Sally. The incoming green tracers flying overhead, matched by the orange response tracers, were the only lights in the moonless night. Will guessed it was near midnight, and the NVA hadn't let up for hours.

"How much longer do you think they can go on?" Will asked Two. Two kneeled beside him, both men clutching their rifles. Will and Two peered into the darkness and listened for signs of an invasion. Their company commander, Sergeant Ze'ev "Wolf" Alperin, came flying into their foxhole from the rear, almost falling directly on top of them.

"I gotta check out what happened," Wolf said between breaths. "I just told Brass and Turner that I have no choice. Cover me. Seems we got a stray out there."

Will and Two looked at Wolf, their eyes asking for an explanation.

"Aw, you know one of our fucking new guys, from New Mexico – Cavallo. Didn't he come on the chopper with you, Will? For some reason, he's out there on some rescue mission he cooked up. I don't know what, but he'll have hell to pay. If he doesn't get shot full of holes first, I'll shoot him myself. Two, when I tell you, flash your light at Brass and Turner. I'll be hauling ass, so cover me. He's somewhere out there, at about one o'clock. I'm gonna grab his sorry ass and drag him back here."

Wolf checked his M-16 and snapped his helmet tight. He took a second to look up at the tracers. Then, on his nod to Two, Wolf jumped over the berm. Will and Two joined in the fury of light and sound.

In moments, Wolf and Cavallo came flying into Will and Two as the two men crashed into the safety of the foxhole.

Wolf let Cavallo know his mind. "What the hell were you doing out there? I gotta protect your ass, and you get fucking stuck in the middle of this hell."

Cavallo lit a match, having first pulled a cigarette from his pocket.

"This isn't the time for a smoke, private," Wolf knocked the cigarette from Cavallo's hands. "Now get back there, and keep your head down. We'll have time later to figure out what kind of moron you really are. Double-time it, soldier."

With that, hunched over, both Wolf and Carvallo retreated to the rear behind Will and Two. Both men broke out in loud guffaws before they caught themselves and lowered their amusement to mere snickers.

"You gotta hand it to that guy; he's not afraid of anything like thousands of tracers to save even a dog," said Will.

"Me, I ain't here for that," Two answered. "Just wanna get through this nightly mess and catch a few zzzs. How long you think they gonna keep this up? Don't they sleep or what?"

The battle that night ended not much later. Since it wasn't their turn on watch, Will and Two collapsed onto their bunks once the shooting stopped, joining Brass and Turner.

"Stanford, are you OK?" Brass asked. They made themselves as comfortable as possible. "I don't know you, seein' as how you just arrived this morning, and all, with the other FNGs, but from the way you look, looks like the shooting got to you."

"I guess," Will answered. "I mean, that was the first time I faced live fire."

"You better get used to it," Brass said. "That happens pretty much every night. You can't be afraid, man, if your time comes – well, it just comes, that's all."

"Yeah, I know that, but – and I'm not afraid, exactly." Will stopped. "I haven't been in country very long and did nothing but load supplies. A third-grader could've done that. Gotta be more here. But at least there nobody was shooting at me."

Will continued, "But today, somebody was shooting at me to kill me for the first time in my life. It's gonna sound stupid, but why would they want to do that?"

Brass laughed. "It's not you, man; it's this stinkin' war. You ain't done nothin' 'cept wear the wrong uniform. You gotta think the same. Shoot at their uniform. Except with them, you cain't ever see the uniform. We shoot at the noise."

"Yeah, but still, being shot at. I could be dead right now."

"They fight their battles at night. We answer them during the day. This thing'll never end." Brass said to nobody in particular. Brass, a nineteen-year-old draftee from the French Quarter of New Orleans, added, "It doesn't really matter. Don't know who cares how it all comes out."

"Yeah, who cares anyway?" That was Two. "My old man could've kept me home from this mess. But no. Instead, he told me stories of World War II and how he has fond memories of the camaraderie with his buddies from the war. Said he wanted the same for me."

Will turned on his side and asked Two, "What's with the name anyway? Who wants to be called Two?"

Two lit a cigarette and stared outside at the night. "Easy - and I must have explained this a million times. Being from an Italian family, the name Antonio stuck. That's my father's name and my grandfather's name, and probably a bunch before them. Antonio – and don't call Pops Tony - he won't even look at you - when he started the restaurant, that is Pops did in the twenties, my dad was always there. Well, to look at them is to see one person. Dad hated the name Antonio, but Pops wouldn't let anyone call him Tony either, so since Dad is the proverbial "chip off the old block," he became "Chip." So, as weird as it sounds, my Dad is Chip Abruzzi. Pops didn't seem to care. Anyway, I'm from the same mold, so it's "Chip Two," but always just "Two.""

"I'm just Will. Always been Will. Never William, Bill, Billy, Willy – nothing like that. It's easy. Maybe boring, but it's me. And you Brass, let me guess, you play the trumpet or something."

Brass laughed. "Yeah, something like that."

Will looked at Turner. "You gotta nickname? Or what?"

Turner – true to his name – turned over on his bunk. "No. I gotta sleep though. I hate FNGs. Why don't you guys forget it? I'm tired."

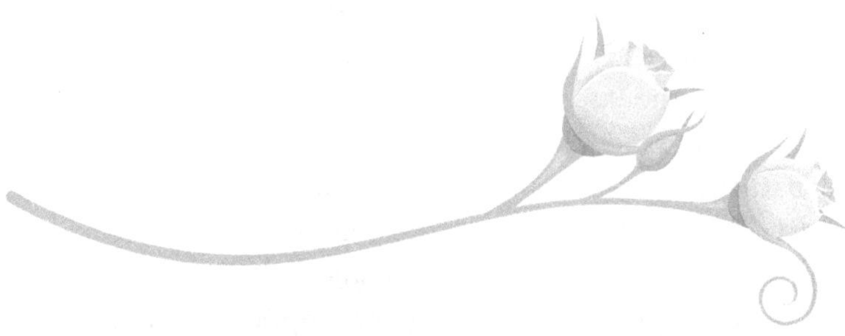

T W E N T Y - S I X

The weather in Vietnam in late April can change in minutes. Calm and clear one minute; quickly replaced by driving rain the next. Then there are days of constant humidity and sun-drenched heat. Alpha Company woke up before the sun the following day. The oven of hot, humid air welcomed them with the rising sun. The threat of showers hung in the low clouds creeping in from the west. That morning was unlike so many others at Fire Station Base Sally when the usual blasts of enemy fire served as the soldiers' alarm clocks. The NVA's pattern was to stage their attacks in the dark of night or as the sun rose. As Will, Two, and the others woke up to begin their day with breakfast that morning, the day was as quiet as a football stadium the morning after the big game.

"Can't understand it," Turner offered to Will and several of the other members of Alpha Company. "Maybe we're in for something a little different this morning. What do you think?"

The answer came from Brass. "You gotch're good mornings, and your bad mornings. Don't seem to matter much; we're still here, in this pile a' dirt. Just get me some gooks. My kill count is getting low."

Will started to say something when a missile cruised no more than a hundred yards away, followed immediately by a second in the same path, their low whistles shattering the early morning silence. The men felt the explosions, knocking Brass's helmet to the ground. The flames at the southern end of the FSB reached up in bright contrast to the gray clouds gathering overhead. Two, Will and the other men grabbed their helmets and weapons and joined the others as they ran to the southern edge.

The missiles hit near the supply tent, destroying two jeeps. Men were seen running from the tent, yelling and searching for the members of their squad who had already been out preparing for the day's activities. Will and his squad walked to the scene of the carnage. They stopped, however, as the supply troop found two of their soldiers, dead from the missile attack. They were carrying bodies. Everyone stopped and watched as the medic treated the wounded.

Captain Harmon, the base's commander, surveyed the scene and called his troops together. "We've been suspicious of recent activity in the area. Obviously, what we witnessed was the result of that activity. Wolf, I need Alpha Company to gear up. We're heading north to find these sons of bitches who did this and take them out. Be ready in fifteen minutes. We won't stop till we find and destroy them."

Will gathered his gear together for the search and destroy mission. Then he heard someone calling his name. The voice grew louder. He saw Pedro and Apopka lugging their duffle bags toward Will.

"I thought that was you, Will," said Apopka. "Didn't know when we'd see you again. Did we Pedro? They shipped you out of camp so fast that we barely had time to say our goodbyes. It's great to see you." Will, Apopka, and Pedro exchanged hugs and back slaps. Apopka and Pedro suffered through boot camp with Will.

"You guys got stuck here too? Did they put you in Alpha Company?" Will asked.

"Yeah," Pedro answered, "I can't get away from you smelly gringos. But if I gotta hang with gringos, 'stead of us Californians, guess you two will have to do." Pedro Benevisto hailed from a long-time Mexican/ Californian family from San Diego. Pedro informed Will and Apopka of his true allegiance - to neither Mexico nor the United States, but to the mythical Republic of California. He told them that he'd suffered through life in the U.S. One day, California would return to its independent glory of the early years. Will never knew Apopka's first name but recalled Apopka's voice describing his small hometown near Orlando, Florida.

"But you're here. I don't know if you're part of the mission, but we're about to head out." Will was interrupted by Wolf, who charged to the men and barked, "Will, you know these guys?"

"Yessir, Sargent."

Wolf looked at Apopka and Pedro. Shaking his head, he said to both, "Get your gear ready." Wolf added, "Looks like I have no choice. Hey, Turner, get these FNGs in line, will you? We're headin' out."

The men gathered at the northern perimeter of FSB Sally. Turner led them at point, the fifty yards of clearing giving way to the triple canopy of Viet Nam jungle. Intelligence from HQ indicated that the big guns lay to the north, maybe five or six klicks from Sally. With no road and not even much of a path to follow, the going was slow. The prize weapon was the machete wielded by Brass. They were told to keep their bearings to the northwest.

The mosquitos proved insufferable. The bug spray helped some, but the soldiers remembered their instructions to keep the amounts low or suffer from too much insecticide. The platoon marched through the overgrowth, hacking their way through the jungle. Will, Apopka, Two, and Pedro tried to keep up a steady banter, but their observations of the jungle prevented idle chatter. Every noise and broken twig increased their nervous energy. Soon their primary task to watch for the enemy wore on the men, and their silence became a welcome ally.

Their trek through the jungle began as expected. Will did not see anything that caused him concern, but he could have sworn that the sway of the trees overhead carried more than the rustle of the wind. The feeling of a presence lingered in Will, and time after time, he looked up, thinking he'd see someone, but saw only leaves, with traces of clouds visible past the canopy overhead.

Soon, though, the rain came down in flowing sheets. At first, Will didn't mind blocking the rain with his poncho. At least the rain dulled the silence and helped keep the bugs away. The morning passed when Will heard Two announce, "Sarge, there's a trail." The troops stopped. A small trail crossed their path, almost completely hidden from the soldiers. The trail looked in the distance to be swallowed by the jungle foliage.

"Sarge, you want us to have a look?" Turner asked. "Maybe that'll lead us to the artillery."

"Okay," Wolf answered, "Take Apopka, Will, Two, and Pedro. Check it out. Keep the lines open. And don't do anything stupid."

"Yessir, Captain. Nothin' stupid. Let's go, guys."

With Turner in the lead, the five men entered the jungle through the trail's opening. The rain slowed to a drizzle, with steam rising from the ground. Now and again, the sunlight touched the men and the lower flora in scattered shards of light reflecting off wet leaves. Keeping watch from every direction, the men followed the path, which more clearly defined itself within twenty minutes, indicating a fair amount of use.

Still, as they moved forward, they neither saw nor heard anything. They approached a village set back in the jungle, but saw no signs of life. Only the sounds of the jungle filled the air.

Through the brush, they saw several grass huts. The men crouched down, hidden from the hamlet, waiting for potential danger to disclose itself. The minutes passed, and nothing happened. The village's loneliness beckoned to the troops. On Turner's signal, they headed into the hamlet.

They found a deserted ring of six grass huts, all facing into the center of the ring, each in decent shape and empty of any life. Remnants of human presence spilled inside and outside the huts, with food, stray dishes, clothing, and garbage thrown about, with spent shells already being sucked into the dirt.

Turner radioed back to Wolf. "Sarge, we found a hamlet, but it looks deserted. Can't rightly tell what happened here. Been empty for a while."

"Roger that. Double check for ordnance, and then check back in."

Turner gave Wolf the coordinates and ordered a thorough search. "Guys, they got tunnels under everything. From the looks of things, the only thing to keep an eye out for is hidden openings. Be careful moving anything that could cover a hole large enough to slide a small man into. Let's check it out, and we'll hook up at the trail."

There was nothing. They poked around the last belongings of the hamlet that had been the home for no more than thirty people. But to Will, it didn't look like much of a home. He had no idea whether this was an old home or had been there a week. Maybe he'd learn in time how to tell, but to his untrained eye, that place could have sprouted up in minutes. It eluded Will as to how a place like this could be anybody's home.

The trail closed upon them as they hiked on. They marched single file, with Turner in the lead and Apopka and Will bringing up the rear. Sniper shots rang out across the jungle. The men dove into the brush. All except Pedro, who fell across the trail. The shots opened Pedro's gut to the jungle; red blood spilled everywhere. More bullets bounced around them. They responded with hot fire in every direction. The thunderous response lasted for a minute until Turner signaled them to stop.

Will watched Two and Turner crawl to Pedro but couldn't see more. With the cacophony silenced, Will found himself shaking. He gathered enough composure to ask Apopka, "You think that's it?" Apopka said nothing.

Will turned around to look at Apopka and saw nothing at first. Then he found Apopka lying at the edge of the trail. Looking closer, Will saw a line of blood oozing from Apopka's head and the torn pant leg and blood above Apopka's boot. Will shouted, "Two, he's hit." The shouting brought more shots from Will's left, which were answered by Turner, the squad's sentry. Two busied himself over Pedro.

"Keep quiet," Turner hissed to Will. "Is he bleeding?"

"Hell, yeah, everywhere," said Will.

"Well, find something to stop the bleeding, 'cause if he ain't dead, he'll bleed to death."

Will looked around, "What about the sniper?"

"Forget it, I think I got him. Take care of Apopka."

"Pedro?"

"Don't know. It's up to Two."

Will crawled to Apopka, strewn on his side, his chest rising and falling but otherwise remaining still. The bullet burned a streak along Apopka's hair, leaving a red slice along his scalp the size of the blade of a pocket knife. Will struggled with the view of Apopka's lower leg, with blood, muscle, and bone nauseating Will. Will had no idea how to do anything about that.

"Hey, Turner, give me a hand here, will ya?" Without saying a word, Turner crawled to Apopka. Will watched as Turner cut off a part of Apopka's pant leg and wrapped what was left of his leg with the olive green fatigues.

Turner said, "Don't know how long Pedro's gonna hold out. We gotta get back to the medic. Grab Apopka, and let's go. I gotta help Pedro."

Turner and Will were the larger of the men, tasked to carry the injured out of the jungle. Two led the squad back down the trail, eyes everywhere, with his gun ready. Turner ran and grabbed Pedro, hauling him over his shoulder. Watching, Will copied Turner and grabbed Apopka. The three men jogged as best they could back to Alpha Company. The medic and several other men met them halfway.

That night, the rains returned, this time with pounding force. As Will waited for his turn on watch to begin at 0200, there was nothing more to do but get what sleep he could. He couldn't.

On watch, Brass huddled with Will against a large tree. He offered Will a cigarette, which Will waved off.

Brass lit up, and Will asked, "Did you hear anything about Pedro and Apopka?"

Brass blew out smoke, dissipating to the canopy. "He didn't make it."

Will felt his eyes water. How could he not have made it? Will felt a boulder drop into the pit of his stomach. Will thought that they had stopped Apopka's bleeding. "You sure, man?"

"Yeah," was all Brass said.

The next morning, Will traded places in line to speak with the medic. Surprise and relief filled Will upon learning that Apopka was okay, except that he'd have a permanent limp from the loss of muscle in his leg and a permanent scar along his scalp. Captain Harmon later commended Will for the job he did with Apopka. "Don't know how he would have done had you not stepped up to bat. Nice job, Private."

It wasn't Apopka who died. Will felt a slight surge of pride knowing that he had helped Apopka. But Pedro didn't make it, as the bullets took out most of his abdominal organs. Will's pride turned into a troubling feeling. Why did Apopka make it and not Pedro?

That question fed more questions in Will's mind. What was he doing in the middle of a jungle in Viet Nam? What was he doing anywhere? His sense of loss, not knowing any direction for his life beyond following the helmet in front of him, felt heavy to Will. Being ever the pragmatist, if nothing else, Will decided that marching in step with the helmet in front was as good an option as any.

Will joined the squad for their debriefing. The rendition of what happened to Pedro and Apopka had no choice for Will but to remind him too strongly of his inability to step forward and do what had to be done, coupled with the fact that the mission itself resulted in nothing. That Pedro had to die to do it troubled Will even more.

At that thought, Will caught his breath. He realized that he hadn't thought of Glory since arriving in Vietnam. Caught up in the fear and uncertainty of the war, a new continent, and his place among the soldiers suppressed all thoughts of Glory. He wondered what she was doing. Did she have any idea what place he was in? Will knew with certainty that she couldn't imagine anything about Vietnam nor his state of mind. Based on his memory of their short romance and marriage back in Chicago, she must be thinking that this was easy for Will. He always hoped that everyone would think that his life was easy. He believed that Glory was no different. Will's fears and doubts were known only to himself.

TWENTY-SEVEN

The Spring semester at Northwestern University was hurtling at full throttle, past mid-terms, with the senior class focused on their June graduation date. It was lunchtime, in between classes and Glory was early for her lunch with Teri. Glory fought the rain with her umbrella practically resting on her head. She crossed campus to University Center, passing a shivering group of protesting students huddled under Old Oak, the University's prize 250-year-old Majestic Oak tree. At the front entrance, she waited for Teri's arrival through the downpour. After a chance for Teri to drip dry when she got there, they went inside. Tacked on the walls of the lobby and the hallway leading to the cafeteria were hand-made posters, remnants of a student protest the prior week, echoing the overriding sentiments: "Pray for Kent State," "All Troops Out of Vietnam," "Support the Troops, Reject Nixon," and so on. They negotiated the cafeteria line, and then a table opened up in the middle of the room. A blast of thunder careened through the room as they sat at the table.

"Have you heard anything from Will?" Teri asked.

"Not a thing."

"He hasn't written to you?"

"Nope. I guess he's not much of a writer. But I guess no news is good news."

"Maybe," Teri said.

Even though they both wrote for the newspaper, they had little time together, primarily for lunches such as this one. This time, however, was different. As they ate their sandwiches, they spoke of finishing their course work, graduation, and Teri's latest love interest.

"How's your story coming?" Glory asked Teri.

"That's why we had to meet now. I'm leaving today after class. Ohio. I don't know if I'll be back for your birthday, so I wanted to give you your gift."

"Kent State?"

Teri nodded.

"You are a dedicated journalist. I admire that."

"That's groovy, Glory. You have no idea, do you, how much I admire you?"

"Me?"

"Yes, you. You're a mom. A top student. Your report cards make me jealous," Teri said and then chuckled. "Seeing the row of As is amazing. I keep getting those Bs. And did you hear anything about the contest?"

Glory shook her head.

"You write amazing poems," Teri continued. "There's no doubt you'll win. I can say I knew you when."

"Yes, you did. You do. I can't believe you're leaving."

"Yeah, I better get used to it if I'm going to write for the Tribune one day. A journalist can't wait for the stories to come to them but has to find the stories where they're hidden. This one's out in the open," Teri said as she waved consent to someone to take one of the empty chairs. "Nixon can't control his own National Guard. They killed four of us. That could have been me getting shot for nothing more than walking across campus. It stirs my soul thinking about the four victims."

Glory watched as Teri sat up straighter in her seat, her eyes narrowing in the way that Glory has seen so often. "You're not going to get arrested again, are you?"

"Why not? If that's the price to pay to get the story."

"But you hated it."

"Sure, we all did. Do. We hate the war. We hate Nixon and Daley, and they hate anyone that isn't a white, Christian, heterosexual, millionaire guy. That's why we marched at the convention. Most of all,

I hate hate and love love. Less of the former and more of the latter, I say."

"I was there," Glory jumped in. "You reminded me of a mountain climber, scaling up the Logan Monument in Grant Park. If you look closely, you can see the back of your head in the newspaper picture."

"Yeah. It was something. We made the news. I wasn't there as a journalist, so this trip should be different."

"They don't lock up journalists?" Glory asked.

"Let's ask Leo," Teri said, looking toward the register as a man waved at them as he was paying. Teri waved him over.

"Glory asked if they arrest journalists," Teri said as Leo took his seat. "I figured you would know better than me."

"Why, if you think so," Leo answered. He had grown his hair past his shoulders, in straight lengths of dark brown, with pre-mature gray showing its colors. "I know Daley does. He hates all journalists, particularly long-hair freaky student journalists."

"Like, Izzie?" Glory asked, smiling at her best friend.

"Absolutely," Leo answered. "Now, Izzie, if it was your gorgeous friend here, she'd probably talk the cops out of hauling her in. Ain't that so?"

Glory giggled and turned her eyes down from the deep look Leo gave her.

"My friend can get away with anything," Teri said. "She's a trust fund baby."

Glory straightened up to address Teri. "I told you a hundred times, I don't have a trust fund. You're just jealous that I'm the baby of the family and you're not. The youngest gets whatever she wants, and that includes me. Would you agree, Leo?"

Leo nodded, adding the crinkle of a smile at the corners of his eyes.

"But still," Glory continued, "you must have hated being in jail."

"Well…I don't know," Teri said to Leo. "Tell her the story you told me. It sounds more fun than the last time we went to Rush Street."

Leo finished the last spoonful of his soup, took a drink from his glass, then leaned toward the girls.

"You should have seen it. It was pretty cool. Teri was in a separate lockup with the women, so she didn't have the chance to see him. Anyway, we're groovin' in there. This young cop was nearby and came to quiet us down. So anyway, we get to talking, and we start rappin' about music. He plays the guitar – well, he's learning to. He asks me what I play, and I tell him that I am a big Phil Ochs fan...."

"The folk singer?" Glory asked.

"That's the one. Well, wouldn't you know it, as soon as I mention his name, a guy comes walking toward us, one of us, also among the waiting. Here's the cool part, the guy walks up to us and tells us he overheard our conversation. 'I'm Phil Ochs,' he says. The cop's jaw drops. I just look at him and go, 'Well, damn, if you don't look just like him.' And we shook hands and had us a grand ole' time. Even the cop. Jordan was his name. From Joliet, I think."

"See there, Glory," Teri said. "It's not the cops."

"Of course, it is," Glory said. "Give Jordan five years on the force, and the next time you're in there, and you call him over, he'll rap on your knuckles and head back to his desk laughing."

"She's probably right," Leo said as he gathered the detritus from his lunch. "They got the cops where they want them. That's why we all make so much noise. It makes news. We may not convince the man, but we can get to the undecideds, the independents, the students who are riding the middle lane. Enough of them come around, and suddenly we're in charge. They need to forget their illusions about McCarthy and get with us. We'll have a new party one day soon. A progressive party. Everybody's invited unless you think you're better."

Leo stood and pushed his chair under the table. "So for your trip to Ohio, Teri, keep it cool. Keep an eye for the younger cops. Could make a difference in where you sleep that night."

He headed off, leaving the girls watching him. "You guys seem pretty close," Glory said.

"We work together on the SDS stuff. He wanted to go to Ohio, but the timing didn't work out."

"When will you be back?" Glory asked.

"Not sure. But in case I can't be back by the thirteenth, I wanted you to have this." Teri reached to the floor by her chair, pulled a wrapped gift from a shopping bag, and handed it to Glory.

"It's not much of a gift, but it's the best I could think of. Still, I know you'll like them."

Glory took the package, almost dropping it from the unexpected weight, shook it, and heard nothing. But she felt the inside items slide against each other. Books. As always. She laid the gift on the table and leaned forward toward Teri, her hands resting on the gift. "Remember what I told you the other day?" she asked. Teri nodded, her mouth set in expectation.

"It came back positive?" Teri asked. "Another one? You're having another baby. That's amazing. When is she due?"

"September 25th."

"So you'll graduate now and then be a full-time mom."

"Yeah, a single mom."

"Glory, he'll be back before that. You know that."

"I don't know anything. He's not here. I'm raising Rachel with Mom. Did I tell you we now have an *au pair* living with my Mom? She's only there to be with Rachel. I don't understand Beth. She's her grandmother? Why would she want Rachel to be with, what's her name…?"

"Is she French?"

"I don't know," Glory answered. "Livia, I think. Something like that. I don't remember where she's from."

"So now she'll be needed even more once number two arrives."

Glory nodded. She had expected Teri to find the news to be a positive development. She was right in knowing her best friend so well. But it gave no help to Glory. Instead, it further contrasted with Glory's emotions being matched by the dark gray outside, drenched in lamentations from the incessant rain. She knew that having another baby without Will around to help gave her few options. When Beth granted Glory's request to take care of Rachel while Glory went to school, it gave Glory a window to attempt to conjure up some kind of future. The only reason that Glory was not surprised is how much Rachel looks like Beth, particularly in her eyes. Glory knew that Beth saw this immediately. What would Beth feel about her granddaughter if she came out looking like Will? Glory didn't want to look too deep at that question because Glory also didn't know how she would feel.

Glory had considered how she could work as a journalist and be a better mom to Rachel than her memories of Beth as a mother. Glory quickly decided she couldn't and switched her major to English Literature. She could see staying home to write and finish the collection of poems she's been working on. With luck on her side, she'll find a publisher. In the meantime, with her degree, maybe she'll teach, but does she want to be around other kids? Perhaps high school English. But now, with a second one in the oven, how can this work? Even when – or is that if? – Will comes back, how can she be a real writer and a mother. Who does that? What she wanted out of life from the time she started college changed dramatically. No longer did she read the news diligently every morning to find a story about which she could locate a spin that only she saw and would be able to lure out into the open, digging into the facts, interviewing everyone involved, and then more. Sy explained that it's one of the reasons he gives her the big stories.

Glory had been staring at the rain outside. Teri was sipping the last of her drink. Then Glory's view returned to the intimacy of the shared moments. A short blast of thunder rang out again outside, interrupting the beginning of Teri's comment. Then she spoke.

"What're you gonna do?"

Glory looked around at the lunchtime activity, at her peers all wrapped up in their world, insulated from the realities that will undoubtedly face them when their time as students ends. But Glory's been there, keeping one foot-dragging to hold onto her life as a student, and the other foot, chopped into several pieces and placed with Rachel, the *au pair*, and Beth, and another part hovering somewhere in Southeast Asia. In the same manner that a search team gives up the mission, that last part repeatedly reports to Glory that there is no sign of her missing husband. And the closer she gets to graduation, the less the first foot keeps hold of the ground on campus. Soon, the fantasy of a student's life, where the only job is to do homework and pass, will give way to her life as she has made it. Can she be Glory? Is she at her end and moving into her new role only as a mommy? Is there anything left for her? Is that why Will left for another life in a foreign land, learning a new language and meeting people that don't look like him. Maybe he's doing it for both of them, with Glory living vicariously through Will, if unknown what such life consists of.

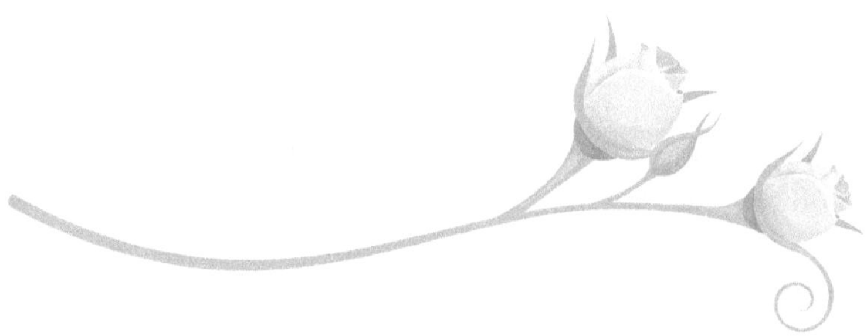

TWENTY-EIGHT

When Will received word that the order came from headquarters to dismantle FSB Sally, he welcomed the activity. With their long time in country, Turner and Brass naturally led the effort for their squad, giving the new guys the tasks that they didn't want for themselves. Will came to find that none of the new guys had any interest in becoming a leader, including himself. They were content to keep busy, knowing that each day they worked and stayed alive brought them one day closer to going home.

All they were told of the order dismantling the camp was that they were transferring to a base near the Cambodian border. Will overheard the lament of his CO that the base he named to honor his mother, Sally, existed no more.

Captain Harmon addressed the troops as they waited for the transports to take them toward Cambodia. "Gentlemen, headquarters has authorized me to inform you that the United States Army, in a joint operation with our South Vietnamese counterparts, will be conducting a major operation that, for the first time, will put you inside Cambodia. We don't know yet where the operation will exactly take us. You'll know in due course. For now, we will be joining the 2nd Squadron of the Blackhorse Regiment at Quan Loi. You will be given your assignments in support of Operation Rockcrusher."

"It makes me proud to look at each of you as we have invoked the confidence of my commanding officers in asking my battalion to participate in a mission of this magnitude. The mission that we are about to embark on is one of great importance. Details will be provided to you as needed. By carrying out our assignments, we will flush out and destroy the COSVN and end the cowardly retreats of the NVA. Your squad, your commanding officers, the United States Army, and the people of the United States of America and South Vietnam are counting on each of you. Now is the time to shine and do the job that we know that you can excel at. Bringing your best to your job, this mission will be a success for which you can be proud."

"We will meet up again at Quan Loi. Good luck, and God be with you."

The base at Quan Loi was near the point of entry into the Fishook region in east-central Cambodia and was alive with activity and motion. When Will, Two, and the others settled in, whey were immediately scheduled for meetings, briefings, weapons checks, and the other matters required to join in Operation Rockcrusher. Will found himself moving from one tent to the next. Facing different officers and differing needs, the entire day was a whirlwind that resembled a puzzle with only pieces of the border laid out. The mission that was the subject of the day's events, like puzzle pieces lying in a box — a mess of parts, colors, shapes, and sizes — didn't seem to Will to have any sense of organization whatsoever.

D-Day was the very next morning: May 1, 1970. Up well before dawn, Alpha Company once again fulfilled the informal motto of the military to "hurry up — and wait." The orders they were given late the previous night required them to jump into Kratie Province in Cambodia and provide support for the armored divisions. They had no idea what they would encounter as the Chinook helicopters ferried them into a landing site somewhere east of the city of Mimot. Landing Zone Zebra smelled of cut grass from work done by the advance troops. By the time Will and the rest of Alpha Company touched down at Zebra, the number of soldiers and arms had expanded to a complete base. Will wondered what was in store for them. At the moment, he followed along and did what he was told.

In its pre-war life, Mimot existed to support the surrounding rubber plantations of the French giant Michelin. Until their transport out that afternoon, Alpha Company provided general logistics support for LZ Zebra. That was a fancy way of saying they did whatever odd jobs were needed, digging foxholes being a primary activity. Shortly after lunch, the squad was given orders for their first mission. The road leading into Mimot was a critical road experiencing moderate to heavy opposition from the NVA. Control of the road was the first key to controlling these eastern portions of Cambodia and, of crucial interest, the COSVN headquarters.

Will looked across at Brass and Turner on the short flight toward Mimot. There was no conversation over the noise of the wind flying around the helicopter. Brass and Turner looked so calm and without worries. Will wondered if they could see the fear that he felt. Well, not fear exactly, but a sense that this was more than dangerous. The first live fire that Will had faced that first day at FSB Sally hung around Will like a shadow, ever reminding Will of his unsuitability for this kind of activity. The thought of his fear that day informed him that he could die at any moment. Will wondered if this would be his last day. Even if it was, his best approach was to hide his thoughts.

The jumping-off point near the battle zone for the Mimot road was absent of enemy presence. They entered the way to Mimot without incident. The squad marched toward Charlie and Delta Companies stationed on the outskirts of Mimot, seeing and hearing the battle. By the strength of the American Army, killed NVA troops littered the highway. The battle for the road produced no casualties for the good guys. Will's squad encountered only sporadic shooting; nothing like a battle for a major road should be. Keeping close to Brass and Turner and Two nearby, Will sensed that he would survive the day.

The Companies marched into Mimot that afternoon. They joined in what was left of the battle — matching fire with fire. Two pointed out to Will that the NVA began their retreat, their small, black-clad shapes fading into the distant grass and rubber trees. The battle ended with plenty of daylight left, and the road was secure, sparing Will from seeing any American casualties that day.

Will later learned they arrived in the firefight as it ended. He thought how crazy that sounded, wasting such manpower for nothing. Brass agreed.

"Don't think they ever get it right." Brass said. "No wonder so many get killed here. They don't know which end is up."

Will sat on his bunk, the pieces of his dismantled M-16 scattered around him. Will studied the scattered parts and began reassembling his rifle. Brass asked him about it. "Why you doin' that all the time?"

"Shit, man. With all this mud everywhere, I can't clean this thing enough. You know, it may be my best friend just 'bout now."

"Yeah." Brass turned and stared at Will. "No such thing as friends here, amigo? Is that what you think? With an attitude like that, you will go home in a bag. Man, if you don't got friends here, you don't got nothin'."

"Brass, I ain't talkin' about you. You crack me up. Never met anybody like you before. But the little I've been here, I've seen guys get shot up. My best friend is this rifle and the bullets right here."

Will stood up, his M-16 hanging from his shoulder, again working as his singular friend. "I'm gonna find Wolf."

Will found Wolf finishing a briefing in the command tent. Wolf spoke first as he spotted Will walking toward him. "What's on your mind, soldier?" Wolf asked. "Wondering how you were holding up, given the first time we met. I can still see the whites of your eyes matching your face."

"Sarge, I know, can't shake it myself. No, got no problem. Never got close enough to the action. I wondered if we could talk."

"Private, talking won't help. You gotta look inside yourself and find the strength to see this through. You think smart and call up the courage that I know is there, and you'll be fine." Wolf continued, "And that's an order, Private. I know you have it. Just show it to yourself. You don't have to impress me or anyone else. Do what you are told, follow orders, be smart, and pay attention. That is all."

Wolf turned and walked away.

Will stood there watching. That wasn't what he wanted to see Wolf about. But now, he couldn't remember what he had wanted to say. He did find the words that Wolf used to be of some comfort. Will ran to catch up with Wolf. Getting Wolf's attention, Will asked for a few more minutes. This time Wolf didn't brush him off. The two men found seats on a couple of large logs lying on the ground.

"What's on your mind, soldier?"

"Sarge, I need to go to DaNang."

"What's in DaNang?"

"I want to find my brother. Lou. Lou Stanford. Air Force."

"What's he doing in DaNang?"

"Nothing."

Wolf turned and looked at Will. "Son, you need to speak what's on your mind. I don't know Airman Lou Stanford, and I need you here. You've just arrived and now want to turn around and leave your post."

"Then can you transfer me? He's been missing. That's why I'm here."

"You joined up to find him? Do I have that right?"

"Mostly. There's more. Anyway, we learned that he was on a mission that left DaNang in January and never came back. I'm going to find him."

"'Fraid not, Private. I need you here. If they looked for him, what do you think you can do that they didn't."

"Don't know," Will said and lowered his head.

Wolf put his arm around Will's shoulders. "I see. It's tough. I'll do some checking, but you need to give me your all. Can we agree on that?"

"Sure, Sarge. I don't want to leave here until I find him or know what happened."

"I'll see what I can do. But for now, stick with me."

"Thanks."

"I don't want thanks. Keep your heart and soul in the game."

"That's affirmative, sir. But still, thanks for what you did."

"I'm not sure I understand."

"Just before. You looked me in the eyes. Your words mean something to me. The guys, well, they talk how you're all business. Cold. Smart, and strong as hell, but by the book. The minute you spoke with me then, I don't know. There's no book for that."

"I do what I have to. My father taught me when you find a man that seems worthwhile, no matter what, you look them in their eyes, and you'll be able to see what they are made of."

Wolf went on. "My father died a hero's death. He was an Israeli tank commander. He died in the war in forty-eight. I still remember him telling me that he always looked people in the eye, especially the soldiers under his command. He determined whether they would serve under him solely from their eyes. I never forgot that. I never knew how he died, but I imagined that soldiers that he would not have chosen were serving under him that day."

"What are you doing here?" Will asked, yet again finding surprise in the men around him. Why was an Israeli serving as a sergeant in the U.S. Army fighting in Vietnam?

Wolf continued, "My mother was born in California and met my Dad at JFK in New York. He was on some top-secret mission in the U.S. When she left New York, she was already pregnant with me. My Dad couldn't stay in the States, but she couldn't be without him and left to join him in Tel Aviv. Years later, after my father died, we moved back to California. She wasn't a Zionist or anything. She was in love with my father. With him gone, she had no reason to stay."

"So you're American?"

"Yeah, and I speak Hebrew, but I lost my accent. When I can, I visit my father's family. But being away for so long, I lost my accent completely. Anyway, everybody thinks this place is a hell-hole. They're right. It's hell here for us. And for these people. But we are here to help them, and where we are right now, doing what we are doing, should help."

Will asked, "What are we doing here? I mean, this is so far from everything. Yeah, we can help, I guess. I mean, they seem so poor. But is getting shot and killed a reasonable price to pay?"

"Will, you got me on that," Wolf answered. "You and I are soldiers. We're here to do the job we were given to do. Saving these people from Communism, from the threat of Ho Chi Minh's tyranny, is the mission that we have been given. If we do our jobs well, maybe we will actually do some good."

"I don't want to get killed doing this," Will continued. "This isn't my fight. I don't know these people. Getting killed so some peasant can have a job in a rubber factory or tending his rice paddies isn't a particularly good idea. This is the only life I have. What do I care, so long as I make it out of here alive."

Wolf pulled a matchbook from his shirt pocket and struck a match. The glow from the flame lit up Will's face against the darkening evening sky. Wolf held the light closer, seeing Will straight through his eyes. "Maybe I'm wrong," Wolf said, blowing out the match.

Snoul, Cambodia, was a small cross-road town on a main north-south road that stretches through Cambodia, lying a few miles northeast of Mimot, where Route 7 meets Route 9. Its small center had supported the local population of plantation workers and local travelers. Snoul would have been of little interest to the generals, but for recent information received by Division HQ: the NVA established a stronghold in Snoul, taking control of the town. The decision was made to capture Snoul and drive out the NVA or, better, to kill or capture as many of the NVA Regulars as possible. The columns rolled through the countryside, ending at the plateaus overlooking Snoul to the east and the west. There, the staff created detailed plans to take the town.

In the early afternoon of May 4, 1970, the lead tanks broke through the jungle into the plains leading toward Snoul. Once freed from the vegetation, tanks, and armored cavalry vehicles rushed toward the town at highway speeds. The trip to the outskirts of Snoul took the entire morning, including three impromptu river crossings requiring bridges to be placed by the Army's flying cranes.

Will's Second Squadron caught up with the heavy vehicles by late morning on the 5th of May, to the south of the town. They watched the villagers streaming away from their homes as they waited along the road. Passing the troops, the refugees confirmed that the NVA had taken over the town. The squad first intended to secure the small airstrip lying outside the city. The heavy vehicles rolled onto the airstrip, taking on rocket-propelled grenades and small arms fire from the nearby perimeter. The 11th Cavalry tanks responded with a barrage of canisters, quickly repelling the minor resistance of the NVA.

In control of the airstrip, the 3rd Squadron rolled through the rubber trees to the west of Snoul. The 2nd Squadron lined up its regiments on the small hill overlooking the town from the east, with a clear view over the wild-growing Eleusine grass. Shelling from the tanks of the armored cavalry and the fire from the armored personnel carriers flattened the town in short order. By the time the 2nd Squadron descended the hill, joining up with the 3rd, there was little left in Snoul that had not been entirely or partially destroyed.

Included in the many squads of infantry troops involved in the invasion, Alpha Company walked through the main streets of Snoul, past the destroyed and crumbling buildings. Word was passed down that the NVA evacuated the area when the first shelling began. There was no trace of the NVA as Will, and the other squad members searched the town. Will took in the level of destruction with a low whistle. The few remaining villagers were barely clothed, their clothes being flaked off from flying debris.

The tanks continued to roll through. Like the second team standing on the sidelines waiting for their chance to take the field, Two, Turner, and Brass stood with Will and watched as the tanks completed the destruction. They watched with astonishment as one of the tanks leveled a children's playground. There was no sign in the playground of any Cambodian children.

Turner was first to join the frenzy that infected the minds of the men of the 2nd and 3rd Squadrons. The few items that remained inside the shops and homes in Snoul became the targets of a looting free-for-all. Turner led the way into the nearest shop - a small market. Will and the others followed. Up and down the streets of Snoul, the other squads were doing the same. Behind a counter in the dusty, darkened store, Will found two bottles of whiskey – at least he thought so, but since the label was in Khmer, it was hard to tell.

Everyone else grabbed what they could. Will walked outside toward the store next door, but stopped to watch soldiers carrying bottles, clothing, radios, bicycles – whatever they could find. If they couldn't find the COSVN, at least they could grab a piece of Cambodia. The Great Cambodian Souvenir Hunt had commenced.

The squad entered a clothing store, the body of a little girl lying next to the frame of the blown-out front door stopped Will. The girl could not have been more than six or seven, with the front of her tiny dress stained red from her blood. Will couldn't tell what killed her. She had been knocked against the front wall, but her face had no damage. Her black hair – cut short – neatly framed her pale face. Will stared at the girl. Her eyes were closed, telling Will nothing. The only surprise for Will was that his tears didn't come faster. Will wanted no part of anything going on around him.

Tuner pushed past Will into the store, Will turned around and returned the shove, growling at Turner as Will stepped back onto the street. Outside, Two watched as Will stopped in the middle of the road, with one bottle in each hand. With his arms full of pop bottles, Two ran to Will and offered one of the warm, dark bottles. "What happened?" Will looked first at the bottle, then at Two, but said nothing, then turned and headed in the direction of the airstrip.

Will marched along with a small convoy of tanks leaving Snoul. Strapped to every tank were the cavalry's pieces of Cambodia. They grabbed more oversized items, primarily motorcycles from the local factory, and also mattresses, appliances, and even a small vehicle towed behind, now and again.

Will waited at the edge of town, clutching the two bottles stuck to him. He looked at the bottles and thought of smacking them against the nearby crumbling wall. Instead, Will decided that those bottles would serve as his reminder of this war and the level of destruction that he saw his Army heap onto this town. Overhead, the noise of the helicopters demanded his attention. He saw more of the loot hanging from cables, flying, no doubt, for the benefit of the officers. It was all Will could do to keep from screaming out of frustration at the complete injustice of this war.

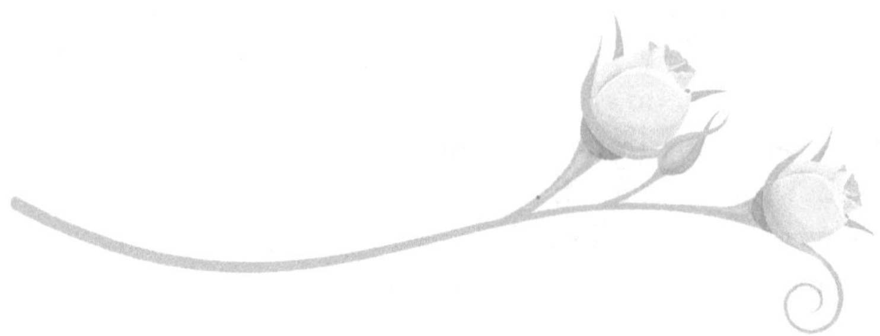

TWENTY-NINE

You saw what it was like there." Will grumbled under his breath to Two as the two men lugged bags of rice toward a waiting truck. "Nothing was left of that town. And what do we do? I mean, you, me, everyone. We take what we want. How are we helping anyone but ourselves?"

Two returned the sentiment with a grunt, the sacks of rice taking more effort than he cared to think about. Their squad had been assigned, along with the entire 2nd squadron that had taken part in the capture of Snoul, to liberate the many items found in the "City", a large supply depot lying further inside Cambodia.

Two and Will were assigned to bunker 156, containing nothing but dozens of bags filled with rice. Two chose not to answer Will's question about Snoul. Taking a water break, the two men perched themselves atop a half removed stack of the bags. Two put his canteen to good use, took a swig, then gave Will his thoughts of the moment. "Ya gotta get over it, man. What's done is done. It's this job that startin' to piss me off. Day after day, we're luggin' stuff to trucks. I'm getting tired."

Will said, "Yeah, but at least we ain't killin' nobody. And from what I can tell, all this stuff can go to some good use. Better we take it than leave it for the NVA or to feed the Viet Cong."

"Good point. But, still, I'd like to get some R&R, soak up some rays at the beach, and drink some beer. Be nice to spend some quality time with those pretty Asian girls now, if you know what I mean."

"In time, my friend. There's nothing better than hanging with you and having a few laughs. The girls, well, I don't know...."

Two jumped down off the bags of rice. "Will, man, let's finish this room, 'cause we'll be that much closer to quittin' time."

The work restarted. Will remembered his earlier question to Two and looked for an answer. "Two, I'm serious; what good is all of this? We're getting killed right and left. The people here are dying or are left with nothing after we've come in to 'save' them."

"Will, you're too serious. Just do what you're told. You want to make decisions, then become an officer in this man's Army, and you can figure out what's best to do. For now, though, we got all these damn bags to load. Let's get this done. Tomorrow we'll figure out a way to save the world."

"Two, you're right. I'll get through today, and we'll start again tomorrow. Before you know it, the days get counted right to the flight home."

Two smiled, his teeth brightening his face. "You got it, man. Just get through each day. Might be your last. Who knows? But when you wake up with the sun, you'll know that you've got yourself a chance to see the next sunset."

The COSVN headquarters continued to elude the U.S. and South Vietnamese militaries. Yet, the amount of material and the capture of many abandoned posts and storage camps made the event worthwhile, or at least that was the official position of the Army. Back in country, however, the deaths occurred as the NVA attempted to hold onto what they could. Many civilians suffered at the hands of both sides, and there was growing and vocal opposition to the invasion. To compound the situation, the rain had become a regular occurrence. The daily rain increased in intensity as a prelude to more severe weather.

Will's Alpha Company was assigned to locate and destroy a claymore mine factory hidden somewhere further into Cambodia, with the stated mission to destroy the entire factory, and whatever was located inside. Anybody found nearby was to be captured, if possible. Harmon included Will for the mission, starting with the chopper ride heading several kilometers to the west.

Will waited in the helicopter, first failing to dodge the rain across the tarmac. The ability of their Huey to fly through the churning thunderclouds rolling toward them evaded Will. But the mission was deemed essential, so rain or not, they'd soon take off for the hinterlands of Cambodia.

Two strapped in next to Will, humming in time to the rain patter. Turner, Brass, and an FNG completed the squad selected by Wolf for the mission. Five men was enough, with Army intelligence reporting the lack of recent activity at the makeshift assembly plant. The only other addition to the mission was the munitions expert who loaded the firepower needed to destroy the factory. For the fifteen-minute flight, Will wondered whether the length of the flight meant they were going into Cambodian territory beyond the thirty-kilometer limit that President Nixon authorized. It mattered not to Will, knowing he only had to follow orders.

The chopper headed west. The blackness of the curtain of weather enclosed the helicopter. The light of day darkened into a premature night sky, limiting visibility outside. Without any warning, the aircraft hit a wall of wind and fell a couple of stories like a wayward elevator. Will felt his entire insides shift and closed his eyes. At that point, he was beyond caring who saw him. He needn't have concerned himself, as each man was fighting the same battle as was Will. The small helicopter fought the winds and the rain. The lifts and drops increased the risk of the mission, at least for the eight souls on board.

The pilot veered the chopper hard right; the mission scrubbed for better weather. Still, the wind kept up its torrent, pushing them up. Then a solid downward draft dropped the small helicopter; like a new kite. The wind drove the machine hard to the left. Suddenly it was pushed back right, then down. The driving wind and rain wrestled the men inside. They were turned to the side while the pilot fought to right the chopper. The thunder and lightning intensified. Lightning flashed long and bright through Will's eyelids, echoed by an orchestra of timpani drums rolling around the lightning and the smell of electricity washing over the men.

Will opened his eyes to watch another bright flash strobe every corner of the chopper's interior. Will looked across at Turner. Turner looked straight back and through Will, the coldness adding to Will's shivers. Glancing over at Two, he noticed the tight grip that Two had on his rifle. Restraints kept him from falling over from the roller coaster ride of the storm.

Will looked to the other side of Turner at the new guy, the only one who looked back at Will. With a little cock of his head, he gave Will a tight grin and shrugged his shoulders.

The burst of a thunderclap gave them all a start. Immediately a flash of lightning preceded the distinct odor of burning rubber. Smoke filled the small cabin. Will heard the gunner in the second seat up front announcing, "May Day, May Day." The cabin spun and continued to drop with the speed of an out-of-control downhill skier. That last strike of lightning blew out the back rotor. With the next flash of lightning, Will saw the treetops rising up beneath them. Their spinning accelerated, the blades shearing the tops of the triple canopy jungle below. The chopper smashed into the jungle floor, crushing the windshield and the two-man crew. Then the cabin spun around, with Will, Two, and the others rising and falling and turning. They held to the shell of the cabin by the strength of the straps. Timed precisely to the loudest thunder heard yet, the large rotor blades broke off as they hit the ground. The metal around them crumpled and folded as the tree trunks proved strong enough to withstand the crash of the downed chopper.

Will wondered why his shoulder blades both hurt so much. Then he realized that he was hanging by his straps, with his shoulders holding his weight. "Two, are you hurt?" Will asked. Breathing came hard. The pain was sharp.

"Uh, man, I think I busted my arm. Owww. Shit, it hurts," Two complained.

"Hold on, then," Will answered. The front of the helicopter had been completely crushed. Will couldn't see the crew in the darkness, only that the crash eliminated the cockpit. "Turner, are you guys okay?" Only the wind answered. "Anybody there?" Nothing. "Shit, Two, whaddya think?"

Two turned to unbuckle the straps, letting out a shrill scream. Catching his breath first, he said to Will, "Get me out of these things. I can't do it with my arm busted."

Will unbuckled his straps and reached for Two when, Will too, burst out a loud scream of pain. He fell to his side, and lay there, breathless. "My leg. Left one. Didn't even feel it before." Will hoped to see something of the three other team members peering into the darkness. He saw nothing but a wall of black. "Two," Will pleaded anyway, "We need some help."

The answer came from Two over Will's shoulder. "I don't think so. Ain't heard nothin' from them."

It was at that point that the fire in the rear flared up. "What now?" Two complained out loud. "Will, we gotta do something. You know that corporal loaded some pretty powerful shit. This whole thing's gonna blow."

Will worked to push himself toward Two. "Yep. Fuck the pain. If we don't get outta here now, we're charcoal." Will had to stop every other moment, muscling through pain in his left leg and chest. "Can't breathe, Two. Must've broken some ribs. Hang tight for a second. I'll get to you."

Between Two's one good arm and Will managing to get within arm's length of Two, they extricated Two from his constraints. The two men collapsed onto the remains of the floor of the chopper. By this time the rain streaming into the cabin soaked the men.

"I'm okay, 'cept for the arm." Two said. "We can get a sling together now, and I should be good to get us both outta here."

They ripped enough cloth to craft a sling for Two. Once secured, Two stood and braced himself to lift Will with his one good arm and Will's one good leg. Thus, linked together, Two and Will, stumbled out of the helicopter onto the wet floor of the jungle.

"Wait," Will said, "We gotta find the radio." The rain stopped, with the wind howling ever stronger. The flames were reaching from the back. They then smelled smoke from the front of the chopper.

"Will, there's no time for that. Put your arm around my shoulders. We gotta move."

The three-legged soldier-pair headed away from the helicopter as the first explosion punched the ground under their feet. They ran as best as they could. Pieces of the chopper flew past them. They fell to the ground but quickly picked themselves up and kept running.

Then they saw the first RPG missile flying overhead. Someone else was there, and they weren't friendlies. Gunfire rang out. The two men fell to the ground with as much silence as their bodies permitted. They must have been past the fringes of the jungle into a rice paddy, as the ground on which they ran, and fell, was inches deep in water. Will hoped he didn't drown before he got shot. The shots kept coming at them.

Will felt the shot hit Two's head and instantly knew he was dead, from the rusty smell of Two's blood. Bits of bone with blood mixed with pieces of brain washed over Will. Will feared he'd be next. By Two's death, though, maybe Two could save Will. Will turned on his back in the shallow water. He pulled Two's body over like a blanket of sackcloth, out of sight to the sniper. Will struggled to stay conscious. He lay in the water, with Two covering him as shots whizzed by him. The last thing he heard through the water surrounding his submerged head was the muffled patter of the rain.

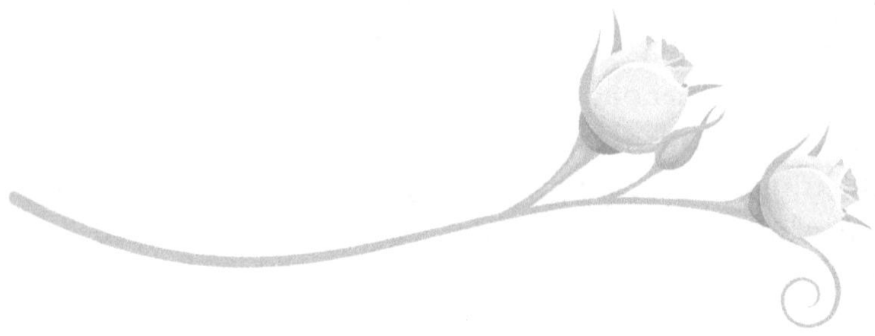

THIRTY

The thunder of a bass drum woke Will. It began as mere vibrations in his gut but then increased to a crescendo that would do justice to an operatic production. The ending to the natural orchestra thrust Will out of his slumber.

Will opened his eyes, or at least he tried. They felt glued shut, and the weak attempts of his eyelids to perform their singular task perpetuated his visual void. With sluggish awareness, Will considered his dream, sensing with more clarity that Joey and Ben hadn't been blown out of the crashing helicopter after all.

The pounding sound overhead of monster raindrops woke Will to his Cambodian jungle reverie. His fog of memory put him back lying in the shallow pond with Two covering him. Will meditated on the rain. He knew that the roof was primitive. The only other clue available to Will was the lack of a pillow or anything soft beneath him. Reaching down, he felt a thin reed mat serving as his mattress. His hand found the dirt floor beyond the edge of the mat. The effort was more than Will was ready for. His next thought was a dreamscape view of one of his last rain-delayed high school football games. Sleep came again from his memory of doing nothing but sitting in his full football uniform, waiting for the rain to end.

Will felt a gentle push to his shoulder, waking him. Not ready yet to face the new day, Will turned away, onto his side. His pain as he attempted to roll away forced his eyes open. He had no idea what he was looking at. Will saw only a tan-colored wall of dried grass in front of him. He knew that if he moved, the pain in his arm would increase. He turned slowly to where he started, taking in the limited view around him. An Asian girl, dressed in a pale brown robe, kneeled on the ground near Will. The girl's black hair lined straight back into a ponytail. Knowing that he wasn't in heaven, Will wondered where he could be.

Will focused on her face as she poured something from a pot into an earthen cup. She brought the cup toward Will. The girl's stoic face told Will nothing. Will first felt the heat of the liquid, then smelled its pungent odor. Will resisted. How could he know what she was doing? Was she the enemy? He didn't know. Will recalled that the last action he was involved in was a war.

The girl said something to Will in a voice not much louder than the outside rain. He didn't respond, not knowing what she said. Instead, he contemplated his setting. The walls consisted of dried grass bound together, rising vertically to the thatched ceiling. The space inside the hut compared to the size of his old bedroom back in Skokie. From the dusky light filtering through the small doorway, Will saw only a simple table, against the far wall, with two small chairs tucked into the sides. Other than his visitor, he was alone. Was this the girl's home? He didn't know. If he could see other mats on the floor, he'd have his answer. Will started to lift himself up with his one good arm when the sharp pain dropped him back onto the mat. Through searing pain, his heart pounded, and Will gulped the air to reduce the pain. The effort knocked Will out. The sleep that overcame him was the perfect anesthetic.

Hours later, Will's eyes sparked wide open. He realized that he was still lying beneath the roof of the grass hut. The morning song of the birds outside amongst the tree canopies told Will that his new home was located in the forest, as sunlight flitted through small cracks in the grass walls. The aroma that seeped in from outside contained the cleansing scent of newly washed leaves and jungle growth.

A thin blanket covered Will. The Asian girl was gone. Nothing in his limited view told him the date or anything about his current location. He attempted to lift himself up, but fell back to the mat from the pain coming from everywhere. Even his head hurt. What had happened? Bandages bound around his chest kept his ribs in place and assisted in lessening the pain as he breathed. His bandaged right arm stayed in place by a sling. The throbbing pain of his left leg caused him the greatest concern. Will reached down to his leg, taking his time, hoping that he'd avoid unnecessary pain. His fingers found only the mat on which he was laying. What was this? He touched his right knee. No pain there. Reaching back to his left knee again, he found nothing but the grass mat.

Will yanked the thin blanket away, throwing it halfway across the room. He saw only the beige striped grass of his mat where his left knee, leg, ankle, and foot should have been.

"Shit! My leg! They took my fucking leg!" In his anger, Will ignored the binding over his ribs and sprang up from the mat, letting his rage springboard him to action. Instantly, he fell, breaking his fall with his hands. His ribs, damaged arm, and what was left of his left leg announced their displeasure with Will's impetuous action.

Will lay still where he had fallen. He caught his breath and rolled to his back and onto the grass mat. "I can't believe this," Will said to the empty room. "Wherever the hell I am, whoever that girl is, she's gonna pay for this. What did she do to my leg?" The words came amidst his labored breaths.

The empty hut stared back at Will without comment. Will forced himself to sit up, gritting his teeth to combat the throbbing that seemed to come from everywhere. Looking down, he took care to unwrap the bandage, stained brown from his own blood (he hoped). The shortened leg showed his stump's scars and dried blood above his knee. There was no knee, nor anything else. How could it hurt? Will wanted nothing more than to find the lower part of his left leg and give it a good massage. That would relieve the pain.

The dark cloth that served as the door to his hut rustled open as someone entered. It was the Asian girl. She held a teapot by a half-circle handle and a cup in her other hand. Will's yelling didn't give her a chance to fully enter the hut. "What did you do to my leg? It's my leg! Whatever the hell you did, you gotta get it back." The pitch of Will's voice rose, losing its normal deep tones. Taking huge gulps of air to catch his breath, Will did his best to keep up his show of strength, but his voice weakened as his strength faltered. "Where the hell am I? Who are you, and what do you want from me?"

The girl watched from the doorway. When Will stopped, she continued toward Will. Will eyed the pot. "Whatever that is, get it the hell away from me." The effort to say those few words surprised Will. Catching his breath took even longer this time. Still, he went on. "You are trying to poison me. That's what all you gooks do." Spent of energy, Will could do nothing more than watch.

The girl ignored Will and poured the hot, pale brown liquid into the cup. Will continued with his complaints, but the girl ignored him, instead reaching the cup toward Will. A swing of his fist sent the cup flying across the room, the hot drink spilling on the ground and onto the girl's sandals.

She said something to Will. It wasn't English. Probably not even Vietnamese, but he couldn't be sure. She shook her head, brushed herself off, retrieved the cup, and re-filled it. This was too much for Will, and he let out a scream. He tried, at least. The hiss that resulted was, in any event, too much for the girl. She turned and ran out of the hut.

Will realized that he had no choice but to get out of there. Nothing but his own pain prevented him from getting up and walking out. Because it hurt to breathe and that he was down to one leg might cause him some difficulty. Will found nothing within easy reach to form a makeshift crutch. Maybe he could hop outside and grab a branch that would serve him. Rising from the ground on one leg challenged Will. The stump of his left leg offered no strength to support anything. Will's attempt to jump up proved a miserable failure. Not only did the pain exceed his power to fight it, but he was so light-headed as to almost pass out altogether.

No, this plan wouldn't work. Even crawling was out of the question, with his broken ribs and the stump being a significant handicap. Will realized then that he was famished. His hunger made a worthy adversary to the exhaustion that invaded Will. He had no idea how long it had been since he'd last eaten. It must have been a while from the hunger pains rolling around in his belly. What was going on? Will was a ball of questions. He had seen only one soul since realizing that he survived the ambush in the Cambodian rice paddy. He had no way of learning anything. Will noticed the two bottles he grabbed in Snuol leaning against the wall. One had been open, now only half full. Convenient, Will thought, for anesthetic purposes. Taking the opened bottle, he helped himself to more of the liquid pain relief.

The girl entered the hut, again carrying the teapot. Entering behind the girl was an elderly version of the girl, no doubt her grandmother. Wearing a similar dress, the old woman's gray hair also brandished a ponytail. The similarity of their faces struck Will, with the aged lines and creases the only discernible differences.

They stopped halfway across the hut from Will. The old woman passed the girl, speaking to Will as she walked toward him. The old woman took the cup from the girl and kept a constant chatter. Even though Will could not make out a single syllable, the woman's tone, coupled with the look in her eyes, searched for a place inside Will that would respond. Will remembered the stories he heard about torture at the hands of the Viet Cong and the NVA. This didn't feel like Viet Cong. The whole scene made no sense.

The woman attempted to hand the cup to Will. Will didn't respond but couldn't take her eyes off the woman. Her unknown comments continued. Will didn't know what to do. Maybe they had helped him. Why he had no lower left leg, he didn't know, but perhaps the old woman could answer. "What happened to my leg?" This was a different Will who asked this question than the one who could only yell at the girl. The woman answered; Will presumed she tried to answer his question. The woman attempted yet again to hand Will the cup. Will shook his head and repeated the question, but knowing that it was useless to continue the charade.

The girl stood next to the old woman. She took the cup from the woman in one hand, and reached for Will's hand with the other. Will didn't resist. He let the girl guide his hand to the warm cup, and took it. The drink smelled unfamiliar to Will. This wasn't the tea his mom used to give him when he was sick. Not unpleasant, exactly, just different, with a bitter scent reminding Will of the cigarette ashes his parents left lying in ashtrays scattered around back home. The memory of the warmth of home invited Will to take his first sip.

"Can I get something to eat?" Will asked. He considered the lack of English, and made eating motions with his hand. The girl looked at the old woman, who nodded back to her. Will hoped that the simple communication worked. The first sip of the tea flowed into Will with a warmth that surprised him. It also was enough. Laying back down, the girl retrieved the cup from Will.

Will hadn't realized that he'd fallen asleep. When he woke, the room was dark, except for a candle burning on the table. He remembered to consider his pain threshold in every move he made, Will took his time sitting up. Someone left him a bowl filled with white rice but no fork or spoon. Will scooped some rice with his fingers. The comfort of his first taste of solid food didn't last past the second scoop. The rumbling in his belly magnified when he finished that bite. The third scoop didn't make it much past his fingers. Not much of a dinner, with the rice shooting out the way it went in. At least the mess missed Will. With no food and no energy, sleep was Will's only solace.

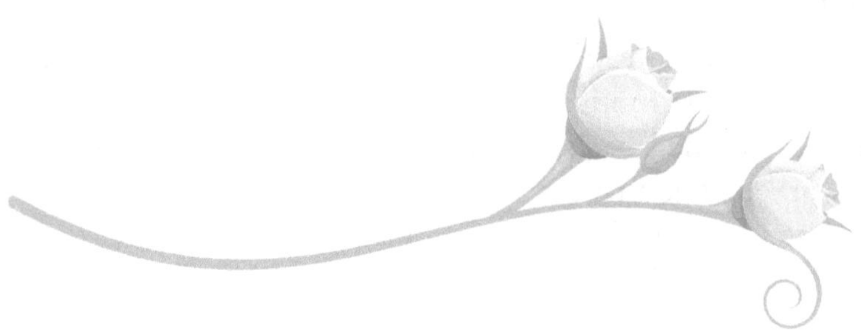

THIRTY-ONE

Several days passed before Will gained control over his weakened body. The rice bowls and the strange brew arrived each day, but he never saw anybody other than occasional views of the girl. Will rarely moved from his straw bed. With little to occupy his waking hours, Will began to cherish the rustling of the crude clothe door that announced the girl's entry, or that of the old woman. Will's strength increased, giving him more energy to pay attention to the girl, hoping to find a way to communicate with her and find out where he was and what had happened.

"Please," he started one afternoon. He sat with his back against the wall. "Do you know any English?" Will spoke slowly, hoping that she understood some English. Her look told him his answer. How was he going to get anywhere this way? He couldn't even move nor ask to find anyone that could understand him. With no better answer, Will kept up his monologue.

It then occurred to Will that not only did he feel clean, but the area around him was spotless. His questions continued. That he didn't pass out after a few words encouraged him. The girl seemed harmless enough, and he noticed that she stole a glance at him now and then. He even suspected that his smile one time caused a similar reaction from her.

A boy entered the room, catching Will by surprise. The boy was only the third person Will had seen. He often heard voices outside the hut, but it was only so much noise. The boy was tall and very thin. Will guessed that the girl and the boy were both in their twenties. The boy stopped at the doorway. The jerky motion as he entered, with the old woman following him right behind, told Will that the boy's entry was less than voluntary. The old woman pushed the boy toward Will accompanied by her instructions.

The boy stopped in the middle of the room. The girl and the woman remained by the door. Moments passed. Then the boy said, "Mamasan tell me talk you." These were the first words in English he heard in some time that weren't Will's own words. "You not good," the boy went on. "Mamasan and Soka fix you." That wasn't right, as the boy shook his head. "Care you."

"You know English?"

The boy looked at Will. The nod came with some hesitation.

"Learn in village. Not use."

"The girl, her name is Soka?" The boy nodded. "Your name?" Will asked.

The boy then turned to speak with the two women. From what Will could tell, the boy fought to get out of this distasteful task, ultimately surrendering to the woman's charge.

The boy turned back to Will. With his hands hanging at his side, the boy did nothing more. His job must have been to answer Will's questions. Will did his part.

"Where am I?"

"Kampuchea," came the delayed answer.

The sounds spoken by the boy didn't register with Will. The boy didn't need Will's words to answer his next unasked question.

The boy went on. "Home. Mamasan, Soka, me - this our home. You very sick. We think you die, but no." The boy stopped, searching for the word he needed. "Doctor - she give you medicine. Bad leg go."

"The word you said first - am I in Cambodia still?"

The boy looked at the girl, who gave him no expression. "Yes - think English say Cambodia."

Will's first real information. That, and the bit about the doctor.

"What happened to my leg?"

"Bad. Doctor - she cut."

"Why?" Will lay back on the mat. The injury must have been worse than he thought. "Was it gangrene?"

"Green?" The boy repeated.

"No — forget it. Can I speak with the doctor?"

"Speak?" The repetition was getting tiring. "Me - I -" the boy stopped, then, in frustration, turned to leave. Mamasan stopped the boy. The noise of the heated discussion floated past the walls of the hut.

"Mamasan say I need learn English more. Doctor - to the city I get her. I get her again?"

At least question marks don't need translating. Will knew there was no doctor there. He needed time to think. What time was it, anyway? For that matter, what day was it?

"What day is it?"

This the boy knew. "Monday."

"Good," Will said. The straight answer to Will's question drew a smile from Will.

The boy asked, "Is Monday funny to American?"

"No." Will looked at each of them. This was a curious group with no discernible hostility. The boy seemed less afraid or angry than hesitant to be the translator. What was this all about? Will asked with a smile, "I mean the date. You know, May 15th, whatever."

"Oh." The boy looked at his fingers, translating the number of days into English. It took several repeats on each hand. "June twenty-nine."

Will thought a minute. When was that last mission? That was a month ago? To Will, the time on this mat had not been more than a week.

He had enough, and turned to his side, away from the Cambodians. Will shut his eyes and listened to their rustling as they left the hut.

Will didn't sleep. After they left, he sat up and helped himself to the tea that he came to expect each day, topped with a shot of whiskey. With the rice, the tea, his drink, and the passage of time, his pain had decreased. He couldn't stay shut in that hut any longer. He heard the rain start its daily romp through the Cambodian jungle. For good measure, the wind joined in the act. The roof held its own. What rain seeped through dripped down the sides of the walls. Will sipped the homemade brew in the deepening browns and grays of the room, brightened only by the flashes of lightning.

He felt what remained of his left leg. The healing process moved much further along. Will leaned forward on his right knee and the stump to test it out. That was a mistake. Healing might be progressing, but not enough for the stump to hold his weight. He fell back to the mat. Maybe he could find a way to get around on his own.

But more significant questions lie in Will's mind. At the top was why he was still in this hidden camp in the middle of the Cambodian jungle. He recalled the Army's philosophy of leaving no man behind. It made no sense that the search team had not found him yet. Except that he couldn't see himself, even, since he didn't know where he was. The lack of modern conveniences told Will that this place was perfectly isolated. Still, with the helicopter going down, and the deaths of seven men, they wouldn't leave them to rot. Or would they? Hadn't they given up on Lou? The mission was aborted; the weather was an issue for further airborne searches. Plus, the location likely put the downed chopper in the middle of Viet Cong territory.

Will could only guess what was going on with his commanding officers. Completely on his own, he had no weapon, no radio, not even any way of leaving. Will could no longer lay on a mat in a tiny hut and do nothing. Will worked his right foot underneath him using his good arm for support. Sitting there, leaning on the heel of his right foot, Will took stock of his situation. How sturdy was the wall? It had held him sitting. Therefore, he could use it for balance once he got on his good leg. If he didn't faint from the effort, he could then hop around the room to the door. At least he'd get a look outside. With the storm out there, he knew that there was nowhere he could go now anyway. Besides, if they had wanted to hurt him, there were plenty of opportunities. What dangers lay beyond that hanging door, he would find out. For now, he needed to break free of, at least, the visual barrier of the grass walls surrounding him.

Will rocked forward. It took all the effort that Will could muster to lift himself unto his right leg. If he leaned too far away from the wall, he had already decided that he'd let gravity do its thing, taking care to break the fall with his good arm. It will hurt, but he'd take the risk. Gulping air, Will lifted himself onto his right leg and leaned toward the wall. His strength held, and even with the light-headedness from the instant jolt, succeeded in grabbing the grassy wall.

He looked around the room. It looked even smaller from that view. He tested the wall to see if he could work a hole near where he was standing instead of hopping around the room. The construction was tight. No, it looked like the doorway was the only exit. With the wall providing support, Will hopped around the room, and with each stop, he conjured an image of himself as a flamingo. standing on one skinny leg

Spent of energy, he stood at the entrance before opening the crude cloth door and took stock of the level of effort needed to cross the room. He had never given much thought to the spectacular mechanics of walking on two good legs. For Will, it was too late for that. His task now was to get along in life with only one leg. When he enlisted, the possibility that he'd leave one leg in Southeast Asia failed to enter his thinking. Will had no great desire to free Vietnam from Communism. He wasn't much of a fighter and becoming an officer — a leader of men, so to speak — held no promise for Will. Now being less than a whole man, he was relegated to a life of a mute girl bringing rice to him in a bowl. Was this it? What was he going to do? What does a one-legged man with a high school education and no fundamental skills do? He was good at one thing — that rifle was cleaned and reassembled in no time.

Then Will realized that he had no rifle. The questions kept piling on Will. A crash of thunder brought Will back to the present. Outside — there was an outside. Maybe he'd begin to find some answers out there. All he knew then was that there were no answers inside.

He propped himself against the door frame, and poked his head between the cloth and the bamboo frame for his first look outside. With some success, the small eaves overhead did their best to block the rain. In contrast to the downpour inches from his face, mist welcomed Will. Four similar huts formed a small square around a smoldering fire, smoking from the rain, the center courtyard being about the same size as a living room of a modest suburban home. Several large pots were turned upside down near the fire ring, the rain keeping everyone indoors. A few chickens and ducks wandered in the area.

The canopy of the trees overhead hid the small enclave from the world's view. The jungle extended past the huts, providing a thick screen to anything beyond. From Will's perspective, this village served more like an outdoor apartment. Other than Soka, Mamasan, and the boy, he still didn't know who else resided with them. If he needed to hide from someone — perhaps the NVA or the Viet Cong, or maybe the Cambodian Army, if there was one — this seemed like the perfect place to do it.

From what he could see, this camp they constructed did not have the makings of a long-standing home, more like a hiding place. They must be refugees of the war. Who were they hiding from? Or what? If they feared the war across the border, were they afraid of him, too? Of Americans? That couldn't be. They knew he was American, and it's not exactly fear he felt from them. Mamasan gave him the opposite impression. And despite the boy's concerns about using English, his body language hadn't conveyed fear. Will needed to learn more. But this wasn't the time. Or was it? Will called out the only name he knew.

"Soka...."

The pounding of the rain drowned out Will's voice. With nature providing so much noise, Will didn't know if the call reached the next hut. The answer came when the door of the hut across the way moved as if pushed by a strong breeze. Then he saw Soka standing in the doorway. Will wasn't sure, but he thought that Mamasan was standing directly behind Soka.

"I need to talk to someone. Please, Soka, who is there that knows English?"

No response. Soka looked at Will; her dark eyes showing through the raindrops, bore into Will. The look lasted a moment, then her head tilted down, her gaze averted to the ground. As fast as she appeared, Soka slid back into the darkness of the hut.

"Is anybody else there?" Will called over the rain. "Soka...."

There was nothing further. Will knew he wouldn't get far on one leg, downpour or not. Maybe the old woman would help. "Mamasan," Will tried.

The weather intensified. With the storm dumping more rain, the wind, thunder, and lightning increased. Will realized that he chose the wrong time to assert himself.

Then a sudden burst of thunder and lightning startled Will. He didn't much believe in omens or cosmic impulses or that sort of thing. In this case, though, he made an exception. Mother nature's fury almost knocked him from his vertical perch. Will had leaned out of the doorway and into the rain. Mother nature's clash brought him back inside.

Will wiped the dripping rain from his hair. For the first time, he hobbled to the table. With abnormal care, he sat down on the crude chair. His left leg throbbed. His arm, still restricted by the sling, and the dull ache of his ribs helped remind him that he was still healing. What a sad picture he imagined. How trapped he felt. Nothing kept him here, yet he can't escape the natural boundaries that locked him in this informal cage. He knew that Soka would keep him from going hungry. Maybe the boy would come back. For now, though, Will remained locked in the small room, guarded by mother nature, and occupied only by the vagaries of his own mind.

Whoever constructed the hut knew what they were doing. The slope of the packed-dirt floor kept the rain from pooling. The roof seemed as watertight as possible, even though it was only made of grass. All in all, the water stayed outside where it belonged. Will lay in his usual spot, while questions paraded through him. Answers remained hidden. He turned to his side to rest, and as he did the wrapped photo in his shirt pocket poked him through the shirt. From his position on his back, he took out the picture, removed it from the plastic, and angled it, so the light from the candle illuminated the image.

There he was, clean, ready for whatever. His view of Rachel propped on the bed between Will and Glory prompted a low whistle from Will. What could they be doing now? He looked at his new stub and imagined walking out of there. Those images turned into nothing but empty landscapes, with the end well beyond his vision. He dropped the picture and did nothing but breathe. It was no use, he thought. They don't need me, and I have no need for them now in my life, whatever's left of it. Will rummaged for the plastic, wrapped the photo, and returned it to his pocket, waiting for the time when he could empty himself of the past.

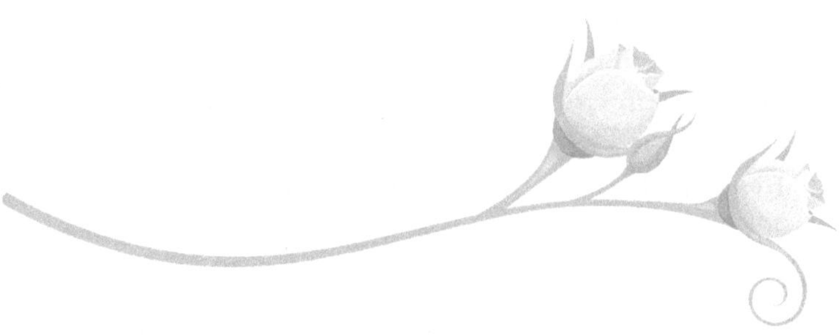

THIRTY-TWO

The first thing he saw when he woke was a candle not far from him, and Soka's face glowing just beyond. In the exact position he had seen her that very first day, she knelt in front of Will with the rice bowl. She remained silent. Will worked his way to a sitting position, taking the bowl from Soka. Will looked at Soka's eyes. Their gaze met, but Soka first broke the connection, looking downward.

"Soka," Will said. "All I know is your name. I wish you knew English."

With her fingers upraised, Soka reached to Will and pressed two fingers against Will's lips. The movement surprised Will, but not as much as what came next.

"No talk now." It was Soka's first words to Will. "No talk," she repeated. Will's ears failed to hear anything more as the pounding of his heart drowned out all other sounds.

She pulled her hand away. Will touched her arm as it passed his hand. The flicker of the candle danced in her eyes. Will feared that pushing her to speak would scare her away. Right now, she gave him exactly what he needed. How could she know? Yet she had been taking care of his physical needs for some time. Maybe that gave her an understanding of some of his other needs, perhaps more than he understood.

"Eat." Soka's soft voice floated through the air. Remembering the bowl of rice cradled in his lap, he glanced down, then looked back at

Soka. Her eyes were dark and wide and seemed to swallow Will hole. He wondered what she could be feeling.

Soka watched Will as he ate. At one point, when he stopped, she handed Will the cup full of tea. Except that this time, she placed the cup to Will's mouth while he sipped its healing contents.

Will finished his rice. He felt more content than he could ever remember feeling. This wasn't like anything he had ever experienced, certainly not during his many months in command of the Army. The washed air blowing in from outside, through the doorway which Soka left open when she entered the hut, seeped deep into every part of Will's body. Beyond the physical comfort and luxury that surprised him, he knew that with the hot meal, Soka brought her caring to him – the very thing he needed.

Soka reached toward Will for the empty bowl sitting on his lap while her dark eyes focused on Will. He leaned toward her, holding her hand, and kissed her. She returned the kiss. Their lips met in longing for more.

For the rest of that day and deep into the night, Will re-played the kiss repeatedly in his mind. Only a moment in time – a simple drop in the rain of his life – yet it was the one drop that found its target in Will. Actually, that drop hit all the right spots at one time. Sleep evaded Will as the vision of Soka's face, glowing from the single flame, urged him to move closer, by some unknown inner force glowing brightly inside Will. Will fought sleep, preferring that the light of Soka shine within him like the mid-day sun shining over a blanket of snow on Christmas Day.

It was only one kiss. How it happened – why it happened – Will failed to comprehend. Tired of all the questions his life thrust onto him, Will decided to let the moment settle inside. That it happened, sufficed. He knew well enough that tomorrow was a new day. For the moment, as sleep crawled in, his slumber grasped that one promising idea.

When Will woke the next day, he knew from the sounds and intensity of the light outside that he had slept later than usual. He lay on the mat in no hurry to break the spell that took over last night. He was surprised to see lying next to him a crutch carved from raw red and green veins of gumbo-limbo tree limbs. Next to the crutch, folded neatly, were a hand made shirt and pants lying on top of a pair of dried grass sandals. They looked functional and only slightly worn from use. Who used the crutch before him? He instantly recognized his increased mobility beyond his hoppings of yesterday.

The rice turned cold on the small table. He wondered when he'd see Soka again, turning his thoughts to Soka and their moment of the night before. Will then recalled his dream. He was in a small apartment, reminiscent of his apartment back in the States with Glory. Except it wasn't Glory and Rachel with Will in that apartment. Instead, he was with Soka and a baby boy. The baby boy cried a lot, and he tried everything he could think of to help him. Soka calmed the boy so he could sleep. Was the boy their son? He didn't know. He did remember touching Soka and taking her into his bed. He knew that he had wanted more, but in his wakefulness, the memory of the dream dissipated.

Will lay on his mat thinking of the dream and the circumstances that brought him to last night and the feeling that had built up in him since then. His mind's eye continuously played images of Soka in his head. Her presence invaded Will. She was inside of him. He held the crutch in his hand, feeling its worn smoothness of the hand-carved wood, Will noticed sunlight reflecting from his wedding ring, the single piece of jewelry he brought with him to Vietnam.

Will contemplated the ring ensconced on his finger. He remembered how Glory had convinced him to marry her. How it was her choice to have the baby and begin a marriage without giving any concern to what he wanted. Now he was half a world away. What was the point? Even if he wanted to go home, he didn't have even the beginning of a plan that would get him there. With the way he felt, with the loss of his leg, he knew that the last place he wanted to be was in Evanston in an apartment, married to a girl he barely knew. He was no husband nor father, unequipped to understand what to do with Rachel.

Now he could shake both of those away as if they were mere autumn leaves falling on his arm. Even if he managed to get back to the States, what would he do? No, there was a bigger world out there for him. The surprise and wonder that life previewed to him beckoned for further discovery. The loss of his leg ironically ignited Will's inner fire. He won't grow another one, but he'd gain a life in losing a leg. The course of his new life didn't yet take shape in Will's mind, other than to put Skokie, Evanston, and definitely Oak Park, and the old Will's life he left there, in a box on the highest shelf. *"You gotta leave. You can't be here."* He heard those words as if Glory was standing right in front of him.

Will pulled his wedding ring from his finger; time to inaugurate the new Will. Will turned on his side, and dug a hole in the dirt near the wall of the hut. When he thought it was deep enough, he dropped the ring in the hole. In no time, it was gone, covered by the dirt of the Cambodian jungle. The new Will emerged. His old life ceased to exist.

Soka entered the hut as he finished smoothing the dirt. She carried a tray with the tea, rice, and two bowls. She put the tray on the table near the door. Walking to Will, she said, "I help get you to table."

When Soka neared Will, she gave him a quick kiss. Before she had the chance to take Will by the arm, Will reached for Soka's waist. He wanted to tell her everything but thought the words would take an effort that wasn't then needed. Instead, he pulled her closer to him, and he kissed her. This kiss lasted. Though still tender, there was passion lying beneath the surface. Both Will and Soka held back, not knowing what would happen if their desire for each other took full effect. Will hugged Soka around her waist. She wrapped her arms around Will's neck, lingering together. Then with a final kiss on Will's cheek, Soka stood up and pulled Will by his arm. With Soka's help, Will stood and held the crutch under his left arm. Will leaned on the crutch and on Soka and walked to the table.

"Thank you, Soka. The table looks good."

They sat together, speaking the best they could while they ate. When he finished, Soka got up and gathered the dishes. Together they walked outside.

They found the fire glowing with Mamasan working near the fire, with two small boys nearby, following her instructions. None appeared much interested in Will. He sat, watching.

Thus began Will's first new day. And it was good.

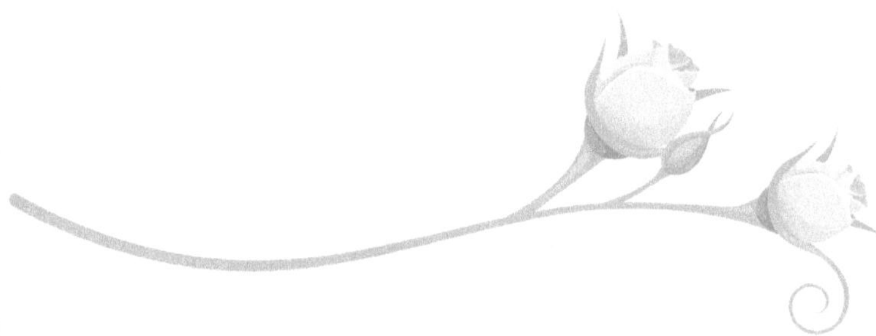

THIRTY-THREE

Glory had completed her coursework. Her graduation ceremony planned for later in the week gave her some time to take care of a few things. Rachel was napping in her room, and Glory took her papers from her desk and went to tell Beth that she'd be back later.

"Where are you going?"

"Just some errands, Mom. I finished my last story. I'll drop it off, and I should be back before Rachel wakes up, but can you keep an eye on her?"

"Of course," Beth said. "Isn't that what grandmothers are for?"

Back in Evanston, Glory stopped first at the University Center to get her cap and gown, complete with the satin purple stole marking her graduation with honors. She walked to Fisk Hall to deliver her final story for the *Daily Northwestern.*

Inside, the newsroom was quiet, with much of the work for the last issue ready for the editors. She left her papers in the in-box. Checking her messages before she left, she heard a greeting from behind.

"Your Teri's friend, right?"

Glory turned and saw Leo. She had seen him several times since they met in the cafeteria.

"Hi. Glory, in case you forgot."

"No, I didn't forget. But I did hear that you are done with journalism. Is that right?"

"Seems so."

"I can see why," Leo said, looking at her belly, showing the small bump of her pregnancy. He reached past Glory to grab a few papers from the slot of his mailbox.

"Do you have to be somewhere now?" Leo asked.

"Not particularly. Why?"

"You probably didn't hear about Teri. I heard last night."

"What about her? What did you hear?"

"She got arrested at Berkeley. There was a protest, and she was there with her friend…."

"Yuna."

"Yeah, I think so."

"What happened. The last I heard, she was in Ohio researching the Kent State murders."

"I think she finished that story and got an assignment to cover the hippie thing in San Francisco. But let's not stand here talking. How about I treat you to lunch?"

"Well, maybe something quick."

"Better than nothing."

They walked off campus into a sandwich shop across Sheridan Street. Leo told the story to Glory of the protest that turned into a riot, as best as he understood.

"What's going to happen? Is it real, or a show for the press."

"Can't say. If what happened at the Democratic convention is any clue, she'll be there a while."

"I always knew that she'd get in trouble. It's her nature to stir things up. I'm going to take a wild guess, that it's as much her mouth as what she did."

"No doubt. She's not afraid to say what she thinks."

They stopped talking when the waiter stopped by with their lunch. As they waited, Glory took a closer look at Leo. His hair was still long, but neatly trimmed, as was his goatee. Their eyes locked, for a split second. It was enough. Palpitations forced her to avert her gaze. Since

Glory became Rachel's mom and lived with worry over whether Will would ever come back, she had given little thought to her own life. Now here she was, for a moment, on her own, not a mom, and sharing a meal with an attractive man. She saw beyond Leo when he caught her eyes; there was something. Leo interrupted her thoughts.

"So, what are your plans?" he asked. "Sticking with writing, I hope. You do know that you have an amazing talent."

Glory put the sandwich down after taking a bite. The time to come up with a response gave her a moment to gather her thoughts. "All I know," she said as she took a drink. "I am a writer."

"That you are. What's your favorite medium? I gather it's not writing for a newspaper."

"Poetry."

"Oh, yeah. I heard about that contest. Well done. We'll miss your striking prose, but the world of poetry is about to hear from its next superstar."

Glory hoped that the red of her blush didn't give her away. "That's very kind, Leo. But I'm hardly a star, super or otherwise. All I know is I constantly have a poem in my head. And have gotten some positive feedback."

"Tell me one."

"One what?"

"One of your poems. I know you have something you can recite. You've memorized at least one, right?"

Glory nodded. "I guess when you like your own work as much as I do, you can't help but know it inside and out. Well, then here goes.

The supple mist eased into place
With morning's rise
Again, a day, the plan keeping pace
Birds cocked their heads…

Glory's chair was then crashed into by a cart from the cleaning crew, knocking the dishes and spilling their drinks.

"I can't do this here."

"I can see that," Leo said. "Then let's go."

"The lake. You have time?"

"So far, I love the poem. Of course, I have time. I need to hear more."

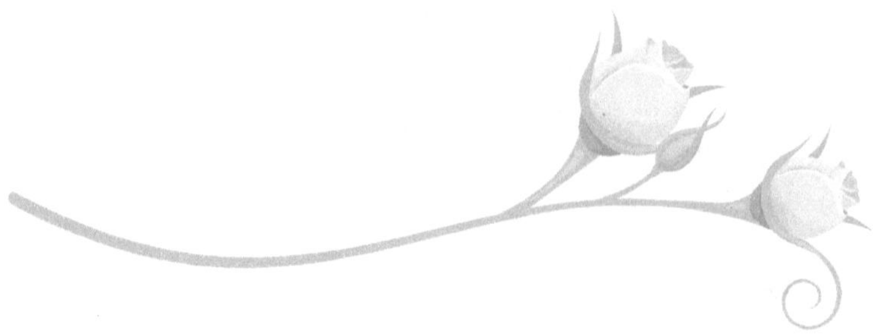

THIRTY-FOUR

As predicted, Teri missed her graduation. At Yuna's apartment in Berkeley, Yuna picked up a second phone when Teri called Glory to congratulate her.

"They let you go?" Glory asked.

"It was nothing. Rehearsal for me for the next time. Enough of that. It's great being with Yuna again."

"I'm thrilled for you guys," Glory said, taking a deep breath heard over the line.

"I love that she's here," Yuna responded, reaching out as if to hold Teri's hand from across the room. The attempted grasp turned into a small wave.

"Yuna's great, and her place is fantastic. Glory, you should be here. It could be the three of us again."

"Too hilly," Glory said. "I don't mind the idea of pushing the stroller uphill; it's the downhill race that concerns me. The thought of me losing my grip and watching the stroller roll downhill shakes my spine."

"I can see what you're saying," Teri said, shaking off the trace of a shiver.

"Glory, are you okay?" Yuna asked. "You don't sound right."

Teri jumped in, "I thought it was just me. What's going on with you?"

"He's not coming back," Glory said and then added, louder this time, "And I'm fine with that. I wish I never met him."

"Who's not coming back? What's going...?" Teri paused and met Yuna's look, each watching the eyes of the other.

It was Yuna who broke the silence. "How do you know he's not coming back?"

"The Army told me. The letter came today. I married a soldier who got lost in the war. He's officially missing in action. Seems to be a family trait. I had no idea."

"What did it say?" Teri asked. "They're still looking for him, right?"

Yuna joined in, "Where was he? What happened?"

"I don't know. There was a mission. Somewhere. Some base somewhere, and the mission of eight men took off by helicopter, and blah and blah. It doesn't matter. And I don't care. Who leaves a wife and baby to go halfway around the world?"

"Glory, dear, he meant well," Teri said.

"They can't find him. Better that they don't."

"I know you don't mean that. Yuna, she's going crazy."

"Maybe she's right," Yuna said. "Life goes on, now doesn't it, Glory?"

"Of course. Oh, I forgot to tell you. I had lunch with your friend Leo the other day."

"Leo? How'd that happen?"

"Random, is all. An accidental meeting over mail, and the next thing you know, I'm reciting poetry to him at the lakefront."

"I always thought Leo was someone you should meet," Teri said.

"But I have no idea what to do. I'm married, at least legally speaking."

"So. Did he already propose to you?"

Glory laughed. "Hardly," she answered. "He did ask me to go out with him. I'd love to, but...."

"But nothing. Go. What did he have in mind?"

"He said he has a thing for open mic night and that I should recite my poetry. He thinks it will boost my career as a poet."

"They'd love you. I've heard some of the poetry, and trust me, you've got nothing to worry about."

"Hey guys," Glory interrupted, "I know you want to figure me out and all, but I have a baby to feed. You guys have fun out there."

The line disconnected, and Teri and Yuna remained in their spots, each holding their receiver.

"We have to do something," Yuna said.

"Let's get out of here. I need some air."

Outside, the dry afternoon air shot their adrenalin awake. They walked down the two flights of stairs to street level and then past the clustered homes to the Castro business district. When they got to an ice cream shop, Teri stepped forward to open the door. Yuna followed right behind.

"Ice cream," Teri said, twisting around as she did so Yuna could hear. "We'll start with the inspirational combination of strawberry, chocolate, and vanilla Neapolitan ice cream."

"Cup or cone?"

"Be serious, please. Always a cup. Otherwise, you don't get the full effect of the Italian flag in ice cream."

Yuna nodded and paid for the treat. They took their ice cream and walked back to the street, strolling through the urban setting. Storefront Victorian buildings, all with apartments in the two floors above, lined both sides of the road. The namesake Castro Theater is the exception on the next block. The people walking around and with them displayed every color and manner of dress. Bright tie-dyed shirts, bandannas, and even dresses were the style of the time, with nobody sporting a short haircut. The cutting smell in the air proved that some of their peers joining them in the ways of San Francisco youth saved water by cutting back on bathing. The music played from an open window the final notes of *Scarlet Begonia*, and with the Grateful Dead's faded last note behind them, in front of them the symphonic rock synthesis of the Moody Blues took its place.

"I feel so bad for her," Teri said. "What she's been through. I don't know if I could handle it."

"She's strong. From the first moment in high school that she looked at me, I could tell there was something different about her."

"That's so true. And she was there for me when we lost Bumba. I want to be there for her."

"Teri, you have a big heart. That's one reason I love you. But you have a life too."

"Of course, of course. I know she'll be fine. Plus, she's got her folks, her brothers. She can even talk with Rachel. Sorta."

"She is absolutely adorable."

"Yep."

"Glory will do the right thing. She'll come out of this stronger. You'll see that no matter how bad things get, or the opposite could be true, how good things can be, always changes. As King Solomon said, 'This, too, shall pass.'"

"He did say that, huh? Well, okay, if that's what Sol says, then so it be. I'll call her tonight."

Over dinner of pasta with vegetables that Teri cooked for them, Teri met Yuna's roommate and girlfriend, Halima. Halima and Yuna met at Berkeley. Halima came over as an exchange student from Tanzania, with family on her mother's side descending from the Hadza tribe of bushmen.

"Teri's here to write about us, Hali. Isn't that right?"

"Well, the assignment didn't say to write the story of Yuna and Halima, but it's not a bad option, given what's going on."

"It's getting bad in the streets. Too many people keep coming in. The money is coming in, buying the houses, and moving us out."

"You should come with us to meet some of our friends," Halima said. "There's lots of stories. Cops attacking. And the politics. That's the problem. We need more like us."

"That's cool, baby," Yuna said.

"So let me interview you guys and then point me to the leader." Teri added, "Take me to your leader," in a deep, theatrical voice.

"We'll start. Tomorrow. 'Cause we gotta go. Yuna wants to cover a protest at some business in the Haight."

"Still trying to perfect the night-time shots," Yuna explained. "There seems to be more drama over protests at night, but much harder to catch on film."

"Yuna, you'll get the shot. You always do, my friend."

Teri spoke with Glory again later that night. Rachel went to sleep quickly after dinner, leaving Glory with some free time. Taking her spot at the desk near the window, Glory pulled out her composition notebook with the black and white speckled cover to give the poem from the morning another reading. One stanza in, and the phone rang.

"I know it's you, Izzie," She answered the ringing of the call.

"Who else would it be? But enough about me. Are you okay? I need to see what's in your head."

"My head's fine. My feet are tired, but I don't sense a massage soon in the works."

"Nope. But how about you tell me where else you are feeling pain."

"Teri. Teri. I don't know. Life is always full of surprises."

"Such as."

"Well, having two babies before I'm twenty-five is one of them. Then there's Beth."

"Your mother?"

"The very one. She is anything if unpredictable."

"Go on."

"She wants me to bring Rachel for us to live at home. They want to make the third floor a full apartment for us. There's room enough for a whole family. And that's what we'll be."

"But, did you think about Will? What are you going to do?"

"Nothing. If they can't find him, they can't find him. Is it a real loss, anyway? From the minute he told me he was joining the Army, I told him I'd be on my own. That must be what he wanted. Or maybe that's the Universe talking to me."

"I can't believe that. Didn't you see that he wants the best for you and Rachel?"

"I don't know. There was once something. Maybe. But I could never leave my family like that. I don't know how he could."

"Well, you know we're all different. Maybe he had to do this. Maybe it's his way of being the man he needs to be as your husband and Rachel's father."

"Or maybe not," Glory answered Teri's unfounded optimism.

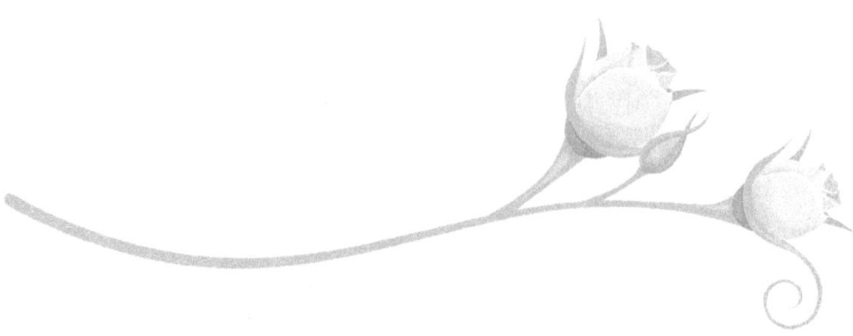

THIRTY-FIVE

Life improved for Will as the days went by. Though the lack of privacy prevented more vigorous encounters between Soka and Will, they found some quiet time together. Soka explained the residents of the hamlet included Mamasan and Soka's brother, Neap, who Will met earlier. Soka's older sister, Chhou, lived in the third hut. The two boys were hers. The last hut was Soka's Aunt Maranet, who never left the hut. Soka explained that this was her entire family. Her father and his brother, Aunt Maranet's husband, and an older brother of Soka's, were killed by Khmer rebels. Through tears, Soka described the forced viewing of their torture and death. Neap had carved the crutch for her older brother, who later died from his wounds.

That left their livelihood to Neap, doing what he could to buy, borrow, or steal food and whatever else they needed. Other than the provisions that Neap found, Mamasan was in charge. They all did what they could for Aunt Maranet, but as Soka said, the killings bothered her so much that they feared that she was waiting to die. She had family members who were killed in a nearby village.

Soka struggled with English to tell Will about her village and this hiding place, but her description didn't help Will know where he was. The names of the villages sounded to Will only like so many syllables, which Will understood were destroyed by rebels, murdering most of the men.

Those left behind had fled. Soka explained that there were many other families also hiding in the hills.

When Will asked about the future, Soka said that they didn't know anything about the future. Only today existed. When he asked if Soka thought their future together lived beyond the camp, Soka failed to answer.

One morning a few days later, Soka brought Will breakfast, which consisted of local fruits and vegetables in addition to the rice. The few chickens and ducks that wandered around were saved for times when there wasn't anything else or for special occasions. Finishing the breakfast at the table in Will's hut, that time seemed safe to Soka to steal a kiss or hug from Will. Such moments were less about their physical desires than a chance for two people to feel close to each other. Soka was sitting on Will's lap, and they were kissing when Neap burst through the door, speaking a loud and staccato Khmer.

The sight of Soka and Will stopped Neap. Will watched anger flare up in Neap, standing inside the door, screaming again, even louder. Will's failure to know the words didn't prevent him from understanding that something significant had happened. Neap barked a command, forcing Soka out of her seat. Clearly, Neap controlled the situation. Soka bowed her head and left the hut.

"Soka," Will called after her. "Neap, what did you do?" he asked.

"American, sister not for you. She live here with us. She not be with you."

"What do you mean? She wants to be with me. I want to be with her."

"Not now, American. Have big problem."

Neap left the hut in silence. When Will stepped outside, he saw Mamasan leaving the hut next door with Soka's sister. The two women were crying. Will walked toward the hut, then stopped. Unclear if there was anywhere he should be, or what was happening, given Neap's last objections to Will being with Soka, he wasn't sure what to do.

Soka emerged from the hut. Her red eyes fought back the tears. Will caught up with her, doing his best to keep pace. He stopped her. "Soka, what is going on? Why is everyone crying?"

"Aunt Maranet dead. Last night. She stop breathing. Want life no more."

Soka spent time with her mother. Will did little but sit near the fire pit. After returning to his hut to rest, Neap walked into the hut. "You must go."

"What are you talking about? Where am I going? I don't even know where I am. I don't want to leave."

Neap said, "You cannot stay. You cannot be with Soka. She stay here."

"So, I'll stay here. There is nowhere for me to be anyway."

"No. Not right for you to stay. You must leave."

"What do you mean it's not right for me. You, Soka, Mamasan, have been good to me." Clearly something changed by Aunt Maranet's death.

"Not right. You – Soka."

"What's not right about me and Soka?"

"You are American. Mamasan choose man for her, from village. Not you. You need to go." Neap looked at Will. "You go tomorrow. I take you to find doctor. I bring food to take."

"But where will I go?" This was too much for Will. He felt comfortable there, making a connection. Now he was told to leave the middle of the jungle with nothing.

"I want to talk to Soka." Will at least had to find out from her what was going on.

"Soon we leave to…how you say…." Neap stopped. "We take Aunt Maranet to family. Say last goodbye. Send her to spirits. You come too. After, we leave. I take you to city. We give you food for trip."

After Aunt Maranet's funeral he would have no choice but to leave. "What city? Where are you talking about? I could be killed. Is that what you want, for me to die? Just do it now."

"No, American, I take you to doctor. She know what to do."

"What doctor? Where?"

"Doctor – she here to help you. You trust her. She know. I go. Tomorrow, we go to city."

This was all confusing to Will. He thought that some things started to make sense, even if his life didn't. Now nothing was clear, except Neap's insistence that he had to leave. She was to marry another. He had no idea. Will wasn't sure he could look at Soka again over his embarrassment. What must she be feeling? Nothing gave Will any clue.

But if he left, he could be in grave danger. Where could he be safe? Neap mentioned the doctor. Since Will's convalescence, nothing concerned Will as to his safety. The doctor knew of Will, yet he had been safe here for the weeks of recovery in his hut. Maybe the doctor could be trusted. He could have some ideas for Will. Will needed some serious planning to know where he wanted to go and where he'd be safe.

Will suspected that any search for him had long ago been abandoned if there ever was a search. How far was it back to Vietnam? Should he go east and hook up with American forces or the South Vietnamese Army? That was way too dangerous. He hadn't seen or heard any trace of the Americans being in the area, recalling the Army's plans to withdraw from Cambodia once they grabbed all the provisions. Soka and her family had treated him well. He had little choice but to trust them.

Will guessed the time to be close to 3:00 a.m. His clothes were drenched by the rain. He had thrown away the last bits of bread that Mamasan packed in his shoulder bag. Will never could stand the sight of soggy bread, much less the thought of eating it. Will's single leg remembered the last three days of walking with Neap as his guide.

Will slept on and off, remembering Neap's final instructions to Will before Neap returned to the jungle. During their walk over the past three days, Neap told him of the daily market and how the village of Chari lay on the banks of the Mekong river. Neap had set Will under a makeshift shelter of Colocasia elephant ears on the side of a hill, in sight of the village spread before Will like a picture postcard. In the valley, the streets of Chari spread out much larger than Neap's camp that had been Will's home. Neap told Will that it was in Chari that he found the doctor who had been willing to make the overland trip to tend to Will. Will reflected on how long ago it seemed since he first woke up that rainy morning in Soka's hut.

Two days earlier, Will thought he found some relief from the constant toil on his one leg. It was when they ran into a boy with an elephant. Neap convinced the boy to give Will a ride. It would have saved time and given Will a break from the constant torture. The boy agreed, accepting the small payment from Neap. Will walked toward the boy, and the tilt of the boy's head looking up at Will matched the sudden fear that crossed the boy's eyes. The boy hopped on the elephant without a word, and they were both gone. Was it Will's size that scared the boy off? Neap didn't know either.

Will's leg throbbed, and his right foot – which took most of the punishment from the walk – bled from cuts and blisters. Being soaked would only make things worse. Neap's last words to Will described where he would find the clinic and the doctor. The rustling of the trees from the wind reminded Will of Neap's sudden disappearance into the jungle.

No trace of sunlight had yet emerged in the night sky. Will had a chance to think about Aunt Maranet's funeral. The scenes that Will recalled stayed with him. Though sad for Soka and Neap and the rest of the family, the funeral struck Will as a dignified and touching ceremony. The words used in the ceremony for Aunt Maranet passed right by Will. That didn't stop Will from knowing the feeling of love and honor expressed for the Aunt's passing.

Aunt Maranet's family camped in the next enclave and hosted her funeral. That there were other people so close was news to Will. The funeral began, and spread out before Will and the other guests were replicas of various items, including a bowl, fork, cup, plate, and a book. A pot holding a ladle, a pair of sandals, and a folded robe completed the scene.

The ceremony began. An older man spoke before the group. Will learned later that this was a holy man for the family. The surprise for Will came when the man placed a burning torch against the table, pot, and the other items. Every item caught fire when touched by the torch, including a pot, a plate, and a bowl. The blaze lasted only a few moments.

The sight of the flames lingered in Will's mind. Neap told him that all of the burned things were of paper. These were all things that had some importance in their aunt's life. It was an ancient tradition to burn these replicas so that the aunt's spirit in the next world would be surrounded by those things that gave her comfort while she was alive. The more things that were burned, the more honored was the person's life.

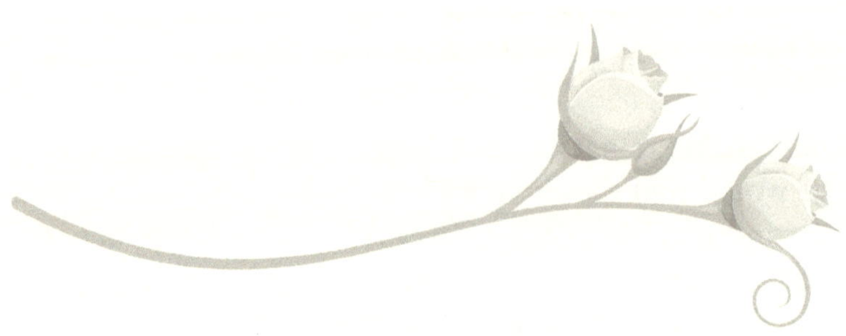

THIRTY-SIX

The morning sky above Chari emerged from its nightly slumber. While Will slept, the rain ended. Upon awakening, he saw a touch of red in the sky, waking up the village. In the valley, the lights winked on and off, giving way to the first rays of the morning sun. The outlines of the homes and shops became more visible. The faint sounds of voices drifted up to Will. Unseen by Will, a truck with an engine in need of a mechanic coughed along its way, the sound echoing in the morning air.

In no rush to get back on his feet - actually, his one foot Will recalled with some shock - he lingered to watch the morning sun brighten the village to start the day. Movement was slow, with no rush for the day to begin. Villagers rolled their carts loaded with goods into the center of the village, as the marketplace filled.

The sound of a distant helicopter reminded Will of the chopper crashing that led him to this moment. He recalled running with Two as the helicopter exploded into a thousand pieces. Neap later filled in some of the gaps. In their stilted conversation during their jungle trek, Neap explained that his two small cousins ran to take a look after the explosion. They came back yelling about seeing a ghost. The helicopter was still burning, but the boys saw Two lying in the water. The boys figured he was dead since half his head was blown off. As they moved closer to the body, without warning the head moved.

Neap laughed when he told the story. The boys came running, looking like ghosts themselves. He would have dismissed the whole thing, except something told him to take a closer look. Sure enough, he saw Two lying there. When he saw Two move, he spotted Will covered underneath Two, almost completely submerged. It was Will who had caused Two to move. As Neap watched, Will took in some of the water, causing an involuntary movement to keep his face out of the water. How Will didn't drown was a mystery.

Neap told Will that he pulled Two off Will and pulled Will to dry ground. Will was a mess and soaked with the briny water, barely alive. Neap dragged Will back to the hut, where he was cleaned up and placed in the hut. They kept him dry and warm, but Will didn't wake up for many days. But, the growing stink told them of a bigger problem. Neap had taken a closer look. The shattered leg boiled with signs of infection. The doctor said to them that if she didn't remove it that the infection could kill Will. There was no choice.

"Why did you do that?" Will had asked Neap.

"You do for me if I dying?" was Neap's response.

The question surprised Will. Would he save a complete stranger and most likely the enemy? He had never hurt anyone.

"I am the enemy," Will said. "Keeping me alive will hurt your cause."

Neap looked at Will and walked away from Will in silence.

"Wait, Neap." Will hobbled to catch up.

Neap stopped and turned to Will. "Enemy? You know nothing. War – fighting and killing – not my war. Only hurt and kill my people." Neap walked on. "You were dying. Need help. I help. No enemy. No friend. Do what I do to help. You do same, no?"

Neap's apathy toward war surprised Will. All along, he thought that Neap considered him the enemy. How stupid he must have seemed to Neap. It doesn't take schooling to make someone more intelligent than another. Neap's family must have been through hell. In truth, the whole clan was part of a prominent tribe of indigenous mountain people who had lived in that area of Cambodia for generations. It was only with the war that the tribal people became targets. The killing did not escape the tribal villages. It was a matter of survival that they were forced to hide in the highlands.

The clamor of the morning market, and the smells of baking and cooking, rising from the valley below prompted Will to consider his situation. Neap left him with enough money for a meal and a night in a room if there was one below. If he didn't eat something and find some dry clothes, his problems would grow out of control.

Not able to avoid pain any longer, Will picked himself up and started for the village. Warmed by the morning sun of the new day, with his first step a touch lighter, as if gates were opening below, Chari beckoned for Will to enter.

A while later, full from the breakfast of warm bread and the sweet slices of dragonfruit, Will found a spot at the edge of the marketplace, sitting on the ground to let the sun finish drying him off. The market wound down from the bustle of the morning. He watched as several vendors packed up and headed away from the village center. Will clutched the two bags – one filled with fruit, bread, and cheese, his lunch, and the other a complete change of clothes.

The clothier had trouble finding something Will's size. Every item was too small by a considerable measure. It took some searching, but he located a shirt and pants, a welcome clean and dry change of clothes for Will. Will chose, however, to wait until he had a chance to shower first. For now, the warmth of the sun would have to do.

Will's memory of Neap's directions to the clinic and the doctor made it seem close and easy to find. Either he heard it wrong – not too far-fetched due to the language gap – or the difference in mobility between Neap and Will was more profound than either of them had realized. Despite his wandering through the town, Will failed to locate a hospital in any event.

After several frustrating attempts to ask for directions, he located the clinic set back in the jungle, away from the village, nestled between the banks of the Mekong river and the Chhlong road. A former church, the orange façade long before faded to a dull yellow, its walls peeling and chipping, initially built in a French style, with its roof of red Mediterranean tiles.

The path overgrown with weeds and bushes led to the front door. Far from inviting, yet to Will, it felt like the entry to the Garden of Eden. Still bleeding and sore, Will wanted nothing more than a shower and a soft place to lie down. There was nobody around him. He thought he heard more than one voice inside. He tried to turn the doorknob, but its refusal to move caught Will off guard. This was not exactly what he expected to find. Will rebuked himself for expecting anything nearing normalcy. The best thing he could do from then on was to expect the unexpected.

He doubted anyone heard his soft knock on the door frame. But too tired to remain standing with his single crutch, Will slumped to the ground and propped himself against the frame. He remained upright and attempted to swing the wooden crutch around so someone would hear him. After several tries, Will found the correct position to swing his makeshift hammer and banged the door loud enough to be heard.

Soon Will heard the sound of the latch opening. He sat back and waited for whoever – or whatever – would next approach him. He closed his eyes, not caring what happened as long as something happened. His exhaustion left him uncaring of whether his plans, such as they were, would amount to anything.

He heard someone step on the fallen leaves covering the entryway, followed by a woman speaking in Khmer (he guessed). Will initially viewed only her white shoes. Her white-stockinged legs were inches from his face. Looking up, Will saw a woman standing over him. Was this the doctor? He couldn't tell. European, her deep brown hair hung straight down to the top of her shoulders. Her black eyes, set in a pixie face, sparkled her light to Will. She looked to be about Will's age. He didn't know if she spoke English, so he tried to remember how to say something – anything – in Khmer that would help explain the situation, but nothing came to him. He asked, "Is there a shower I can use?"

Instead of answering, the woman stepped back inside and closed the door. Gazing up at the trees overhead, Will didn't know what to think. Before he could decide whether he was angry or ready to cry, the door opened, and the woman came out.

The words came to him in a heavy accent. "We have a bath, but you look like you need much more than that." French, was Will's guess.

Without another word, four boys lifted Will – teenagers, perhaps, each with the bronze skin and Cambodian features as were prominent among the local villagers. They carried him inside and placed him on a small bed, little more than a cot. The inner room held many beds occupied by children, boys and girls, with many others wandering around.

Will's entry provided the entertainment of the moment, watched by all the children. Some approached Will's cot. Several of the teenage boys stood taller than the woman. The French woman followed Will into the room, providing the instructions for Will's chaperones.

"Before I give you a chance to get cleaned up, you must answer my questions. Who are you, and what are you doing here?"

"I am an American," Will blurted, unsure what he should say.

"That is obvious. Okay, American, tell me why we find you lying on our doorstep, all bruised, in dire need of a shower. Who knows that you are here?"

"My helicopter crashed. I was the only survivor, and I ended up in a small camp in the hills. A family hiding in the hills took care of me, but my leg was amputated. They told me that they found a doctor here who fixed me up. I was told where to find the clinic and the doctor."

"You are here looking for a doctor. You certainly need one. But you can't stay. If they know you are here, we could all be in danger."

"Who?" Will wanted to know about the danger of just walking up to a local clinic. "Are you the doctor? Can you help me?"

The woman looked closer at Will's leg and remaining foot. "Before I answer that, tell me, did anyone follow you here?"

"I don't know. I don't think so, but if they wanted to without me knowing it, they wouldn't have much trouble hiding from me."

"We must wait then and see if anyone's outside. We must hide you. If they suspect that we have an American here, it could be a huge problem. You will have to leave. This is not a hospital. Well, not exactly. This is home for these children. We take care of them as best as we can. They have nowhere else to go."

Will looked around. Most of the children lost interest in him, busying themselves with other things. But some continued to stare at him. It was easy to see that these children were casualties of the violence that defined their short lives. In Will's view, many of the children did not have all four limbs intact. Catching the eye of a small boy across the room, the boy didn't move but kept staring straight at Will. Will looked away.

"You don't like looking at them?" She asked. "Well, give some thought as to how they feel. Most of them have no family. Many went through horrors that you could not even imagine. This may not be easy for you, but it's a complete disaster for them."

Considering that manners likely exist in the Far East as well, Will said, "My name is William Standord. I am from Chicago. And you?"

"My name is Gabrielle. I come from the south of France, from a town near Nice."

"Gabrielle, that is a nice name. Who pays for all of this?"

"We get help from many sources. The UN relief agencies play a big part, as do various church groups and private donations. It is a struggle, but we survive. Enough talking. We need to move you."

They managed to squeeze his cot into a storage closet. Will wasn't crazy about being in another small room with no windows, but he was promised it was only for a few days.

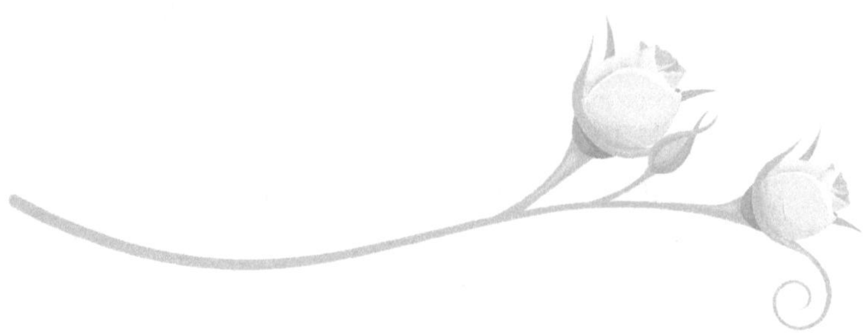

THIRTY-SEVEN

At least he was given food to eat. The best part was the bath that felt like no bath had ever felt. Gabrielle told him that she closed the front door when he first knocked because of how bad he smelled. But she also figured that someone who smelled that bad could hardly be dangerous.

The days passed, and there was no indication that anyone noticed Will or was looking for him. They moved his cot back to its original place on the third day. Gabrielle found a pair of modern crutches, complete with padded armrests. With his athleticism, Will quickly mastered his mobility using one leg and two crutches.

In those first days, Will had little to do. With so much time on his hands, he found the children open to being with him. Their communication mainly was non-verbal, but the common fact of their injuries made for an instant connection.

At the end of the third day, after everyone finished dinner in the small room that passed for a dining hall, Gabrielle sat with Will.

"You need to make plans to go soon," Gabrielle said.

"Why?" Will asked. "I need to speak with the doctor. Unless you know how to get me out of here?"

"No. I know that we are here to help the children if you haven't noticed. We'd have trouble with our donors if we start housing adults.

Especially injured American soldiers. You should contact your Army. They would know what to do."

The Army. To them, he must be listed as KIA. The chopper went down, and everyone in it was killed. Will had no illusions that they were searching for him.

"Where is the doctor? Maybe she can find a way to help me."

Gabrielle stared out the window, searching for something. "We don't know. She hasn't been here in weeks. We sent someone to search for her at her home and clinic in Chhlong, but she seems to have disappeared."

"How can that be?" Will wondered out loud.

"This is a dangerous place. Nobody is safe. Especially anyone who the Khmer regime sees as a threat. Maybe she was more than a doctor."

"So who's taking care of all these kids? I've seen new ones come in every day. Do any leave?"

"Some, now and again. But we are nearing a crisis. It will be tough to recruit another doctor, especially one as good with the children as Dr. Morra."

Gabrielle sipped her tea. Will didn't know what to say.

A change came over Gabrielle's face. "You need to leave as soon as possible. It is dangerous for the children if you stay. You will be in danger. I can assure you that the calm will not last. I have to protect the children. Please, tomorrow, we will find a way for you to go to the city if you like, or maybe on the road to the border is better. But you must leave."

Will didn't have a chance to speak as Gabrielle stood up and walked out of the room, leaving her tea as her unintended exclamation point.

His options were down to almost nothing. Perhaps his best chance at a future was to make contact with the Army. If he can get back into Vietnam, then he'd hook up with an outpost. It wasn't much of a plan, but there wasn't much else available to him. Maybe he'd come up with a better plan in the morning.

Will's cot had been placed near the front door to minimize his impact on the children. At night, with the room darkened, he lay awake for many hours, waiting for the noise of the children to subside. The darkness provided no answers to Will. With a good night's sleep and the sun in the morning, he'd come up with a plan.

The morning sun's light cast a dim glow across the large room when an explosion blew through the room. The blast shook Will out of his cot. Will's heart thumped in his chest with displeasure. Forgetting that he was down to one good leg, Will shot up from his cot, intending to find out what happened. The cot broke his fall. Will grabbed his crutches and walked across the room.

The children screamed with abandon. The bomb blasted a large hole where a window used to be in the back of the room. Will rushed to the scene, taking care not to poke any of the kids with his crutches. One of the girls lay on the cot nearest the window, bleeding heavily over her entire body. The bomb singed her hair and pajamas. Other children were injured, but the girl – she couldn't have been more than five – was by far the worst hurt.

The teenage boys who had pulled Will in that first day stood nearby. One of them reached for the girl. Will pushed him aside and kneeled down to check on the girl. As he checked if the girl was breathing, he felt a hand pulling him away by his shoulder. Wrapped in a robe, Gabrielle had run across the courtyard. She caught her breath, then pulled Will away from the girl.

"Leave her alone," Gabrielle barked at Will. The claw of Gabrielle grabbing at Will forced him to the ground.

"I hope she's okay," Will said, catching his balance.

"Nobody cares what you hope. Just get out of the way."

Gabrielle and the older boys tended to the girl and the other injured children. Will backed away along the floor, watching the chaos around him.

The kids still carried on. One of the boys tended to the injured girl. Gabrielle kept busy comforting the children. Will wanted to be helpful. He followed Gabrielle's lead and sat with several of the children. Even though he knew they would not understand him, Will spoke words of kindness, hoping that the tone and the sounds would help at least a little.

Gabrielle walked to Will on his cot, with a child under each arm. She said something to them, and they headed off; the tears ceased rolling down their faces. The children left the two adults alone.

"You must leave, now. I know that was because of you."

Pushing at Will toward his cot near the door, Gabrielle asserted herself against Will.

Another blast startled everyone, again shaking the room. This time glass flew everywhere.

Will reached for his crutches. "I'll check it out," he yelled over his shoulder, catching the eye of one of the boys. Will motioned that he should follow.

The second blast found its target across the small courtyard, blowing the door off of the frame of the small cottage that served as Gabrielle's apartment.

He stopped near the door and held up his arm to prevent the boy from entering the courtyard. A small fire started inside the blown-out door. Will saw no signs of any attackers, and hobbled as fast as possible to the cottage. He ran to the door, but Gabrielle startled him by blocking Will's entry.

"I told you to leave."

"You said that…"

"Quiet. It is a good thing she's alive. If not, I would turn you into the Khmer myself."

Will stared at Gabrielle and walked around her to the cottage.

"Stay away from here. This is off-limits to you."

"I can help," Will said, sizing up the situation. Talking wasted time as the fire could quickly flare beyond their ability to control it. He pushed passed Gabrielle, through the door, and toward the rising flames. Gabrielle moved past Will. Like racers nearing a tie for the finish line, they reached for a blanket spread across the single bed in the small room. Will grabbed the blanket, and covered the flames. With Gabrielle finding a large towel, the two managed to put out the fire. Gabrielle grabbed a pitcher of water for extra insurance and thoroughly doused the smoldering embers.

They watched the steam rise, but no words were spoken. Gabrielle stared at the wall and the door. Will couldn't keep from watching Gabrielle.

"I don't think that was because of me," Will said. Gabrielle looked up at him through her reddened eyes. Then Will saw the tears well up in her eyes. He reached for her, and she didn't stop him.

"It's too much." Crying, she turned away from Will but stood where she was.

"What is?"

"The horror. We were lucky this time. We lost three of the children a few months ago. Blown to bits."

"Who would do that?" Will reached his arms around Gabrielle from behind. When she pushed his arms, Will pulled her even closer. Giving up the struggle, Gabrielle leaned back against Will, brushing up against Will's cheek.

"I'm sorry," she said, and gave Will's arms a gentle squeeze.

"I'm not hurt. You need not apologize."

"I'm sorry for yelling at you. I'm sorry that I can't protect these children."

Gabrielle turned her face toward Will. "William…."

"Please, call me Will."

"Will." She looked at Will. Turning toward him, she kissed Will's cheek. Before he could return the kiss, she lay her head on Will's chest, and closed her eyes.

They remained still for a moment. Then Gabrielle said, "You are a kind man. I didn't mean to be harsh with you."

"I just wanted to help."

"I know. There are so many problems here. With the war and with no money, I am scared. These children are helpless. I am helpless here with them."

Gabrielle started crying again. Will walked Gabrielle to her bed, and lay her down. When he turned to leave she pulled for Will to stay. He stopped. Gabrielle settled back on the bed and looked up at Will. She had hold of his arm. She reached for him. Will responded. She pulled him toward her, still crying softly, Gabrielle again kissed Will. When Will kissed her as well, the passion mounted. They lay together, absorbed in each other, hoping – somehow – that the evil out there would keep its space away from them.

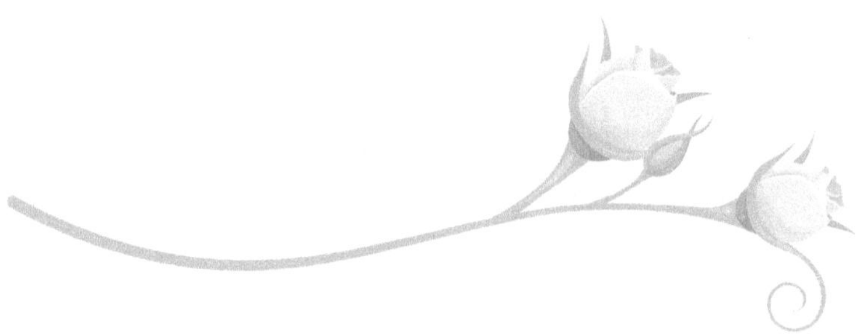

THIRTY-EIGHT

Dad, are you okay?" Glory asked Fred. "You're not breathing right."

"I'm fine. It's the excitement. Plus, the fact that your mother is late."

"She'll be here, and there's no rush. Yet." Her face contorted from the next contraction. The door to the garage then opened, and Beth entered the kitchen carrying packages.

"I need two minutes," Beth said, rushing through the kitchen. "You can hold out that long, dear, can't you?"

"Mom, I'm fine. We're all set, so we can leave as soon as you're ready."

Fred drove them to the hospital, dropping Glory and Beth at the emergency room for them to check Glory in. He'd meet them in the maternity ward.

In her wheelchair being rolled through the hallways to the elevator by a staff member, Glory held Beth's hand as they moved.

"That last one was pretty strong."

"Mine were too, with George. With Abe, it happened so fast that I don't remember it. By the time you came around, I didn't give it much thought. Plus, there were some new drugs then. That helped."

"Well, I'm staying away from the drugs if I can. Ugghhhh." That last was brought on by another contraction.

Up in the room, Glory settled in and hooked up, waiting as her body made its move to bring her baby into the world. Fred came in, carrying a bouquet of white carnations. A nurse followed behind, made adjustments, and let them know the doctor would be there soon.

Glory delivered her baby through the pain as the contractions quickened and deepened. Then there he was. A new baby boy. A few minutes later, Fred and Beth joined Glory and the baby.

"Teri's on her way. And before you say anything," Beth said, "George said to call him as soon as you feel up to it. Abe wants to come by, so I told him to wait. Jerry is on his way, I think."

The nurse waited for Beth to finish. "Everything looks good. We want to keep an eye on his jaundice, but that should clear up soon. These are your parents?"

"Yeah, my parents. Where's my baby?"

"We'll bring him to you as soon as he's ready. It shouldn't be long. But now you need to rest."

It wasn't more than a few minutes later when Teri came in the room carrying Rachel. "Look who it is, Rachel. I told you we'd see Mommy." She walked closer to the bed, and as she did, Rachel leaned out of Teri's arms, practically falling onto Glory. Teri grabbed her back. "We need to be careful. I told you that Mommy's baby came out of her belly. So we have to be gentle." Teri sat Rachel on the bed next to Glory

"Mommy, where's our baby?" Glory smiled, but it was Beth who answered.

"You'll see him soon," Beth said, leaning toward Rachel for a hug and kiss. Fred copied Beth.

"You look so pretty," Glory said. "Is that a new dress? Did Aunt Teri take you shopping?"

Rachel shook her head up and down, her smile wide across her face.

The nurse came in again.

"Where's Brian?" Glory asked.

"Who?" the nurse asked, with Fred and Beth asking the same question.

"My baby," Glory said. "Teri, I'm naming him after Bumba – well, based on his real name, Bryant. I hope you don't mind."

Teri rushed to Glory at her bed and smothered her with a hug.

"Ow, you nut. Did you not see that I had a baby?" Glory said and laughed.

"You didn't tell me. When you talked about names, you never mentioned Bumba. Wow. I'm speechless."

"Doubt it. But he's Brian Walter Stanford."

"Glory. This is an amazing thing…."

Then the doctor entered, interrupting Teri. "So how is Mom? Let me take a look." He kept up a monolog while performing the examination. "You're baby is doing well. And soon you can take him home. Would you like that?" he asked Rachel. She nodded her agreement.

"Can I see the baby?" Rachel asked.

"Soon," Glory said, then turned to the doctor. "Can I see him?" The doctor turned to the nurse behind him and gave her instructions.

Two days later Brian's condition cleared, and they went home to Oak Park.

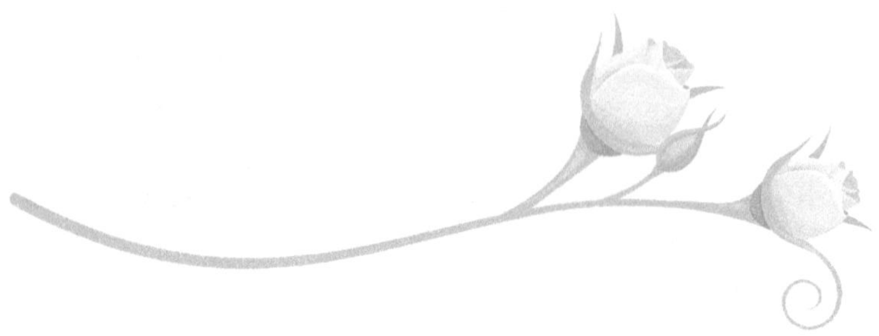

T H I R T Y - N I N E

Gabrielle Honoré chose Cambodia. Or was it the other way around? She liked to say that it pulled at her heart even before she knew where it was. She had to convince first herself and then her parents that despite all the problems of the war, there was little risk that she'd get hurt. More important was to fulfill the mission that had grown inside her since she heard a talk given by United Nations relief workers.

This was one way, she said, being a nursing student could be put to good use – now – when there are children in pain who need her help. Graduation could wait. Besides, as always, she could live on her trust money. No, this was something she had to do.

By the time she found herself face to face with Will in a blown open cottage near the Mekong River, Gabrielle knew that she had left out the possibility of her own emotional pain. Her first-hand views of the torture of children with no parents, no homes, and in some of the worst cases, blown off arms or legs was worse than if she was the one whose legs were destroyed. But she knew that these kids needed someone, and for those that came to their small home in Chari, she had to be there for them.

She didn't like Will when she first saw him. She didn't want him there at all. But when she saw him that day after his first bath, she saw him not as a soldier but as one more soul in pain. Her first impression of Will was wrong. He ignored his own pain. Will was great with the children. She never heard him complain about his leg. She saw a man who knew that life was more significant than his little problems, even the loss of a leg. In the way he looked at each child as they tried to talk with one another, something in his eyes told Gabrielle that this was a man of great compassion. She didn't realize it until he burst through the flames to save her apartment.

Dousing the flames together sparked something else between them. Gabrielle welcomed Will into her home that very day. In the short time caring for the children, Gabrielle developed resourcefulness to get things done. She used that ability to surprise Will.

At the end of one day, several weeks later, Will returned from his supply run into town. "Glad you're back," Gabrielle greeted him as Will entered, pulling a cart behind him. "I ordered you something. It arrived today, and I can't wait to give it to you." She turned to a small group of children behind her and nodded. From the back of the pack of children the bustle grew forward. One by one, each child passed to the next a package wrapped and stamped for shipping from France. The last child then handed it to Gabrielle, and the children sat as prompted by Gabrielle's downward hand motion.

"Some ceremony," Will said. "I have no idea what you're doing."

"That's what we had in mind. They all want to be part of this. You'll need some help, so don't think when you see it that you're going to get it to work."

"What do you mean?"

"You'll see," and Gabrielle handed Will the package. Unwrapping the gift like it was Christmas, the torn paper revealed a box labeled in French. "I don't know about this," Will said with a smile.

"Open it."

Will reached inside the box and pulled out half a plastic leg, formed from above the knee to the end of the foot. Will turned it around in his hands.

Gabrielle said, "It's a prosthetic. I arranged for a doctor to stop by. He should be here soon and will fit it on you. I can help you learn how to walk with it."

Will sat on a nearby chair. He lifted his pants above his absent knee and tried to work the prosthetic onto the stump of his leg. "I'll need some help." Then he placed the leg on the table, rose from the chair, and hopped to Gabrielle. "You are incredible." Will hugged Gabrielle as the children clapped and cheered. "I had no idea," he added. "This is wonderful." They kissed, long and deep, enough for some of the children to turn away.

"It's for you," Gabrielle said. "It's the least I could do. My dad was great at making it happen. I can't wait for you to walk on two legs again."

"Me too."

They spent most of their time together at the orphanage. By day Gabrielle taught school, homemaking, and everything the children would need inside a home. Will occupied the children outdoors, teaching different sports and a junior version of the skills of a soldier. Still, when they could, they found time to be alone. With the river nearby, they often chose a spot near a small leafy beach circling a lagoon carved by the swirling waters. There they would talk and share moments of romance. The life they made in those times could not have been better if they had designed it from scratch.

"I love our time together," Gabrielle said, sitting by the river with her feet splashing in the water. Will lay by her side, his head in her lap.

"This is a beautiful country," he shared with her. "Look up. What do you see?"

Gabrielle leaned back, tilting her head for a better look skyward. "Trees. Leaves. Lots of leaves."

"Yep. Oxygen. The breath of life. With so many leaves, it's no wonder that I feel so happy."

"Really?" Gabrielle answered, taking Will's hat and hitting him with it. "I thought it was me that made you happy."

Will laughed and grabbed his hat. "Sure. But leaves - they are our constant companions and giver of the breath of life." He leaned on his arm and kissed Gabrielle, covering them with his hat.

Gabrielle leaned back and said, "You are so poetic. I am in love with you, William Stanford. One day, we'll go home together. My home. And we'll be married."

Will felt his muscles freeze in place, reminding himself to breathe. He recalled the first time someone told him that he should get married. Again, the physical attraction between Will and Gabrielle was the match that lit the fires that burned around him. He once got burned by that fire after he added fuel to lift the flames ever higher.

"Are you all right, Will?" Glory asked. "What's happening?"

He rolled off her lap and sat upright. His hat fell to the ground, and instead of picking it up, Will swiped it further away. Will sat upright, rocking. Gabrielle matched Will's position, sitting with her feet under her.

"Did I say something wrong? I know you feel the same about me."

Will looked at her, but the smile that he could have given to Gabrielle stopped somewhere between thought and movement.

"I can't," Will said.

"What?"

"Why can't we just be? You and me. Here. Now."

"We are."

"So we'll leave it at that."

When Will got up, Gabrielle reached over to stop him. "Will, please," Gabrielle said. "We have plenty of time. Please talk to me. Something happened in you; that's obvious. But if you know, and I don't, then there is a gap between us. That gap will keep growing unless we both understand what that gap is."

Will fiddled with grass near him.

"You know," Gabrielle said, seeing Will's reticence to speak. "Sometimes, the strong, silent type is not such a good idea. Strong is good. Silent…maybe now's a good time to modify that. Tell me what I don't know."

"I'd rather not," Will answered Gabrielle.

"Oh, but you must. What we have, Will, I know you feel it too. But if you keep secrets from me, then we really don't have much, and perhaps it's better if maybe you went on your way. Or you can tell me what's so deep and dark in you that you freeze like a popsicle."

"Are you sure?"

Glory nodded.

"Back home," Will started. Then he stood. She let him this time. Instead of walking away, he reached with his hand for her and helped her stand and join him. "Let's walk," he said.

They walked along the river path. The movement helped get Will's mind back on solid footing. He could see that Gabrielle was right, that now he has a choice to make, to be wholly a part of her life into which she has welcomed him, or once again move on and be the loner that has apparently been the suit that has best fit him for so long. But something felt tight around him, and there was only one way to loosen it and allow him to truly breathe free.

"Back home. Chicago. In the suburbs, I left a wife."

"You never said anything. What's her name?"

"You want to know? I don't understand. Why?"

"Will, why I want to know is because she is a part of you."

"But that's the thing. She is no more. I haven't been a part of that life for a whole lifetime."

They reached a crossing, where a stream broke off from the river, heading inland. Will and Gabrielle negotiated the fallen tree trunk someone thought to put over the water. After they crossed, Will went on speaking.

"Her name is Gloria, but she is known as Glory."

"Sounds lovely. Is she?"

"You're kidding, right?"

"What do you mean? What would I be kidding about?"

"You like her name? I thought…."

"You thought that because you have a past and that your past is too hard for you to face; that I would reject you."

"Wow. A psychologist."

"No, Will. I'm just a girl who happened to fall for a guy. What the guy is about, what happened in your life to make you who you are today, with me, is also a part of that guy. Do you understand that?"

"I suppose I do."

"So tell me about Glory. Tell me how you ended up thousands of miles away and years apart. Oh, where's your ring?"

"Let's head back," Will said. "I'm getting hungry."

"Are you avoiding this, still?

"Gabrielle, I don't think I am anymore. But I do want something to eat. I need fuel for the fire. Soon, you'll know everything. First, though, I need you to know that what's past is past, and for me, even the fact that Glory and I had a baby together doesn't change anything about you and me."

"Wait. A baby. You're a father."

Will nodded.

"I see that smile that is fighting to get out of you. What's her name?"

"Rachel. She must be around four by now. Yeah, that's right. It's been that long? Anyway, she was something. But I wasn't. I didn't know anything, and from the moment she was born, when I first saw her, I felt lost."

"Why would you feel lost?"

He didn't wait for their walk back to the orphanage but told Gabrielle the story on the way. Gabrielle stopped them as they neared the building. "So you feel like you have no value because of her parents?"

"That's the basic idea. They made it very clear to me – mostly her mother – that I may have impregnated their daughter, but they did not choose to let me in their world."

"So that's why you stay away?"

"Not just that, but that's the main thing. When I lost my leg and the family in the jungle nursed me back to health, it gave me plenty of time to think. I also felt that the change in me was more than physical. And now, since we've been together, I feel like a real person again. Not someone who's required to be part of something. I choose you. I choose now. What happens next, where the future will take me, remains to be seen. That script is not yet written."

"Should we try to write it together, then? Are you sure you don't want to go back to see your daughter? What about Glory? Don't you wonder?"

"Not really. She has her world. It's not mine. Never was."

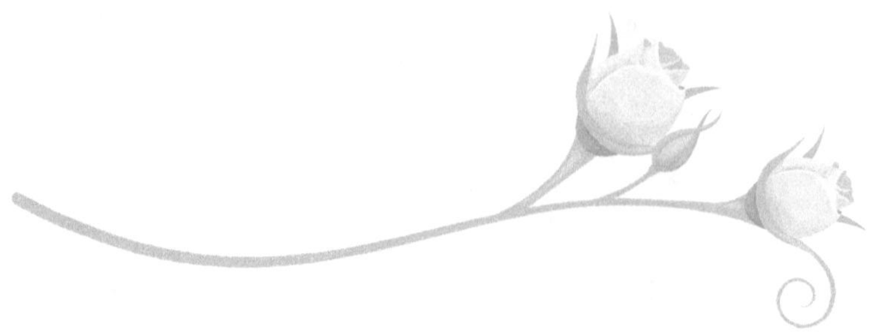

F O R T Y

It was a clear spring day. The morning fog had since lifted, giving Glory the chance she had hoped for. In her bedroom, she finished dressing and then went into Rachel's room.

"Are you ready, pretty girl?" Glory asked Rachel as she sat on the bed. Rachel was sitting on the floor, playing with her dolls. She looked up and smiled.

"Can I take Katie and Cindy with me? We're playing school." Rachel asked.

Glory shook her head. "Not this time. Tell Katie and Cindy that it's time for them to go home. It's a lovely day outside, just like you, so I thought we'd walk to the park. Where's your jacket?" Rachel pointed right next to where Glory was sitting on her bed. Glory laughed and stood up, taking the jacket with her. "Okay, baby-cakes. You ready for the playground?"

Rachel nodded and turned around so Glory could put on her jacket.

"I also have a little surprise for you," Glory said.

"Another doll?"

"No," Glory answered and then chuckled. "It's not a thing. I want to show you something."

"What is it?"

"You'll see. So let's go. The park is waiting. Maybe you'll see one of your friends there."

"I want to play with Debbie. Can you ask her mom?"

"We'll see who's there. For now, it'll be you and me."

Field Park waited a few blocks down the street, adjacent to the Horace Mann School. Glory pushed Rachel in her single stroller, leaving the double-wide stroller for later when Brian woke from his nap. They crossed the street and strolled through the winking sunshine that filtered through the young leaves overhead.

At the front of the school, Glory stopped and kneeled next to Rachel.

"Remember I told you that one day you would go to a big girl's school? Well, now that you are five years old, this will be your school after the summer. Do you like it?"

"It's so big, Mommy."

"Yes, it is. And there will be lots of kids there, many new to the school just like you'll be. Debbie, and I think Gina, will be with you too. Would you like that?"

Rachel smiled. "But no boys. They are mean."

"Rachel, maybe some boys are mean sometimes. But not all boys are mean. Weren't you playing in the sand the other day with Sammy? I saw you, and he was not mean."

"I like Sammy. Can we go to the playground now?" Glory nodded and then pushed Rachel around the corner to the playground.

After a while, the clear skies gave way to wind and cloud cover. Glory pushed Rachel on the swingset when a blast of cooler air told her it was time to go.

Back at the house, Glory gave them both lunch in the kitchen.

"You remember what I told you we're doing tomorrow?" Glory asked Rachel. She shrugged.

"You are a silly girl," Glory said. "Of course, you remember. You remember the white dress with the lacy sleeves?"

"I can wear it?"

"Yes, you can. And Brian is going to be very handsome in his little blue suit. You liked that, didn't you?"

"Mommy, is Leo going to be my new daddy?"

"So, you do remember? Yes, dear. Tomorrow you will have Leo as your Daddy, and Brian's too. You can call him Daddy because he will be here with us. We will be Mommy and Daddy and Rachel and Brian."

"And Lidia. She's part of the family too, right, Mommy?"

"Of course, she is. She takes good care of you guys."

Until the Army finally cut through the red tape and resolved Will's status as missing in action, the lieutenant that Glory had been working with finished putting together the dossier on Will. The Army finally issued the certificate that confirmed that Will was dead, and releasing to Glory the death benefits. Glory and Leo's hold on their plans to marry had finally been lifted.

The two families put together a classic wedding at the church that Leo had attended since childhood, with the reception at the country club near Leo's family home in River Forest. Leo's parents joined Beth in the front row of the church, with Beth holding Brian. They watched Rachel walk up the aisle tossing flower petals from a basket. Then she scooted herself next to Beth. The lyrical tune from the organist changed to the pomp of Mendelsohn's *Wedding March*, and at the back of the room, Glory stood next to Fred. Up the aisle they walked. To see all of the Walters and Fillmores would be to watch people with permanent smiles.

After the wedding, the music of the orchestra filled the reception ballroom. For their first dance as Mr. and Mrs. Leo Fillmore, they chose Al Green's ballad, *Let's Stay Together*. With their inauguration as a married couple completed, the band picked up the pace, moving right into their rendition of *Joy to the World*. Teri and Yuna joined them on the dance floor bringing Rachel and Brian. Glory held Rachel, and Leo had Brian as all six of them danced a circle dance in time with the music. The laughter and smiles decorated the scene as pink fringe frosting lines the edges of a cake. After the dance, they sat at the main table, their appetizers awaiting their return.

"I am so happy, Mr. Fillmore," Glory said, leaning over the children.

"Mrs. Fillmore," Leo answered, "It was worth the wait. I would've waited another three years for you."

"I know, sweetheart," Glory said and then pulled Leo closer for a kiss, with the tingle of forks on crystal ringing around the room as their guests marked the moment.

While they were in Acapulco for their honeymoon, Beth worked with Leo's parents to move Leo's things into Glory's room. Happy to give up his bachelor days with his roommate, Leo had moved back home to stay with his parents until the wedding. Glory and Leo returned, sunburned and covered with smiles. Leo immersed himself in Glory's world yet kept busy with his job covering the Lake Michigan marine beat and the waterways of Chicagoland for the Sun-Times. Glory's life filled with poetry and children.

PART III:
NICE, FRANCE –
AUTUMN, 1979.

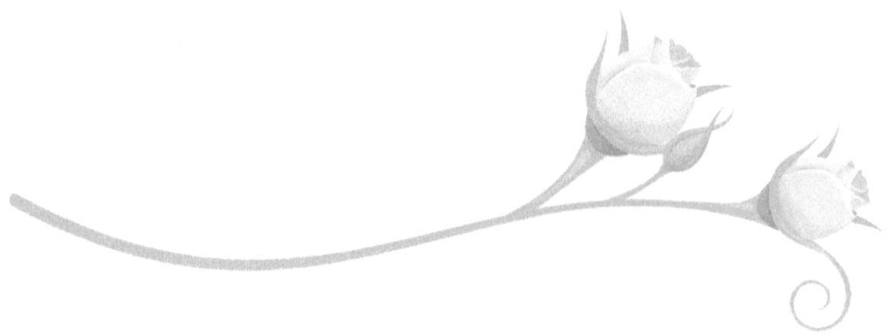

F O R T Y - O N E

Years passed by. Many children continued to call the orphanage their home. Gabrielle and Will did what they could to keep it running. In the village, nobody seemed to care that a tall American with a fake leg often arrived pursuing supplies for the children or strolling in tandem with the lady of the orphanage.

One November afternoon, Gabrielle and Will walked through the market in Chari filling their cart with ripe oranges that never turn orange, a giant jackfruit, bananas, rice, and other supplies.

"I remember the first time I saw this place. It looked so peaceful. I must be blocking any memory of the pain, the fear," Will said.

"I'll never forget it. You were a wreck. Never mind. Let's stop for tea. I need to rest my feet."

At the far edge of the market by the river, the fishing boats tied to the docks, they entered an outdoor café, *Koh Rong Café* set on a wooden dock. They were led to a table with seats along the edge of the Mekong River, with views north and south. "A fine spot you found," Will said.

"We've been here before. Don't you remember?"

"I do. Sort of."

Will lay his menu on the table. "You don't want anything?" Gabrielle asked. "The family that owns this place has been growing their own tea for generations. You should try one."

"Tea's okay."

"Will, it's a drink of healing, and meditation, two things I know mean something. Even the tea ceremony adds an entire layer of culture."

"So?"

"So, we're not just drinking tea. We're experience a cultural event."

"Well, then lead us on."

"But, you get to choose."

"Naw," Will declined. "I'll leave it to you."

They ordered their food. Gabrielle sat back to watch the activity of fisherman unloading their morning catch, residents commuting to town, along with the arrival of typical map-holding tourists.

Near where they were sitting, a kayak pulled into a space near them. With the craft tied to a piling, a man in his late twenties, with a bushy beard and long, unruly hair, stood and stepped one foot onto the dock. "Careful, Syd," the man said, in American English. With the man's help, a woman, Syd, took his hand, and pulled herself up, encumbered by the addition of her mid-term pregnancy.

Safely lodged on the earth-bound dock, Syd remained still, holding tight to the man's arm.

With the scene unfolding, Will leaned back in his chair, as Gabrielle leaned forward, intensifying her view with her instinct as a healer. "You might want to get her tea, and some salmon," Gabrielle said to the couple.

"That was my plan," the man said. The couple walked toward a table that the restaurant's owner had indicated to them.

"You speak English?" the man stopped near Gabrielle and held out his hand. She shook it. "I didn't mean to be rude. I'm Marc. We're from New York, upstate, near Albany."

"Will Stanford," Will said, accepting Marc's handshake.

"You're American?"

"Yeah, Chicago originally. This is Gabrielle. We run the local orphanage."

"That is so far out," Syd said. "My name is Syd. Sydney. Marc sometimes forgets his manners."

"Sorry, hon."

"It's, okay dear. I already know that about you." Marc leaned down and kissed Syd.

"We're on our honeymoon," Syd continued, smiling as she did. Will and Gabrielle returned the smile but couldn't help turning their view to Syd's belly. Seeing this, Syd went on. "It's not what you think. We were planning on this trip as a traditional honeymoon, but my mom got sick so we had to wait."

"And things just happened," Marc completed the thought. "And now Mom's fine."

"Well, that's wonderful," Gabrielle said. "When are you due?"

"Not for another three months, so we should be fine. Do you have children?" Syd asked.

"Us?" Gabrielle responded with a chuckle. "No."

"Well," Will started. "We do have children. Quite a few, actually. The orphanage holds more than fifty kids, with new ones every week."

"I don't see us having kids any time soon," Gabrielle added. "What we do takes a lot from us. As long as the children are well, we are happy. Isn't that right, Will?"

"Of course. They need us. And we have committed ourselves to their care," Will answered, with Glory nodding.

"And we're not married," she said.

"Oh, sorry. I didn't mean anything," Syd responded, then sat up and surveyed the area around the restaurant. "This is beautiful here."

"It's our hidden corner of the world," Gabrielle said. "And it's not far from paradise." The group chuckled. Then Will said, "But be careful. It may look like paradise, but the secret's in knowing what's in the dark corners."

"Will, cut it out, you'll scare them."

"It's okay, brother," Marc said. "We have no use for dark corners. No problems so far."

"Knock on wood," Syd answered, doing just that.

Their tea arrived with two bowls loaded with baked pastries the shape, size and color of a pointy lemon. The meringue, baked sugar, and vanilla among other spices masked a malodorous scent rising up from the hot desserts.

"That's an interesting smell," Syd said from the next table. "What is that?"

"It's a choux puff," Gabrielle said. "I've been wanting to make something from the durian fruit, but couldn't find any in the market. It's better known as a stinky puff."

"I can see why. Or smell why."

"It's gotta taste better than the stink," Marc added. "Kinda like bleu cheese."

"Here," Gabrielle said, cutting a pastry in half and handing one each to Marc and Syd. They both bit into the warm dessert.

"That's amazing. Inside, like a custard, maybe vanilla," Syd said.

"I'm tasting almond," Marc said. "With a sweetness, like sugar, or maybe honey."

"So," Will said, finishing a bite of the pastry. "What about this tea?"

"What do you mean, Will?" Gabrielle asked.

"Pretty strong smell there, too." Will took a sip. "Tastes familiar. What is it?"

"It's a rare tea from Malaysia. Drink it slow." And they did.

By the time the newcomers' food arrived, it was time for Will and Gabrielle to resume their errands. They left the newlyweds to their privacy, walking back toward the market. "Nice couple," Will said.

The clouds overhead blocked the yellows of the sun as the wind pushed the couple further into town. "Something's different," Will offered.

Gabrielle pulled her sweater closer around her. "It's colder, I guess." Passing a newsstand, Will stopped and picked up a newspaper, *"Militants Storm US Embassy in Tehran."* Will scanned the article, then mumbled, "This is not good."

"What?"

Will showed Gabrielle the newspaper. "Something doesn't feel right," Will said as Gabrielle scanned the print.

She dropped the newspaper to its rack. "Will, let's get back. The children."

They returned at the beginning of the lunchtime chaos and putting away the groceries, Will and Gabrielle stopped and surveyed the scene. The old blasted-out windows had long before been replaced by plywood. Covered at its lower reaches by stick figures, color splashes of paint believed by the children to be trees, elephants, tigers, and birds with occasional flowers and fruits in colors never before seen anywhere.

The raucous sounds of children grabbing lunch filled the air. Two pre-teen girls ran toward the couple, crashing into Will. The older girl made her claim. "That's not fair. I saw you first."

"Now, Sophal," Will said in broken Khmer, "you saw that Tep was here first." Will peeled the two girls off his leg as he moved toward a table. "Anyway, are you ready for your lessons? I am the English teacher, yes?" Both girls nodded. "Then you must be ready to learn." Will took an easier tactic. "One, two, three, go," and Will took their hands and marched them to a nearby table.

Gabrielle followed. "You really are good with them. At least they have that." Gabrielle joined them at the table and watched Will help the girls settle into their chairs. The view cut through Gabrielle. "Your daughter," she said, taking Will's arm. "Rachel, right?" Will looked at her and, after a pause, nodded.

Will handed Sophal and Tep their notebooks and pencils. Watching them turn the pages, Will remained silent. Finally, he turned and looked at Gabrielle. "I told you. That's the past. I won't go back there."

"Will, you should think about it. She's your daughter."

"I'm no good to her. All these years."

"If Rachel was a boy, I think you would feel differently."

"It would be the same."

"Perhaps. You are good to all the children. Why not Rachel?"

"It can't be good. It's been too many years. Besides, there's this other person."

"The mother-in-law. Yes, I know."

"I can't. That life is gone. I'm here now. With you."

Gabrielle looked Will over, checking for any vulnerability to counter his words. The girls' lessons replacing their impromptu debate, Gabrielle saw only what she knew to be one of Will's best qualities, patiently imparting English to his two Cambodian charges. Gabrielle realized that she had to get back to work and oversee the children's chores to clean up from lunch.

The burst of the door opening from outside shocked Gabrielle. The surprise crash caused a few of the children to cry out. Their cries intensified as a squad of Khmer soldiers swarmed into the room, rifles at the ready.

The commander barked his instructions. "The children are all to come with us. Now. If everyone cooperates, nobody gets hurt." Gabrielle walked toward him, with Will not far behind.

"Who are you?" the commander asked.

"We are taking care of these children," she answered. Will walked past her as she said that, but Gabrielle reached for his arm to stop him. The soldiers in front had the same notion, thrusting their rifles forward and aiming directly at them. Helpless to do anything, they could only watch their children led by gunpoint outside and gone.

The wind echoed the silence that lingered beyond the former gaiety of dozens of children. Will and Gabrielle stood frozen by the shock of what they had just witnessed. To mark the moment, a gust of wind blew a loosened sheet of plywood off the wall onto the floor with a thunderous crash.

Their only response was to keep breathing.

The devastation they felt masked the fear of the worst for them. With no reason to remain, and with the help of connections from Gabrielle's family, Will had papers made up for him that would allow him to travel to France. It had always been a given that Will would someday accompany Gabrielle back to France. There had been no contact from anyone even remotely associated with the United States Army. Given the circumstances, Will Stanford of Skokie no longer existed. The opportunity to make a new life was not lost on Will.

They found happiness in France. Will had never experienced a place as colorful and lively as Gabrielle's family home near the town of Grasse. At first, he was lost as to what he'd do. Gabrielle made it very clear that he need not worry himself about money. Her trust fund provided more than enough for both of them. Gabrielle finished nursing school and took a job in the pediatrics ward of the local hospital. Will tried working in the hospital, but with no training and, at best, a poor command of the French language, he found the work challenging and frustrating. Instead,

Gabrielle got him a job working for her father and uncle in the family's perfume factory. It wasn't much, but Will found the activity in turning flowers into perfume to be a better fit.

It was indeed a better fit. Will took to the perfume business in a hurry. Immersing himself in his work and life in southern France, the language soon no longer hindered Will. It became his second language, much more so than the bitter memory of his meager attempts at speaking Khmer during those years in Chari. He worked hard and, with Gabrielle, played hard.

She didn't need the money from her job and wanted to do more. Gabrielle quit the hospital, convincing her father to establish a foundation to open a home for orphans and other children with special needs. With Will's support at every step, Gabrielle spent her family's money and built the children's home in the hills not far from their home in Grasse. Will was involved daily with the children. And Will fit right into Gabrielle's family.

With a solid command of French, the support of Gabrielle, and a work ethic unlike any that the family had ever seen, Will soon became an essential part of the family business. It was the opportunity that they had been hoping would come along to expand their line beyond the European continent to North America. The shelves of department stores throughout Europe had been stocked with the family's best-selling perfumes – long-time household names in Europe such as Bleu, Soleil, De Jeu De Paume, and Rouge Fleur. Honoré Perfumes was a perennial leader in European sales for fifty years. Sales overseas was another story – virtually nonexistent. Will convinced Claude Honoré that he could help them break through the barrier, not with his knowledge of perfumes but his familiarity with American customs. Will learned that they were selling to Americans as though they were Europeans. He provided them with a sales approach that better worked in his native country.

Will found a place inside him, tapping into his dormant interest in learning to be a corporate buyer. Through grit and a new, raw interest in learning, Will's help guiding them into American stores and dealing with American wholesalers was the key that Honoré Perfumes had been missing. The American success of Honoré Perfumes promoted Will to a corner office, a huge bonus, generous salary, and benefits – all the trappings of success. In short, life was good. Even Gabrielle found success with the center built for foster care and as an orphanage. Her new donors allowed them to open orphanages in other cities throughout France.

Together they bought a villa only minutes from the perfume factory in Grasse. The luxury of the pool, the tennis court, and the beauty of the grounds surrounding their home was more than Will had ever allowed himself to dream, much less live as his reality. Their lives merged at the intersection of their home at Villa DeBrus. Their world of perfume and helping children felt perfect. They had what they wanted, making a difference in the world. But still, through all of it, something felt off inside Will. He ignored that little something that insisted on clinging to him for so long, sending a repeated message that he didn't want to receive. Could he keep ignoring the apparent trouble that stirred inside him? When the century turned, giving Will pause to consider the enormity of a change that happens only every thousand years, a new era had to mean something, from a global level down to his small corner of the world.

"Gabrielle, you're right on time," Will said, when Gabrielle entered the kitchen coming home from her work at the Lucien Honoré Children's Care Center. "The *coq-au-vin* is almost ready. Smells good, right?"

"I guess," Gabrielle answered. She stopped at the entryway, her coat remained buttoned.

"Are you going somewhere? You know we allow our patrons to remove their outerwear. As our best, and only, patron at the Café Will, you are certainly not the exception."

When Gabrielle maintained her stare across the room, Will put the dishes that he was carrying on the table, and walked to her. "Right. Not funny," he said, unbuttoning her coat. "What's going on with you? You usually love my *coq-au-vin*. Come. Smell the wine." Nothing. He nudged her toward the table. "Okay, give me your coat, rest your feet, and tell me what's wrong." She followed his lead, and with her coat safely draped over another chair, sat and accepted the glass of wine Will handed to her.

"He came back. Gideon."

"Again? He's, what, only six. He's been with you more than with his parents."

"Seven. Still, this time might be permanent. I don't know what happened, but we had to get him stitches. He was hysterical, so I had Carter sit in the room with him."

"That was smart."

"Yeah, Carter is the only one who connects with the kid. Took a bit, but he finally fell asleep. But Will, It's so sad."

"It is. You're an angel to care so much."

"You think so?"

"Why do you doubt it? How many have you seen come through? And if not for you and what you created, what would happen to them?"

"You're right. It takes a lot, and when I see them like this… oh, inside I want to choke somebody."

"Not me."

"You? You're my rock, Mr. Stanford." The first smile of the dinner hour crossed her face. "I need you. You give me energy."

"And you, them," he said. "You're mom to so many."

"Too many to count since we started. But giving so much every day, you know I'd have nothing left, except when I'm around you."

"That's so beautiful," Will said. "And it feels real, the give and take. But I see why you always tell me you that your life is too full for you to have kids. Still, are you certain that you never want to backtrack a bit? We'd do it together, you know," he finished, getting up to set the table. "Let me get dinner."

"Will, we have a good life, right?" He nodded with his back to her, ladling out the dinner. "We aren't getting any younger?"

"That is a fact."

"And you see my kids. They are incredible. Through every challenge, every bump in their road, which becomes a mountain for us, you can't know how much love they give, how hope flows from every pore of their being. They are too young to know what we know, how hard life is. But they don't have to know it, 'cause they lived it. And I feel it, too. These are my kids. With them, and with you, I am, Will, a fulfilled person. Too many children have no home, no parents – far more than we can help. No, that's enough for me." The cup of wine emptied with the last syllable.

"For you, my loving partner," she went on, "you may feel some of that too. But in your case, it would be only to one, to your daughter. But also what you give me, the feelings we share, I know will last, no matter what may happen."

Through the steam rising from the dinner-plate he placed in front of Gabrielle, Will leaned down and kissed her - slow, sturdy, and deep.

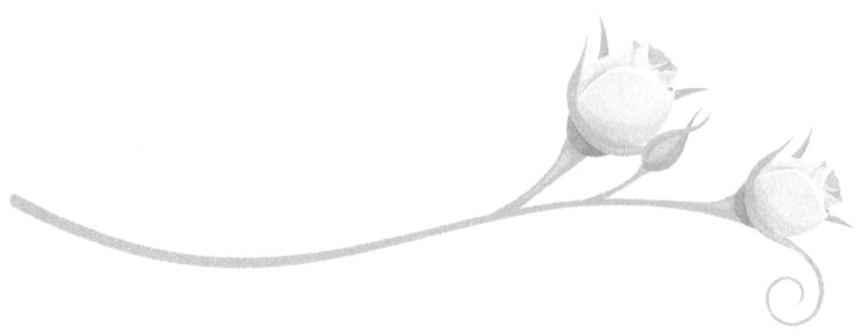

FORTY-TWO

Too chilly even in mid-day to ride with the top down, nonetheless, down it went, exposing Will and Gabrielle to the cold wind. They closed their jackets around them to better combat the chill. They cruised along the coastal road to enjoy the views of both the ocean to the south and the villages and occasional fields of flowers passing them. Traveling into Nice, a row of swaying cypress trees opened up before them to display a park, the emerald grass leading to sporting fields beyond, teeming with the activity and sounds of competition, fragranced by grilled American style picnic cuisine. A baseball game was in full progress.

Will veered the sports car to the edge of the road, slowed, and turned onto an access road. He stopped the car by the picnic area near the field, and turned off the engine.

"What are you doing?" Gabrielle asked.

"Nothing. Just watching."

"Why?"

Scattered about were players wearing the uniform of the U.S. Navy. Will opened the door to step out. He saw the two matching sneakers, one at the end of the prosthetic fitted over the remnants of his left leg. Will stopped, and instead looked toward the fields.

"What is it? Why are we stopped?"

"It's baseball. Seeing them play reminds me of summers back home," Will said. "Sorry. I mean, back in Chicago."

"You have nothing to apologize for. It was you, not me, who said your days as an American are behind you." Will turned his look toward Gabrielle's eyes. Gabrielle had to bring up her concerns. "Whatever you need to be happy, even if it's avoiding your entire past if that's what it will take. That's what I want for you. But I think you need the opposite. The past cannot be ignored. Your daughter cannot be ignored even after all these years."

"I buried the past long ago in the dirt of Cambodia."

"Will, you can't bury your daughter," Gabrielle said. "We're not getting younger, you know. When will you finally decide that Rachel is a part of you? By that time, it might be too late."

Will responded by starting the engine, shifting gears, and gunning the accelerator, thrusting the couple forward along the road to Villa DeBrus.

Later that day, with the dusk of evening settling in, Will, alone in the car, pulled into the parking lot of Honoré Perfumes. He pulled the Peugeot into the spot marked on the bumper with his name. He rushed straight to the credenza inside his office against the wall, opened the middle doors, and began his search.

"It's here somewhere. I'll find it," he said out loud.

He threw items to the floor. He found what he was looking for, pulled it out, and made his way to his desk. He placed on the desk the photo that Glory had given to him the day he left for Vietnam, the plastic wrapping darkened by the dirt and blood from the conflict. Brushing the plastic, Will removed the photo of that long-ago day when he left Glory and Rachel.

Will stared at himself through more than thirty years. The photo of Will, Glory, and the infant Rachel woke the seeds of Will's memories. The image of Glory revealed a reminder of her figure that had caught Will's attention so long past. He stared out the window at the factory's grounds and the trees in the distance beyond. Finally, Will put the mess back inside the credenza. Then he walked out to his car, with his memory firmly lodged in his pocket.

"Gabrielle, are you home?" Will called as he closed the front door.

Gabrielle emerged from the kitchen. "I'm right here. But why are you yelling?"

"Sorry, my love. But it's time." He showed her the two tickets he had purchased for their flights to Chicago.

"What do you mean….?" Gabrielle stopped herself. She walked to Will and wrapped her arms around his shoulders. She saw something new, different in his eyes.

"Are you sure?"

"Yes. But you have to promise to stay with me."

Gabrielle pulled Will to a nearby sofa to sit together. Gabrielle leaned into Will, kissed him, and hugged him again as she said, "Will, my dear. I'm with you. Whatever you need, whatever you want to do." She looked up at him. "What are you going to do?"

"I have to see her. Somehow. There's something there that I need to see. I can feel it. I don't know what it is or what will happen. But when it does, I want you with me."

A sliver of the light of sunrise crept through the curtains, reflecting off the water of Lake Michigan into the darkened hotel room. Will turned on the bathroom light, hoping not to fully waken her yet. Dressed and ready to go, he searched through his suitcase, the desk, and the dresser. He needed help.

"Hon, do you know where I put the rental keys?"

Gabrielle stirred, lifted herself up from the bed, and answered, "Are they in your pants?"

"I looked." Will then spotted his jacket on the chair and found the keys in a pocket.

Will left Gabrielle back in the room and drove northwest from the city in the rental car. In Oak Park, he stopped in front of Glory's home, the place of their first passion, still dark from the night. Will shut off the engine and rolled down the window. Remaining in the car, he watched a woman jogging on the far side of the street which ran past him, turned at the front walk leading to the house, and scampered up the steps to the front door, letting herself in with a key. The lights then streamed from inside, startling Will's view. Unsure what to do, Will rolled the window back up, started the engine, and drove away.

"I can't do this," Will said as he and Gabrielle strolled along the lakefront later that morning.

"We can do it together." She said. A young couple pushing a stroller walked by, interrupting Gabrielle. They stopped to let them by and watched the young family stroll into the distance.

Gabrielle continued. "How difficult this must be."

"Why, Gabrielle?"

"In some small way, I have always known that you would do this. You cannot avoid your family forever."

"That's not what I mean. You never complain."

Gabrielle walked to a nearby bench, sat, and beckoned Will to join her.

"We have talked about this. I learned long ago to take life as I find it. I took you, all dirty and smelly that first day. I don't regret a single minute of our time together."

"You might. Starting today."

"Will, I have always wanted this for you. Leaving Rachel, well, I wondered how long it would take for this to get to you."

"I came here for her," Will said.

"And I came here to be with you. For you. I can be here for her too if that's what you want."

Will nodded. Lake Michigan stretched to the far horizon, reminding Will of the great chasm that lay before him. Somewhere beyond his view lay the far shore, a landing of safety from the dangers of the deep waters. Would he land on safe ground with Glory? Maybe seeing the lake so close portended instead a warning to leave this place and return to the other side of the pond. But where did he belong?

It was evening later that day. Will parked the car in the same spot as the morning. Gabrielle sat next to him. The lights shined bright from Glory's home across the street, glowing onto the trees and bushes.

"Looks like they're home," Will said as he turned off the engine.

"It's time, Will. You've come back."

"That's their home. Not mine."

"Your daughter is there. In a way, it's your home, too, at least in spirit. Are you ready for this?"

With a deep gulp of the night air, Will turned and looked at Gabrielle. He nodded through a forced smile, and opened the door.

Through the decorative glass at the front door, they saw lit candles on the table inside. Will did not hesitate to ring the doorbell. After a moment, they watched through the glass a woman approached the door, wearing surgical scrubs, the same woman who Will had seen earlier. She stepped to the door and opened it.

He saw her immediately, the same girl that he left behind a lifetime before. She was, of course, a larger version of herself, but he looked into the same eyes. Her hair hung long and was a lighter shade than he remembered of Glory's similar hair color. The slight upturn of her nose dominated the few freckles on her face. Then when she spoke, the way she moved her mouth conjured up long-dormant memories of Glory.

"Can I help you?"

"Rachel?"

"Yes." Rachel edged the door closer, leaning against its side. "Who are you?"

"I don't know how to tell you this…." Will stopped, unsure how to continue even though the scene he had often imagined stared right at him. Will reached into his coat pocket and pulled out the photo as he caught his breath. He studied the photo yet again, and then handed it to Rachel. She took the photo and glanced at it. From behind her, a voice called out, "Rachel, who is it?"

"I don't know, Mom." Rachel looked back at the photo. She then looked up at Will and Gabrielle. That's when Glory came up behind Rachel and, with her hands on Rachel's shoulders, studied the two strangers. Rachel stepped to the side, and as Glory stepped next to her, Rachel showed her the photo, and then asked, "Is that you, Mom?" Glory looked closer at the picture.

Will interjected, "That's me," but stopped as the frog in his throat came to life. Gabrielle added, looking at Rachel, "Yes. That's you. The last time you were with your father."

"Let me see," Glory said, taking the photo and examining the images. Then she studied Will more closely.

"Oh my god," Glory gasped, taking a step backward.

"Where did you get this?" Glory asked, peering at Will. Will removed his Irish cap to give her a better look.

"I always had it," Will answered.

She turned and walked into the living room, pulling Rachel with her. Rachel asked in bewilderment, "Mom, what is it? What's going on?"

Glory found her way to the love seat, and as she sat, she handed the photo to Rachel and said, "He died. In the war. That's what they told me."

"My father, you mean?" Rachel queried.

"Many years ago."

Together, they resumed their study of the old photo. Glory pointed to the picture and said, "That's you, and that's me."

Will called from the foyer, "And that's me." They looked at him. "I survived. Barely."

"Oh no." Glory lowered her head into her hands as Rachel pulled her closer into a hug.

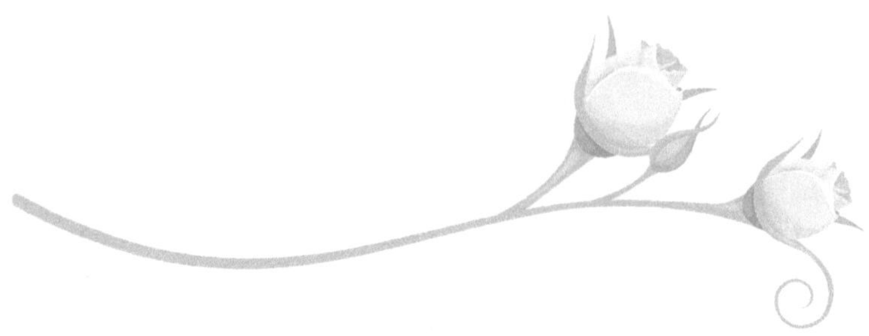

FORTY-THREE

The warmth of the coffee aroma attempted to remove the chill from the air, notwithstanding the moderate room temperature. Through the steaming brew, Will continued his story. "And I've been living in France ever since. I…couldn't come back. I was young. Stupid, I guess. Definitely afraid. You name it."

Will looked at Gabrielle. "Gabrielle always wanted me to come back. For you, Rachel." He added, looking down at the drink, "I couldn't find it in me."

"It must have been confusing for you," Rachel said.

"At best. I buried my old life in Cambodia." A sob came from Glory as they all turned to look at her. Rachel squeezed her mother's hand that much tighter.

"I have been in France for a very long time. And if not for Gabrielle and her family, I may not be alive."

Silence took over for the moment. Then Glory asked, "What about our marriage? Leo and I have been married for a very long time."

"I don't know. We'll have to figure that part out."

"I'm stunned. You have no idea what seeing you sitting here, hearing you speak, is doing to me."

"You can't know how sorry I feel. And I'm happy for you. How long are you married?"

"Twenty-three years next month."

"A lifetime for some. You deserve happiness. I only knew that I would get in the way of that. I don't think that anymore."

Glory felt Rachel next to her lean forward. Rachel picked up the photograph from the coffee table and peered closely at it but said nothing. Glory asked her, "Rachel, you've been quiet. You must have something to say."

With all eyes watching her, Rachel returned the photo to the table. She stood and walked out of the room, then ran upstairs, with Glory calling after her. "Rachel, where are you going?" Glory said, looking back at the group, "I hope she's okay. Maybe I should check on her."

Glory stood up, and Rachel returned and resumed her seat and took the photo. "It is you. You're old. But I always had this." Rachel opened her fist and showed in her palm the old wooden peace sign necklace with the wooden beads, then let the peace sign slide off and hang with the wooden beads. "Look," Rachel said, "it's the one in the photo, laying on the bed. That's the only thing I ever had from my real dad." She looked at the photo, then handed the picture and the necklace to Will. "You," she concluded.

Will took it and, over his tears, said, "I'm sorry."

"Rachel, dear," Glory said.

"Don't be sorry. Will? Do I call you Will? Mom, what do I call him?"

Will answered instead, "Will is just fine," and handed the necklace back to Rachel.

Glory cut in, "Rachel, Will was near death. I can't imagine the trauma."

"Mother, I am okay with it. I know it happens. I see trauma every day. The way I see it, now I have two fathers." This spoken sentiment drained Rachel as she slumped back on the sofa, leaned her head back, and closed her eyes.

It then occurred to Rachel that there was more to the picture than they were all seeing. "But what about Brian?"

If exclamation points and question marks could be seen, they would have filled the unspoken dialog clouds that hovered above all of them.

"Mom, I always had you. But Brian never had his real father. Dad has been Brian's father forever."

"Why couldn't you come back for him?" Rachel asked. "We both would've like to know our birth father. Isn't that right, Mom?"

Will didn't know what to make of this. He could only stammer, "Brian? You mean…."

Will looked at Glory. He looked around the room to try to make sense of what he thought was happening. He saw a table piled with assorted photographs. Without fanfare, Will rose and walked to the table, peering at the photos, various groupings of smiling faces with Glory and Leo, Rachel, and images that were likely of Brian.

The group watched, Rachel ask her mother, "What? Mother, he didn't know about Brian?"

"I couldn't. Before I learned that your father…Will …sorry …was missing in the war, I dreaded him coming home. The war. I hated the war. I was afraid of what it would do to him."

Will held a picture of Brian from the table and stared at it. It was a classic pose of Brian in a football uniform on one knee holding his helmet. Will figured it was a high school photo. The bewildered smile that angled toward the helmet hinted at Brian's place in the world at that moment. Zooming in on the face, Will saw a more chiseled version of himself. Turning, he asked nobody in particular, "Why?" He could only shake his head.

"Rachel," Glory said. "You better call him."

Before Rachel called Brian, they all agreed that it would be best for Will and Gabrielle to wait in another room when Brian arrived. Moments later, a screen door slammed at the back of the house. His jacket unbuttoned, a young man, tall and robust, rushed into the living room. Catching his breath, Brian viewed the scene and asked, "What's the urgency?"

Glory sat with Leo. They both stood and started toward Brian. "Brian, have a seat." Removing his coat, Brian popped himself into a chair. "So, what's wrong? Who died?"

Glory stood near the chair and leaned toward Brian. "You remember about your father?"

"What about dad? What's wrong?"

"Not Leo. He's fine. I'm…we're…talking about your father, Will Stanford."

"He died in Vietnam. I know that. So?" Brian took a moment and looked around the room as they all stared at him. He spotted the photo and the choker lying on the table. Nobody said anything.

"What, Mom?"

Leo stood up and spoke to Brian, "What your mother means to say is…."

Glory interrupted him. "Let me. Brian, your father didn't die in the war?"

Brian looked up at Glory and saw Rachel watching him, rubbing her eyes. "Rachy, what do you know? He didn't die in the war? Where did he die?"

Glory answered, "He didn't."

"Didn't die."

"No."

The news did not seem to penetrate Brian initially. He rose and headed in the direction of the kitchen and asked, "Mom, what is this?" Glory stepped toward him and reached her arms around Brian. He shrugged her away. "Mom, no hugging now. Just tell me what this is about."

She grabbed his arm, stopping him. "All right. He's alive. He didn't die."

"Of course he did."

"This is quite shocking to all of us. Come, Brian, sit with us." She took his hand and led him to the sofa to sit with Rachel. Standing at their side, Glory called out, "Will, Gabrielle."

Will and Gabrielle were holding hands as they entered the room. Glory walked toward them and took Will's hand. She turned to Brian, "Brian, this is your father, Will."

Brian retorted, "Yeah. Okay. Who's that?"

Leo offered the answer from the love seat, "That's his…That's Gabrielle."

This whirlwind surrounded Brian no differently than a winter storm. The snow of emotion flinging around him made it difficult to see. Brian jumped to his feet, "This is sick. What kind of joke? I'm not a fool, you know." Not knowing where to turn, Brian remained where he stood. "My father died. Dead. Dead. Mom. Dad. What are you doing?"

"It's no joke, Brian," Glory said.

Will started forward, stopped by Gabrielle. "I'm so sorry," Will said, shaking his head, "I didn't know."

"You're Will Stanford? My father?" A plan came to Brian, and he moved toward Will. "I don't care. Get out. Who are you to do this?" Veins bulged from his neck and his fists clenched. Glory stepped in to provide interference.

"He was almost killed. He was left for dead."

"Good. That would've been better."

Rachel stood on the opposite side next to Brian. "C'mon. He's alive." She reached down to the table and lifted the photo and necklace. "Look at these." She took Brian's fist and tried to pry it open. "Brian, please stop."

To Will, Glory said, "Show him your leg. Brian, he even lost his leg. Take a look." Will pulled up the pant leg to display the prosthetic.

Brian stared at it and then looked at Leo. "I have my dad. You're nobody. You can leave now. And never return. Like you did so well before."

Nobody moved. The grandfather clock ticked its witness of the event.

Brian turned to leave. "I don't believe this." Off he marched through the kitchen, the screen door slamming his goodbye. Rachel followed into the kitchen. From the kitchen, Rachel called out, "Mom, where did I put my keys? Never mind. I see them." The screen door announced Rachel's departure.

Through the cones of light painted along the street from overhead, she saw Brian running down the street. She knew his destination, and chose to drive.

Brian made it to Oak Park High School in just minutes and then sprinted across the tennis courts.

At the concrete of the basketball courts that led to the playing fields was a solid brick wall, which composed the outer wall of the high school gymnasium. Marked on the wall at separated intervals were vertical rectangles spray painted in single line outlines, displaying a standard strike zone for the expected batter intended to face away from the wall. A batter standing at the wall facing out to the field would face his opponent pitcher, and a two-man baseball game of fastpitch could then commence.

Rachel parked on the side street and watched Brian standing several yards from the wall, throwing a rubber baseball at one of the batter strike zones and then catching the rebound. In the solid form that Brian showed as a former pitching sensation from high school, the solid thwack of the ball striking the wall reverberated across the yard.

To avoid startling Brian, she called out for him as she approached. "Thought you'd be here." The only response was the call and repeat of Brian's windup and throw, followed by the crack of rubber hitting brick and the cascading bounce of the ball back to Brian.

A throw later, Rachel pulled the photo and necklace from her pocket and held them out for Brian to see. "Look." Another strike against the wall. Rachel moved closer. "Brian, stop doing that. You're not a child." Brian froze, the ball bounding past him onto the grass blackened by the night.

Rachel pushed the picture closer to Brian, forcing it into his hand. "Don't you see? In the picture, Brian. It's him."

Brian grabbed the photo and angled it to the light for a closer look. Rachel continued, "Talk to him. He seems like a good person. Haven't we always wondered about our real father? How many times did you tell me that you wanted to go to heaven to meet him? Remember that. It's not so long ago. Well, heaven brought him to us. We don't have to wonder any more."

He handed the photo back to Rachel and turned to chase after the ball. From the darkness, Brian asked, "Why? He quit on you. Don't you know that? Where's that damn ball?"

"Brian, grow up. When were you ever shot at? Almost killed? I see trauma in the ER every day. He lost a leg. That's more damage than most people can handle. How do you think he felt losing his leg, lost in the middle of the jungle?"

Emerging from the dark, Brian again toed it up and resumed his pitching. After the first pitch, Rachel moved directly in front of Brian to impede the second. "It's me. Rachel. I'm a bit scared myself. Of what I might learn. Brian, this is adult time. He just wants to know who you are. You'll see."

"What's the point? He'll go back to his hole, and we'll never see him again."

"You don't know that. You can make it more than that if you want."

"I don't even want that. He should have never left you and Mom in the first place. He deserted her for the army. He chose that. That's why he almost died and lost his leg. It's his own fault. I don't feel sorry for him. I feel bad for Mom and you and everything Mom had to deal with on her own. She must have been devastated when he left and never came back. What kind of man leaves his wife and baby, not to mention that Mom was pregnant with me. Think about that!"

"That's all behind us. We're adults. We have no idea what hell he must have gone through. Give him a chance."

He gave up on his imaginary pitcher's duel, and walked off toward Rachel's car. "Come, Rache. It's getting cold out here." He stopped and waited for Rachel to join him. "I'll think about it, but it's tough to swallow all of this."

"Okay, that's something," Rachel said.

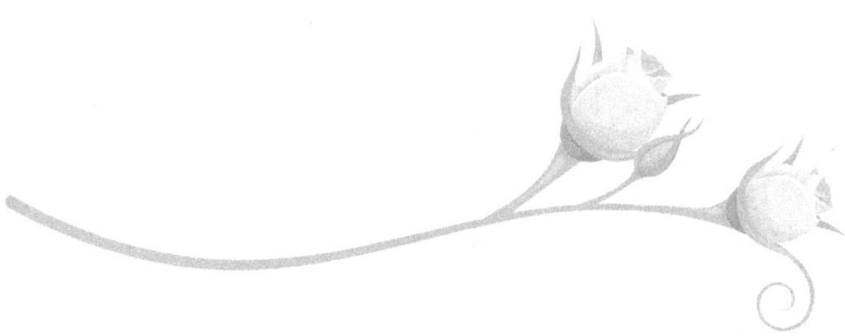

FORTY-FOUR

Inside the airport, Will and Gabrielle stood on the up escalator to the departure gate to take them home to France. Will held his cell phone to his ear, listening to Rachel on the other end.

"Brian said he would join us last night. But I think he's avoiding this whole thing."

"It's okay. At least we had some time with you. Rachel, you're a beautiful woman. How I hate the years I've missed. Now…" He couldn't continue, choking up the words. Will handed the phone to Gabrielle.

"It's Gabrielle."

"Is he okay?"

"I don't know." Gabrielle looked closer, checking that Will was breathing normally. "When will we see you again?"

"We'll have to see," Rachel answered. "This has been very difficult. But, we'll figure something out, I suppose."

Will took the phone. "Please talk to Brian. I'd very much like to find another way for us to connect. Maybe you can both visit us in France. Anyway, keep in touch. Let's talk soon, and maybe you can help work things out with Brian, too."

"Yes, Will…Father."

Rachel sat on the back deck beyond the kitchen, watching the distant blues and oranges of the twilight sky. Rachel, Brian, Glory, and Leo, with Beth taking the place of honor at the head of the table, just finished Thanksgiving dinner that took her and Glory all day to prepare. Rachel was once again astonished that a meal that took hours to prepare could be fully consumed in minutes. The swiftness of the meal gave Rachel little time to locate the ball of courage somewhere inside her to bring up the topic that had been on her mind for many weeks.

She contemplated how she could convince Brian to look past himself and spend time with their newly emerged father, Glory opened the door and peeked her head out from the kitchen.

"Can you heat up the pie? And we could use a little help in here." Rachel stood up and retreated into the kitchen.

Over dessert, with the table cleared of the dinner plates, serenity flowed through the small family, the result of a full turkey dinner. Rachel took a bite of the freshly baked apple pie with its warm crust topped by a dollop of vanilla ice cream. Letting the hot-cold blend slide down her throat, Rachel felt the warmth to speak her mind.

"I think we should invite Will to Brian's birthday party." Forks were placed on plates as Glory, Brian, and Leo looked at her, with silence holding fort. "And if they want, they can stay a few more days and be with us for Christmas. This table is big enough for two more people for dinner."

Glory looked across the table at Brian, occupied with sipping his coffee and peering over the rim of the cup at Rachel. Rachel sensed Brian's gaze, turned to him, and said, "Brian, you told me that your therapist thinks it would be good for you to learn more about your father. Right?"

He put the cup down and gathered his thoughts. "I know she said that, and I can't find any logical reason why it's not a good idea."

"So then you would welcome him at the party?"
"I don't know," he said. "Mom? Don't you think it would be kinda weird?"

"Brian," Glory said. "I've been trying to tell you, but you seem to find all kinds of ways to cut me off. When we were together a whole lifetime ago, your father seemed like a good man. Yeah, he had issues, but don't we all. When your sister was born, I saw something in the way he used to look at her that told me that he could be a good father. But, he was very young and had no job. He didn't know what to do. I got on with my life and had a lot of support from Teri and Yuna, from Mom and Grandpa Fred, and then Leo, and everybody. But things didn't turn out so well for him, as you know. The world can be a harsh place. Perhaps we can make it feel a touch less harsh for him."

"Brian," Beth opened up for the first time, "I'm old, but I am still your grandmother. I knew him back then. Believe me, I didn't like him. Glory can tell you that I wanted nothing to do with him. But now, we're getting old. I don't know how much longer I'll be here. Neither do you or any of us. Just like my Fred." She paused, wiping her eyes with her napkin. " If he's asking to be part of your life, do you really have it in you to deny him that, after all he's been through? Glory, how do you truly feel?"

"I never once doubted his intentions. And he wasn't perfect. God knows I'm not. Still, this feels right; to celebrate your first thirty years with you could be the best way to begin the next phase of life for both of you. And all of us."

"You think he'd want to come?" Rachel asked.

"I have no doubt. You've been speaking with him. You should answer your own question."

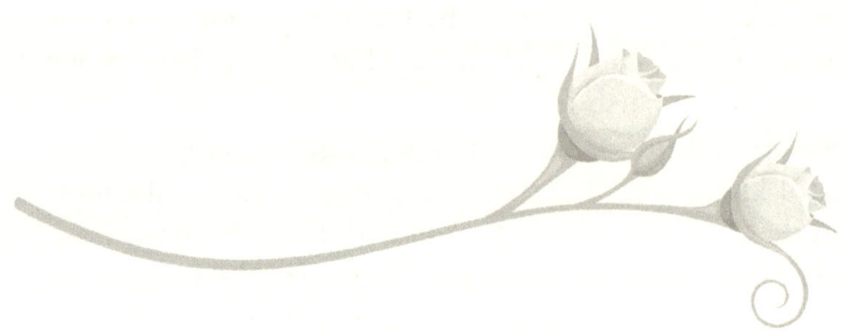

FORTY-FIVE

On a late December day, Rachel pulled her car onto the driveway and parked. She opened the trunk and removed the shopping bags bulging and overflowing with decorations and food for Brian's party. Brian opened the front door and skipped to her, taking the bags.

"Brian, you know I can handle them," Rachel said. Brian laughed, joined by Rachel's own chuckle. "You think you're so tough," Brian said as he rushed up the front steps to the door, still holding the bags. Inside, they both removed the items. Brian opened the packages. Rachel grabbed them from his hand, and nudged Brian aside. "This is your party. You're not supposed to do the work. Get lost, Bud."

Brian rushed past Rachel, patted her head, and headed upstairs. "Mom," he called, "What do you want me to do? My therapist told me that I need to keep busy instead of moping around. Rachel won't let me help her. Give me a hand here."

Glory came down the stairs, pulling Brian with her. "Rachel, does it really matter? He wants to help. So let him. Besides, he's tall." Glory grabbed a package of streamers and pushed them to Brian. "You got something to do, big guy. Get to it. Oh, and Brian, you sure you're good with seeing them?"

"It's perfect," he responded, stepping on a living room chair. "I remember very clearly what my therapist told me, that I can't pretend anymore that he doesn't exist. It's like, at first, when she pretended to be him in role-playing, I just yelled and yelled. I'm about yelled out. No, it's better than that. He needs to be here."

"My, what weeks and weeks of therapy will do for a man's soul," Glory said.

"Yeah, but I still have a lot of questions."

"And your temper is not too far hidden either," Rachel said.

"I know. Sorry about the other day. Couldn't control myself."

Glory added, opening up a package of plastic plates, "You know it's really not his fault."

"I can think that, sure," Brian said. "But still, there's a big part of me that doesn't understand. It's a good thing that nobody read that letter I wrote. It needed to go nowhere but straight into the fireplace. Dr. Morris said it would help to get my feelings out on paper. But sure didn't want anybody to see them. Not even me. Couldn't get the fire started fast enough."

"So, yeah," Rachel added. "I've seen a big change. You sure you don't want to go to the airport with me? It would be a great start for their visit."

"There's a limit to what I can do. I better save myself for the party. I know you'll take good care of them. Just don't be late. Don't want you guys to miss the party."

The party was in full swing by the time Rachel returned from the airport with Will and Gabrielle. Cars filled the driveway and were parked along the street near their home. Rachel thought that it would be better to first go inside the back door so as not to disturb the party.

They entered through the kitchen, which was empty except for the mess left from preparing the food and drinks. Rachel took their coats.

"Do you need a few minutes?" she asked.

Will answered, "No, I think we're good for now, right, sweetheart?"

Gabrielle gave Will a small hug, stepped to Rachel, looked straight into Rachel's eyes, and said, "I don't think you can truly understand what a wonderful thing you have done." Rachel lowered her head with a smile crossing her face.

"How could I have not? You don't know how much we've done to work through this." Will started toward Rachel, but she put up a hand to stop him. "No, Father. It's not what you think. Brian wants very much, I believe, to know you. But he's struggling with a lot of issues, and it hasn't been easy."

Will said, "I know. I really do. This is more than most people could ever dream that they'd have to handle. That's why I am so happy…so proud of you. And Brian. He's inside, right? I hear the party. Sounds like everyone's enjoying themselves."

Gabrielle cut in, "We're thrilled to be here and to be part of this. Is he ready for us? For Will? Maybe this isn't the best way to enter his life."

Rachel laughed. "It's the best time. You'll see. Why don't we join the party, yes?"

They passed through the swinging kitchen door. Inside, a group of people was sitting and standing around the couches and chairs in the living room. The lights were lit to a daytime brightness to give the room a liveliness they all felt. The Christmas tree sparkled in the corner, its lights blinking in approval of the festivities.

At first, they were not noticed, so Rachel led them through the gathering toward the front, where Brian stood surrounded by his friends. Rachel called out, "Brian, I'm back. They're here." They stopped at the edge of the group.

Brian turned and saw Will and Gabrielle standing next to Rachel. He didn't move and waited. Brian did not know exactly what he was waiting for. Like a Texas standoff, Brian stood and looked at the three of them, who waited, smiling. Then he heard someone call out, "Brian, are you going to just stand there?"

Rachel broke the ice. "Hi, guys. We have two exceptional people here. I guess they are so special that Brian has no words. And maybe that's appropriate because without this gentleman standing next to me, none of us would be here, together, celebrating Brian's birthday. I would like to introduce Will Stanford and his wife, Gabrielle. Will is our father, who was lost to us for all of Brian's thirty years until now; a victim of the Vietnam War. Will, these are Brian's friends."

One of them spoke out, "Were you in Vietnam the whole time?"

Will looked at the questioner, a man sitting on the couch, the same age as Brian. Will tried to speak, but no words came out. Rachel stepped in. "It's a very long story. But a story that has given me and Brian a lot, now that Will, and Gabrielle, are in our lives. Of course, our Dad is still our Dad; always will be. But now we have both dads. Will and Gabrielle just came off the plane from France to be here with us."

"Brian, that is so cool," another of his friends said. "Why are you standing there? Give the man a hug." Others joined in. Someone behind Brian gave him a little push toward Will. Brian laughed and said, "Okay, guys. That's cool." He looked at Gabrielle and Will. Will took a step and, with open arms, met Brian. Together, they hugged. Applause rang out from Brian's friends. Rachel's smile could be seen clear across the room where Glory, Leo, and Gabrielle stood, taking in what had happened.

Will didn't want to remain the center of attention. It was Brian's night, and Will was happy to be at the party with Brian, Rachel, and his friends. They sat together with Glory and Leo in the kitchen as the party continued. In time though, the ordeal of the intercontinental travel along with their emotions drained both Will and Gabrielle. They decided to make it an early night and head to their hotel.

That week they took in some of the sights of Chicago. Gabrielle wanted to see the places of Will's history before Vietnam. Together they toured around Will's old houses, his schools, and even Sears, circling back to where it all started. The stop at Sears wasn't precisely on the itinerary. Will slowed the car as they drove past Sears. "There it is. That's my Sears."

"You want to go inside?"

"No." He continued to drive and suddenly let out a short laugh.

"What's so funny?" Gabrielle asked.

"Nothing, really. I think…" He suddenly turned the car into the parking lot and drove back to park near the entrance to the department store.

"I'll be right back. Just wait." Will left the car running and headed inside the store. A few minutes later, Gabrielle watched Will leave the store carrying a large bag.

"What did you get?" she asked as he returned to the car.

"You'll see. Keep in mind the history of all this."

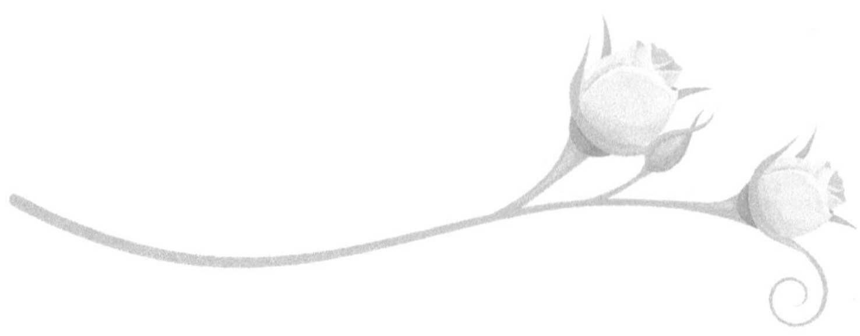

FORTY-SIX

Christmas day dawned with Will and Gabrielle enjoying a continental breakfast in their downtown hotel. Outside the café windows, they could see that a dusting of snow had coated the city streets overnight. It was too early in the morning for most people, and other than their waiter and someone back in the kitchen, they were alone. The plan was to take the drive into the suburbs to be at Glory's home for a late lunch. They lingered over breakfast, given plenty of time to relax before heading out. Having said everything, they sat within their own thoughts.

Later in the rental car, Will drove away from the city. They marveled at the beauty of a fresh blanket of snow coating the spindly trees bare of leaves and creating a magical view of winter, perfect for Christmas day. Snow started falling as they ventured further into Chicago's suburbs.

Inside Glory's home, aromas flowing from the kitchen combined the heartiness of the turkey simmering in the oven with the sweetness of dessert. The decorations celebrating Brian's 30th birthday had been replaced with Christmas lights lined across the ceiling overhead. Leo greeted them at the door, leading them inside as they brushed off snow from their coats. They gathered in the living room, the spot where so much of their emotions had been brought forward for them. A few minutes later, Glory joined them with Brian and his girlfriend holding

Brian's hand as they walked into the room. Leo, Will, and Gabrielle rose, and they all enjoyed a family greeting.

"We are so happy you are here," Glory said. "It's very different without all of Brian's friends everywhere. That was fun, but this is real."

"I know. I already thanked you for welcoming us here. No, for insisting that we be here," Will said. "But thanks much the same. This is lovely, really."

Brian walked with his girlfriend toward Will and Gabrielle. "Will, Gabrielle, I would like you to meet my girlfriend, Robin. Robin, this is Will and Gabrielle."

They shook hands, and Robin responded. "Brian can do nothing but talk about you two. It's a pleasure to finally meet you."

"Why don't we all sit and relax," Leo said. "Dinner will be ready in a while, so we can enjoy being here with each other."

"There's more than that, Dad," Brian said. "Now that I know my father, I want him to have something." Brian reached down to the floor and pulled up an old, brown grocery bag, wrinkled and frayed.

"Before you do that, Brian, we have something for you," Will said. From the end table, Will took a box wrapped for Christmas. "This is something you probably already have, but I wanted you to have this from me, even though it's about twenty years too late. I also have something for Glory and Rachel." Will turned to Glory and handed her a box, also wrapped, no larger than a bedside alarm clock.

Will handed Glory her gift, and said, "This is something that you asked me about a very long time ago, Glory. I never answered you. Perhaps if I did and became your friend before falling for your beauty and charm, things might have turned out much better. I hope you can now be my friend." He then turned and gave Brian his gift. Brian handed Will the old grocery bag.

"But I didn't get you anything," Rachel exclaimed.

"Never mind," Will said. "My gift, what I want, is all right here in this room. Brian, before we open these, let's let your mother open hers first." Taking the direct cue, Glory pulled open the wrapping paper and held up the gift. "A tennis racket. Did I want a tennis…?" She lowered the racket and held it, turning it in her hands. "I did want this. You never did tell me that day which was the right racket. I guess now we know, huh?" She walked to Will and hugged him. "I am glad you're back." A single tear slowly danced down her cheek.

She stepped back from Will, wiping her eyes. She walked back to where Leo was sitting, sat down next to him, and held his hand. "We are not reliving the past but creating a great future," Glory said. "This is special in a very unique way." Glory turned to Rachel, and asked, "What do you think it is?"

"I have no idea." She pulled off the ribbon and ripped off the paper. The box was wrapped in clear plastic, showing a box in solid lavender. Across the front of the package in gold letters, Rachel saw her name, written in a familiar script.

"What is this?" She held the box to her nose. The scent of lavender mixed with a citrus undertone floated through the package. Rachel pulled off the plastic, opened the box, and pulled out a perfume bottle shaped like a vertical hockey puck. The top sprayer was the same violet color as the box, and the same script of her name was engraved in gold letters across the front of the bottle. Rachel recognized the script as her signature. The light of recognition crossed her face. On seeing this, Will said, "That is our newest perfume. We finished developing it last month. Gabrielle helped me convince her father to name the new line Rachel in your honor. I took your signature from one of your letters. What do you think?"

Rachel sprayed the perfume on her wrist and rushed to Will and Gabrielle. She hugged them both together, tears running down her cheeks. "I've never experienced anything like this. This is amazing. You are amazing." She leaned back down to them and pulled them both closer.

Glory said, "That is so thoughtful. What a great gift. But what about Brian and Will? What are you two waiting for? Open your gifts. Let's see what you got. Both of you." The two men opened their gifts at the same time. Brian pulled out a professional-style baseball glove. Brian ripped the glove out of the box, slipped it onto his hand, held it up to his face, and sniffed the fresh leather smell. "That's so incredible," he said. Brian recognized the look on Will's face, watching Will open the grocery bag. Will pulled out a well-used leather baseball glove.

"I'm in shock," Will gasped. "My old glove." Like Brian, he put the glove on his hand and smelled its old essence of glory days of yore.

"You kept this?" he asked.

"Not me," said Brian. "Mom. She had it locked away. I never knew until a few months ago. Mom pulled it out as part of my therapy."

"I can't believe this," Will laughed and reached inside the bag. He felt the smooth roundness of a baseball, then another. He pulled one out and looked at Glory. "Is this the one?"

She nodded, then said, "Your very first gift to me. But keep looking."

Will pulled out the other ball. He turned it in his hand, and there, in blue ink, and faded, his handwriting, *WS,* stared back at him. "I can't believe you kept this too. This is embarrassing."

"Why would you say that?" Glory asked.

Will tossed the ball to Brian, who caught it with one hand. "Brian, have you seen this? What do you think of it? She made me sign it."

"Well," Brian started to speak, then paused. "That's Mom. We all know she gets what she wants, even if it's a worthless autograph."

A smattering of *oohs* came from the family. "I didn't mean that."

Will smiled and caught the ball as Brian tossed it back to him. "No, Brian, you're right, to everyone else, this is a worthless autograph, but here, now, I think it's something. You must, too. Right, Glory?"

"Like the day you gave it to me."

"Oh," Brian added. "There's this, too." He reached for the bag, dug to the bottom, and handed Will his old Sears name tag.

Will looked at it and grinned. "She kept this too? I hated Sears."

"Mom told us how you met," Rachel said.

"I've seen pictures from her hippie days. I'll bet she was cool," Brian said.

Will nodded and asked, "Any other surprises? An old man can only take so many at one time." Brian shook his head.

Will returned the glove to his face and again inhaled the memories. Then a thought came to him. "Brian, with my old glove, your new one, and this worthless baseball, that means only one thing?"

"What's that?"

"We have to start breaking in that new mitt and work the kinks out of this raggedy old thing," Will said.

"You want to have a catch? Now? It's winter. There's snow."

"No, Brian. It's springtime. Look." They turned to look out the front window. The snow stopped falling and the sun streamed through the clouds. Brian ran out of the room and came back with their jackets. Together, the two men walked out the front door and into the front yard, shuffling through the thin layer of snow.

"It's good," Will said, winding up and throwing the ball to Brian.

"It's all good," Brian said, making the catch.

THE END

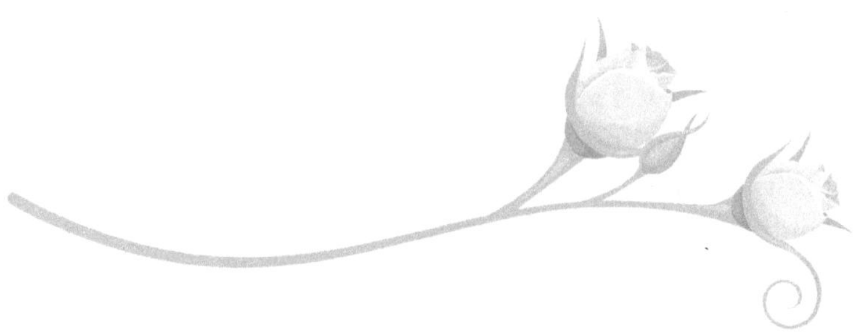

ACKNOWLEDGEMENTS

Like any project that is truly worth doing, this is one that involved many people without whom this work would not exist, and would not have the polish that I believe it does.

As a father of five adult children (and recently three more adult significant others), and grandfather to Isla, beauty and cuteness defined, who each are marking their place in the world, I receive much from our small group. That we may be far apart does not create a gap in the emotional connection we have. To Molly and Arian and Isla, Leah, Laura and Lakish, Jessica and Brad, and Chloe, thank you for what you give me, whether you mean to or not.

My mom, Janice, (may she rest in peace) read an early version of the manuscript. She isn't with us to see the final results, but her spirit rests on many of the pages. As an avid fiction reader, when she told me she liked it, was enough for me.

Many thanks go to Mali Miller, and her husband, Eddie, may he rest in peace, who put up with a very long oral rendition of my story. Eddie's comment to me after he read the draft novel will forever stay with me. "Why did you write about your experiences in the war?" he asked. I didn't. I was too young for the war, relying for my knowledge of the war, instead, entirely on other people's writings, videos, and movies, and on a few short conversations with a couple of war veterans. But the compliment, intended or otherwise, is a personal chart topper.

Thanks go to Kevin Hainsworth, writer and director, who's thoughtful and comprehensive review of an early draft forced me to make welcome changes to the manuscript.

To Marc B. Fried, New Paltz, New York, writer and historian, thank you for your openness and pithy advice, accepted and ingested by me, from which my writing improved, I think, in leaps and bounds.

Leah Orr, children's author and thriller novelist, thank you for giving me an insight into my characters that only a fellow writer of quality work can offer.

My thanks go to Elliot Kleinberg (BMF), South Florida author, writer, lecturer, and blogger, who never hesitated to read the manuscript and offer his comments.

To Nichole Heydenburg, author, freelance editor, and business owner, thank you for not holding back. What I learned from you will go far beyond the improvements it allowed me here.

And first in all ways in my life except on this page, is my ever, ever, ongoing thanks, but more, appreciation, to my wife, Debbie, who I consider my partner in writing as well. Much of what happened between Glory and Will, Will and Gabrielle, and Will and his children, his family and friends, his colleagues, and the Cambodians, resulted from her views of their lives exposed through our many talks and sessions together. Not only is she the best wife ever, but the best muse. Debbie, thank you with all my heart.

If there are any errors in this work, they are entirely on me. And to those out there who have a deeper knowledge of the history of the places, times, and events, that I attempted to create in *Because of Rachel*, please forgive the errors that I have a feeling exist inside the book. I did my best, so, again, it's entirely on me. But it's a work of fiction, so I can do what I want, right? Of course, right.

Finally, as always, I give my undying gratitude to God - for all of this.

Alan Grossman, Plantation, Florida, June 30, 2022.